10th anniversary edition

The Hail Mary

by USA TODAY bestselling author

GINGER SCOTT

ILLUSTRATIONS BY KATY MENDOZA

For the diehards.
Damn, do I love you.

Chapter One

Reed Johnson

THIS LIFE...IT'S hard on a marriage.

I get to see the young guys come in here on the first day of camp, a lot of them just like me—their high school sweethearts walking them to the front office and kissing them goodbye, wishing them a good day. Those walks, they don't go on for more than a week or two. Money starts to flow, vehicles get bigger, lives start to separate. Pretty soon, I see those same guys kissing other women in cities far from home.

Nolan never walked me up to the offices, or camp, or anything; that just ain't her style. Never was. If she showed up for something, it was because she had something to say. "We're pregnant!" or "Your mom...she passed." If I see Noles anywhere near the practice field, I brace myself for big, and I hold on for a ride that's either going to cut me down or make me fly.

Maybe that's the reason we made it longer than most. We didn't have some false expectations or fairytale dizzy dreams going into this life. We knew it was hard because *us* was always hard. In high school, life ate us up. In college, the same. I have constantly had this

1

other commitment that ran right alongside the one Nolan and I have, threaded right through the heart of every obstacle and decision we've ever made together.

Football.

My heart beats out a hard count. My pops says it's been beating that way since the day I was born. But I don't know…I think my rhythm was always off just a little when Nolan wasn't around. She set the tempo, kept me in time with things.

I forgot that. Maybe she did too a little. I've told her that I'm nothing without her but the thing is, I'm nothing without this game either. I'm really not. I'm just some thirty-eight-year-old beer-drinking loud-mouth, who likes Jeeps, plaid flannels, and complaining about how bad my damned joints hurt all the time. I've gotten old. Time—my so-called prime—was here, and then I blinked. This game and me, though, we're not done yet. We have unfinished business. My right hand is missing a championship ring. Three years ago, that title was in my reach, one blown pass away.

That fucking pass.

I never threw Otis Rutgers under the bus for his missed route, but that young hotshot did fuck up his path. He was a good five steps late, but really…it wouldn't have mattered. The coverage was there, and it outsized him no matter where I would have dropped the ball. Twenty-yards in the air, seconds on the clock, and a Super Bowl in my heart—all stolen away by my goddamn college roommate.

It was hard not to hate him for it just a little. He wasn't cocky about it, 'cause that's not how Trig is. It's why he got paid the big bucks and finished his career with a cache of awards and two bowl rings. Both championships were won by his interceptions—the first, a pick from me, and then two years later one off a Green Bay legend. Damn Giants loved him, made him franchise. He'll probably get a job in the front office one day, if he doesn't screw that up.

Trig retired last year. Body couldn't handle being hit high and low in two directions mid-air anymore. Thing is, though, his heart? It couldn't handle life without the game. In less than eleven months, his marriage fell apart completely. Stacia and he got married about a year after Nolan and I did, and they have three kids—all girls. Trig barely sees them right now. Things are…ugly.

Stacia's back in Maryland and Trig's in LA, "living the life." He blames her for never getting to have fun or cash in on his fame. He's a fool. I love him, though, so I'm not done trying to save him. If I can save him, maybe I can save me somehow, too.

I don't want *ugly*. Neither does Nolan. That's why we're just sticking through this *whatever it is* we have now. We should probably really talk about it, but that only makes shit slip away more, so I spent camp keeping my head low, being a "leader" like I'm being paid for, and trying to keep myself in one goddamned piece.

"There's my favorite client!" My brother's voice echoes in the locker room, and a few of the young guys finishing up glance our way wondering why I matter. Punks. It may hurt like hell, but I can still out gun them.

"I'm your only fucking client, which really dude…you should come up with a game plan for after this season. If you want to be in the publicity business, commit. You're not living in our basement."

I've been sitting here daydreaming and feeling sorry for myself so long, I haven't even gotten my shoes on yet. I gesture for Jason to sit down and wait. He drags a chair over from the corner and turns it backward so he can straddle it. He used to do that at the dealerships; he said it was a power move. I've never seen it work on a single person, and it only makes me want to kick him in the junk.

"Gonna be hard to live in your basement when you two get the divorce. I mean, who would I pick? No offense, but Nolan's a better cook," my prick brother says.

I give into my urge and stand up, pushing the chair leg with my foot, knocking him off balance enough to force him to stand.

"Like my wife would seriously cook *you* dinner," I grumble.

"Hey, hey! Don't take your mood out on me. My relationship is just fine," Jason says, tugging on his jacket front to straighten it.

"You don't have a relationship," I throw back, returning my focus to my things, shoveling whatever's left into a bag just to get out of here. I hear two of the new line guys chuckle, and I decide to let them have their jokes this time. They're probably making fun of my brother, and that's fine by me.

"Maybe I do have a relationship…and I just don't want to tell you about it, because all you'll do is shit on it. You ever think of that?"

I tug my bag up over my shoulder and shove my feet into my shoes without tying them. Squaring myself to look Jason in the eyes, I seriously consider his thought for exactly two seconds before dismissing him.

"No. You don't have a heart, and your soul is bleak as fuck, so no…I've never thought of that." I leave him sniggering to himself as I punch open the locker-room door. He follows me a second later, and I hate I have to make this drive with him.

He's right about one thing. I'm taking out my mood on him. I'm glad he's here to take my shit. I need to get rid of this hostile feeling before we make it to Arizona. Maybe Jason will exhaust me so much there won't be anything left for Nolan and me to fight about when I get to the ranch. I'm tired of the fighting. It never gets us anywhere, because we never really *say* anything. *I miss us.*

"You need to stop by your place to pick anything up? Or you just want to hit the road?" Jason beeps his Porsche as I approach it, and I toss my bag into the small space behind the passenger seat and then flop my tired body inside, pushing the seat back as far as it will go.

"Let's just get on the road. Straight through—we should be there by tomorrow morning. And dude…what's with this tiny car? We're the same height. This can't be comfortable for you!"

I kick my feet around the small space surrounding them; like a kid too hot to sit still, I finally find a decent spot to rest my right foot. I lean my body into my door when I pull it closed. I hope Jason's good to drive for a while so I can sleep like this.

He slips in through his door next, folding his jacket and twisting to rest it behind his seat. It's a shiny gray, and I can't fathom riding halfway across the country in a pair of slacks made out of that material. But that's Jason. Always quick to show people he's on the job and someone important.

"Fits me like a glove, bro. Don't know what you're talking about," he says, smirking at me from the side as he pulls his sunglasses from the small box above the mirror, slipping them onto his face. I stare at him for a breath then chuckle once and wiggle again in my seat, finding room for the seatbelt.

The drive from Oklahoma City to Coolidge, Arizona takes a little more than fourteen hours—if we're not in a Porsche 911. Jason's made this drive in around twelve hours. That's the only reason I'm willing to fold myself up into this thing.

Nolan used to make these moves with me. Rather, she made the move twice. We had a good run in California. I was with San Diego for seven years. The politics of sports got in our way, otherwise that's probably where I would have retired. Ownership loved me, until they sold their piece to a team of investors with other things in mind. Peyton was four when we moved to Minnesota, and I think if we could have stayed there, we would have built a good life. The Midwest suits us—suits Nolan. She was doing some great work with the university, building on her animal-therapy studies for kids on the autism spectrum. Her brother lives on the Wisconsin border, and we saw him all the time.

Then my dad had his last stroke.

Nolan and Peyton went back to Arizona, which is really where my girl's heart has always been, and I went on to Detroit. Long flights followed by even longer fights turned into bad habits and eventually silence. We quit talking about real things and just started existing. I wasn't even mad at her. How could I be? She'd moved her entire life into that ranch to keep my dad at home and help Rose take care of him. He slurs his speech, can't control his hands, and his day is spent moving from the bed, to the kitchen, to the patio while two women—who are better people than I am—make him smile as best he can and keep him happy and fed.

Even Jason sees them all more than I do. He manages my business, which frankly isn't much now, and then spends the rest of his time lounging by pools in Vegas and L.A. and wherever else I see him posing for selfies on social media like he's the next bachelor. He still finds his way home, though.

Home.

What's that?

I need to let go of my anger so I can get back to that place. Home will never feel like home again if I don't. My head won't let go of some things, though. And neither can my heart. Nolan and me, we were always forever. Until she betrayed me. With one tiny email, she took away my only other reason to live. Even now, two years later, I get her reasons. She was afraid. She was terrified the next hit I took would be the last, would be the end and turn me into a monster—or worse—a stranger. So she sent one rogue doctor's medical opinion to the man offering me the contract of a lifetime with the guarantee of getting back to the playoffs, and as it turned out the Super Bowl. She did it all while I was asleep in our bed, and as a result, she turned me into something that's proving impossible to overcome—a ghost of a man.

The irony of it all is I haven't taken a hit in a game since. I haven't stepped on the field for a game. I stayed in Detroit, riding backup to the backup, throwing drills to receivers in practice to get them warmed up for the real QB. That's probably what I'll do in OKC. I probably should have hung it up, but I cling to this goddamn hope that I'll be that Cinderella story—the backup who has to step in for the young hotshot who gets injured, then proves he's got just a little more life left in his bones.

My bones, though…they ache. My heart aches.

My brother's stereo is humming his weird EDM music; rather than argue with him over it, I settle in as deep as I can, pressing my head in the space between the seat and window so I can feel the thump of the base in my muscles. I try to remember how I felt when everything in my life was great.

Chapter Two

Nolan Johnson

REED'S GOING to be so pissed when he sees his Jeep. It's too late to do anything about it; call him halfway between here and Oklahoma and tell him to turnaround or just let him make the rest of the trip, see us, then fly back. Honestly, I want to see him, so I decided to just let it be what it will be. Feels like maybe it took his precious vehicle to get him to make the trip out here.

That's not fair of me to think. I won't say it. I'll keep it in my head.

Peyton's locked herself in her room. She's been in there for three hours—grounded. At fourteen, this girl has somehow sucked me back in time, and I am suffering through every last growing pain all over again. Only now, I'm Mom, and I "couldn't possibly know what it's like."

My daughter snuck out last night to go to a desert party—in her father's Jeep. Three years before she can legally drive.

"Two and a half."

That was her response. She didn't have a follow-up though, when I asked about the enormous gash that covers the passenger side. After an hour of tears, she finally gave in about the cactus she "didn't see."

I'm just glad she wasn't drunk.

She's her father's spawn. Not an ounce of caution in her chemistry, and now that she's a teenager, I can't help but feel like I'm raising a mini-Reed in almost every way. I suppose I should be grateful for the roadmap. At least I know what's coming, and I can try to head off the worst.

I'm not sure what car I'm rooting to round the driveway first—Jason's or Sarah's. My best friend isn't exactly helpful when Peyton goes full Peyton. She's more of her usual self—the influence.

"You make good pancakes, Nolan. Good...damn...pancakes."

I smile while my gaze drifts from the front window to the place where my father-in-law, Buck, runs his fork sloppily along his plate, soaking up every drop of butter and maple left.

"It's not my pancakes you like, Buck. It's the sugar."

I wink and he chuckles as I walk over to him and take his plate. Buck's wheelchair-bound now. That last stroke stole away most of his motor control on the left side of his body, and it's made a lot of things impossible. Not everything, though. That man still shows up to every CHS Bears home game. When Rose can't take him, I do. To be honest, I kinda like going. I'm a glutton for the nostalgia, or maybe there are just a lot of things I miss a whole hell of a lot.

"Ah..." He holds both hands up, one much higher than the other, as if he's been caught stealing from the cookie jar. "You got me."

I lean forward and kiss his cheek, then carry his plate into the kitchen. I worried at first that it would be hard to be here alone with Buck. He doesn't talk as much as he used to. The words take so long to come out. But we've found this really comfortable rhythm with each other. Maybe he and I just don't have to talk. He always seems to know exactly what I'm thinking, even when I try to hide it. It's why he didn't go to church with Rose today. Reed's coming home, and Buck wants to be here for me when he shows up.

"All right, bitches. Let's get this party started!"

My eyes roll at Sarah's arrival, but I'm still relieved she's the one who got here first. I'm not ready for Reed just yet.

"You're almost forty, Sar. Time to drop the partying…and why does everyone need to be called *bitches*?" My friend hugs me and promptly moves on to Buck, who leans with his cheek out ready for a pretty woman to plant lips on.

"I'm thirty-nine. Quit with the rounding-up shit. And besides…I plan on partying until they drop me in a grave. Ain't that right, Mr. Johnson?" Sarah kisses Buck and his mouth pulls up high on his right side.

"And this, woman…" she moves into the kitchen and sets an oversized canvas tote on the table, unsnapping the top and pulling out two bottles of the best Pinot Noir in the world. "…is the reason for the party."

"Okay, you make a good case," I say, smirking at her and pulling one of the bottles into my hand. Reed used to bring this home when something big happened and we needed to celebrate. I haven't shared a bottle with him in a few years, so as revved as my palate is to pour a big glass at ten in the morning, I can turn down the temptation that will no doubt come with an overwhelming side of feelings.

"Tonight. If that's okay?" I take both bottles and move them to the corner of the counter.

"Fine by me." Sarah shrugs and follows me deeper into the kitchen to snoop through a few of the cabinets on the hunt for a snack.

"In the fridge. Rosie made fresh blueberry muffins," I say.

"Rosie's the boss!" Sarah doesn't hesitate, reaching in and grabbing the biggest one on the rack. She takes a bite of the top, eating it like an apple, and I grimace because Rosie's muffins are meant to be savored. It's practically criminal to just kill off the muffin top like that without truly appreciating it.

"How's the old man?" My friend talks while she chews. I lean into the counter, folding my arms over my favorite T-shirt. It's the last Coolidge High one I have from when I went there. There are eight, almost nine, holes in it. I can't bear the thought of throwing it away. This shirt, it feels like my marriage—holding on by a literal thread. I'm sure there's all kinds of deeper meaning behind why I chose to wear it today, for Reed, but on the surface, it's just the perfect amount of wear for the cotton. People try to mimic this feel —*vintage*. You can't fake real vintage, though. A thousand loads of laundry have tumbled with this shirt to make it the masterpiece it is now.

"He's doing pretty good, considering. I mean…I know he's frustrated. He does physical therapy three times a week, and the progress has been so slow. Deep down, I think he knows that he's never going to really be able to leave the chair for long. But you know Buck—stubborn as hell." I glance to the main room where Buck's back has turned to us and the hum of Sunday morning football echoes.

"Apple doesn't fall far from the tree, huh?" Sarah says.

I shake with a single laugh and blink my gaze to my friend's. I don't really have an answer for her because as much as she's being funny about it, I just can't joke about what Reed's put his body through. I lived it—I still live it in my nightmares. It's a bye-week. I almost wish his team's off week was later in the season, so I could spread out my worrying. Reed's been injured for most of preseason and the first game, because of a calf strain. I hope like hell that nagging injury nags just a little longer. Not that Reed will get on the field much. Duke Miller's the young stud, head still on his shoulders —for now. Reed is backup.

The team didn't have a problem with Reed leaving. This trip is about more than just his Jeep. His name's on the deed for the six hundred acres we just sold to a developer on the north end of town. The lawyer's coming out with the documents later today. The Jeep just inspired Reed to do this in person, rather than by DocuSign.

Somehow, I missed Jason's car pull in while I was talking with Sarah in the kitchen, but the unmistakable *purr* followed by a slam of a Porsche door has triggered the flop sweats.

"Jesus, you look like a teenager, nervous sweats and pale face." Sarah snorts a little with her laugh. My friend is the queen at letting anything heavy just roll off her chest. Her response to Reed's defiance of what's best for his head and body is "suit yourself, hope like hell you don't die." That's how Sarah is about everything—it's why she's not dancing with a company, and why she teaches at our old high school where she can practically get away with murder, but still keep her benefits because the principal is in love with her.

I don't have the luxury of being cavalier. I love that ass-hat, despite wanting to throat-punch him for this last contract.

"Come on, let's cut them off at the door. I wanna drive Jason's car." My friend skips from her chair to the door in a few long strides, looping her arm through Jason's just as he's about to say hi to me. I'm left face to face with the man of my dreams, and I can't think of a damn thing to say to him, because I know the moment I open my mouth I will inadvertently start a fight.

His shoulders sag, and the overweight duffle he's carrying on one arm slides to the floor where he pushes it with his foot over to the side. His eyes are so tired. If I brought that up, though, he'd just tell me it was from the car ride here, when I know it's not. I know how bright and hungry those green eyes are supposed to be, and I know they've been dimmed for quite some time.

Reed paints me with his gaze before his lips part slightly and his eyes move on to the very different home behind me. Sometimes, I forget that he grew up here. It's nothing like the bachelor pad—albeit *enormous* bachelor pad—that he spent high school and college summers in; now his dad and Rosie stay in a master bedroom they converted from most of the garage, because there's no way his dad is making it upstairs. Clear pathways determined what furniture stayed and what had to go, and assistance bars are mounted on almost every wall.

My hands automatically run up my face, like erasers. I hate this uneasiness. There's no reason we can't just talk, but I overthink every single subject, and I know he's doing the same.

"Hey!" Buck's drawn-out celebratory welcome comes to both of our rescue. My husband's face contorts into a strained smile—it kills him to see his dad like this. Buck knows, and it's the reason he always rests extra before Reed comes home. There are a lot of things Buck can't control, but he still tries to, for his son's sake.

"Hey, Old Man." Reed grabs his dad's hand in his palm, wincing when their grip doesn't align quite right. The touch is different. Reed leans down and hugs his dad with his other arm.

"You get here in that—piece-of-shit car?"

I chuckle out loud and Reed's head turns enough to catch my eyes. The brightness is there for just a moment, and it's while we're both laughing at his brother's expense.

"It's an expensive piece-of-shit, Dad. But yeah, Jason drove," Reed says through a crooked smirk.

"Shit can still...be expensive," Buck says, laying his hand on the controls for his chair to move back and make room for Jason and Sarah to swing the front door open wider.

We all get silent and look away, but Jason already knows.

"Dad made a joke about my car again, didn't he?" Jason says, his words drawing a bigger laugh from Reed that breaks the rest of our silence.

Right now, everything feels so good. It's all too good, and I know it's fleeting. I make the most of it and step over to Reed's back, sliding my hand down the familiar curves of his shoulders and bicep until my hand reaches his wrist. I give it a squeeze, closing my eyes as I bend down for his duffle. Reed leans into me enough that the moment I stand straight, we're chest to chest.

"I got it."

His eyes move from my right, to my left, and everything we are flashes between us. It's the same every time I see him. This is where most couples would kiss, standing close like this. But we don't. We haven't kissed, really kissed, since the day he left for the airport to visit the "miracle specialist" on brain-and-spine trauma. A positive report turned into a one-year deal, and I didn't know a thing about it until it was too late—ink on paper, news on *Bleacher Report*.

Instead...now, we have quiet. A thickness settles into my chest, and the heaviness takes over my lungs as Reed's mouth closes and the delicate smile that was there for that small second fades.

I blink, then look down, stepping back as my hand falls away, giving up its tentative hold on Reed's arm. I wish I could uncork one of those bottles of wine right now, drink it down in one breath, then maybe relax for the first time in years.

"Awkward," Sarah says, her special brand of cringe-worthy humor.

I roll my eyes at my friend and Reed moves on with his bag, heading up the stairs to our room—Buck and Rose's old room. I instantly think about the night, and how we'll both pretend we're exhausted and roll over facing opposite walls so we can avoid talking for a little while longer. It hurts to think about and predict, but not nearly as much as it hurts when it happens and I'm in it. There's this invisible layer covering us and keeping us apart. I don't know how to tear through it. I miss him. Why can't I just say that and mean it, and him accept it for what it is—love?

Buck and Jason move back to the living room; I retreat to the kitchen and wait until I'm alone with my friend so I can scold her.

"Can you just not..." I flash my eyes wide and hold my open palms out to my sides. There are so many words to finish that phrase. The options are too many, really. Could you not be you? Could you not make me feel sick for your own amusement? Could you just not add drama to what hurts for once in your freaking life?

I don't have to finish that statement, though, because those are all things I've said to Sarah over two-plus decades of friendship. She's untrainable.

"You didn't tell him about the Jeep."

I spin to face my friend and press my hands flat on the counter as I blow out heavily and slide my palms across the surface, letting my head fall forward until my hair covers my face.

"Nope. I didn't." I lift my chin and blow away enough strands to spot Sarah through my hair. She circles the kitchen island and heads right to the stash of wine, picking up the closest bottle and sliding it gently toward me.

Without a word, I grab two glasses from the cabinet behind me and pour a generous amount for both of us, then raise one glass for a toast with my friend. I let my glass hover as she does the same. The longer we sit like this, the harder it gets to hold in our laughter. Neither of us can think of good things to raise our glasses to. Eventually, we shrug and press the rims against our lips drinking as if we're on vacation in Vegas.

Sarah sets her glass down before me, more than half gone in the first drink. She sighs heavily, then levels me with the most sincere, deadpan gaze she can muster.

"We're gonna need more of those muffins."

Chapter Three

Reed

WHENEVER I'M in someone's office, or someone's house, or a hotel, and there's a picture on the wall that's a little bit off—slanted —I can't help but try to fix it. A little nudge usually does the trick, but sometimes, it's just the way the nail was hit, and there's nothing I can do.

That's what this place feels like. It's one, enormous, desperately crooked picture, and I can't do a damn thing to make anything in it straight and level again.

I toss my bag on the floor and collapse face-first into the bed, reaching up to unbury one of the pillows as I breathe in the scent of the bedspread. It smells of honey and lavender—Nolan's favorite lotion. Eyes closed, I live in the past for almost a full minute before cracking my lids open and twisting my head to the side to stare at the open closet filled with her clothes.

There's a wide space where her things are pushed to the left and mine, at least the clothes that I've left here, are pushed to the right.

Fucking symbolic.

My phone buzzes a few times in my pocket, so I eventually give in and roll to my side to pull it out and read. They're messages from my agent, Tom. I'm not crazy about the guy personally, but he gets the job done. He got me this contract—every penny from my last one, too. I miss working with Dylan, though. She had become like family, but when she and Jason broke up, it became almost impossible to deal with the tension, and I'm more committed to my brother's career goals than to being faithful to Dylan.

Funny thing is, Nolan wishes I stuck with her. What started as college jealousy turned into a pretty tight friendship between the two of them. And when Nolan was pushing for me to retire after the neck surgery, Dylan was in her corner.

I click through Tom's string of texts and get the gist—he has some interviews lined up for me when I get back to OKC—and I text him back OK.

"Are you sleeping?"

I'm tempted to fake it and scare Peyton when she gets close, but I miss her too much to waste time on that. I roll to my other side and find her clinging to the doorway, her body hidden by the hallway wall.

"Hey, Champ. Nah, I'm up. Just…" I breathe out a laugh as I prop my head up with my elbow and rest my cheek on my palm. "Decompressing from the all-night drive with your uncle Jason."

My daughter laughs quietly and looks down, bringing one of her feet inside the room and sweeping it back and forth on the floor. She's wearing jeans and one of my old sweatshirts, but her hair is a tangled mess, which probably means she slept in that.

"Get in late?" I lift a brow.

She glances at me, and her eyes widen. Something about her reaction tells me to sit up, so I swing my legs around and face her with my feet on the floor and head tilted suspiciously to the side.

"Mom didn't tell you?"

Her fingers go right to her mouth, fingernail lodged between top and bottom teeth.

Oh hell.

"Tell me *what?*" I ask hesitantly. My head somehow leans even more to the side, so much so that I have to strain my eyes to keep my gaze on her. My heart has also sped up. Last month, she got a tattoo. A rose with something flying around it that she says is a hornet but looks like a dirty fly to me. She got it from some high-school tool in a garage band, who is still on my watch list for the day he turns eighteen and I can pound his ass. Nolan made her call me and tell me herself. I'm braced for a piercing this time.

"I dented the Jeep." Her words come out quietly, through crooked lips and only half her mouth. Her eyes flit to mine then right back down the spot on the floor where her foot is now nervously painting side to side.

Frozen, I'm glad she's not looking me in the eyes because I can feel the way they're bugging out. I'm relieved she hasn't let some douchebag put a hole in her body, but I'm also preparing myself for this new turn—the one where she somehow dented my Jeep.

"You hit it with a ball or something?" I throw this sad attempt out quickly, knowing that's not the case. She grimaces at me and rolls her eyes; I dip my gaze and force her not to look away again.

"I take that as a *no?*" I blink slowly and she shakes her head.

"I took it to the desert," she croaks out.

Of course she did. My mouth gasps out a "Ha" and I relax my shoulders. Clearly, she's already been punished. Nolan always takes care of that—bad cop to my good cop. She's here to play on my sympathies, and I hate that it always works. Daddy's girl is a legit real thing.

"You get hurt?" I sit up straight and fold my hands in my lap.

"No. I didn't even go that far. I didn't see one of the barrels when I pulled out from the river bottom though, and I kinda… sorta…" She doesn't finish, but really, is there a need?

My head tilts back as I stare at the ceiling, and I let my mouth fall open.

"How bad is it?" I keep my focus on the ceiling beam until I can calm down.

"Grampa said he'll have Jerry fix it up. Said it's mostly paint and a little body work." I'm almost proud that my girl actually nailed down a solution before I got home. I also know that body work will probably take a week, because Jerry was one of the first body shop guys my dad ever hired when he opened the dealership in Tucson. Jerry's the best, too, but he's also slow as hell. And I'm supposed to head back to Oklahoma in two days.

I nod as I right my head and look my daughter in the eyes.

"I'm not mad," I lie. I'm steaming mad, but what the hell good would that do.

"I'm…disappointed," I say next, and the sound of it makes me laugh internally. How many times did my mom say those words to me when I did something dumb. My pops was never really much of the disciplinary—probably because he didn't usually set the best examples.

"I'm really sorry, Daddy."

And there it is, the stake to the heart that makes every father give in.

I pat the bed next to me, urging Peyton to come closer, and she inches her way into the doorway. When she sits next to me, I put my arm over her shoulder and palm the side of her head as it falls into my arm. This feeling never gets old.

———

Nolan told Peyton she was grounded for uncertain terms that would be set by me. I told her she could work off the cost of the Jeep repairs by helping her mom with the horses. When she put enough hours in, she'd no longer be grounded. That's the one thing Nolan and I haven't let fall apart—our parenting. Even though she usually lets me play good cop, we agree that we won't ever let Peyton off the hook for things.

I got let off the hook too often, and when I look back on the things that could have gotten me arrested or worse, killed, I think the odds are pretty high that I've wrung out every ounce of good luck due to me in life. Which explains a lot of my bad luck as of late.

I've been watching Nolan work with a family out in the ring for the last hour. If she didn't have this session, I think she'd probably be napping in the living room with Sarah, who seems to have had most of the contents from the empty wine bottle sitting in the center of our kitchen island. Noles doesn't look tipsy at all, which means she probably had less than a glass. She's never been able to hold her wine well, zipping from buzzed and sexy right to sleepy and passed out.

Jason and Pops are invested in the late-afternoon games. I used to be just as obsessed on my off days, but who knows when I'll have to deal with any of those other teams on the field. And if and when that time comes, they'll be a totally different force than what they are today. It's still too early in the season for anyone to have their rhythm. There's a lot more important work for me to get done out here.

When Nolan moved back to Arizona, she brought the animal therapy business with her. It's perfect for this land, actually, and the large section we're selling off to a developer is going to fund even more buildings and staff. It's the one thing we can talk about without arguing—her work. She has a vet on staff and two assistants. They help with one-on-one sessions guiding these kids with disabilities and their families around the ranch on horses or one of the donkeys. There's still a lot that Nolan does herself, though. Somewhere—sometime soon—something has to give. She can't keep burning at all ends: caring for my dad, managing Peyton's wild side, and running this business.

She needs to hire more help. Hell, we can afford it. We're not lavish—that's never been our thing. We don't spend on garages filled with cars, or trips to Europe, or clothes. For us, the goal has always just been to live the life we want and to have a cushion there to let us do it.

Noles tips her head back with a laugh as one of the girls covers her face, blocking the stench from the horse poop. The scene draws me out onto the back porch, and soon, I find myself walking over. Nolan's eyes catch mine, and her smile softens as her laugh quiets.

Goddamn is she beautiful. Her long brown hair is twisted from day-old curls she probably put in last night. Her skin is soft like cotton, sprinkled with cinnamon freckles that travel across the bridge of her nose.

"We used to call those apples," I say as I step up next to a boy who looks like he's about Peyton's age. He's wearing a long-sleeved T-shirt and jeans, the dirt from the ring muddying up what looks like a pretty expensive pair of basketball shoes.

"I got boots you can borrow," I say, expecting him to rush back to the house in relief that his sneakers can be saved. Instead, he simply shrugs.

"It's just a little dirt is all," he says, running the back of his hand over his forehead. It's barely fall in Arizona, which means it's still hot as hell outside.

"Nick loves coming to watch his sister. He's a good brother," says a woman I'm assuming is both kids' mom. She leans in front of her son and stretches her hand to me. "I'm Wendy. My husband's a huge fan, and he's going to be so mad he didn't come to therapy today."

I give out a short laugh and take her hand in a firm shake.

"She's way more impressive than I am," I say, nodding toward Nolan. She's been watching us talk while one of her assistants walks along the side of the horse with the little girl.

"She's amazing with Lily."

Wendy looks back at her daughter, and I follow her lead, watching as Nolan kneels next to Lily and talks softly for a while until the little girl willingly gives Nolan her hand to press against the horse's side. They freeze like that for a moment, and I feel both mom and brother pause their breath beside me, waiting for Lily to react. Where most kids might light up and cheer or laugh, though, Lily's experience with the horse is different. With Nolan's hand on hers, she moves slowly along the horse's side, stretching her arm up the neck until her body is close enough for her to press her ear against the animal. Her weight shifts, and her other hand comes up, this time on its own—without Nolan's help—and a few seconds later, she's standing, holding the beast, completely on her own.

"She's making such great progress," Nolan whispers at us with her head turned to the side. She stands slowly, backing away until she's with us and Lily is alone with only the therapist and Soldier, our oldest horse.

We watch in silence, all of us completely rapt as this little girl—with her hair pulled back tightly into a ponytail and her clothes draping on her skinny arms and legs—gives herself over to the love of this animal. At one point, Wendy runs the butt of her palm under her right eye, drying up tears.

"Is she on the autism spectrum?" I keep my voice down because I've learned that some families prefer not to talk about it in front of the child. This doesn't seem to be the case here, though, and Wendy nods rapidly, smiling when her eyes reach mine.

"She was diagnosed late—at five. She has such a hard time making friends, and being…just calm, I guess," Wendy says.

"She sure looks calm now." Nolan glances to Wendy first, then to me. My mouth stretches proudly, and my eyes blink slowly—a silent "Good job, Babe."

We all watch as Lily spends several minutes touching the horse with her small fingers. It's such a brave thing to do, and it makes me think of the men I've faced off with over the years who have stared me down with hot breath and juice in their legs, ready to tear my head from my shoulders whether it was part of the game or not.

This life here, the one Nolan's made…it should be enough. But somehow, I can't accept that.

"I bargained you some free labor," I say to my wife as she leans against the fence on the opposite side of me.

"Oh yeah? How so?" She turns to make eye contact, and I cock my head and lift a brow.

"It's the least our daughter can do," I say.

Nolan's lips get tight and a smirk starts to form slowly.

"You're such a sucker," she says, and my face draws in.

"Hey, I thought that was a pretty good sentence. She wrecks my Jeep and has to work off the cost." I fold my arms as Nolan snorts a laugh.

"She's terrible at helping out here, and it's probably going to end up being more work for me. I was thinking maybe something like she has to wait an extra six months or a year to get her license." Nolan twists to face me and mimics my stance, her arms folded, too.

I laugh out once.

"A year! That's...well...oooof, that's just..."

Honestly, that's probably a way better punishment, but Nolan's right—I'm a sucker. I got to drive so young, and in this family, getting your license was such a big deal, and I have a car picked out for her already, and I don't want that all ruined because she got a little excited about a party. It's high school.

"See?" Nolan says, reaching forward and patting my shoulder. "Sucker."

It's like she heard my thoughts in my head. I hold my ground for maybe five seconds, staring into her wide brown eyes that I know are functioning because of that tumbler full of coffee she downed.

"Fine, okay? I'm a sucker." I hold up my open palms and her judgmental stare softens into that sweet look she gets when I let her know she's right but she feels bad about it.

She turns around and leans into the fence again. Her hair is blowing in the breeze, so I catch a strand with my fingers now that she isn't looking. I miss this hair. It slips from my fragile hold in seconds and I start to drop my hand away, but she scrunches her shoulders up in a sign I should rub them. I'm not sure if she knew I wanted more time or if her shoulders just hurt. Given how little it feels like we touch anymore, I jump at the chance, first gathering her hair in one twist and then sweeping it to the side before running my thumbs along that perfect curve the back of her neck makes into her shoulders. She tenses at first, but her muscles relax under my hands. It's easier like this—with other people here, with something to distract us. We play the part of NFL couple who have their shit under control. No one would know how shark-infested the water is that we tread, or how close we've come to drowning in it.

We stay like this until Lily's session is done. Wendy's husband, Patrick, has rushed to the ranch to meet me. After a few photos and some reliving of my best and most heartbreaking games with him, we walk them back to the driveway. Nolan and I hold hands until their car disappears around the line of trees. When her pinky falls from mine, it feels like a rope giving way, and life comes tumbling down.

"You really didn't punish her?" Her question comes out with a yawn.

"Look at how exhausted you are. You could use the help. And make her earn it—make her really do the work. It'd be good for that girl to learn how to earn something," I say. Such a hypocrite. Nolan doesn't call bullshit on me out loud, but she does squint her eyes just a little bit and glare.

Behind us, my brother's voice bellows over some touchdown I'm sure he'll tell me about the minute I step inside. For as much as I love this game and it gives me life, I really hate talking about it like a fan, though. It's like seeing behind the scenes at Disneyland—magic gets lost.

I know Nolan won't want to talk about the Sunday games.

"You wanna go for a walk?" I say without giving my brain a chance to stop my mouth from asking.

Nolan laughs at first, but when she sees I'm serious, she glances over her shoulder then looks back to me.

"All right," she smirks.

I nod toward the driveway, and we both step at the same time. As much as the area has grown, our family's place is still set off from most of the rest of town. That won't be the case when we sell off the back acreage, but it's the right developer and the right time. Still —I'm going to miss the lonely feeling of our main road one day. Lonely isn't always a bad thing. Sometimes, it clears the head.

"Please say this wasn't the tattoo boy that made her go to the desert party," I say, feeling my fist tighten in my pocket just at the mention of him.

Nolan laughs lightly.

"No, Reed. You'll be glad to know that this boy is a quarterback," she says.

"Ah, hell," I roll my eyes and look up at karma.

"Yep. He's fifteen. Sophomore."

I want to finish her sentence with "…and he's dead," but that's just my daddy blood boiling.

"She's a freshman, and she's not allowed to date," I say instead, knowing that's not true and won't be enforced. Nolan lets my rant go without acknowledgement, so we walk a little longer in silence, our legs turning on instinct to head into town.

"Is he good at least?" I grumble my question, and when she doesn't answer me right away, I glance to my right to catch her grin.

"What?"

"Nothing," she says, teasingly. "It's just…he might have broken your freshman record for passing yards. And he maybe wears your number. And his name might be Ryan."

I stop walking and she takes a few more steps away from me before turning and walking backward to face me.

"I'm kidding…" She points at me and laughs. All I can do is shake my head. My relief is short, though, because she's only kidding about that last part.

"His name's Bryce. He's a nice kid. Just a little…misguided." Her eyes dance on mine with that word—the same one her mom used to say about me when we were in high school.

"I'm going to hate him," I say, catching back up to her stride.

"Nah…" she says.

"I disagree." I'm firm about it. I don't care if the kid ends up winning state. I won't like him. Wait… How'd they do at state last year?" I ask.

She doesn't say it out loud. It's in the expression she wears, mouth higher on one side and eyes lifted. My daughter is dating a mini me. Dammit all to hell.

The sun is getting higher, and I know Nolan's starting to feel the heat on our walk, so I offer to turn around, but she insists we keep going. I don't fight her on it; these roads have a healing power to them. It's why Nolan wouldn't let my dad sell everything and move into a care place, why she moved in and why she and I both agreed this was where we wanted Peyton to go to high school. We can afford for my dad to be anywhere, which means we can also afford to bring therapists and doctors to us. This little piece of our history is too important.

The press box comes into view and the scent of barbecue hits my nose at the same time, making me salivate.

"Fundraiser?" I ask.

"It's homecoming week." Noles flits her gaze to me for a few seconds, and a thousand memories flood in. I'd give anything to get a redo on some of our school dances. On homecoming, especially.

That's why she was all right with the heat. She knew this destination would scratch at my soul. It does the job.

"Come here," I say, slowing down my walk as she gets a few paces ahead. She turns to face me and I reach out my hand.

Bashful eyes haven't aged a day, I swear to God. Her mouth curves in suspicion—as it should. I curl my fingers, gesturing for her to take my hand, and my head tilts to the side.

"Come on, I won't bite," I say, and her head turns a fraction to the right as her eyes dim.

We stay in this standoff for a few seconds, eyes locked and every chase in our past flowing through our minds. I don't mask it well, and when I reach for her, she squeals and takes off in a sprint toward the field.

"You know I'm going to catch you!" I call after her as she rounds the fence and swings the gate closed behind her in an effort to slow me down.

I grab the top and swing my legs over in a jump, a little impressed with myself when I don't biff the landing or get hurt. Noles glances over her shoulder, her long hair a twisted mess that covers most of her eyes, but she still sees me. Her laughter gets wild, this giggle that's so damned reminiscent of the school girl I fell for two decades ago.

We make it to the track and she slows up, giving in for my arms to lift her up over my shoulder and walk her the rest of the way into the end zone. I spin her a few times until I'm dizzy and then I let her body slide back down to the damp grass, my arms still around her.

This feels good.

It won't last.

"Why can't we be kids like this, huh?" I say, my hands roaming down until they find her hips. I loop my thumbs in the belt loops of her denim shorts and sway her side to side. Her hands flatten against my chest, starting up high and sliding down to my stomach

29

where she grabs two handfuls of my shirt in her fists. Her lips tighten as she fights saying all of the things running through her mind behind those eyes.

One neck surgery. A few—more than a few—concussions. Two agonizing minutes lying unconscious on the field while she held her breath more than a thousand miles away, her phone clutched in her hand waiting for my brother to call and say everything was fine.

Her fists swing with my shirt, tapping against my body a few times before she lets go and moves from my arms. Our old high school band is blaring out in the distance, the songs the same. Nolan's hands reach for the curve of her lower back and she slides her palms into her back pockets as she paces a few steps away, back to the dry track. Small bits of grass stick to her ankles. I breathe in deep, staring at her back, her hair flapping in the breeze.

"Jeep probably won't be done for a few days. I got the week. Maybe...I stay home until it's ready? Catch homecoming, visit the team—see coach." I chuckle nervously.

Nolan turns until our eyes meet, her smile still stretched and flat, hiding problems—our problems.

"You know how I feel about that. Of course, I want you home." What she doesn't say is "for good." It's there though. And I should give it to her, but it scares the hell out of me. Me and that field have unfinished business, and I know pretty soon the game is going to decide for me. Maybe it already has—it's not like I'm taking snaps anywhere that matters.

It's just...I've seen what leaving the game did to Trig. He's so lost, I don't know if he'll ever be found. It's hard to be around him, his nervous behavior and messed-up emotions. He's so depressed, but he won't get help. His kids hate him.

I don't ever want Peyton to hate me. I like playing good cop.

"You're gorgeous, you know that?" Her mouth curves and her cheeks round where they grow pink.

"You always did know just the right thing to say, didn't you Reed Johnson." Nolan walks backward a few more steps but I catch up and pull her arms loose from where they wrap around her midriff.

I don't want to mess up this little slice of peace we have going on because Nolan's wrong; I don't always say the right thing. I have learned, however, when to shut up. I do that now, tugging my girl's hands toward me until she's close enough to kiss. I spend a full breath remembering every little nuance to her face and noticing the tiny things that have changed in the twenty-three days it's been since I saw her last.

I vow to kiss each change, starting with the small worry line that's started to form between her brows. That one's my fault anyhow.

Chapter Four

Nolan

Four Years Earlier

THE IRONY IS NOT LOST on me that my only child likes to cheer. I've actually gotten into it, at least the competition aspect of it all. I don't think I will ever get into the music. This sport, for whatever reason, breeds horrible musical scores of mashed-up, knockoff pop hits fused with techno-whiz that sounds like it's pulled right from an electric piano sold at the toy store. And they blast it so loud!

I reach into my purse to dig around for the two stray Advil I know I threw in there. My head is pounding, and my claustrophobia is being tested. Peyton's team is up in fifteen minutes, so I just have to hold out until she sticks the full twist and they leave the stage.

My fingers finally locate the two pills, and I pop them in my mouth quickly, ignoring the dust and dirt stuck on them so I can dry-swallow them down. If I could mainline them into my forehead by pushing them through my ears, I'd go that route.

"Anissa said Peyton's hungry." Morgan, Anissa's mom, is stuck against my right shoulder. She flips her phone to the side to show me her daughter's text. I roll my eyes.

"Tell her we're all hungry. Get over it," I say, feeling my own stomach roll at the thought of lunch.

Morgan types my response, and as she does, I fish into my bag again to get my phone out and ready to film the girls' routine. My entire body sways and my head goes light when I see seventy missed calls.

Seventy is a big number. It's not an "I'll just catch you later" kind of number of calls. It's incessant and means that someone needs to reach me *now*. I instantly think about Buck, and I'm expecting all of the missed calls to be from Rose. Those expectations make what I see even harder to grasp.

Jason's calling. He's calling right now. *Seventy-one.*

My hand vibrates with the buzz of my phone, and I wobble my way backward until I can find a small enough space to work my way out of the thickest part of the crowd. I shove one finger in my left ear and press the phone against my right.

"Jason. What is it? What's wrong?" My heart is slapping inside my body, beating its way out. I don't hear him at first. By the time my feet get into the hallway, my body instinctively slides down a wall until I'm sitting on the floor. He's already well into his message.

"Start over. I missed that. You said…you said neck?" A wave of sickness knocks into me, and my face begins to perspire, beads of sweat dotting along my hairline.

"Noles, he took a big hit. He's being taken to University Hospital, and I'm right behind the ambulance. I knew you'd want to know. I didn't know how else to call you, so I just kept dialing…"

I hear bits and pieces. Reed was trying to take the ball in himself. Some Matthews guy broke through the line. The hit was helmet to helmet. His neck twisted as his body fell, and when Reed was pinned between the ground and this defender, another player hit him from the other side. He laid there for several minutes because they didn't want to move him too quickly. His neck. His back. Spine, spine, spine.

"Meagan's already working on getting you a flight. I wasn't sure if you'd want Peyton to come too—so if I should cancel hers, let me know. Noles…"

He says my name a few times, each time it sounds like he's calling out to me from a long tunnel. Music kicks in from the gym across from me, and the heavy thud of bass drums at my ribcage.

"Noles," Jason says again.

"Yeah, no…flights. Thank you. Yes, I want Peyton to come. She's competing. I don't know what to do. Do I pull her right now? Do I let her finish? Is he alert? Jesus, Jason…was he talking and moving? Oh my God…"

My mouth waters as my body shudders. This is my worst nightmare. It's why I can't watch Reed's games anymore. So many concussions…all when other players' wives are telling me stories about how their husbands are changing from their head injuries. This is his last extension. He's done—this was it. God don't take him away from me now. We have plans. We have dreams.

"Listen, Noles. He's okay. He's alert. He's in a brace, and this is probably just precautionary. But he might have a fracture. He was moving, though." Jason's voice holds calm and steady, and that's the only reason I don't cry.

I nod and whisper, "Okay."

"Let me find out from Meagan when the flight is. There's no reason Peyton can't finish her competition. Just keep the phone handy, and I will call you right back. And Nolan…it's going to be okay."

I nod again, knowing he can't see me. I can't verbalize; all I can do is picture the absolute worst. If Reed can't walk, or if he loses some part of him…I stop myself there because I know none of it will matter. I will be right there, holding his hand through every single moment until he feels whole again.

Jason ends our call, but I sit with the phone pressed to my cheek for several more minutes, angry at myself that I wasn't watching. If I was watching, maybe this would have happened differently. I know he would have been hit no matter what, but if I'd just seen it, then I would know how bad it really is. My mind conjures up visions that are far worse than what probably happened.

My phone buzzes against my skin and I let it slip down to my lap so I can read the message. Nothing from Jason yet. It's a text from Morgan.

The girls are starting. I'm doing my best to hold your spot.

My legs feel numb, but I drag them into my body so I can stand anyhow. I clutch my phone in both palms against my chest and wait for it to buzz with news, for Jason to call me back. I can't fake it. I've never been good at pretending I'm fine when I'm not—so when I step back into the space next to my friend, her eyes widen in concern.

All I can see to do is shake my head at first.

"Are you okay, Nolan? You look awful. If you're sick, I can take video and just share it with you." I reach out and grip Morgan's wrist, unable to lift my gaze to hers.

"Reed's being rushed to the hospital. He's hurt. He's really hurt." I glaze over as I say the words out loud, shouting them so my friend can hear over the heavy bass and music.

She says something back to me, and I'm not sure what it is, but within minutes, my daughter is running out to the center of a stage in Minneapolis so she can finally land an element she's been working on for months. I bring my phone to my face and position the camera right on her as I begin to record. I keep my face blocked from her view. She's in bliss right now, and she will be for the next seven or eight minutes.

Then I am going to ruin it all with chilling news about her daddy.

Chapter Five

Nolan

Present Day

MY FINGERS still smell like apples, and there is no amount of perfume that's going to combat that. I massage my hands into the back of my neck and just go with the fragrance. I spent three hours slicing apples and baking the cobblers for tonight's booster cookout. It's still the only thing I make just as well as my mom, so whenever Peyton has to contribute for a bake sale, this is what she gets.

It's hard to believe Reed has to leave again so soon. He spent Monday at Peyton's practice. Tuesday, Coach Baker got wind that he was in town and held him captive all day and well into dinner with the team that evening. This trip home for him is so temporary. I hate it. But at least he isn't leaving me to go get sacked all week. The Jeep will be done by morning, but Reed was planning to stay through the homecoming game anyhow, driving through the night and rolling into the stadium in time to report Saturday—still on that disabled list.

Thank God!

"You about ready, Suzie Homemaker?" Reed smirks at me in the reflection of our bathroom mirror. All I can do is glare at him because he knows I hate to be teased over anything domestic.

"I baked two fucking cobblers; I'm hardly a Suzie anything."

I step into him and kiss his lips lightly. He slaps my butt as I walk by him and out the bathroom door.

"You know I love it when you talk dirty like that…*Suzie*." He laughs at his own teasing and I shake my head and roll my eyes.

"Please don't embarrass me by being all gross in front of my friends," Peyton says, overhearing us from her room.

"We wouldn't dream of being gross in front of your friends," Reed says, tugging my hand to pull me into his chest so he can kiss me and dip me backward to overexaggerate and needle at our daughter.

"I'm walking," Peyton huffs, slinging her backpack over her shoulder and moving toward the stairs.

"She's going to take that out on me, you know." I bump my elbow into Reed while he chuckles as we follow our daughter down the stairs.

He shakes it off, but there was more to my comment than just chastising him, and he knows it. I don't mean to rattle off little passive-aggressive things, but they just slip out sometimes. Like just then, when I subtly pointed out that he won't be here.

Despite Peyton's threat, she climbs into the backseat of my Tahoe and slams the door shut while she waits on Reed and me to drive her to school. I carry the stacked cobblers and hold them on my lap when I get in the car, letting Reed drive. It's strange riding to our old high school like this. The familiar memory—of so many trips we took just like this—needles at me along the way.

"So, this Bryce kid…he ask you to homecoming yet?" Reed leans up to stare at Peyton in the mirror, and I sink my neck in between my shoulders a little embarrassed on her behalf. Sometimes, Reed really reminds me of my dad.

"It's not like that," Peyton says, her words clipped. I know my husband isn't dropping this topic, though. One day she'll see his questions like this coming. Not today, though.

"Not like what? A guy doesn't have to ask a girl out?" Reed glances at me and all I can do is shrug with tight lips.

"Oh my God!" Peyton's frustration comes out with a heavy breath.

"I always had to ask girls out," Reed starts, and I can't help myself—I laugh hard, my head jerking back with the force.

"What? I did…" he starts, but I cut him off there.

"Bullshit!" I twist in my seat and look to Peyton for a second. She folds her arms and looks out the windows at her side, but her mouth smirks. She's glad the heat's off her for now.

"Reed Johnson you never directly asked a girl out once in your life. They simply fell in your lap." My mouth hangs open with my personal shock, and when Reed's mouth twists and his brow wrinkles in disbelief, the fire in my chest grows a little wilder.

"Ummm, you didn't," he says, and by some miracle, I don't tip the glassware filled with sticky apples and crust onto him while he drives.

"Only because your lap was already taken up." I move my neck to emphasize my words and gnash my lips together as I mentally run through every swear word I want to throw at him right now too.

"Okay, that's not fair. Besides, you were dating Sean." Reed glares at me as if he's made a good point, and I start to unravel his logic, but before I can, Peyton reminds us she's still here.

"Oh my God, Mom went out with Uncle Sean?"

I glance sideways and take in enough to see my daughter's eyes opened wide with shock. When I look to Reed, he nods slowly, and my eyelids flutter in frustration as I twist and sit back in my seat. We never told Peyton about things like that because none of it was real —it was adolescent high-school stuff, just like she's going through now. I guess at the time, though, it seemed like everything to us.

Maybe some of it was. Reed—he was everything to me then. He still is, and that's why I hate being apart so much.

The three of us ride the rest of the way to the school in silence, and Peyton escapes the car the moment Reed shifts into park. We both sit and watch her walk away in her too-short shorts and over-sized sweatshirt that, deep down, I know she stole from Bryce.

"You really think girls just fell in my lap?" Reed's gaze stays on the scene out our windshield as he speaks. It's been two decades, but the setting and the players are exactly the same. Boys pull up in pickup trucks, their friends piled in the back still hungover from the party the night before. Girls stare at other girls with judgment on their faces, and the shy ones find corners to hide in. Peyton disappears into the crowd, and I think about the heartbreak that is coming for her. It's a rite of passage, and if not this boy, then the next one. I'm jaded.

"I guess it just felt like that to me, because I was always off to the side waiting for you." I feel him look at me, so I don't turn to meet his eyes. It's old wounds that Reed has spent twenty years healing. He's a good man, and he did a lot of dumb things as a teenager. That's what growing up is—it's learning from our mistakes.

"Come on; let's take your cobblers inside." He reaches over and takes the dishes from my lap. I lock gazes with him for a few seconds.

"I'm sorry. It's just that I know you're leaving, and I think I maybe took it out on you a little," I say, breathing in deep and letting the air spill out slowly through my nose. I hold Reed's stare for as long as I can in silence, which is only a few more breaths. "I hate this," I confess.

His eyes flit down to his lap, and he nods slowly.

"I know you do."

We both let that conversation sit in the air for a moment before finally leaving it behind in my car to suffocate behind our closed doors. We'll have that same talk again, I suspect. I'll hate it then, too. I hate it when he leaves, and I hate it when that game clock starts and I have to pray for three hours that he doesn't step foot on that field.

I hate this game that we both used to love. I hate it for putting him in jeopardy.

And I hate Reed a little for being so addicted to the high it gives him that he can't let himself leave it behind.

Most of all, though…I hate that I hate him—even that tiny little bit.

Chapter Six

Reed

THERE'S a bond that happens between a coach and his player. It's always there. Sometimes, it's coach yells, player listens. Other times, it's coach ignores, player quits. The bond isn't always a positive one, but for me and Coach Rudy Baker, it's rare. I won't say he's like a father to me, because he's not. But there's this thing that happens for us, no matter how many years pass between visits—all it takes is a handshake and a hug, and it's like we've been shooting the shit for years.

That happened at practice last night. I watched him work with the little turd who wants to date my daughter. Damn if I didn't miss the simple life—district lights, hand-mown grass, and stripes painted by the janitor on the morning of the game. I promised I'd come by today to check out some films.

I left Nolan with the other booster moms in the cafeteria, and from the glare she gave me, I know that I can't leave her alone in there for long. There was a hot debate happening over what shape the tables should be pushed into for tonight's dinner. There's always some control freak in every squad—my wife isn't it. She's merely the victim, held hostage. If films didn't bore her half to death, I would have told her to come along with me.

The same buzzing sound that shot panic through my sixteen-year-old heart echoes through the halls now, sending the last rush of students squeaking their sneakers along the dirty floor as they race to first hour. Coach Baker's door is propped open, the lights off—just like it always was.

"Still teaching health, huh?" I tap on the glass inset of the door as I slip inside to announce I'm here.

"Ha. Yeah, more like teaching 'please don't make the same sex joke they make every year for this unit.'" Coach clicks the remote to pause the television and leans back in the chair until the front legs tilt up.

I nod toward his angled seat.

"You know, it's true what all those teachers told me. If you're not careful sitting like that, you'll crack your head." I chuckle and rub the back of my skull, remembering the time I fell back in art my junior year. I got an enormous lump from the table behind me, and I hid it from my coaches because I didn't want to miss from the concussion I'm sure I had.

Not much has changed. Still hiding my wounds and leaving shit up to chance on the field.

Coach tips his chair back and drags the nearby chair over for me to sit next to him.

"Nolan didn't want to come?" He laughs at his own question because he knows better.

"It was a tough call for her between this and dealing with Cathy Tolbert," I say.

"Christ, that woman's up my ass every morning and night. Someone gave her my cell number, and I'll be damned if she doesn't text me her every thought and whim about the team and her boy Zach." He rubs his face at the thought of the stress she causes him.

"Why'd you make her president then?" I ask, and he starts to laugh instantly.

"I didn't! Crazy woman was the only one to run!"

We both chuckle at the politics of high school football for a few seconds, but soon his face turns more serious. A tightness takes over my chest, probably because I sense it coming. I try to head it off anyway.

"So, what'd you want to show me?" I prompt his attention toward the TV. He chews at his lips for a few seconds and eventually gives in, clicking the video back to play and pointing at a formation on the screen.

"We play St. Mary's in two weeks. It'll be our toughest game, probably tougher than whoever we end up seeing in state, since we're in different divisions. They've got this kid—six-foot-three and fast as hell."

Coach quiets for a second while we watch. He runs his hand over his mouth and chin, chuckling lightly. His mouth ticks up on the right. "He catches everything, and I don't think we have the manpower to cover him. This crop—they're small as shit, Reed."

I puzzle over where this is going. I'm not really much of an expert on strengthening defenses. I'm more about seeing the holes and maximizing the passing game...or at least, I was...before.

"You've gotta get to the ball before it leaves QB's hands, I guess," I say, circling my finger in the air in a signal for him to play the film back for me one more time.

"That's what I was thinking, but I just figured, since you played with Trig and all..."

I start to nod, and he doesn't have to finish. I see it now, watching this kid on the screen. He's just like Trig, only younger and going up against boys instead of amped-up men. I watch the play through again two more times, then let Coach show me two or three more. It's almost like watching an alternate past, and I start to smile.

"What's got you so amused?" Coach asks.

"Ah, sorry. It's nothin'. Just...I was thinking this is what it would be like if I had Trig to throw to in high school." I let myself imagine it while Coach hums at the thought.

"Nah, that woulda made things way too easy," he says, clicking the pause button and tossing the remote on the metal table in front of us as he leans back again to perch on two chair legs. I do the same, only leaning a little less and keeping my hand close to the nearby desk so I can catch myself if things start to go the wrong way.

"Nothing wrong with easy," I say, meeting his eyes. His mouth forms an amused smile while his eyes wrinkle at the edges, the lines matching the ones filling the skin on his forehead and cheeks. Years of waking up every morning with the sun to run seven miles have kept him fit, even into his sixties. He's got the build of an active army general, but his smoking habit has taken its toll on his skin. I can smell the Marlboros on him even now.

"So, what do you think? Double team? Force them to run? Give up the two…three…maybe four touchdowns he's going to get even through our coverage?"

I consider his question and shrug because if it were Trig Johnson out there catching those passes, there's nothing any team could do to stop him.

"Ah hell, that's what I thought," he says, pulling the pencil from its perch above his ear and tossing it at the paused TV screen.

After a few more seconds of silence, his focus lands on me again. I look up to find his scrutinizing eyes waiting and I try to shirk his stare off a few times before giving in.

"Just say it."

I let out a heavy breath as my chair rights itself and my posture sags into the plastic seat. Coach's eyes drill mine for a few more quiet seconds before he talks.

"You're being stupid."

I start nodding and discounting his critique the moment he begins to deliver it.

"Right, says Mister Two-Packs-A-Day," I say, throwing his careless regard for his health right back in his face. My nickname makes him laugh, and he pulls a half-smoked pack from his front pocket and throws it into my lap.

"You think I should quit? Here…my last pack. Take it—I'll quit. I tell you what…I'll quit if you quit. Sound like a good deal?" His tone is hostile, and I shrink a little because it reminds me of my youth—of those times when our relationship was he yells, I listen.

"Reed, I don't have a family. Hell, I barely have a life outside of this stale-smelling classroom and that football field out there. My brother's the one that had the kids, and I went right from the military to teaching and coaching. I've been here in the same place for thirty-two years, and I'm tired son. But you know why I keep doing this? Why I show up?"

He waits for me to answer.

"Because you love this goddamn game," I say, leaning forward to stare him in the eyes, elbows on my knees.

He matches my posture, his voice getting louder.

"You're damn right, I love this game. I love it! It's my family, son. You, your teammates, those boys I'm coaching right now —family."

I stand up and circle the chair as I thread my hands together behind my head.

"Exactly," I say. He's proving my point—this game is family. It's life. It's air. It's what I know.

"But when I go out there on that field for practice…on Friday nights…" He leans back in his seat again and crosses his arms, the tattoo of a weeping rose faded on his forearm. "There's no question for me, Reed. I show up. I do my job, and I go home. I call every shot because I get to. I get to say what's best for my boys, and I get to see them safe. That's my job, Reed."

He stands and paces a few steps toward the wall where he flips on the lights. The harsh glare makes me squint for a few seconds.

"You don't get that luxury." Coach stops and leans into the wall, hooking his thumbs in the pockets of his shorts. "Your job is different. It isn't safe—not any more. And if I didn't tell you that, I wouldn't be doing mine."

I breathe in hard through my nose, exhaling heavily in frustration. He had to say it to me because yeah, it's his job. This is his family. It isn't mine.

The blaring sound of tubas and drums echoes through the hallway, and the disruption is just enough to break up this moment that is making me feel trapped.

"I should go rescue Noles," I say, not liking the way Coach is looking back at me. His face is full of expectations for me to ride this season out, play up this injury and finish up clean. That fire in my belly is still begging for a single shot, though, to prove I've got a few thousand-plus yards left in this arm.

Coach stretches forward with his hand and I grip it. He holds me captive with a firm squeeze for a beat, a silent deal made between us that I'll really think about things.

The halls are filling up between classes and the band is starting to snake through the hallways, a tradition on homecoming week. It's hard not to feel young again hearing the sounds, and I find myself high-fiving players as they walk by me, feeling like I'm a part of their team. Weirdest fucking thing in the world is the fact that I'm somehow their hero.

I catch Nolan's eyes across the parking lot, and I hold up my hand to tell her I'm coming. I weave through the crowd, but just before I pass the last building, I catch sight of something that stills me in my tracks. Between two portable buildings—in the exact spot I would have gone if I were in his shoes—that little shit Bryce is kissing my baby girl.

"Mother fuck," the words come out under my breath. Without pausing to wait for reason to kick in, I change course and am walking toward them. I get to the edge of the building when Peyton hears my steps coming. She flips her hair from her eyes, glaring at me.

"Mr. Johnson...sir..."

Little shit is wiping his mouth on his sleeve. I'm gonna hit him.

"God, Dad. Don't you have some place to be?" Peyton picks her backpack up from the ground and jerks it over her shoulder. The irony of what she said punches my funny bone.

"Uh, don't *you?*" She bunches her lips and brushes past me. I wish like hell I could swap places with Nolan right now. This is not a situation for a dad, not a dad like me—not a dad with a daddy's girl.

"I'm real sorry..." Bryce stammers and his lips keep moving even though he's not saying any words. Or maybe he is, and I'm deafened by rage.

"Big game Friday." I decide to keep it cool with my words, even though I know my mouth is a hard, straight line and my eyes are narrowed on his jugular.

"Yes, yeah. It's against Liberty. They're number one."

I watched Bryce practice, and he does look smooth out on that field, but he's built like a feather. Liberty's gonna hurt.

"Rankings are just numbers. You know their defense?" I can't believe I'm thinking what I'm thinking. I still want to strangle him, but damn it—it's like a fucking mirror.

"They're big," he says, his mouth dejected. He sees the hurt coming.

"Big means slow," I say.

"That's what Coach says."

I catch Nolan in my periphery, so I take a step back to let Bryce off the hook and unblock his way out of this very narrow pathway —in which he was making out with my baby girl!

"Coach Baker knows what he's talking about. You got lucky to be his QB." I put my hand on his shoulder and squeeze a little, mostly to drive home the point that I can still crush him anytime I want to.

"We moved here just so I could play for him," he says, and the coincidences pile on even more. The only thing missing is for this kid to tell me his last name's Johnson and he's my long-lost baby brother…which would be good, because then he couldn't date my daughter.

"I tell ya what…" I stop next to Nolan and catch the bend in her lips as she silently laughs at me. "How about we meet up on the field today before practice—you guys still go at five?"

"Yes, sir." His formality is winning some brownie points.

I glance at Nolan and she tilts her head in a subtle warning that I ignore completely.

"Be out there and ready at four," I say, and this baby-faced punk lights up.

"Cool," he says, the word half teenaged giggle. Jesus Christ.

"Who's your next class?" I ask, noticing the hallways and walkways are completely empty now. He's late, which given who he is and the jersey he wears, he probably won't be in trouble anyway, but just in case.

"Lit, with Walker," he says, and I catch the little roll of his eyes. Mrs. Walker's tough. She's also probably close to retirement. I could walk him back to class and give him an excuse, but I've been too easy on him. I can't let him off the hook completely.

"Ah yeah, she hates late students. I tell you what…" He leans in, eyes widening like a kid on the precipice of the best show-and-tell moment of his life. Nolan's gonna kick my ass for this, but it's worth it. "Just tell her I caught you making out with my daughter and spent a little while making sure you don't do that again. Think that'll work?"

His swallow is audible, and I recognize the forced smile and laugh he gives. I've given those.

"Sorry, sir." He gets my point. That isn't for his teacher. It's my warning.

I wink and nod over his shoulder, shooing him along. His scrawny body looks smaller now, or maybe it's just the dad-colored glasses I'm wearing. I wait for him to get his hand on the hallway door handle before I give him an inch of room to breathe.

"And don't forget. Be there at four," I remind him as his eyes are still on mine for a few seconds before he turns back to the door.

My shoulders roll and Nolan's hands find them, her palms sliding down my long-sleeved T-shirt until she's wrapped them around one of my biceps. I flex to show off because I can't help it, and she nestles into that space under my arm as she loops my arm over her head. I kiss the top of her head as we walk back out to the lot and her hand comes up to pat my chest a few times.

"You didn't have to yell at your daughter's boyfriend," she says, and my gut tightens at that word—*boyfriend*. Ugh!

"Hey, look…what I want to do is make plans with him and not show up, just to make him wait out there for an hour all nervous and shit…"

"But you won't do that because that isn't nice," Nolan cuts in, and I wince remembering all of the times someone did something like that to her. This would be for entirely different reasons, and I think this Bryce kid will be just fine socially, but I get what she means.

"I won't stand him up." She squeezes my arm in approval. I bite my tongue and keep the follow-up to myself. I won't stand him up, but I'll work his ass really hard and maybe throw a little extra zip in those hard-to-catch places.

We reach the Tahoe, and I open the passenger door for her to get inside, wondering how I got so lucky to have a girl like this in my life at all. She's the same sweet girl who's at her happiest in a pair of jeans and wearing Chucks. I reach down and tug the top of one of her mismatched socks that shows when her jeans rise up. I know she put them on this morning because they were the only things she could find that were clean.

"They're Peyton's," she admits. Somehow, that's even cuter.

"We should go on a date." I kneel down next to her and twist her legs so they're facing me, which makes her giggle.

"Wouldn't that be amazing." Sarcasm always suited her.

"I'm serious," I say, wrapping my hands under the underside of her knees. She quirks her lip up as she looks down at me then runs both of her hands through my hair, grabbing hold and leaning forward just enough to meet my eyes.

My phone blares from the center console and the light dims behind her eyes.

"Hey," I lift my chin and move one hand to her face. "We're discussing our date."

Her gaze sits with mine while Drake repeats for a second time through. They'll leave a message.

"Go on. Answer," she says.

I know exactly how long I have before that call slips to voice-mail. I should wait it out, but I give in and lean around her, grabbing my phone in time to answer. I catch a glimpse just before I bring it to my ear. It's Stacia. The only reason she would call me is because she needs help with Trig. My stomach sinks and I stand and walk away from the car a few steps, automatically bringing my fingers to the bridge of my nose to prepare for the worst.

"Hey, Stac. What's up?" These calls used to begin with her

yelling at me because Trig wasn't around to yell at. Then they slipped into her calling me because she couldn't find him. I haven't talked to her in a few months though now, so I'm thrown when the only sound I hear coming from the other line is heavy, choking sobs.

"Reed…he's gone. He just…I don't know what to do, and I didn't know who else to call. Trig…they found him."

My eyes lift just enough to find Nolan's, but my mouth doesn't know what to do. I'm barely able to breathe, and there's a good chance I'm not. I just talked to him four days ago…maybe five. He was getting ready to go on some yacht with some girl who wasn't Stacia. He was living "the life," as he said. To think of life without him…it cripples.

Nolan's hand is on my arm and I have no idea how she got here. Stacia's been repeating the same awful truth. And I'm frozen.

Chapter Seven

Nolan

NOTHING IS CONFIRMED. They don't confirm things like this for months, because there's always a chance that their guesses are wrong.

They're not wrong.

Trig did get on a yacht like he told Reed he was going to do. He never had any intention of getting off of it, though. They found an empty bottle of the Vicodin he'd been taking for back pain for years and Oxy that he didn't have a prescription for. He washed it all down with Jack, then fell into a forever sleep with the boat tethered to the dock. It wasn't his boat. He didn't even know the owner.

Reed keeps playing their last conversation over and over again, looking for something he missed, and I don't know what to do for him. I don't think there's an answer to be found. Trig didn't want anyone to think he was anything other than in love with the life he'd finally gotten. But there was so much self-destruction.

I don't know.

I don't know.

"I'll be back in time for the dinner," Reed says, suddenly

standing from the chair he's been glued to in the living room since we got home. He made calls from that chair, consoled Stacia as best he could, told his dad and Jason, and stared into my eyes waiting for me to tell him what to do next. Mostly, he just sat there staring into empty space…avoiding.

It's like a switch flipped suddenly. He has his keys in his hand, the Jeep's keys, and he's smooshing his head into a hat that's too small—one he hasn't worn since college.

"Where are you going?" I'm cautious as I stand, treating him like a feral cat that's just getting used to my scent. His eyes don't settle on anything—on me—for long. Instead, he looks around at everything and nothing, forcing expressions in an effort to show me nothing's wrong.

Everything's wrong.

"I promised Bryce I'd meet him at four, so…ya know…" He flashes me a tight grin and lifts his fisted keys as a gesture of goodbye.

"Reed!" Long strides get me to him before he can swing the side door closed. There's no way I'm letting him leave the house right now alone. He's not driving, either. And I don't give a shit if now's not the time for a fight.

He turns halfway, expecting me and my words.

"Bryce would get it. You don't have to…"

"Noles, I'm fine. Really." His eyes still can't fully connect with mine, and he's palming his keys so hard that his knuckles are turning white. He's avoiding feeling things and dealing with this by going right to that masculine aggression of his. The only way for me to combat it is to speak his language, so I hold his stare and take small steps toward him until I can feel the heat of his breath.

"I just wanna go do something normal," he says.

"Then I'll drive you." I hold out my open palm.

"I'm fine," he argues, but I flex my fingers and flash my hand again, my face growing more serious.

"Not. A. Debate."

He blinks finally and his eyes flit down to my hand. One heavy sigh and they're in my grasp, my husband already marching to his precious vehicle.

I'd rather drive my car. I hate the Jeep. It's been rebuilt twice now, and the motor idles so damn hard I can feel the fillings in my molars jostle against my nerves. My husband is already climbing into the passenger side, though, and I think if I made him change cars at this point he would scream obscenities and run his ass to the field.

That might actually be good for him.

I consider it for a second, and dismiss it quickly, opening the driver's side door and lifting myself up. I catch his smirk as I struggle my way in.

"You know I can never get in this thing gracefully," I say, shimmying my hips into the very well-worn bucket seat. I buckle and shove the key in and realize he's still smiling at me, that special kind that's subtle but sorta just for me.

"What?" I whisper.

"I was remembering you driving this thing pregnant. Sometimes...ha..." He rubs his chin and relaxes back in his seat, amused with our past. "Sometimes, it would take you three or four attempts."

"Or six...or seven," I add, remembering how embarrassing it would be at the grocery store. Reed thought he was being kind when he bought me the super-responsible "mom car." He was so proud of doing something so responsible. I didn't want to tell him it was hideous, that it smelled like hot plastic, and that the interior color made me look jaundiced in the rearview mirror. I just told him that I missed the Jeep, but damn this thing—it's sentimental, but it rides rough as shit!

His cheeks lift with the slight growth in his smile and his eyes dance over my face until I blush. Somehow...still, after all these years, this guy can make me feel special just by the way he looks at me.

"You're beautiful."

His compliment warms my chest, and I take it in quietly, the golden glow of the falling sun touching off the red in the ends of his hair as it shines through the side windows. I can't even imagine my life if I lost this man. He's half of me, even when we're living a thousand miles apart.

I back out enough to turn the Jeep around, and that little moment of bliss slips away. Reed's eyes trail back into nothingness, never leaving the space inside this cab. He'll be leaving soon, and then I suppose we'll both meet again in Santa Fe for the funeral. Trig's parents still live there.

It's close to four in the afternoon when I pull around to the backside of the football field, parking behind the bleachers just like the visiting team does. Bryce is standing out in the middle of the field running patterns and pretending to take snaps. I bet he's been here waiting for an hour just to impress Reed.

My husband starts to open the door before I completely put the Jeep in park, so I grab his arm to get his attention. His eyes move my direction but don't meet mine. He's on auto again.

"Hey, take it easy on this kid." There's double meaning in my request. Bryce might deserve a little more ribbing from his girl-friend's father, but he doesn't deserve the emotions that accompany the grief inside Reed right now.

Reed nods to acknowledge me, then slides out from his seat, pushing the door closed behind him. There's no way I'm leaving, and Reed knows that. I drive around to the other lot, though, and pull into a spot to watch from more distance. Peyton's practice is starting on the other side of the field, and I hope like hell Bryce clued her in on this impromptu session her dad set up this morning. I hope Peyton gets in the Jeep before Reed's done. I want to be able to prepare her about Uncle Trig. It's going to crush her.

Tucked deep in the driver's seat, I pull out my phone and take one last look at my tiny little family. My daughter is fearless, so different from me in some ways. She's a flier, and it makes my heart stop every time those boys throw her in the air. I'd feel better having the other girls catch her, honestly. The boys are stronger, but damn is their attention span pathetic. She's tumbling now, flip after flip along the track. Every time she stops, her eyes go right to Bryce and Reed.

My eyes go there mostly, too. It's like we've both slipped into a time machine and I'm still the girl watching him from far away. His body is bigger, but those moves—the way he can step back and just see. He's always been special.

I thumb through my contacts list and press Sienna's number when I get to her, giving my attention back to Reed. She answers a little out of breath, and I'm sure I've caught her rushing from one of her girl's activities to the other. Her and Micah had their first girl soon after they were married, and a few years later wanted to try for one more. They ended up with triplets—every single child a girl. Sienna's life is spent between dance and swim and diving and piano lessons. They're all incredibly different, but also incredibly gifted in some way.

"Noles, what's up?" She's trying to mask her panting.

"Let's see…Thursday, so is this swim to dance?"

My friend laughs, but only as much as her breathing will allow.

"Close, it's piano to swim. We're running late, and by running… I mean we're *running*. The damn van won't start, and whoever decided to build the swim complex on top of the hill was an idiot." Her phone slips and I hear her girls yelling at her to hurry in the background.

"It's okay, just call me back when you can." I walk through the mental list of everyone else I need to call.

"No…no…hold on." Her phone muffles again, but this time by her palm. She tells her girls to go ahead and after a few seconds her end of the line clears up, and her breath seems to finally catch too. "They don't need me. They're eight. Talk to me."

I smile and rest my head on the window, realizing how much I've missed my friend being close. They live up north, outside of Flagstaff, and it's only a four-hour drive, but life makes that trip seem impossible lately.

"Trig passed away." I don't know another way to say it, but that's not the entire truth. I'm being sensitive, but maybe I shouldn't.

"Oh God." I hear how it smacks her just like it did me. Her

voice loses something as she speaks. It's because this is the first time we've all been faced with mortality like this. Trig…he was one of us.

"They found him…on a boat…" I let Sienna work out the details in her own mind, and I sit in silence on the phone with my friend for nearly a full minute.

"How's Reed?"

I swallow at the question.

"He's not good. He's gone into robot mode, and we haven't talked about it—just the two of us. He's actually out on our old high school field right now showing Peyton's boyfriend some of his old moves." I look up in time to see Reed clapping loudly at one of Bryce's throws before jogging out to collect a few of the balls.

"What's he doing in town?"

"Retrieving the precious Jeep, signing the deed; we met with the lawyer a couple days ago out on the property. It's pretty much done. And he's still on the ole disabled list." I forget the last time Reed's been around for one of our get-togethers, and the idea strikes me all of a sudden. "Hey, actually…it's homecoming tomorrow. You think…"

"Hell yes, woman. Micah's mom owes us big time! And I need a break. I'll call him now, and we'll be down there by morning. We'll bring those breakfast burritos you love. I'll freeze them tonight and they'll be thawed by the time we roll in for breakfast."

My mouth waters thinking about the fresh chorizo.

"You sure Micah's okay taking off that early?" I ask.

"If not, I'm leaving him at home." I laugh at her answer, but I'm fairly certain my friend is dead serious.

I hang up with Sienna and let her work out the details on her end while I send my next round of texts to Sean and Becky, who both call me back at the same time—from separate rooms of their San Diego house. I leave them both to figure out the how and when, and by the time Reed is done working with Bryce, I have a mini reunion set in motion. I did it all so fast, so caught up with the excitement of it all, that I didn't really give myself a second to consider how he might…actually…hate it.

In a perfect storm, he climbs into the Jeep just as Peyton finishes practice, and now I'm stuck trying to sort out what type of conversation to have next. I get the wrong one out of the way first, and I know it is, but it's easier to have.

"I did a thing," I start.

His response comes in a heavy breath, and I turn in time to see his fists twisting in his eyes. They look tired when they open on me, tired for different reasons. His eyes are tired from holding in everything he needs to let out.

"Becks and Sean are driving in, and Micah and Sienna are coming down. Sarah's already here, so ya know...I thought..." It was a stupid idea. This isn't the time to celebrate.

Reed barely reacts, a crooked smile dimpling one cheek briefly while dead eyes blur out on my face.

"I didn't think. I'll call them back, tell them maybe next year, or..."

His hand falls on top of mine.

"No, it's cool. They can stay with us. It'd be nice, really. It's been a while." He's feigning enthusiasm, and he's a bad liar.

"They'll understand," I say, giving him the option of an out.

"I know," he says, drawing in another deep breath. You'd think he'd been sacked a thousand times today by the way every breath seems so heavy. "I'm being honest, though. I'd like to see everybody...and it's homecoming."

Peyton taps on the window next to him, and he turns enough to give her a smile as he puts his hand on the door handle to let himself out.

"I'm gonna walk home with her, let her know about Trig. I think maybe that'd be good for both of us."

I give him a nod, and he steps out of the Jeep, dropping Peyton's bag in place of where he was sitting. Peyton glances at me, and in that small second, I catch the panic in her eyes. She hasn't said it directly, but I know she's been worried about her dad and me. We don't fight in front of her. We don't really fight. Sometimes that long silence can be harder to handle, though, and I know she's felt the wall we've both put up. She was with me when Reed was in surgery, when I got the news he had possible spinal trauma. She's watched me break down in fear that something awful is going to happen to him, and when those studies started to pile up about brain injuries, I wasn't particularly good at keeping my opinion out of breakfast-time conversation.

I drive away thinking of how my daughter, for a second, thought her parents were about to tell her they were getting a divorce. In my mirror, I see her crumble into Reed's arms over the truth. I'm not sure which hurt would be better for her to have.

Chapter Eight

Reed

"WHAT DID you talk to him about?" Peyton finally bursts with the question she's been biting onto behind those tightly closed lips. She jerks down on the sleeve of my dress shirt in a frustrated move to stop me from walking into the school auditorium for the booster dinner.

"We talked about football, honey. I swear...that's it." I bend down and kiss the top of her head, eliciting a sigh. She doesn't believe me, and I'm okay with that. I like her being apprehensive and nervous. Maybe it will keep her from doing something stupid.

Peyton walks ahead of us, the glimmer of her pompoms flashing wildly with her pounding steps as she quickly marches away to join her friends.

"When did she get so...teenagery?" My shoulders sag, and Nolan weaves her hand in mine.

"When she became a teenager," she answers. I shake out a small laugh.

We're still hidden in the refuge of the dark parking lot, and part of me wants to turn around and hide in the Tahoe until Peyton's done. I'm sure that would be her preference, but I promised Coach I would talk to the parents and maybe help boost morale. The Bears are still good, but the spirit hasn't been the same for a few years. Honestly, what they need more than me is my dad. He had a way of getting people to volunteer and pledge their undying allegiance to anything, including a Division Three high school, in a rural area still about fifty miles away from any real sprawl.

Nolan and I make it about three steps inside before we're swarmed by other parents. It's funny how their boys have the ability to treat me like just another human, but when I interact with the adults, they just get stupid.

"Hey, Reed. I don't know if you remember me, but I caught your last pass during practice drills before our final run to state senior year." I take the hand of the man talking and search my memory bank for anything that might clue me in, but nothing's there. He's my height, maybe about forty pounds heavier than me, and bald.

"Yeah! Hey, how's it going? How's your boy doing?" I fake it, and I see I've been caught in the way his eyes dip and his mouth bunches.

"Daughter. She's on cheer," he says.

"Oh, that's right. Sorry," I say, pointing to my head and sticking out my tongue in an effort to accentuate how clueless I can be.

"That's cool. We're proud." He shrugs with his words. The way he answers me is lifeless, like he's disappointed that he isn't the father of a football player as well. I think of Peyton, and suddenly this guy pisses me off.

"Honestly, I'm so glad I have a girl, and she cheers. Us dumb jocks could never do half the shit they do. Too much coordination. We'd break our necks."

It's the wrong word choice, and I feel it in the way Nolan squeezes my hand. It's too late though, and Mr. Pass Catcher is already being joined by four or five other dads all standing around waiting to talk to me about getting knocked out of my last big start, and surgery, and the chances I might get the ball a few times this season. My wife slips away in the chaos, and after indulging the small crowd in my well-practiced answers about feeling lucky to be a part of the OKC organization…and the talented young quarterback I'm mentoring—lie, lie, lie—I excuse myself.

Nolan's seated at the center table near the front, doing her best to make small talk with women I know she doesn't really have a thing in common with. She pretends well, though, coming to life for shared frustrations over having teenagers when the topics sway that way. I should join her, but I'm stuck on the last question one of the dads asked me before I stepped away.

"What do you think happened with Trig Johnson?"

I've thought millions of things in the few hours I've had to process the news. It still doesn't feel real, and I keep pulling my phone into my palm surfing my texts, expecting one to be from my friend—asking for advice on what exotic place to take his latest fling or what car to blow his next sponsorship check on. I'm so mad I deleted his old messages because I can't even look at them to pretend now.

"How you holding up?" Coach Baker slides in next to me, our backs to the entrance and our eyes on the nearly full banquet.

I raise a shoulder and spin my phone in my palm one more time before pocketing it.

"Haven't really gotten through that first step yet…realization… is that?" I tilt my head toward him and he shakes his head.

"Denial is first. Sounds like you're right on track, too." He brings his hand up to my shoulder and squeezes once.

Denial. Yeah, I guess that's what this is. It's not as literal as they tell you in therapy. I know what happened, but I don't want to.

"You ready for this little speech thing? I appreciate it, but if you're just not up to it, nobody knows it's happening, so we can just…" He makes scissors with his fingers.

"Nah, I like the distraction. Keeps me in denial." I breathe out a pathetic laugh.

I follow Coach up the short row of steps that lead to the stage where they announced our homecoming king and queen every year I was here. I wore that crown every time, thinking that paper and glitter put together by fifteen-year-old girls on a committee really meant something. I bet Bryce wins tomorrow night.

"Proud Bears Families," Coach gets their attention through the mic. It squeals a little, so he taps the side of it and one of the parent volunteers rushes to the edge of the stage to turn down the amps. "Thank you all for coming out for tonight's Booster Dinner."

He knows when to pause; he's done this song and dance so many times. Everyone applauds and the team stands and slaps their hands on their tables, a roar of thunder culminating with a growl.

"I hope you can bring that energy to Liberty tomorrow."

Coach is answered with a swift "Yes, sir!" in unison. He's trained them well, and I look down at my red suede shoes as I mouth the words with them and smile. Some things are hard to unlearn.

"Normally, I spend this time telling you all of the things we need to accomplish to get to state this year, and the jobs we're going to need to fill and money we need to raise, but..." He pauses to step to the left a little and hold an arm out toward me. One eye squints more than the other with his smile, and I feel my heart pound a little heavier with nerves. I haven't been nervous in front of a crowd in years.

"It's not every day that we get a seven-time Pro-Bowler and future Hall-of-Famer in our humble cafeteria-slash-auditorium." His description gets a wave of laughter, and I step close enough to speak into his mic for a second.

"I heard I still have a delinquent account with the lunch lady," I add, which drags the laughs on a little longer.

"I'll wave your fees if you sign my shirt!" A woman stands up in the middle of the room and holds her Bears shirt out in front of her, stretching it across very ample breasts. My eyes bulge a little and I look at Coach.

"Reed, meet Abigail Loman, our cafeteria manager," Coach says.

I nod and smile, turning my eyes back to my fan.

"Nice to meet you, ma'am." I say, bracing myself for her to yell at me for calling her ma'am. Nolan kicks me when she catches me doing that, but I get stuck sometimes wanting to be respectful and not knowing what word to use. She says women don't like to be called that, but damn it…these rules are hard.

"You spent time with my boy today. We're huge fans, and he started playing because of you. So, thank you." She says, nodding at me again as she folds her hands over her chest now in appreciation. This tall woman with big, blonde hair and hoop earrings is Bryce's parent.

I smile and mouth "No problem" while I make a few mental notes about other things, like the lack of a husband sitting next to her, and the years she seems to have on the other women in the room. She's at least fifteen or twenty years everyone's senior.

Bryce has a story.

"Well, I could waste ten minutes on some introduction up here, boring you all with old stories I have about what it was like to coach this guy when he was a pain-in-the ass punk…no offense," Coach says, holding a palm up to me.

I give one back.

"None taken," I say.

"But I'm pretty sure everyone in this room has a good handle on his story. It's hard to live in Coolidge and not know Reed Johnson. Hell, you might just be in our history books now, son. So, go on, take this thing from me." He tips the mic my direction and I pull it into my hand, chuckling under my breath.

"Thanks, Coach…I think." I scratch at my head, a few loose strands of my hair flopping over my forehead. I run my fingers over my head and smooth it back, my nervous tick starting already.

"I'm glad I got to be here for this tonight. These dinners…I always loved them. Mostly because my dad didn't cook worth shit and this was the one time of year I had really good food."

Everyone laughs with me, and my eyes go to Nolan's. Dark hair frames her pale face like a heart. Her smirk puts me at ease, and my pulse settles in, but my palms continue to sweat. I've realized too late that I'm not sure what to say to this group of young athletes, to these families. The tears hit me unexpectedly, and with force. I run my wrist over my eyes and breathe out an embarrassed laugh. I can't believe this is happening here.

"I'm sorry…" I shake my head and plaster on a wide smile. It's so fake it hurts my cheeks to form it. "It's been a really hard day. Trig Johnson…he was like a brother to me. He was a special player, an athlete and a friend. And today's news…"

I break down a little more and when I search for Nolan, I find her a few seats closer, ready to come up to stand with me. She's chewing at her nails, her feet curled under her chair in the nice shoes she doesn't get to wear very often. She's in a dress I haven't seen before. We were supposed to have a date. I shake my head slightly and hold my hand out a bit in front of me to let her know I can make it through this.

"Woooo," I puff out, blinking my lids dry. The entire room is silent, and this is the last thing this team needs before heading into their final sleep before their most important game of the season. Trig would smack me for this, tell me I'm "dulling his jam." That's what he'd always say when I got moody in college. In the pros, he'd Tweet it to me as a joke when I had a better week than he did.

"I've always been proud of where I came from, which…I know. 'But Reed, dude, your dad owned a dozen car dealerships. You didn't come from anything very adverse.' But I know that I was fortunate in having parents who saw talent in me, who knew that me playing for a school like this, for a coach like this, would be the difference maker. This place—it's community. You look around here tonight and I'll tell you what you see—you see the people who've got your back."

I didn't think about any of this. I felt it, the words, and what I'm about to do. I didn't talk it over with Nolan, and I hate that because not talking things over has been the cause of most of our trouble in life, but I know she'll be all right with this.

"Trig had my back. Always. He caught that damn pass—oh, y'all know the one," I trail into a chuckle. They join me. "You know what he said to reporters in the media room after the game? He said he got lucky because he just happened to be in the right place for the only mistake I ever made.'"

My mouth tugs in on one side and I put a fist against my chest, tapping myself a few times with it.

"My wife can attest to you all that's just a damn lie. I make mistakes all the time. I've been making them for years," I say through a growing smile. I look to Nolan who's nodding and gazing around the room to affirm what I said.

"Trig said that because, even in his moment, he wanted to make sure some of the praise came down on me. He spun that game so it wasn't one of my worst, and I don't know…maybe it wasn't, but that selfless moment right there, giving me that…"

I look to my feet and hold the mic against my chest now. I wait for the wave to pass, the one that threatens to choke away my words, and when I feel like I can, I give back the only thing that feels fitting.

"Y'all know that grass you play on is shit, right? And those bleachers…tell me, parents, what do you think about those bleachers?" I hold my palm open and lift it over and over, encouraging their participation, and eventually I'm serenaded with nodding heads in agreement and shouts of "the worst" and "splinters" and "so uneven!"

Glancing to Nolan, I meet her eyes and do my best to convey what I'm about to propose. I could be wrong, but I think her nod means she understands.

"You pull off a win tonight, you win out the season and make that run through playoffs and bring home that state title—an undefeated state title—then next year's games will be on a field of dreams, with a stadium worthy of a school like this. This town is getting bigger, and this football program needs to be equipped to keep up because there are some serious titles in its future. If you keep producing the talent, then you should have a house that fits. Buck Johnson stadium, home of Trig Johnson field. I like the sound of that, and in my head, I see it clearly. You all better not fuck this up!"

I mouth an apology to coach and a few parents sitting nearby, but nobody seems too upset with my F-bomb. It was fitting the moment. I don't know a damn thing about contracting or tearing down and rebuilding a football field, but I know that guy who bought our land does—and I know he's good people. And I've got eight million coming to me guaranteed, so might as well spend it.

I think they call this stage of grief *bargaining*. The reason it's in the middle is it doesn't work.

Chapter Nine

Nolan

"REED'S not going to start walking around your corn talking to old-time football players from, like, 1910 or whatever, is he?" I knew Sarah would think this was nuts. It is nuts, but it isn't really a bad kind of nuts. We both have always liked the idea of charity and giving back, and our old school is falling apart. I actually adore the gesture and the outcome.

"First of all, we don't grow corn. Second, the NFL wasn't around in 1910, and third, Reed is not Kevin Costner. And you know what? The book was better than the movie!" I throw that last part in because Sarah's frustrating me.

"*Field of Dreams* is a book?"

I lean my head forward into the cabinet and moan while the coffee finishes dripping.

"Girl, you were the smart one with all that reading and stuff. Don't act all snobby all of a sudden," Sarah says.

"She's not the smart one. I'm the smart one!" Sienna's voice cuts through Sarah and my spat. We all start squealing as we rush our missing piece at the doorway, not even letting her get her bags inside before we carry her off, arms linked with ours, to the couch where we can make up for too much time apart.

"Don't worry; I'll just get all these bags that we, for some reason, needed for a weekend, that doesn't require jackets or snow boots, and far fewer layers than we're used to," Micah calls from the doorway. We talk right over him.

"I got you," Reed says, stepping up behind him. He's been wandering around outside since the sun came up this morning, half of the time spent with his phone pressed to his ear making the field pipe dream happen. I know it never depended on the Bears winning or losing homecoming, but there's no need to take the carrot away from a bunch of teenage boys who look ready to work harder than they ever have in their lives. Reed has a lot of legwork to do on this thing if he wants to pull it off anyhow. I don't need another project landing on my lap, so the more hiring he can get done now, the better.

Reed grabs half of the bags and winks at me as he passes through the living room with Micah.

"Looking good there, old man," Sienna says, followed by a whistle.

Both Reed and Micah shout, "Thanks."

"I love that they're both fighting to be called old men," Sarah says, swinging her body over the couch to the cabinet where my favorite wine is still hiding—at least what's left of it.

"I say we trade the coffee in for something more our speed." My friend helps herself, navigating my kitchen as if she's our live-in chef. Honestly, she's probably in that room more than I am.

Sarah pours three glasses and delivers them to Sienna and me, the rest of the bottle tucked under her arm. I give a short laugh looking at the glass because it's not even close to lunch time yet, but what the hell. I'm never a rebel. I take a small sip and sink into the soft couch cushion while Sienna takes the opposite end and stretches her legs out to my lap.

"So, catch me up. How's everything going?" She asks.

I shrug and glance to Sarah.

"He's still a stupid boy who doesn't talk," Sarah answers for me.

"It's not that…" I add, but then stop because really…it's still a lot of that, too. "I think his problem is he doesn't know *how* to talk about it. It's all too close, ya know? Trig dying…"

"It's like a version of himself," Sienna finishes. I swallow hard and stop breathing because she's nailed it. It's exactly that, and I know it. Reed knows it, too. It's why we don't know how to dissect anything that's happened over the last twenty-four hours.

"Reed's entire identity has been about the game, and I'm guessing Trig's path was exactly the same. But neither of them gave a single thought to what they would become when the game was done." Sienna's words float between the three of us, and I realize she said everything that's been worrying me—worrying my husband.

Is just being someone's husband and father enough for him?

It wasn't enough for Trig, or if it was, he didn't give it a chance to feel like enough. He blew it up like a child throwing a tantrum—with bitter divorce and drunken escapades with girls that looked nothing like his ex-wife—that made regular weekend headlines. But this life, it's enough for Reed. I know it is.

"I'm gonna check on Buck," I say, leaving the conversation I know Sarah and Sienna are dying to have about Reed and me when I leave. I'm okay with that, too, because maybe they'll come up with some grand solution that will make this knot in my gut untangle.

Buck's already dressed and sitting in his chair when I get to his room.

"Rose got you ready before she went to the church this morning, huh?" I lean in to kiss my father-in-law on the cheek.

"I did this myself," he says as I step back, impressed.

He works his right hand down the middle of his chest, two buttons still needing to be redone, off by one hole. It's still amazing, and proof that the intense physical therapy he's been pushing himself through is paying off. Reed is so much like his dad.

I fix the mixed-up buttons for Buck then stand back to take him in again. His lopsided smile is proud.

"Well, damn." I fold my arms over my chest. "Handsome as ever."

"Bull—shit," he coughs out with a laugh. I chuckle with him but shake my head and reach forward to reshape his thinning hair across his forehead.

"No bullshit." I smile and hold his gaze for a breath until he rolls his head and eyes a little, reluctantly letting me have my way.

I take the handles of his chair and direct it toward the door of his room, but before we get there completely, Buck starts to grumble excitedly. I stop and kneel to look him in the eyes again. His speech has gotten so much better, but I find it's still easier when I'm looking right at him.

"Let me walk. Just…to the…door," he says.

We've been trying to do this a few times every week. He calls it his "extra practice," still thinking he's out there on that field somehow, even though *he* hasn't been out there in years.

"All right," I say with a shake of my head.

Buck clicks the brakes and shifts his feet until they find a steady balance on the ground. This is always the hardest part, so I wait with my arms flexed and carrying a lot of his weight as he pushes himself up from the chair and works to find his center.

"I got it," Buck barks. He still gets frustrated with me sometimes, and despite the temptation to just let go, I don't because I know that "I got it" is often wrong.

I loosen my hold, but keep contact until I feel him sway less. He stands taller when he feels it, rolling his shoulders sloppily and stretching his open palms out at his hips. I reach to take his hand but he slaps at me, which only makes me laugh. Stubborn as shit!

"I've got this," he says, his lips twisted in concentration.

His breath is struggling from the start, but it doesn't deter him. Buck uses the strength he's worked hard to build on his right side to compensate, his body dragging on the left, but still moving forward. It's the switch that always gets him. I stand behind him with my hands out and ready. He doesn't see me, because he'd only slap me away if he did. With unsteady feet, he shifts his weight to his weak side and grunts as he pushes his right foot forward. His limb moves well on that side, but it depends on so much strength from his left that it's difficult for him despite being stronger.

We move in inches, but those inches double with every shuffle. By the time his hands can safely grasp the doorframe, he's able to nearly pull his right foot fully from the ground.

"That's right!" Buck shouts, reaching forward and taking the doorway firmly. He belly-laughs, the gravelly nature of his voice crackling as he tips his head back and howls in celebration. I clap behind him, and the sound draws Reed into the room.

"My wife trying to pinch your ass again?" Reed teases, and I grimace at him.

"Your dad just walked to the door all by himself." I lower my brow and purse my lips before crossing my arms.

Reed's eyes widen, then glance behind his father seeing the short distance. His expression morphs a dozen times within a second, from sadness that his dad can no longer do something so simple, to pity and guilt that he's not here to fix this—that he *can't* fix this.

"That's nothing," Buck pauses, working his mouth to make his words. "I'm taking my seat…at the game tonight."

I cover my mouth and run my hand over my chin thinking about the logistics. Buck's seat is on the field, in a special set of bleachers and chairs set up behind the western end zone. He hasn't sat there in a couple years because the field isn't exactly *accessible*. The entire stadium isn't accessible, which is why he hasn't gone to see the games live, instead living vicariously through the crappy live-stream put on by the media club.

"All right," Reed says, nodding. His eyes flash to mine for a second telling me he's going to find a way to make this happen. I don't know if he realizes how hard it's going to be. Those same holes and divots in the grass that he mentioned to the team—why he said they need a new field—those litter the way to Buck's special seat.

I don't want to be the negative one, though, so I nod in agreement behind him, instantly craving more wine. I might need something stronger tonight to get me through what I know is going to be draining. There are so many things Reed hasn't seen, and when his dad can't just walk out to that field, it's going to kill him.

"You want to keep walking out to the couch?" Reed forces a

smile while he asks his dad, full of hope that they'll just keep on walking for the rest of the day, all the way into the night.

"I think I better save my energy," Buck says, reaching back toward the chair I've already pushed up to him.

I can't help myself as I blurt out one last excuse not to go through this.

"You know I can always FaceTime the game to you…so you get a better stream." Both Johnson men shoot me a stare, and I let my eyes flutter and roll back into my head. "Fine…fine. We'll do this your way. You're in charge, Buck."

"I haven't…been in charge…in years." He puffs out a grunt as he sits heavily into the chair. I step to the side to make eye contact with him. "But I missed…the last two home…coming games."

I nod as he breathes, and my fingers instinctively reach for Reed's as we stand side by side. His hand weaves into mine almost nervously, with a little desperation. Even though they talk on the phone constantly, it's different watching Buck have to navigate things in person.

"I missed, and look…what happened," Buck finally adds.

I smirk and shake with a single laugh.

"We lost," I say, letting my eyes fall closed as my smile grows and I nod.

"That's right…I miss games…we lose."

He has a point. And far be it from me to be the one who stands in the way of a damn football game.

Chapter Ten

Reed

NOLAN LEFT with the girls and Peyton about an hour ago. I told her I had this, but I don't have a damn thing. Rose isn't strong enough to help, and my brother is off somewhere and only texts me vague answers about showing up to the homecoming game. Hanging around our old school has never been his thing. I think he feels like he failed the legacy somehow because I was the better quarterback. He's better at business, which is why I gave him mine.

I could use him to check his ego tonight, though, because my dad was a handful before half of his body betrayed him. Now he's a belligerent handful that still thinks he can move around like a forty-year-old.

My only hope is that Sean and Becky somehow make it through Phoenix rush hour in time to get to Coolidge. I need one more set of hands besides Micah, who isn't really very…well…he's a musician.

"He's still getting ready," Rose assures me as I call my best friend one more time, hoping he's close.

I nod at her and mouth "Thanks" before stepping outside to

pace around the driveway while the phone rings in my ear. I should move my Jeep so my dad doesn't get some crazy notion that we'll drive that to the game.

"Hey, man. I'm almost there." My neck releases about a thousand pounds of tension at Sean's words.

"Thank God," I say, pinching the bridge of my nose. I close my eyes and let myself breathe in and blow out.

"You're making this harder than it is, man. We got this," Sean says.

"Thanks...yeah. You're right." He is right, but I don't think that tonight is what's pushing my chest in so hard and sucking me into the dirt. It's part of it, but it's really just...everything, I think.

Trig. My injury. My marriage and contract, and the nothing I get to do on the field. My age.

Fuck. I'm having a mid-life crisis.

I start to chuckle to myself when I see headlights spill over the desert brush out in the distance.

"That you?" I start to walk down the driveway, suddenly not getting to my friend fast enough.

"Yeah, that's me." I can tell by Sean's voice he misses me too. Grown-ass men still wanting their best friend to play with. If only the rest of life were this simple.

I begin backpedaling my steps as Sean pulls up closer to the house, and when he gets out I march toward him with wide arms and this strange choking sensation holding my lungs hostage.

"Goddamn, it's been too long." Sean's hands pat my back hard as we hug, and I squeeze him enough to lift him from the ground before letting go and moving to the other side of the car to hug Becky.

"Thanks for coming straight here," I say, scratching at the side of my face to mask my emotions.

"Of course," Sean says, his eyes settling on mine for a few long seconds, his mouth in that same slight smile that he always got when we did this—when we spoke without words. Two people in this world can read me this well, and I'm married to the other one. Sometimes, Sean sees things just a little deeper, too.

"Thanks," I say with a hard swallow. He doesn't speak but only nods.

I help Sean with his bags and the three of us head inside where Rose and Buck are waiting in the foyer. My father reaches his hands out for Sean the moment he steps inside, pulling my best friend to his chest as he bends over to hug my father in his chair.

"You lose that hair...or just shave it to be...fancy?" My dad teases him, and my friend throws a fake punch softly into my dad's arm.

"Remember when you used to tease me about spending so much time styling it?" Sean responds.

My dad's quick back to him. "Styled it right off...your damn head," he says.

My friend laughs and reaches out a hand, prepared with his other one to take my dad's awkward shake firmly. He always thinks about those little things, the ones that require extra care of feelings.

I help Sean take his and Becky's bags up to their room, the smallest of our guest rooms and the one that used to be Jason's. When we come back down, Becky is laughing with Rose at something my dad said. It almost feels normal. I guess this actually *is* normal now.

"You ready to get this show on the road, folks?" Sean moves to the back of my dad's chair, and I wrinkle my brow at him.

"Abso-tudily-ludily, Skipper!" I tease him for being so colloquial.

"I'm being polite. I didn't want to call you all ass-hats," my pal says, guiding my dad out of the house and to their SUV.

"Ass-hats would definitely...be accurate," my dad says.

I shrug and laugh.

"He's right...Skipper," I joke again, dodging his fist as it flies to my arm.

I chuckle my way to the car, getting into the backseat and sliding to the other side making sure everything's ready and out of the way before stepping out again. My dad has gotten good at getting into vehicles as long as there is enough room and nothing unexpected, like arm rests. Sean helps my dad into the vehicle while I move his chair to the back and fold it up as small as it will go. My friend helps me get it in after my dad is settled, and he brushes his hands together after he closes the back hatch.

"See, that was easy," he says.

"It's not the driveway I'm worried about navigating," I answer.

I climb in the backseat with my dad, and Becky takes the front passenger side. Sean starts in quickly with small talk about the team, and the new quarterback, and I fill him in on the fact that we might have to kill the guy since he's dating Peyton. Sean makes a few jokes about how this is the ultimate payback for me, but Becky's mostly silent. I don't ask why, but I have my suspicions. They've been trying to have kids for years, and Nolan told me a few months ago that they're on their last attempt. I wonder if that attempt has come and gone.

Nolan and I had our struggles too—before and after Peyton. But we have Peyton. She is our blessing, even when she makes us yank our hair out.

When we get to the school, I direct Sean through the back gates. I step out of the car to swing the security gate open when we get to it, and he drives through until we're parked right next to Nolan's car. This lot is for the boosters, which means we technically get a spot here, but we told them we'd need two tonight since Buck was coming.

Everyone's waiting in the lot for us, along with a cluster of parents anxious to talk to me. I must wear the frustration, because Sean jumps from the driver's side and holds up his hands before anyone can step closer and start firing away with questions and autograph requests.

"Hey, folks," he says, glancing at me over his shoulder. I bite my cheek with my laugh. "Wheelchair coming through, so if you all could give us some space for just a little bit, I'm sure Reed will come over and visit for a few minutes."

I'd rather sneak in and never come back out, but I get it. And normally, I don't mind. I'm just so high-strung tonight that my mood is less...grateful athlete. I'm more depressed has-been.

"How you doing?" Nolan's arm slips around me and she hugs me tightly as my lips find the top of her head.

"I don't know," I breathe out.

"It'll be fine. Even if all of us have to carry your dad in his chair like some king of an empire," she says, and I cringe at the thought.

"Yeah, that'll be *real* subtle," I say, letting go of her and pacing a few steps while my dad works his way from the car to his chair.

"Your dad doesn't give a shit what people see. Is that what's bugging you so much? That people will see your dad like this?" Nolan steps in front of me with her arms crossed and hip jutted out.

"No…it's not that. I just hate that he has to go through this," I lie. She's always more right than wrong.

"No, you're not." She calls me on it and steps in closer so she can speak in a whisper. "You hate that people will *see* him going through this and start to talk about how you're getting older, too, Reed. Well, guess what?"

She steps back with her arms outstretched and palms up.

"We all get older. Some of us just age with a lot more fucking grace." Her eyes narrow and I feel the chill that's meant from them.

"Noles, stop. That's not it…" I put up a pathetic counterargument and give up quickly when she catches up to the other girls and walks away.

Sean, Micah, and I begin maneuvering my dad through the thick gravel and onto the weed-filled grass. If I had any sense, I would have come here this afternoon and smoothed all of this out or laid plywood for a ramp.

"Not very ADA compliant," I mumble.

"It's fucking…Coolidge," my dad jokes. Sean laughs with him, but all I can do is stew over the fact that this is hard when it shouldn't be.

We get my dad to the track and the edge of the field, and most of the old-timers have gotten up from their seats to greet him. He's been insistent that he'll walk to his seat from here, but with dozens of other senior citizens surrounding him, I don't know if he'll ever make it. I'm not sure he cares anymore, either, because his face is smiling larger than it has in months—at least compared to the times I've seen him.

I step back and thank Micah, sending him to the seats with the girls while Sean hangs back with me. My dad's in his element, talking with people about his physical therapy, but more about what a damn good-luck charm he is. If the Bears win tonight, my dad will take full credit.

Maybe he'll deserve it.

"He's gonna be busy for a little while. You wanna go do this with me?" I point over my shoulder to the now doubled-in-size crowd clustered around the concession area.

"Sure, man. I'm like your personal body guard. This is awesome." My friend rolls the sleeves up on his sweatshirt and puffs out his chest, trying to look bigger than he is. It makes him walk stiff, though, and the entire visual makes me laugh, genuinely.

"What? I'm a tough guy," Sean says, adding a little skip to his step along with a fake piece of gum that he chews on one side of his mouth.

"Yeah, you're tough. Like the way a kitten is when it can't quite climb to the top of the couch yet," I say, barely getting the last few words out between laughs.

My friend spins on his heels and flips me off while we make our way back to the crowd. Sean manages to stay close to me at first, despite the dozens of pens and random pieces of paper people thrust at me to sign. I think one of the papers is a bank statement.

"You playing this weekend, Reed?" One of the older guys shouts his question from the back and I squint to focus on him.

"Hard to say. Depends on how my MRI goes tomorrow." I hand back one pen and paper and take another.

"Yeah, like you're not playing just because you're injured," someone heckles from my side. I ignore him and keep signing, but I can feel the burn start in my chest.

"How's the leg feeling?" An older woman I sort of recognize asks me while I sign a stuffed football for her and hand it back.

"Good…thanks," I say, scanning her face in an effort to jog my memory.

"Mrs. Stetson," she says, seeing my struggle. Her reminder sends me back to my junior year physics class.

"Oh wow, how are you?" I relax a little and put my hands in my pockets to get a break from signing things being shoved at me.

"I'm good. I retire this year, so I'm glad you came back now. Next year, I'll be in Costa Rica." She holds up the ball I signed. "Thanks for this. My grandson just loves you."

I nod.

"That's some retirement…wow!" I mentally flash to my own life, imagining it in some remote place away from here.

"It's a lot more affordable, and ya know…teachers," she shrugs in jest at her pathetic salary.

"That's why I went into football," I joke.

"You should have retired this year, buddy." The voice comes at me from my side again, and this time I give in and turn to find out the source. I was half expecting to recognize him as some old team-mate or something, but this guy is definitely a stranger, and he's embarrassing his son, who's standing next to him and getting smaller by the second.

"Maybe," I say, faking out a laugh and deciding to be the bigger man. I am, by the way…the bigger man.

I turn my focus to the kid standing next to him and make the gesture for the old Chargers hat he's holding with a pen in the other hand. The kid's maybe a freshman, but he's small, so I'm guessing he's still at the junior high. He smiles enough that his teeth show, but as I reach to take his hat, his dad pushes it back down.

"No maybe about it, Johnson. You're a shit quarterback, always have been. We don't want your signature on nothin'."

I breathe in slowly through my nose above my tight-lipped grimace, and I spot Sean a few people behind this guy, making a gesture with his hand to tell me he's pretty sure the dude is drunk.

"That's okay, man. I know not everyone likes me. Your boy play?"

I probably should have just left it there, with the bit about liking me, but I don't know—something makes me want to string this guy along. It's a bad idea, and I know the second his face sours because I dared to talk about his son.

"He's gonna start here someday…break all your records," he says, and I keep it positive and start looking for a way out.

"I hope so," I say, nodding and lifting my hand to say goodbye and make my way back to my family. Before I turn and join Sean, I make eye contact with the kid.

"Best thing you can do is take your practice seriously. Do that, eat right, and lift a lot." I reach out and pound the kid's fist, and his mouth quirks up in a faint smile as I begin to walk backward. I make it a full three steps before the jackass sets me off.

"You should be riding around in a wheelchair like that old man, Johnson!"

Everyone hears it. I know they do because everything gets hushed. Or maybe the switch flips so hard in my head that it rings my ears and renders me deaf. In a blink, my fist is smashing into the side of the guy's face, and in a beat, he's scrambling backward away from me, sliding on his ass and feet and palms while yelling that he's going to sue.

He will, too. Maybe that's all this was, but I think it was more than that. I think this guy's a drunk, and probably a gambler. Maybe I threw an interception that cost him some serious cash. Perhaps I only cost him pennies, or was a source of jealousy behind his failed marriage.

Whatever it is that drives him to be a dick, it shouldn't happen in front of his kid. And it sure as shit shouldn't be an insult to my dad.

"You're going down, Johnson! You broke my face, you fucker. That's bank!" The man stands and spits blood on the ground as he pulls his phone from his pocket and begins dialing the police. The resource officer shows up during his call, though, so I stand back and wait while this enraged man begins swinging his arms around and pointing fingers.

"If you didn't hit him, I would have," Sean says as he leans into me.

"I probably should have waited for that," I say, sucking on the sore set of knuckles that met his bone. They're gonna bruise, but not badly.

I sigh as I look over my shoulder and catch Nolan and Rose watching me. It was far enough away that my dad didn't notice, still surrounded by old friends and talking about the good times. But everyone else saw.

Nolan saw.

And she already thinks I'm a mess.

Maybe she's right.

Chapter Eleven

Nolan

REED GAVE A STATEMENT, and I overheard a lot of the other witnesses talking to the officers when I went to the concession stand to get my husband ice for his hand. It sounds like this man is going to have a hard time getting someone to back him up, which is both good and bad. If something got Reed suspended, that would be one more long break from stress. Stress for me.

Selfishly.

That's a terrible way for me to think.

From what I heard from Sean, Reed had every right hitting that guy anyway. Not that violence is a solution, but people shouldn't say things like that about anyone. Especially about Buck. And that man has no idea how many nightmares I've had where Reed's been confined to a chair like his dad, or worse—been brain dead.

Dead.

The clock is dwindling, and it looks like the Bears have made good on Reed's challenge. They aren't just winning, they're killing Liberty. Reed's falling a little more in love with Bryce, too. It's fun to watch him watch someone young be so good.

"Look at his steps." He's giving Sean play-by-play, and Sean is just as invested. Per the norm, Sarah tuned out after her dance team performed at halftime. Now that the clock is showing just seconds left, she's antsy for making plans for whatever comes next.

Peyton slips under the bleacher railing and climbs up a few levels to where we're sitting. She moves into the space between Reed and me, and before she can try to work the daddy's-girl angle, I beat her at her own game.

"You're going straight home. Don't even think about it," I say, garnering a heavy breath that pushes the stray hairs from her face. It's strange how much she looks like me but acts like her father.

"But everyone's going!" The lip pout follows, and I lean forward to ignore it just in time for Sarah to guarantee my daughter will go directly home.

"Oh my God, yes! Let's go! Desert party! Becky, Sienna… Reed…" She dips her chin and puckers her lips, taunting my husband into reliving his youth. "You *know* you wanna go. It's our thing, y'all! We invented this shit!"

"Uggg," Peyton huffs, slipping back from the bleacher steps and onto the track with the rest of her cheer squad.

"Thanks," I say through laughter. "No way she's showing up if there's even a threat her parents will be there."

"Girl, I'm not threatening. I was legit making plans. We're going. In fact, Becky and I are leaving right now to get the beer. We'll see you bitches there in an hour." Sarah tugs Becky to stand by her arm, and our shyest friend shrugs in obedience, knowing there's no use arguing with Sarah.

It actually sounds kinda fun, and it would be nice to spend a night just being all of us—like we used to be.

"I gotta hit the road early; I don't know…" Reed stands to stretch his arms, and I can tell by the lost reflection in his eyes that he's not really present. "Besides, maybe I'm wanted by the law."

"You are not. And maybe you come out to the desert with us and for once," I pause with an exaggerated gasp as I cover my mouth. "Perhaps you play this party sober."

His lips draw into a tight smile, one eye smaller than the other as he looks down at me.

"I'm not eighteen anymore," he says with a roll of his eyes.

"That's the truth," Sean says, standing and grabbing at his belly, which has grown a little—*a lot*—since high school. "Come on, man. We won't stay late."

Reed rolls his head side to side, finally staring off at the score-board as he considers it for a few long seconds before finally giving in.

"Maybe an hour or so. Okay, fine," he says. I stand and squeeze him at his side. I step away enough to look up at him, and for a small breath, everything else goes away; we're just us. He leans forward to touch the end of his nose to mine, and I lift myself with my toes to press my lips against his, a welcome warmth in the growing frosty air. The desert at night is cold; it's been so long that I had almost forgotten.

We all caravan back to our house to get Buck and Rose home before we climb into the Jeep. It takes a little longer to get out of town than it used to. More stoplights have popped up, and more stores have crowded street corners. A lot of our favorite parts have given way to more of the same, and we pause at what used to be our favorite corner where nothing but concrete footings remain.

"I can't believe they tore down MicNic's," Reed says, his arms folded over the steering wheel.

"I can," Sean says from the backseat. "That place was a serious health hazard."

I laugh.

"It's true. I'm pretty sure the cook dropped actual ash from his cigarette into the meat once." I fake a gagging sound, but Sienna makes a real one behind me.

"Sounds like it was amazing," Micah says. He never had the pleasure of the MicNic burger, so Reed assures him he wasn't missing out, but the rest of us all know the truth. MicNic's had the best burgers ever, ashes or not.

Reed peels out at the last stop sign, and I grip the handle on the passenger side and laugh up at the moon as my hair whips violently around me.

"Drive, baby!" I scream, righting my gaze in time to see the smile stretch across his face. It's a wild abandon that he hasn't had in years. I think maybe I'm the cause of it disappearing, or at least part of the cause.

We weave into the night around the cactus-peppered hills, the road only lit a few feet in front of us at a time. It could be pitch dark and we'd all still know the way. It's burned in our fabric, and time hasn't caught up with this part of our home yet. No homes built around here, other than the eastern stretch of property that now belongs to Reed and me.

"Do you remember when we walked home through this?" Sienna reminds us all. I hear her begin to explain the memory to Micah, not wanting him to feel left out, while Sean, Reed and I joke about it.

"It was always so much farther than you said it was," Sean says, pushing the back of Reed's seat. "You ass!"

Reed laughs and looks his friend in the eyes through the reflection in the rearview mirror.

"You were just lazy," Reed says.

I remember that first walk, and I know Reed's thinking about it now. I can tell by the way his smile softens just before he reaches for my hand, gripping it and pulling it to his mouth to kiss the back of my hand. He holds his lips to my skin for a few seconds and when he sets our tethered hands down on the center console, he flits his eyes to me to make sure I'm all right with this memory now, too.

Reed was dating Tatum then. It all seems so stupid and trivial now, which I suppose it was, but at fourteen, that night was my whole world. Feelings were bigger somehow, and things cut deeper. I was a girl with a crush, and he was a boy just figuring out how to deal with desire. And Tatum...well...she's a stripper now, so I guess not much has changed.

"You know I saw her in Vegas, bro," Sean says, drawing loud groans as Sienna and I fall back into our seats. I twist my head to make eye contact with my girlfriend, and we both jerk in a disgusted laugh.

"Becky know that?" Reed says over his shoulder.

"Not like that, dude. I mean I ran into her. I was there for business, and she was on the strip heading somewhere. She looked good." Nobody speaks after Sean gives us that update. I think maybe we're all glad she's all right, even though she put us through hell when we were young—me more than most.

Tatum always wanted to perform, and I had heard during college that she spent some time in New York and L.A. trying to get gigs in theater or commercial work. She was on a soup ad for a while. It even aired during the NFL playoffs. Reed never brought it up, but I know he noticed. It was a year he was watching them next to me on the couch. My mom's the one who told me she eventually started working in Vegas. She ran into Tatum's parents just before they moved to some retirement place in Florida. They said she was starring in a show, but my mom had this feeling they were leaving out a few details. It only took her ten minutes surfing online to find out that show was topless.

"She always had great boobs." Sienna's quip is utterly sincere, and it breaks the thick silence as we all burst into uncontrollable laughter.

The dim lights start to reflect the dust behind the thick brush, and pretty soon Sarah's car comes into view, her trunk already popped open with way too much alcohol dumped in the back for seven adults, two of whom won't be drinking.

"I couldn't decide what to get," she says, already starting in with excuses as she cracks open a can of the cheapest beer in Coolidge for me. I wasn't planning on drinking, but I take it in my hand knowing if I hold onto it over the next hour, she won't harass me.

Reed reaches in and kills the lights on his Jeep, crawling up on his hood and stretching out a hand for me to join him.

"So much for date night, huh?" I tilt my head as guilt shrinks his smile a little. "It's okay," I shake my head, feeling bad.

I take his palm and plant my foot on the tire, letting him lift me. A little bit of my beer spills on my arm, so Reed takes it in his hands and sucks it off.

"I still can't let you waste it," he teases.

My back rests on his chest as he draws his knees up on either side of me and I hook one arm under his thigh. I take a sip of my beer, which is bitter and possibly stale if not a little warm, but I hope it helps me relax. He leaves in hours, and I want to soak up this last moment.

For the next hour, we all take turns warning Sarah that it's a bad idea to cross the gulch where the actual teenagers are, but it doesn't stop her from trying with every new song that blasts from someone's stereo.

"Has she always been this crazy?" Reed speaks into my ear, his lips stopping at the edge of my skin long enough to dust a kiss. It still sends shivers down my neck, and I tilt my head inviting him to do it again.

"She's actually tamer than she used to be. I'm just shocked she's never been arrested," I say, swallowing hard when his nose draws a line from my collar bone up to the space behind my ear.

He nuzzles me there for a few seconds, his breath hot and his chin scratchy, reminding me he's a man now and that this is not twenty years ago. This is now. I lean into him more, feeling the heat of his chest against my back, the rise and fall of his wanting breaths. I can't remember the last time we've been together—*really together.*

"I miss you," he finally says, his hands running along my arms as he folds them over my chest, his thumbs dragging in secret across my breasts. I draw a sharp breath as he pauses with his knuckles over my now hardened nipples that have turned to pebbles from his touch and the cold air.

"I miss you so much," I breathe out, my head falling back into his chest and turning enough to find his mouth waiting hungrily for mine. He kisses me with *our* kiss, taking my top lip in and sucking slowly until I feel the rough edges of his teeth grab hold of my skin. My lip slips out with a slight pant and Reed pulls me against his body more, this time so I can feel what this is doing to him.

"We should go for a walk," I whisper. He nods, his rough cheek rubbing against my soft one, and we slip away just as our friends are all shouting over one another about who can handle more shots.

I start to giggle as we break into a run, and Reed holds his finger over his wide smile as he turns to take my hand and jog backward.

"I can't believe it's come to this. We're almost forty, and we have to sneak out in the desert to have sex," I laugh out.

Reed's laugh shifts into a growl as he reaches for my other hand and draws me closer to him, urging me up a few steps to a large boulder embedded on the opposite side of a wash that's been dry for months. My back against the rock, Reed cages me between his arms and leans to the side to test how hidden we are.

"They're drunk as fuck," he says, his eyes glimmering with the moonlight. I don't bother to look. I'm too mesmerized by the movement of his Adam's apple, and every dip it makes with his laugh. It stalls when his gaze shifts to me, his lips closing with the heavy swallow of his growing desire.

"Reed," my lips quiver out his name and my eyes work to seduce him more, sweeping closed at his chest and opening wide on his.

His gaze circles my face, painting me with the adoration that's never left, but has only been buried by life—by all of this shit that the game brought with it. The game isn't with us right now; it's only me and him. I shift my body up enough so my eyes are square with his, and I wrap my fingers behind his head, threading through his thick hair. It's courser than I remember. These months apart have aged it, but it still submits to me, softening to silk in my hand as he takes his time closing the distance between our lips.

His eyes flit from mine to my mouth, licking as he parts his just before falling into me with a possessive kiss that forces my chin up as his hand comes to the side of my neck. I whimper as his fingers follow the curve of my jaw, neck and arms then grip at my sweater, gathering it in his fists from the bottom until his palms are cupping my breasts.

If the ground were softer, we maybe wouldn't have noticed the crunch of gravel and brittle snaps of brush under someone's approaching feet. Reed's eyes widen and he presses two fingers to my mouth, holding my nervous laugh inside, but barely. I can feel his body shake with his silent laugh as his head falls to rest against mine, and after a mood-killing round of hearing two teens trying to sneak off into the darkness to do the exact same thing we're doing, we make our escape and slowly walk back to our friends.

"You all went to make out, didn't you?" Sarah is slurring her words and stumbling toward us. My friend is a sloppy drunk, and it's late and the early morning will be here way too soon.

"You caught us," I smile at her as I shoot a glance to Reed over my shoulder. I slide my arm under her to hold her weight and hold out my open palm, our universal sign for her to give me her keys.

"I'll see you at home," Reed says, and as everyone else loads up in the Jeep, Becky, Sarah, and I climb into Sarah's car. Together we all make our way out of the dry river bottom to the main road.

My stomach sinks the moment I catch up to the Jeep, now parked near our house in our driveway, the lights beaming high on the front door that Reed is ripping through as I shift Sarah's car into park.

"Who's here?" Becky's question is so sweet and innocent. It's exactly how she always was in high school. Peyton, however, is more like me. And that extra vehicle parked in our driveway belongs to a certain high school quarterback that should not be at our house while we aren't home.

I sit back and grip the wheel, debating whether I should join Reed or wait this one out and let him handle the shit-fest that comes with parenting a teenager.

"That's the boy," I say in a flat tone.

Becky's chuckle starts to boil into hard laughter.

"I know, I know. This so serves us right," I say, grabbing the keys and my phone and moving my attention to the backseat where Sarah is now completely knocked out.

"Should we just leave her here?" Becky sits on her knees in the passenger seat and stares over the seatback at our friend. I do the same and shrug. It isn't hot out, and all of the extra beds are taken.

"Yeah, why not. She'll just let herself in like she always does if she wakes up anyhow," I say.

Becky pulls off the flannel shirt she was wearing over her T-shirt and drapes it over our friend like a blanket. We both exit the car and push the doors closed as quietly as we can. I'm shocked when I don't hear yelling or see an embarrassed boy rushing from our house while Reed's ears smoke from the sides. I catch up to the rest of our friends and stop in my tracks when I see Buck sitting on the sofa next to Bryce watching old film of Reed on the TV.

Peyton catches my gaze and leaves her perch on the sofa arm to come talk to me.

"I asked Grandpa if he could come in. He was up. I promise," Peyton explains away the situation quickly. I nod, not really caring if it's plausible or not. I'm too invested in everything I'm seeing.

Reed is standing a few feet behind them and off to the side, his thumbs hooked in his pockets and his eyes hypnotized by the boy making miracles happen on the screen. Buck gives play-by-play for every single movement of the ball, knowing every game by heart. It's been years since we've watched Reed's scouting video. I put it on a disc a few years ago, and the only person who has ever gotten it out is Buck.

"He sure was something, huh?" Sean's arm brushes against mine as he moves into the space next to me.

"He still is," I say, admitting to myself that I'm talking about both the man and the player.

Chapter Twelve

Reed

I'LL CRACK the border into Oklahoma just as the sun is setting if I can get on the road in the next half hour. It's feeling impossible to leave this bed, though.

Curled up in my arms, Nolan hasn't even stirred once over the last two hours. Maybe she sleeps silently like this when I'm gone, but right now, I'm taking complete credit. I reach to my right to tap my phone screen awake so I can turn off the alarm before it sounds, but my movement makes Nolan wake up. Her arms stretch out, one to the empty side of the bed and the other across my chest, which she then places a flat palm against to help her lift her head.

"Good morning," she says, eyes all sleepy and smile crooked. I run my thumb over her eyebrows, which always somehow get a little bent overnight. She looks up at them while I do.

"Brows go rogue again?"

I breathe out a soft laugh in response.

"Just a little," I say.

Her eyes settle on mine again, so I live here for several long seconds. Once I leave the warmth of our bed, everything will go back to how it was—I'll be a thousand miles away, and she'll be here, and Trig will be dead, and we won't be talking like we should.

I don't want that. I don't want any of it, but there's really only one piece of it I can control.

"Noles, I'm so sorry." I let my eyes fall into hers as they start to form tears in the corners.

She sucks in her top lip, and I run my thumb under her eyes this time, sweeping the moisture away. She gives me a small nod before finally speaking.

"It was the worst thing I've ever survived," she says, and though we've had this talk before, it's never been quite like this. My insides crack, like poorly plastered walls in an earthquake.

"I know it was," I whisper, drawing her head close enough to my mouth that I can press my lips into her hair. I inhale her scent, remnants of the desert and the fire pits still smoldering in the strands.

"I shouldn't have sent that email," she says, and I let my eyes blink closed. My pulse speeds up just a little from the pain.

"It's okay," I whisper into her, my own body quivering with emotion. I blink away tears, and I'm ashamed because they're a mix of fear and anger still. Not completely, but those feelings still poison me.

"I love you," I breathe out instead. She whimpers—those easy words have become too hard to say. We need to speak them more. She needs to hear them…now.

"Always have. From the very first moment. And through everything…this…now. I love you."

"I love you, too," she cuts in. I needed to hear those words as well. I swallow hard, consuming them.

Nolan adjusts her hold on me, sliding her arms around my body and shifting her weight until she's lying completely on top of me. Her eyes sweep closed and her lips close softly on my chin, her tongue peeking out just enough to taste my salty skin. She moves up me in fractions of inches until her kiss finds lips, and my hands tangle in her chocolate-colored hair.

"Mmmm," she hums, the sound coming out with a cry of pleasure when her hips roll against me. My hands slide down her back and find her ass, feeling her perfect contours and gripping hard enough to pull her center over my aching cock.

She braces her weight with her hands in the center of my chest and moves her knees up until she's straddling me. My head falls back as her hips grind and her body squirms for relief. I glance up in time to see her grab the opposite sides of the bottom of one of my old college T-shirts as she drags it up her naked body and tosses it to the floor.

"Jesus Christ, woman. Your body is the same garden of the gods it's always been," I say, leaning up enough to take a soft bite of one hard nipple.

She whimpers when I do, and my cock flexes beneath her, forcing my hands to rock her hips up and down. Eventually she takes over the movement for me and I let my hands paint every inch of her skin with feather-light touches at first until I pull hard on each nipple and send her body cascading down on top of me.

"Please, Reed. Now." She moans at my ear, and I obey, sliding my boxers down just enough to feel her bare skin against me. I reach between us and tug the cotton strip of her panties, now wet with her own needs and wants, to the side, giving my cock enough room to push deep inside her.

"Ah," she cries, and the sound of her pleasure sends a rush from my spine into my shaft as I push up and into her again.

Pushing herself up to sit, she begins to move up and down, meeting me with each forceful lift of my hips. Her eyes drift into bliss, but they remain focused on mine. I don't want to look away, but I'm so drawn to the art of her—the way her breasts quake with our crashes, the muscles in her arms as they work against me, the curve of her hips and thighs. I'm a fool for not thinking any of this is enough, that I need more to prove who and what I am.

Nolan brings the knuckles of her right hand to her mouth and bites down on them as her eyes flutter closed and her cheeks blossom with a pink flush. Heavy breaths turn into panting and we both move slower and slower until eventually she's collapsed in my arms, our bodies damp with our actions and our hearts craving more.

We lie together in total quiet until the tension of all the words we aren't saying starts to make it hard to breathe. I reach again for my phone, knowing more time has passed than I planned. It was worth it.

"I have to go."

It hurts to say out loud. Nolan doesn't move from the spot where her body is practically glued to me, our legs intertwined, hair splayed on my skin, fingers spread covering as much space on my chest as possible. It's seven in the morning. The team is going to want me to fly. I'll be late.

It won't matter anyhow.

"I thought you were dead." She says it so matter of fact, as if it's in the middle of a conversation we've been having. Maybe it is; we just haven't been having that conversation out loud.

I swallow hard, trying to be quiet about it but the movement is jarring and it causes her to curl her fingers on my chest. They form a fist. I cup it in one of my hands, covering it completely.

"You were miles away from me, and all I could do for so long was hold my phone in my hand," she says, her head shifting against my shoulder as she looks down at where our hands are linked. I let go of her palm and she opens, flexing, before closing it again.

"I stared at it…for hours. I don't know what Peyton did on that stage, I don't know how I told her the news, and I can't remember how I got from that building to the airport. I can't remember a single word your brother said to me that day, Reed, but I remember how desperate I was and how my heart stabbed with searing pain and hope and despair every time he called."

She moves to sit up and I join her, turning to face her as she puts a little distance between us so she can look me in the eyes. The ghosts hiding behind hers are frighteningly real. She's like a crystal ball right now of what could have been, and I know it's the reason she sent that email. I know it's the reason we aren't where we should be.

"I started making plans, and I was terrified Reed, because I didn't know what I was going to do. I could function. I could pay bills...file documents...plan a funeral. I could talk to the press and do stories about how horrible it was to be me—*for Peyton and me to be us.* I knew how to do all of that, and yeah...my mind went through it all. I made a list. I made lists of lists. I sat on an airport floor lying to your daughter that things were going to be fine, that this was something routine. But not once in any of those lists did I write down how I was going to be able to live...without...you."

She shudders and loses her breath, tears forming quickly at the corners of her eyes. It guts me, and I reach for her, but she pulls away, standing up and waving with her hand.

"No, I'm fine. We're...we're fine. I think we're fine, but..." She pulls the sheet around her body and turns and paces before steadying her nervous feet and looking up at me again. I stand on the opposite side of the bed, nearing an hour late for the road, willing to make it hours more.

"I needed to say all of this out loud because I feel like you don't get it. I need you to understand why I did what I did, and why I am so mad at you sometimes. I'm afraid you're not going to come home. It's made me hate that game, Reed. And I hate that you love it so much. I just feel..."

"Stuck," I fill in.

She nods, repeating the word.

"I don't want to feel this way," she says, trailing off and looking down at her feet...the floor.

"I know. Me, too."

I can feel it coming. This is the place I should stop. But that would be lying, and she's been so honest. This won't be real dialogue if I don't hold up my half.

"I feel guilty...for wanting to be who I am, to do what I do." I glance up to check if she's still looking down. She is, but she's chewing at her lip. She wants to yell. She probably should. I'd still feel this way, though.

"I don't want to quit."

There it is. It's heavy in my gut, and her stillness makes it feel as if I swallowed concrete. I want something that is in direct conflict with what the love of my life wants. We both have our reasons, and I am picking my reasons over hers. She hates that I am. She probably should. She understands anyway.

And this dance shall continue.

————

It felt good to be talking at least. It also felt good to leave her with a house full of friends. They'll stay through the weekend, and we all promised—*I* promised—not to let so much time go by before we do this again.

I keep replaying hearing my dad talk with Bryce while they watched my clips. It was like I wasn't really there, like they were talking about someone else.

Like I was dead.

I don't remember that guy on that screen. I love the game just as much as he did, but something changed with my surgery, with those last few big hits. I'm playing afraid, and it's the reason I'm not playing at all. I don't know how to lose that fear, and what I was trying to tell Nolan this morning was that I think I need her to remove it for me.

She packed me a small bag of snacks, a cute thing she used to do in college when I'd drive back from her college to mine. She handed it to me in the rolled-up paper bag, but the smirk on her face gave it away. I got about a mile away from the house before I opened the bag and pulled out the orange crayon she shoved in there.

I didn't want to call her about it right away, so I waited until now—until I passed through our favorite mountains in Southern Arizona and the place where we slept together for the very first time. Until I got to the spot that the orange crayon was all about in the first place.

I pull over in the same lookout as I did twenty-two years ago, the campgrounds a little more formal than they were back then. The Jeep slides to a stop in a graveled area marked with concrete, and I get out to look down a well-manicured trail below that leads to numbered spots, only two taken up with tents. The scene makes me laugh to myself, because it's nothing like the remote and rustic location I remember taking her virginity in. I wonder if I remember things differently.

Her phone rings about six times before sending me to voicemail. She's probably out with the horses. I nearly hang up, but before I press the END CALL button and shove the phone in my pocket, I decide maybe she deserves to hear how I remember that night. I've actually never told her.

I wait for the tone to prompt me.

"Hey. I got the crayon...nice touch," I say, pulling it from my pocket and rolling it between my thumb and finger like a joint.

"I was hoping you'd pick up, but you probably have a lot to get done today. I'm sure I put you behind with things. Oh, and hey... make Peyton help you with the horses. That was part of the deal; don't let her forget that."

I lean back on the front of the Jeep and look at the rolling valley where a thin trickle of water somehow exists. It snows up here in the winter, and rain can collect when there's a lot of it. We must have gotten just enough.

"So, I'm in *the spot* right now." I pause to laugh. Nolan never liked to talk about our first time. She'd blush and cover her face, tell me to stop. She can't really do that to me right now, so I decide to push on. She can always stop my message, but I kinda think she'll hear it all the way to the end. It's in her nature to be curious.

"I never really got to tell you what that night was like for me. *Someone* gets all embarrassed. But *someone* should have picked up the phone if they didn't want a long-ass message about it. And since you did give me the crayon..."

———

Reed - Twenty-one years ago

This trip—everything about it—it needs to be perfect. Nolan's birthday, the gift I'm giving her, the lie we're telling her parents so she can spend the night away from home…

It all needs to be perfect.

When Nolan asked me about other girls during our bus ride home from the track meet near the end of the season, a shift happened. My honesty with her was key, and I know it left a scar. But that scar—it was going to happen eventually.

I knew what I was risking the minute I slept with those other girls. I was gambling away my chances to ever be with Nolan. And when she asked me, point-blank, to my face, to tell her every girl I slept with, I knew I was rolling dice again by telling her the truth. I knew that some details were more painful than others—some girls more of a betrayal than others. One girl in particular was going to break her heart.

And I broke it.

I saw it break, watched it fall into a million tiny pieces with the tear that slid down her face before she tried to wipe it away. Seeing that, it broke me, too. But I felt the odds in my gut; somehow, I knew that not telling her about Sarah's sister, that lying to Nolan, would be the fatal error.

So, I confessed. I confessed and then I held her, and begged her not to run. And she hasn't; not yet. But every time I'm with her, I feel her urge, her questioning of herself, wondering if she's worthy, wondering if this is a trick, wondering when I'm going to drive the knife into her heart. She's been questioning herself, questioning us, for a month. And that…that is no one's blame but my own.

I've hurt Nolan, and I'm the biggest dick in the world for doing it. But this trip, it will lay her doubts to rest, a do-over for our first date, a second-chance for that epic beginning. It's everything she deserves. Or at least, it's a start. I think about the time I've wasted, how Nolan's been there for everything in my life—even just the time's she's sat there in those stands while I was on the field, my head not where it should be at all. I was focused on partying, getting laid, having some girl make me feel like a king for five minutes. I wanted to be the guy everyone told me I was supposed to be—the hero, stepping into my brother's shoes. All that time Nolan was there…watching.

I should have been looking back.

I ditched my last class so I could be here for this moment. Her backpack is weighing down her shoulders while she walks to my Jeep, her overnight bag already packed and tucked in the backseat from this morning. She thought it was strange when I asked her to pack a full change of clothes, sweatpants and sweatshirt, toothbrush, her favorite music, a flashlight and an orange crayon. When she questioned it, I told her we might be doing something that would get her a little messy, but I didn't breathe a word about the fact that it might just take about twenty-four hours too.

I put the orange crayon on her list just to mess with her, because I like the way she bites her lip before she pushes me and grins. It's just one of a million tiny things she does that I like. I doubt she'll actually pack it, though. Nolan—she's always been good at reading my bullshit, and I don't think she'll fall for this one.

I watch her every move as she tosses her heavy bag into the back with a thump and pulls her other bag to her lap, clutching it as she buckles herself in, her fingers working the bag's zipper back and forth with nerves. I stare at her hands, and for a brief second, I flash to my fantasies, to that little thought buried in the back of my head about tonight—Nolan is going to be in my arms all night, and there's a chance…

"So, where is this mystery date?" she asks, snapping me back, my lap more than obvious what I was thinking about. I shift my weight, rev the engine, and move the gear into reverse, hoping she doesn't notice I have the hard-on of a junior high boy in health class. I take a deep breath, then look at her, her eyes full of hope that I'm going to give in and tell her early. I wish I could, because maybe, just maybe, she'd be as excited as I am over the thought of sleeping together, and maybe…

I stop myself there. I know better. If I tell her we're leaving town, that I've concocted a lie with her friends so she can sleep out under the stars with me alone, she's only going to spend the entire trip trying to talk me out of it. Nolan's a rule follower—one more of the million tiny things I love.

Love.

"No, no…all will reveal itself," I say, catching a glimpse of her bobbing leg, the nervous energy seeping out from her. She's anxious. Anxious is a whole lot better than being doubtful and worried. So far, this gamble is paying off.

Traffic is in my favor today. Our trip through the desert highway is quick, and we're buzzing south on the interstate in no time. I can tell that Nolan's anxiety is picking up, though, and I'm pretty sure she's realized that this date I have planned—it's not going to be over by curfew.

"Reed, maybe I should call my dad? I think he was thinking I'd be home by nine or something?" Nolan asks, her nail-biting picking up at a frantic pace.

She's legitimately worried now, so I cut her a break. "Not a problem, already got it worked out," I say, unable to help but smile while I talk. I hope like hell she's smiling after I tell her this next part. "See…you're spending the night at Sarah's tonight. She worked this whole thing out with me."

Shit. She's not smiling. Her face looks shocked. I think I've shocked her. I also think she might think she's actually spending the night with Sarah, and that makes me laugh a little. I keep my focus straight ahead, on the car in front of us, for the next mile, until I can get my massive grin under control.

When I finally sneak a look at her again, her brow is pinched, that small worry line forming on her forehead. I don't like that line —I've put it there too often.

———

The entire trip takes about two hours, and we're right on schedule when I make the turn off the interstate into the mountains outside the city. I'm watching Tucson's lights fade in my rearview window as we climb higher into the desert hills. Soon the cacti give way to pines and forest brush. I always loved coming here with my dad and brother, the way the desert hides this forest oasis is almost like a fairytale. This place doesn't feel like it should belong, like it's fleeting and might disappear at any second.

That's sort of how I feel about Nolan. The way she's been carrying her doubt, like she might give up on us and run. To think that my time with her might be fleeting hits me in the pit of my stomach, and I push the gas a little harder, like I'm racing against two clocks now.

I think maybe this feeling is regret.

The turn is coming soon, so I start to slow the Jeep down again after a few minutes, hunching forward on the wheel to watch for the small wooden sign marking the road. I've never driven this road at twilight, but I remember the sign is crooked, leaning just enough into the roadway to make it hard to miss.

My bright beams glimmer off the metal post, and I hit the break a little too hard, Nolan gripping her seatbelt and pushing her feet against the floor to stay in her seat. On instinct, I reach my hand over her chest, bracing her, holding her in place, and she wraps her hands around my forearm.

I leave my arm there for a few extra seconds. I like it—her touch. I like that it feels like she needs me. This girl...*I could marry her one day.*

The campsite comes up quickly, so I pull off into a thick section of trees, kill the motor, and practically leap out of my Jeep. I sprint to the back and pull out my large hiking pack, the sleeping bags tightly rolled and tethered to the top, then race over to her door, my breath held waiting for her to react.

When the realization of what we're here for hits her—the coordination it took to pull this off becomes worth it in an instant. Her lips make that slow curve up, quivering with emotion until her smile stretches the width of her face.

That smile—that's the one I did this for, the one I'd do anything for.

I don't even wait for her to speak, instead spreading out our camping equipment, setting up the tent, dumping pieces from my pack. At one point, I actually laugh lightly to myself, the kind of release that comes from giving, and my heart is pounding so hard that my ears are practically thumping. I've never been so happy making someone else so happy.

Huh…

"Are you just going to sit there, or are you going to help me set up camp?" I tease, snapping her from her daze. She actually shakes her head, like people do when they wake up from a dream. And I love that, too.

Love that.

I love that I made her do that.

I love Nolan Lennox. And I'm going to give her the stars to prove it.

"Oh! Yes, sorry. I was just taking it in," she says, leaping from the Jeep and rolling up her sleeves to help me. As much as we need to set up the tent, I can't help but waste the minutes away looking at her—touching her. The second she's within reach, I drop everything and pick her up, holding her to the sky, spinning her so the stars swirl around her face, her hair blowing in different directions, her cheeks blushing with happiness, her smile making me feel whole.

"Happy birthday, Nolan!" I say, letting her body slide down into my arms, my lips finding hers, my forehead resting on hers, my breathing matching hers. Everything—her.

"Reed?" she whispers.

"Uh huh?" I say back, my hands finding her hips, swaying us side to side, my eyes closed while I think of how this small piece of her feels under my touch—how badly I want to feel her, more of her. But I won't cross that line with her, not until she's the one asking for it.

"We probably should set the tent up," she whispers again, my eyes opening enough to catch a view of her lip, tucked in her teeth. She's thinking about that line, too.

"Oh yeah, that's what we were doing," I joke, closing my eyes again while I flex my fingers once more, just enough to burn the memory in place before letting go.

The tent is pretty simple, so we have it set up within minutes, and I get a fire working quickly while she sits on the sleeping bag I've rolled out next to the wood, her arms hugging her backpack to her chest. Her eyes practically paint me with their stare, and as disarming as it is when she studies me, it also feels so damn good. She's been looking at me like this for years now, like I'm someone. She did it the first time our eyes met, and it filled me up with this strange sensation that I ignored.

Goddamn how many things I've ignored.

"What's up?" I ask, her eyes still watching my every move.

"I was just thinkin'," she smiles.

"Yeah, I get that much," I say. "Whatcha thinking?"

"Well, I get the clothes and the toothbrush. And the flashlight?" She furrows her brow. She's trying to figure out the bag, the list of things I made her pack. She's working up to the crayon, and it's so damned cute. Holy shit, I think she actually packed it!

"Oh, yeah. Thanks! I'll need that. I don't have one of those," I grin, grabbing the flashlight from her backpack and pushing it into my pocket, turning around again quickly, hiding my grin because I know she wants to know about the rest.

"Why my music?" she asks next.

I pause at the fire, the sparks finally kindling enough for the flames to take over the work, and pull Nolan up to stand in front of me, my lips dusting hers. "Duh, so I can dance with you under the stars," I say, teasing her and tilting her chin so her eyes can take in the sky.

"Okay, okay," she says, a breathy giggle escaping her mouth. "But...orange crayon?" She asks, her eyes coming back down to meet mine. She pushes from my arms just enough to reach her backpack by her feet, pulling the small crayon from the bottom. It's brand new, probably from a box she had to buy just to get it. And I can't help but start to chuckle, my lips hurting from trying to hold my laughter in.

"Damn it," I yell, my arms limp at my sides and my face parallel to the sky. When I look back at Nolan, I can tell she's confused, and maybe a little worried. "Oh, it's nothing really. I just owe Sarah twenty bucks."

She's still staring at me, and now she looks suspicious. Crap, that's not the direction I want tonight to go.

"Sarah said you'd pack anything I told you to, and I didn't think you would. You know, because you're so pigheaded," I say, pulling her hair lightly. "I threw that on the list as a test, and she won!"

I bend down and open up the cooler I brought, pulling out a few sandwiches and fruit slices I prepped for dinner, but quickly notice that Nolan's still staring at me, her bottom lip sucked in tightly.

"I could just sort of pretend I didn't bring it, you know," she says, willing to lie just so I can win a stupid twenty-dollar bet. I look at the crayon, then to her, and smile, tucking it into my pocket with the flashlight. "No, that's ok. I don't go back on my bets," I say, pressing my thumb to her lip. I hand her a paper plate with half a sandwich on it, and we both kneel down on my sleeping bag for our makeshift picnic.

Once our dinner is done, we take a small hike by flashlight, not as far as I wanted to go, but I didn't really think out this whole *walking over loose stones and tree roots in the dark* thing. More than once, I lose my footing. I'm extra careful to go slow for Nolan.

We make it to the small lake—the same one I fished at with my dad as a kid—and skip stones across the water. We get a little carried away at the water's edge, splashing water and kicking our feet in with our shoes in our hands. When Nolan starts to physically shiver, I get her out, wrapping her legs around my front and carrying her back to the campsite. I sit her down, lying on the sleeping bag next to her, my head resting on my elbow while I watch her look at the sky.

Her brown hair is blowing across her face, and her smile could light up the moon.

"So, do you want your present?" I ask. This part is like ripping off a Band-Aid. It's the moment all of the tiny moments leading up to it were about. I've almost chickened out on giving this to her a dozen times, even as recently as the drive up here. But fear hasn't served me very well when it comes to this girl. I think it might just be time for a dose of courage.

"Okay," she says, closing her eyes and holding her hands out.

She's mimicking the same thing I did when she gave me a gift for my birthday. I sure as hell hope my gift can measure up to hers. I still have the state championship patch that matches the one my dad earned pinned to my wall.

I pull the folded paper from my pocket, clutching it one more time, realizing this is it. When I place it in her palm, it suddenly becomes harder to breathe.

"You...wrote me a poem?" she asks, and it makes me laugh, probably because I'm nervous.

"Oh, God no. You don't want me to do that, trust me. It'd be awful!" I say. "It's a letter."

As she starts to unfold the creases, pressing the paper flat against her chest, my heart picks up, faster than ever before, and my body is suddenly on fire, my head a little dizzy.

I can taste the panic.

"Wait!" I say, my hands quickly covering the first words on the page. Nolan looks up at me, her eyes...happy. Everything about her face is an angel. I know, despite how absolutely terrified I am, she's going to read this letter, laugh in my face, and hotwire my Jeep to leave my ass in the woods. It would still be worth it to show this girl exactly what I think of her. She needs to know I think of her—and only her. If she stays, I'll know she's mine. But she'll also know I'm hers. "Wait...you need to know something first. You need to know when I wrote this."

"Okay? So...when did you write this?" she asks, her hands trembling now, the letter shaking in her fingers.

"That night after the winter dance our sophomore year," I say quickly.

Pull the Band-Aid off.

I keep my eyes on hers as long seconds pass, her gaze locked to mine, like she's looking for proof. She's still looking for the trick, the gotcha! There's no trick here, though. It's just me, being honest...for once in my goddamned life.

Finally, her head falls forward, and she begins to read the words I wrote a year and a half before, words I wrote when I wasn't even sure what they meant. I read them while I waited for her in the school parking lot, and over the last week, I've read them so many times that I have them memorized, my lips moving along with certain parts when I know Nolan's reached them.

She laughs lightly when she gets to the funny parts, but it's when her eyes flutter, when her fingers wrap even tighter around the collar of her shirt, gripping at it, that I know she's found the reason behind it all.

"Tonight, I danced with a girl that stole my breath away," my lips speak silently, Nolan's eyes glazing over. As she reads on, I let my eyes go to the letter, my mouth still reading the words along with her silently. "You're not mine. But what's strange is it felt like you've always been mine … as beautiful as you were tonight, I think maybe you've been beautiful all along. And I'm just stupid."

I've. Just. Been. Stupid.

When her hands lower the letter, her eyes give way to tears, and I pull her into my arms. Finally, she feels like she's mine.

"I guess I knew I loved you then, too," I say, my heart full and happy, the feeling strange but welcome. "I'm sorry it took me so long," I whisper, my lips grazing her ear, her heartbeat reaching out from her chest, reaching out for my own.

"That just kicked the shit out of my scrapbook and the varsity patch," she says, a small laugh escaping through tears, her hands moving to her face to wipe them away. That scrapbook she made me, the letter she gave me from my father's varsity year—I knew that I loved her then. So much energy wasted talking myself out of it. So much time…

I kiss her softly, afraid to kiss her any deeper, afraid I won't be able to stop. She takes one step backward, our lips part, and her hand is flat on my chest as she pushes away. At first, I think she's just giving us the space we probably need, being the responsible one. And then her hands reach for the bottom of her sweatshirt, pulling it slowly up and over her body, her hair falling loose in all directions over her bare arms.

I swallow once, choking down any stupid something I feel the urge to say right now. Now is not the time for clever, and now is also not the time to be a gentleman. Now is the time to wait—the time to hold my breath and talk both sides of my conscience into coming to an agreement about what I think might just be happening right now!

Her shirt comes off next, followed by the small tight tank top she was wearing underneath. She's standing here before me, her breasts damned near the most perfect things I've ever seen, and all I can think about is how much I want to touch them, touch her, taste her.

Do not…be an asshole, Reed!

I wait for permission. I wait while she reaches for me, pulls my shirt up over my head, and slowly slides her bare skin up against mine, her lips leaving a trail of kisses along my shoulder, neck and face.

That's enough waiting.

As soon as her teeth graze against my ear, I reach my hands deep into her hair and pull her face to mine, kissing her hard and rough. And she responds, her tongue and mouth just as hungry as mine.

This is the single greatest feeling of my life. And my mind races several moves ahead, hoping and wishing. Yet, when I feel Nolan's hands working to unsnap the button on her pants, something inside me clicks, and my heart surges, those balanced scales in my head warring with one another again, trying to keep me from fucking this up.

I slide my hands down her arms, gripping her wrists and holding her still. "Nolan, you don't have to do this, that's not what tonight was about," I say. Tonight was about me being honest, about me proving to her that she's my girl, that she doesn't have to compete with anyone. And I don't want to cheapen that, but my God, does her skin feel amazing next to mine.

"I know," she says, stepping away from me again. She keeps her eyes on mine, her breathing now heavy, her body quaking. At her final step, she reaches down and slides her jeans from her body, followed shortly by a small pair of white, cotton panties.

That war happening inside my head—it's over now. I lost. Or maybe I won. I'm not sure what side of the war is right, and right now, I don't fucking care. Seeing Nolan stand out here, in the middle of the night, out in the open, completely naked—this is the single hottest thing I've ever seen, and it is going to take every ounce of control in my power not to make this end in seconds.

I move to her slowly, my hands starting at her leg, sliding up along every curve until I'm standing in front of her. When I unbutton my jeans, I notice her body tense, her hands not sure where to go, her breathing picking up pace, filling her chest quickly, then escaping just as fast. I kick my pants down my legs, letting my clothes fall into a pile with hers, and I step closer so we're touching.

This is going to be the most difficult thing I've ever done. I throw passes to moving targets, take hits from three-hundred-pound lineman that are, no doubt, leaving bruises on my body and brain every time I get punched and pressed to the turf. That shit—it's hard! But football's got nothing on this moment right now.

Nothing has ever been this important.

And nothing ever will be again.

I kiss Nolan's neck, and she shivers. "You're cold," I say, her head nodding *yes* slowly as her eyes close. I sweep her up into my arms, walking us to the tent while my lips find hers again, and by the time I move us through the open flaps on the tent, Nolan begins to move again, her hands circling my neck until her fingers find my hair. I lay her on top of the thick comforter I put down to soften the tent floor, then reach for my wallet, pulling out the condom I put in there because of that little hope and wish in the back of my mind that this would happen.

I still don't know if it's right, and I'm not sure I deserve to be the guy taking this from her. But fuck me if I'm going to let someone else touch her like this for the first time. The last guy wasn't worthy of holding her hand.

Once the condom is on, I move over her, her eyes wide and looking at me for something. I think its permission. I'm going to grant it, I'm going to talk her into this, and I'm going to be selfish, because I want her—all of her—like this. I want to feel her and have her ache for me. And I hate myself for giving in so easily, but I have to have this—have to have her. But I promise to love her long after.

Yes, I'll love her. I'll love her for fucking always.

"I'll be slow. And if you want, tell me to stop," I say, looking at her, knowing if she says so, that I'll have to do it. I won't lie to her. And I won't hurt her. This girl, she's my reason…period.

"I know," she says, a small nod of her head, her voice soft, shaking with nerves. But her eyes aren't afraid. Her eyes—they're on fire. She reaches her hands up my arms, sliding her fingers into my hair as she pulls my head to hers, kissing me softly at first, but the need growing with every pass of her tongue. As her hands slide down my neck, to my back and sides, I feel her legs relax beneath me, her hips rocking upward, her stomach meeting mine. The roll of her body is the sexiest thing I've ever seen, ever felt, and I know that even though she's scared, she also wants this as much as I do.

I lower myself slowly, reaching with my hand to guide myself in place, then I push into her slowly, stopping to let her body get used to the feeling of having me inside her. Her eyes close tighter, and I can tell it hurts, and my chest tightens knowing that I'm hurting her.

"I can stop, Nolan. We don't have to…" I say, not so sure I can really keep my word now, all of my base instincts taking over, my arms threatening to weaken their hold, to let my weight fall fully into her.

"Reed, I love you. I want this, with you," she says, her eyes opening just long enough to look into mine, to give me her consent.

My thumbs graze both sides of her face, my elbows caging her body, my weight held by my tingling arms. I take her bottom lip in-between mine, holding it in my mouth, my tongue tasting her quivering lip as I lower myself completely, falling into her, and her insides squeeze against me. I can feel her body tense, so I wait a few seconds before rocking slowly out of her and moving into her again. With every shift, her body grows more willing, until finally, I feel her hips begin to rock into me again, meeting my rhythm.

Our kiss never stops, and it only grows more intense as our bodies move together faster. I let my hands slide down her side, gripping the side of her leg and bringing it up around my hip, letting me push into her even deeper.

As much as I shouldn't do this, because it threatens to send me over the edge with every new movement she makes, I can't help it. My hands want all of her. My mouth—it wants all of her. She feels fucking perfect, and I am going to have to do this again.

This…this isn't one of those things I can have only once. This is addiction, in its finest form.

Nolan isn't my first. But holy shit, nothing compares to the way she feels. Her arms and legs only give into me more, until I finally feel her hands grip at my biceps, her back arching as her breasts beg for me to touch them. I slide my hand beneath her, pulling her hard peaks to my mouth as my hips work slowly, my mind actually counting seconds slowly to keep me from ruining this, from going too fast—from hurting her.

When I lower my head and pull her nipple into my mouth, sucking lightly, Nolan gasps, her breath a whimper, and like a siren went off, my body reacts. Knowing I'm only seconds away from losing control, I work her breasts with my tongue, sucking on each until they're hard and raw, and Nolan's breathing has fallen into a pant. When her teeth dig into my shoulder, her mouth letting out a small cry of pleasure, I finally let go too, everything escaping me in one massive rush, my head dizzy as I collapse next to her, finally falling away and breaking our hold on one another.

That was selfish.

What I just did, it was one hundred percent for me. I had to have her, and I will forever be her first. I just took something from Nolan, something that I know I've taken from others, but for some reason have never stopped to think about like I am right now.

What Nolan gave me, she can only give once, and I am not something that will ever go away. I'm a permanent memory. I've tattooed myself on her heart and soul. And the gravity of all that—fuck. For once in my life, the weight of a moment isn't lost on me. And all I want to do now is deserve it.

Deserve her.

Rolling to my side, I reach my arm over her, pulling her into me, my fingertips touching the moist skin along her back, my ears content to listen to her breathe. Nolan looks up at me, and that worry—the mark on her face I left there from so many mistakes—is gone. Doubt—gone. Happiness all that is left.

————

Present Day

"I love you, Nolan," I whisper into the phone. "And I swear to God I always will."

I end the call and note the time. I just left her a sixteen-minute message. I rambled, and I went on and on about her body and what it was like to be a teenage boy in her presence back then. Fuck, I see how those high-school seniors look at her now. She's the kind of woman they write rock songs about.

I hope she listens to the entire thing.

I'm now a full two hours behind schedule, not that anyone is really waiting for me. When I called Arlon, OKC's head trainer, he almost sounded surprised. I think maybe he forgot about my scan. I'm not really a priority, and they have another backup.

A *younger* backup.

Climbing back in the Jeep, I decide to spend a few extra minutes staring at the mountainside where I once promised a girl I'd be hers forever. I've done a shitty job at that, I guess—almost snapping my neck and all.

Glancing up at the clouds that are starting to form, I talk to Trig.

"You better help me figure this out, man. Just cuz you left doesn't mean you still don't have a responsibility to this friendship. Brothers 'til the end, and I'm still here, Trig. I'm still here."

My head falls forward and I ready myself for the mind-numbing drive that lies ahead through some of the flattest parts of this world, taking one last look at the place where the earth is all beautiful and uneven.

I'm still here.

Chapter Thirteen

Nolan

I HAD to hide in our bathroom. I was completely alone when I got to Reed's message, and even still…I had to hide I was so embarrassed.

Maybe that's not the right word. I blushed. Embarrassed means shame or regret, and there isn't a single thing about that time that I regret. It's because I'm modest, I guess. And hearing him say things about me, that he felt back then…still feels. Well, damn, I guess it made me hot is all.

Reed was out of reach when I tried to call him, and I know it's later where he's at now. I sent him a text. I kept it simple.

I love you.

I spent most of the day working with the horses and cleaning the stables. I was able to persuade Peyton to do a little bit of the work, but as I predicted, it doubled mine. I'm glad I missed Reed's call, though. I would have stopped him from telling his version of our first time, and then I never would have gotten to hear it. I'm glad I did. It makes me love him more.

There's a bonfire tonight. It's funny how this town plans things to celebrate wins way before they've secured winning a damn thing. I can attest that they still party over losses too. Those parties get a little rougher, though. I promised Peyton we would go. As much as I give Reed a hard time for being a softy, I'm just as bad when it comes to some things.

Bryce is planning to go, and the thought of missing it was killing her. If I don't let her make memories, then she won't get those phone calls from someone she was with reliving the moment. She deserves it, even when she messes up.

My friends have been sitting at the edge of our pool for most of the day, minus the few trips Jason made to run out for more beer. I take the last cold one from the fridge and step out on the patio to join them, a noticeable presence missing from our group.

"You guys don't have to come to this bonfire thing. I'm just chaperoning, really. We probably won't even stay very long," I say, dipping my toes into the cool water. It's still warm enough to swim in Arizona, but not without covering my body in chills.

"I love the bonfire! We're going." Becky's enthusiasm isn't shared by Sean; I can tell by the flatness in his eyes and forced smile. But he plays excited for her. He'd take her to the moon if that's where she really wanted to go.

I lean into my old friend—my first real boyfriend—and whisper-mouth "That's nice of you."

He shrugs and wraps his fingers around Becky's. My eyes stay on their hands for a little longer than they should. I miss Reed. I hate missing him. So much.

"I think Micah and I are going to head back when you guys head out. The grandparents have the kids for one more night, and we never get to be in our house alone…" Sienna pauses just long enough for Sarah to corrupt everything she's in the middle of saying.

"You guys are going to do it in the kitchen; aren't you?" Sarah shouts, turning our friend seven levels of bright pink.

"Oh my God," Sienna says through the fingers now covering her face.

"Dude, you totally should! That way every time you're in there for like…the next month…all you'll think about is how that one time when you were home alone you boinked on the counter!" Sarah says.

"I'm sorry…boinked?" Micah says, trying to defuse the attention from his wife. It was a mistake, but I didn't have time to warn him. I shake my head anyway, though, because I feel it coming.

"Yeah, you know…like *fucked?* I just didn't wanna say fuck and all cuz, you know…I'm classy," Sarah says.

We all sit in silence for a few seconds, and Sean is the first to snort out a laugh. Soon we're all lying on our backs, kicking at the water and repeating our favorite parts of everything Sarah just said. The sound of all of us is so familiar, like no time has ever been missed. I used to wonder what it would have been like—*life*—if I'd spent it all still in this town, surrounded by all of them. I wonder if none of the bad things would have happened. But then…who would any of us be now if we never left.

"I should hit the road, actually. My flight's in a few hours." Jason stands and unrolls his jeans so he can put his socks and shoes back on and look more airport-ready and less carefree.

I look up at him and squint from the sun.

"You'll take care of him?"

I ask him this every time he leaves to go be with Reed. Not that there is anything extra Jason can do, but somehow just the little promise he makes by squeezing my hand and nodding makes me feel better.

———

Our party starts to break off slowly as the afternoon wears on. By bonfire time, it's only Becky, Sean, Peyton, and I headed to the practice field north of the school.

"No Sarah?" Becky leans between the front seats while I drive. I glance at her and shrug.

"She was so gung-ho, but then said she had a headache. I honestly think maybe going to these things makes her sad. I think maybe she's missing youth a little…if that makes sense?"

Becky laughs.

"Aren't we all," she says, leaning back into her seat. I nod at her in the mirror.

"Seriously," I say.

I pull around to the side gate, taking advantage of my parking privileges and avoiding the muddy tires the dirt lot usually leaves me with. We all climb out of my Tahoe together, and I see it just a flash before my daughter does—not soon enough to protect her, though.

My heart breaks for her as if it were my own all over again. Bryce's hand is deep in the girl's back pocket, and his mouth is devouring her neck. Their backs are to us, but their friends are facing us. Almost amused that they get to watch some major drama unfold, they nod in our direction, smirking a warning to Bryce who jerks around quickly, taking a step back from the girl he was with, flashing a face that is nothing short of guilty as sin.

"Peyton—" He doesn't know how to finish that, and I knew he wouldn't.

My daughter holds up a hand and instantly climbs back into the SUV, slamming the door quickly. We all follow her, not even questioning it, and as Becky and Sean lean in toward me, I whisper "Boyfriend."

Peyton adds quickly, and much louder, "*Ex*-boyfriend."

Her tears sit in a heavy well under her eyes, threatening to fall, but holding firm until I can turn the car on, pull around and hide her face from anyone's view. As soon as we leave the school parking lot, she falls apart, and I put my arm around her and pull her to my side, driving slowly because she's completely left the safety of her seat.

Nobody says a word; not as we pull in the driveway, and not as we all file back through the front door into the now dark and empty house. I glance back at my friends with pained eyes that they understand, then get Peyton upstairs and into her room. I sit on the side of her bed while she cries into my lap for nearly half an hour before she speaks. It's the silent shakes that hurt the most to feel. *It will get better, baby…I promise.*

"I'm so mad." Her voice is dry, so I offer water. She doesn't want it. I smooth hair that looks just like mine behind an ear just like mine. My mom did this for me more than once.

"I'm sad, too," she says, her body filling with a slow breath that she holds for several seconds. A tear slides down her raw cheek and she pulls her blanket into her fist to dab it away. "I'm more sad than mad now. I just want to be mad and that's it."

"I know." I trace her arm down to her hand so I can squeeze it. I would give anything to make this better, to go through this for her and erase the feeling from her memory, but I know I can't. Some painful things have to be survived when a person's young and learning about love. She'll be stronger—find herself.

I hope.

"Tell me again. Tell me about what you did to daddy when this happened?" I chuckle lightly, but even still, the stab at my side aches. This is a hard one to talk about, especially now. I've always been honest with Peyton, and when she started to notice boys and ask questions—even questions about me and my freshman year and beyond—I always told her whatever she wanted to know. She got the truth.

She's fascinated with Reed and my story. She says we're a fairy-tale, and as much as I don't want her to have a false illusion about life and love, I do think we are. I think girls deserve fairytales—and I think good guys deserve time to screw up and get second chances. There's a fine line there, though. It's a different line for everyone. When I first told Peyton about the times Reed and I broke up in high school, or before we got together and he dated other girls, she was adamant that she would never put up with a boy doing any of that. She came to the realization on her own that she wouldn't have this amazing man in her life now if I hadn't practiced a little forgiveness, though. *A lot* of forgiveness.

I loved Reed recklessly. I loved him blindly. I loved him despite every little and big thing that got in our way. And when I made mistakes of my own, Reed loved me right back. I'm sure to always remind her of that, too. That we make mistakes too. All we can do is learn from every hurt and misstep. For Reed and I, we learned to talk.

We learned to listen.

"I was mad as hell every time. And I was sad...just like you," I say, bending forward and kissing her head. I sweep her hair more, hoping the rhythm will soothe her.

"That's when you dated Uncle Sean," she says, and I lean my head to the side thinking back, my lips puckering into an embarrassed smile.

"Yes, I guess it was, but..." I lean back on my palms as she crawls up in her bed, burying herself in her covers. "It was a lot more complicated than that."

"Yeah," she sighs. I don't know how to explain this part to her. Sean was my first kiss, and when I look back on it all with the wisdom I have now, yeah...I kissed Sean and became his girlfriend as a way to get back at Reed. It was a really shitty thing to do, and the woman I am now would never do that. But if I were fifteen and faced with the same circumstances, I'm sure I would do the exact same thing. I don't regret any of it, and maybe that's because of how lucky I got—Sean became a forever friend. I grew as a person. It brought Reed and me closer.

"I messed up too, you know," I say, tipping her chin up enough to meet my eyes. "And you'll mess up someday. More than messing up your dad's Jeep." I tuck my chin as I stare at her, and she rolls her eyes, but smiles on one side.

"You'll hurt someone on accident, and you'll feel terrible about it because right now—this moment—you know how it feels. You'll keep this somewhere inside, and what hurts will turn to muscle. It's okay to be mad and sad, and it's okay if you want to march up to that boy on Monday and punch him in the face. It's okay if you choose to forgive him later, and it's okay if you don't. Just don't let yourself fall into the trap of thinking that any of this means you aren't enough, because you are. He's just not ready to deserve you."

Her long lashes blink slowly over her wide eyes.

"Your grandma always told me to wait for the ones who were worthy. I just waited until your dad was," I say, running my fingers through her now spread-out hair on her pillow. "He was worth the wait."

Her phone *buzzes* with Bryce's call—his hundredth, at least—and she rolls her head to the side to stare at her phone on her night table.

"Turn it off."

I reach for her phone and power it down, leaving it just out of her reach.

"I'll never mess up like this," she says, rolling herself up in her blanket and turning on her side.

She might be right. But that's another thing she gets from me—we have a hard time seeing when we might just be wrong.

She won't sleep, so I don't even suggest it when I leave her to lie in her bed, chewing at her nails slowly while her eyes stare off into nothingness. I've stared at that nothingness before. I've been in this same exact position—both emotionally and literally. This won't be her first heartbreak, and I can't say or do anything to make it better. But I can be here. That does somehow help.

I slip through the door quietly, mentally noting to call my mom in the morning and talk to her about this. She gives great advice, and I wish they didn't live so far. After decades of desert heat, they finally escaped to the pines up north. It's the greatest gift we were able to buy for them when Reed got his first huge contract —retirement.

The shower sound cuts out, so I hover in the hall, expecting to catch Becky on her way back to the guest room with Sean. The door opens without a lot of time passing, though, and it takes my head a few seconds to catch up to what I'm seeing and feeling. It's not Becky. And it's not just one person. It's two.

More specifically, it's Sarah's naked ass. Her legs are wrapped around Jason's waist, and they're both steaming hot and pink from the shower. And they're kissing.

Oh, holy fuck!

"What the ever-loving hell?" I shield my eyes, but not enough. It could never be enough.

Sarah awkwardly slides down Jason as he wraps his arms around her, pulling her close in attempt to hide both of their...*parts.*

"Oh my God!" I shout again, spinning and dizzy.

133

"My flight was cancelled," Jason says, and I start to choke as I cough.

"Yeah, umm, that is *not* the shocking thing right now!" I cover my eyes with both hands, and amble my way down the hall trying to get distance.

"Oh my God!" Becky's voice echoes mine from thirty seconds before, and I grab her as I feel her run into me in the hallway. We hug, and whisper disbelief to each other on repeat, spinning in shock.

Sean has started to laugh, and a few seconds later, Peyton joins in.

"Peyton, get in your room!" I just need to be in control of something.

"No way," my daughter laughs out.

"My clothes are in the bathroom," Jason says, his hand held out of the linen closet door that he and Sarah have hidden themselves in.

"So are mine, you ass!" Sarah shouts from behind him. Her hand slides through the crack just below where his is.

"I am not touching anything in that bathroom. Everybody is walking away. I'm going outside. Peyton is going in her room." I stop and point firmly at my daughter, who rolls her eyes but finally obeys. "Doors are being closed, and you guys can put your own damn clothes on. And you know what? Clean my shower. And the floor!"

I link my arm with Becky's and we guide each other down the stairs where Sean is already waiting, laughing so hard he can barely breathe. I walk immediately to the leftover wine from our weekend and pull the cork out, flinging it somewhere over my shoulder. I tip the bottle back and gulp, handing it to Becky who does the same.

"Sarah and Jason." Beck says out loud what I keep saying in my head.

"They hate each other," she adds.

I nod slowly with wide eyes and the bitter taste of cheap wine on my tongue.

"They were naked, Becks. So very naked." I hum, reaching for the bottle to add to the sour in my mouth.

"Yep," Becky says. We both lean back into the counter and lock gazes, trying to make sense out of this night. The weirdest thing of all is that Sarah and Jason actually *do* make sense. They make a lot of sense. I just can't believe none of us saw it coming. And that both of them were able to keep their mouths shut.

I wonder for how long.

My phone vibrates in my back pocket, and pretty soon, Reed's favorite song starts to play. My mouth starts to curve on the edges, just like Becky's, as I pull my phone out to answer his call.

"He is going to shit himself," my friend says.

I nod and bring the phone to my ear.

"Hey, babe..." I answer, unable to wait through his greeting on the other end. The words just have to come out. My other half has to feel just as confused as I am.

"Yeah...almost there...good. So, your brother and Sarah are boinking."

Chapter Fourteen

Reed

JASON HASN'T CALLED me back. I don't blame him. He knows why I'm calling, and that's fine. I'll wait. He can't avoid me forever. His paycheck guarantees that.

"All right, Reed. You know the drill."

The tech is nice. She's the same one I've had for the last two ultrasounds. The results always come back with "inflammation," and I'm starting to think that's just my new life—one big, fat inflammation. Doctor Williams, the team doc, is hovering around the computer, waiting for images of my muscles and joints to populate the screen. He's not much of a talker, but he's serious about the work he prescribes. And when he tells people to lay off the work for a while to heal, he's serious about that, too. I've listened. If anything, I've gotten lazy I've laid off my calf so much.

I pull myself up on the table and flip on my side while the tech rolls up my shorts until I'm showing *way* too much leg. My phone vibrates in my palm just as she's slapping the cool jelly on my skin, so I wince when I answer.

"You goddamned asshole," I say, tucking the phone into the crook of my neck and mouthing to the tech "not you."

She giggles and lifts a brow.

"I figured," she whispers. "Hi, Jason." She says that part for my brother a little louder.

"Oh hey, that's Wendy. Tell her hi." My brother is acting like this is any other day rather than the one after I now know what I know.

"You don't get to do that. No, no. What the hell, man?" I twitch a little when Wendy starts to move the wand around. Six-two, two-hundred-twenty-five pounds, and I'm ticklish as hell.

"See, this is why I didn't want to say anything," Jason says, a very audible sigh punctuating his response.

"What is why? I might be critical? I might wonder what's up with the flirting? I might wonder why…out of every woman between here and Arizona…you had to pick my wife's best friend to screw over?"

"I love her."

My brother punches the air from my lungs with three words. I part my lips but only a gasp escapes, and only Wendy can hear it. I'm blinking and my head is spinning, and the length of silence between us over the phone is ticking longer and longer.

"There aren't other girls. I'm not flirting with anyone, and if you really thought about it, if you *really* think back over the last six months, you'd realize that I have been so completely not into any other woman." Jason's voice is almost angry. It's definitely defensive. Shit. This…it's the real deal.

"Six months." I lock onto that detail.

"Officially," he adds.

I echo "officially" with a whisper and a breath of a laugh.

"Don't do that. Don't belittle it. Yes, officially. I asked her…officially. I asked to be real and to try this, a *me* and her. And we both decided to keep it to ourselves because we wanted it to have a shot without all of our friends and family throwing darts at it."

I wince with guilt. He's not painting a flattering picture, but it sure as hell is accurate. We would have. We're dart-throwers.

"I love her, man. I go back a lot more often than you think I do, and half of those times I tell you I'm at conferences, I'm not. I'm holed up in the apartment here or back in Arizona, with her." I can actually picture his expression from the way his voice softens and rasps with that hint of desperation. This is how I talk about Nolan.

"I thought she hated you," I chuckle out.

"Yeah, she may have at one point." He's quiet after that. I think because this…it's hard for him. He really loves her.

"There are things I should say…for Nolan. But I…"

My brother interrupts me.

"I'm not going to fuck this up. It's real. I, uh…" His pause seizes my chest.

"You…" I can't get my own mouth to form the rest of the words.

"I bought a ring. I asked her dad. I've booked a beach house. I hired a fucking cello player, man. I'm in deep." His swallow is audible. I burst into laughter. He joins me.

"Wow," I say, overexaggerating the way the word moves my mouth. "When?"

"Thanksgiving. I have to tell Dad I'll be missing it," Jason says.

"He won't care, dude." I don't add how dad and Rose will think this is a miracle. Jason having a family was something our pops just about wrote off. This is going to make his day. If anything, he's going to insist he travel to California and hide in the bushes to watch the proposal go down.

"Congrats, man. Honestly…I'm happy for you." I sit up, my leg wiped clean with a warm towel. My feet dangle from the exam table.

"Hey, I gotta go. But I'll see ya in a few hours. And do me a favor…just keep this with us for now. I want to tell people," my brother says.

"I got you," I say, and we exchange brief byes then hang up just in time for Doctor Williams to slide around so he's facing me, his long knees jutted up in the air because his body is too big for the tiny stool he's sitting on.

"Give it to me straight, Doc," I say, smirking. The doc and I have a long history. He was with Detroit for my big injury, and he's delivered some seriously tough news to me in the past. This calf thing—it's nothing.

"You're clear."

I blink a few times because clear isn't what I was expecting. Honestly, I was ready for chronic arthritis, splints, spurs, hairline fractures, tears. Clear? Not even a word I recognize.

"Clear," I repeat.

"Yup." He stands and holds out a hand, his mouth a tight smile that says more than the words he's saying. I pull my brow in and take his hand, sliding to a stand as I do.

"Look, I can't make them put you in a game, but if QB1 goes down, you're a viable option."

I puff out a snort of a laugh at his overly scientific prognosis of my future. I'm a...*viable option*.

"That's a lot like saying I'm a hail Mary, Doc," I say, taking the printout of my results from the tech.

"I suppose it is," he says, his mouth still not quite smiling.

"Is there something you want to say?" I tilt my head, wondering what else he saw in that ultrasound.

His chest lifts with breath, and his nostrils open a little more than normal. Our eyes meet, and after a second, his flutter as he crosses his arms and looks up at the ceiling with a huff.

"Your leg will be just fine, Reed. That's what I'm saying. Your leg...it will be fine..."

"But my neck...my head..." I fill in, kinda knowing all along what he meant. He's never been committed either way on this subject. I never asked him, instead getting first and second opinions elsewhere. There's a reason I did that. He knows what it is.

He gives it to me straight. Straight would take away options. Straight...is cautious.

His chin drops so our eyes meet again squarely, and we stare at one another just long enough for his to flicker with warning. He won't say it. He'd never do that to me. Doc knows the danger that comes along with putting risk in a player's head. Doesn't mean that risk isn't there, though. And his ethics can't ignore it completely.

"Right." I nod and thank him again, leaving in a way that I'm sure has made him uneasy. I'm uneasy. All of it is for nothing, though, because the odds of me getting in a game are so incredibly slim.

I stop in at the head office and deliver the paper to Coach Jenkins, our quarterback coach. He's not even fully aware as I enter and leave his office until I'm six steps out the door.

"Thanks, Johnson. I'll let him know," he shouts, busy with his coordinators working out tonight's plan. I wave my hand, sure he doesn't see it.

The rest of the guys won't be here for a few hours, but I'm not really interested in going home to my empty, sparsely furnished rental condo. I should probably call Noles and tell her the news, only it's the last thing she wants to hear. I'm not sure I should worry her for no reason, either.

I kick through the main doors out to the lot where my baby is parked in the middle, few other cars here this early. I pull my foot up and step on the top of my driver's side front tire and stretch the calf that's just been stamped with approval. It hasn't hurt in a while. It'll hurt again. Practice is enough to knock me on my ass for a good two or three days.

I switch legs and stretch the other muscle, then lean through the passenger window and grab my ear pods so I can go for a short run. I pop on the latest playlist Peyton sent me, and do my best not to sound like an old man in my head as I wonder why she likes this crap. Every song sounds the same, and the lyrics don't mean shit. A mile in, I get to a few songs I know she likes because *I* introduced her to them. Back-to-back Eminem gets me to the middle of the downtown, and I start to jog where the shade falls from the buildings.

A few people recognize me and give me head nods as I rush by the Starbucks. "They probably just think you're a regular there," I muse to myself. I turn down the alley I discovered last week and dip in to the greatest sandwich shop known to man, pulling my ear pods out at mile three and wiping the sweat from my forehead with the bottom of my T-shirt.

"Usual, Reed?" the owner says. His name's Tony, and his Italian beef is to die for.

"Yes, sir," I say as I pass through the kitchen and to the hallway for the restroom. A few fans have started to fill the joint, and I run into two or three guys who want to talk strategy with me at the urinal. Why conversations should happen here is beyond me.

I give them my take on the Atlanta defense, which is probably dated, then turn my back a little when I feel their eyes wander a little too low. *Not cool, dudes. Not cool.*

By the time I wash my hands and sign their jerseys—which are Duke Miller jerseys—Tony is waiting at the end of the hallway with my wrapped meal.

"Here you go, Boss," he says, his accent thick. He's from Philly originally, which is why his food is so damn good.

"Ahhh, I love you," I say, taking my sandwich in my fist and pushing through the back door on the other end. Crates stack up to form makeshift tables. This is where Tony and his brothers eat between the lunch and dinner rushes. He lets me sit out here because I can't really enjoy my meal with people constantly stopping in to get my commentary on the team. Sometimes, it's guys who have followed me for years, and they want to relive the past. I don't mind indulging when I have time, or at least, I don't mind being nice. But when I'm hungry, I just want to fucking eat.

I stuff half of the sandwich in my mouth within three bites and spend the next six minutes chewing and swallowing. The rumbles in my stomach quiet, and I pull my phone out to get up the courage for what I have to do next.

I pick at the meat, taking a few small tastes while I open Nolan's info and press CALL. She answers after a few rings, out of breath.

"Hey, bad time?" I ask.

"No, no...one of the horses got out. Kid got spooked. Or maybe he just thought it was time to set him free. I was talking to his mom, and he wandered over." She breathes a few more times, loud enough that it rattles against the phone. "I'm good. Sorry."

"You chased a horse. You sure you're all right?" I chuckle at the thought. I have a visual in my head to help. I've seen her do it twice, and once was my fault.

"Yeah, I'm fine. It was Paisley, and she's slow."

I smile to myself, a little sad I missed it. Not because it was funny or anything, but just because I missed it and it's familiar—*home.*

"I talked to Jason." I wait for a second as her breath normalizes and her throat makes a soft grunting sound.

"Yeah?" She's still pissed. She's going to be hard to convince.

"They're in love, Noles."

My wife laughs so loud and hard that she starts to cough. I squint and brace myself for her knee-jerk reaction.

"No, they're not."

And there it is.

"I said the same thing to him. I threw down the bullshit card, but he had an answer for it all. He didn't bend or break. There wasn't a joke to be found, or some dirty comment or crass thing he said about hookups. Have you talked to Sarah?"

"I think she's too embarrassed because they got caught. She hasn't answered my text yet, and this is the first morning since I can't even remember that she wasn't scrounging for food in our fridge. This isn't love, Reed. Your brother is good at bluffing, and maybe they're caught up in the game of it. It's new, ya know?"

She's going to be hurt when I tell her this.

"Six months."

Sudden silence takes over the other end of the line, and I start to think I lost her when I hear her breathe out.

"He got a ring, Noles."

"Wow," she says, her voice soft and sincere.

"Right? That's what I said."

"In love, huh?" She sounds sort of detached. I think she's hurt that her best friend kept this from her. For a minute, I felt the same way when Jason told me, but I got his reasons. I would have been relentless. Maybe Sarah thought Nolan would have forbade it. She might have. Jason…he's not easy. She would have wanted to protect her friend.

"You can't say anything about the ring. He has it all planned

out, and I was sworn to secrecy, but me and you don't have secrets."
I swallow my words too late. That right there is a lie, or at least, it
has been. We *did* have secrets. Those hidden things are what got us
into this place we are now. She caught that, too, which is why she
hasn't answered.

"Sorry," I say finally, and she knows what for.

"I won't say anything," she says. Her words are raspy, heavy with
thought and double meaning.

I'm no longer hungry; it has nothing to do with Tony's food. I
wrap the other half of my sandwich up, stand and raise my hand as
I pass by the open doorway to gesture thanks to his brother as I pass.
I need to walk for this next part of our conversation.

"In other news…" That's such a lame transition, and I scrunch
my face and wish I'd brought sunglasses now that I'm moving along
the main road. A few cars honk, and the number of OKC jerseys on
the street is growing by the minute. I'm the famous has-been, which
means I'll be nice and always say "Sure, I'll take a selfie."

"Hang on," I say, while two drunk men in Atlanta jerseys sandwich me for a photo that I'm sure they're going to hashtag with
some unflattering shit later, but whatever.

"Reed, you sound busy. It's okay…"

"No, no…" I excuse myself from the cluster of football fans
starting to congregate near a beer garden and duck into a conve-
nience store, weaving into the aisle that sells motor oil and paper
towels.

"I was out for a run, and it's game day." I glance around with
relief when the store is virtually empty minus the steady stream of
people buying beer. No wanderers; if I stay here, I'll be fine.

"Out for a run, huh?"

I didn't really mean to leave her a clue. I haven't been running
much, which I miss. I wouldn't run, either…unless it was okay for
me to.

"Yeah," I sigh, and let the silence fill in the blanks for a while.
She's not going to ask for details. There really aren't many. If I give
them to her, she'll feel better.

"Calf is all good to go. Not that it's going to do much more than pace around behind Jenkins, nodding that he's giving Duke good advice. Really, it's just a formality that I'm quote-unquote healthy." I end with a nervous laugh.

"Yeah…yeah. I know. I guess I just wasn't expecting it. I got used to injuries taking longer, I guess…" Her volume falls with those last few words, probably at the realization that I am always the one living with those injuries—living *through* them.

"Anyhow. I just wanted to tell you before…"

"Before I saw the ticker during pre-game or heard it come out of Terry's mouth on TV?" She's joking, but only partially.

I laugh a short sound to acknowledge her.

"I have a good part to this, though," I start.

"Reed, I'm glad you're healthy. It's good news," she interjects.

"I know. But…" I stop there, because we could do this back and forth all night. I'd miss my game standing here in the four-foot automotive aisle rehashing our guilt. I won't. "The good news is I'm traveling to L.A. with the team. Backup quarterback duties and all. I thought maybe I could meet you in Santa Fe for the services and we could make a road trip together."

"That far…in the Jeep?"

I laugh loudly this time, and I pop up from crouching down to make sure I didn't blow my cover. One guy looks my direction, but he turns his attention right back to his phone. Cover intact.

"We can take the Tahoe," I say, a little sad because me, her and the Jeep have history. And if we take the Tahoe, she has to drive it to Santa Fe alone. I don't want her to be alone on that stretch of highway.

She hums, thinking about it for a few seconds, and finally agrees to my idea. It's actually the first thing I thought about when Doc said I was cleared. It's been years since I traveled anywhere far by road with her. This might just be our shot to right this ship.

"How's Peyton?" My chest hasn't stopped twisting with this adolescent need for vengeance on her behalf. Nobody wants their kid to hurt, especially in their heart.

"She'll live," Nolan says.

"I can't believe I liked that kid. I feel so…duped."

145

Nolan laughs softly.

"You know…you weren't exactly perfect either when you were that age." There's a wryness to her tone that cuts right into me.

I sniffle and look down at my feet, then glance up again at the sound of the bell tied to the store door. If Bryce is anything like me, he's feeling like shit right now. I wasn't ignorant to the effects of my actions. I just lacked that little kick in my brain to stop me before I carried through with the bad ideas. I always felt guilty after. More than guilty—I felt unworthy. I wanted to punish myself, and protect her from me hurting her again.

"Things I will spend a lifetime making up to you," I say, dead serious.

"You already have," she answers.

The heaviness in my chest says I still have a long way to go, though.

"I gotta get your dad moving. Call me after the game?"

I quirk my lip up in a half smile. I remember when she used to watch, not willing to miss a single move I made on that field. I thought for a while she took notes, because our late-night conversations included so many details. She knew every damn play I made. Nothing for her to watch anymore.

"Tell him I miss him," I say, adding "Love you." She says it back, and a second later I'm standing by trash bags and wiper blades all alone.

Chapter Fifteen

Reed, Early Spring, Junior Year of High School

THIS MUST BE what real love feels like.

Nolan's body feels warm against my skin, the heat somehow radiating through our layers of sweatshirts. I wonder if other people on this bus are looking at us. I've never actually sat by myself during one of our track team bus trips. There's always been a girl, and I think most of the people in our school think I just need someone. Maybe I do. This, though…it's different.

This isn't needing someone. This is needing Nolan.

She's doing the cutest thing with her hands. She keeps bunching the front of my sweatshirt in her palms and squeezing it, like it's a teddy bear or something. I love the way her knuckles feel when they press against my stomach. I just like feeling her close—the connection.

Constant.

I thrum my fingers along her arm and she shifts her head, tilting her chin up to look me in the eyes. I brush away her hair, tucking it behind her ear, and I spend the next few miles staring at her. She's all shadows and reflections now that the sun has gone down. The moon is out enough to highlight the curve of her lips, the lift of her cheeks and the softness of her hands. I could ride around on this bus forever under this light. We're surrounded yet all alone.

Her forehead wrinkles, and I press my thumb along the small dent, trying to erase it. It makes her smile, but her lips flatten out again when I go back to stroking her hair.

"What's on your mind?"

She bites at the inside of her cheek. This is how I can tell when she's nervous.

"Nothing," she says. That's a lie.

She nuzzles into me more, hiding her face; I tickle her and make her giggle and move. When her lips are free, I bend down to kiss them. She tucks her chin, so I rest my head on hers and graze the tip of her nose with my mouth.

"That doesn't look like nothing," I tease, but gently. "Come on, you can tell me. Just say it; you think I'm cute, don't you!"

I poke at her side again, but she doesn't laugh as much this time.

"You're all right, I guess," she says, rolling her eyes to make fun of me.

"Hey, you're no looker either, sister. We uglies have to stick together," I shoot back, trying to maintain a serious face. I can't keep my smile in check, though, and pretty soon it's stretching across my face. When Nolan sticks her tongue out at me, I lift her enough to catch her in a kiss. It turns into more than just a short peck, the feel of her lips taking over my self-control. Every time I taste her, it's like her mouth was meant for mine. There was never a moment of figuring out where we belonged. Our hands always knew where to go and how to hold, and our bodies have been the same. Nolan just fits in all of my empty spaces.

Our hands remain twined as our lips fall away, and I lean back in the seat while she rests in my lap, her legs curled up against the window—our own little paradise rolling down the road at sixty-five.

I fall into the trance of our hands together, taking in the way they look—her skin against mine. Where she's freckles and pale, I'm tan and strong. Her delicate fingers are cool to my warm, and all I want is never to let them go.

"How many girls have you slept with?" Her question comes out of the blue, but in a way, I felt it burning in her. It's been on her mind for a while, maybe since we met. At least since I dated Tatum.

"Oh my God, I didn't mean to say that out loud." She's cupping her mouth with both hands and her eyes are wide. She wasn't ready to ask me, but really...she deserves to know.

I sweep her into a hug against my chest, letting out a nervous laugh.

"You're adorable, you know that?"

I kiss against her hair and take a deep breath in, not wanting to talk about any of this. It hurts to share. I'm not proud, but I can't take any of these things back that I've done. I thought I was making the right choices when I made them. I was fifteen...sixteen...seventeen. I was a teenaged boy in a locker room full of other teenaged boys all obsessed with losing our virginity, with bragging about it, with feeling satisfied and grown-up like a man, even though we couldn't be farther from mature.

"Four," I say quickly. I feel a hammer hit my chest with the word.

It hits Nolan, too. Her once-loose body has grown rigid in my hold, and her breath has paused. She's staring at our hands, no longer moving.

There's no way she'll be surprised by Tatum. She and I weren't exactly quiet or discrete. She was my first, and she and I were about all of the wrong things. It wasn't fair to her that I let our relationship go on that long. Even with the mistakes she made, she deserves better.

"I'm not proud of it," I say, nervous about this conversation. I don't want Nolan to think less of me, to doubt us. "I would take all of them back if I could. You know that, right?"

I lift her chin to look into her eyes. Her lips part to speak, but she closes them again quickly. I've surprised her—*disappointed her.* It feels terrible.

I graze her cheek with the back of my hand.

"I don't want to hurt you, Noles, but I'll tell you anything you want to know. Anything you need to know and deserve to know. But

I'm not asking you to have sex with me, not unless you want to. I'll never be that guy."

Every bit of me wants her, to touch and feel her. But it's different. It's this need to be close to her that grips at me, and as hungry as I am for it, my love for her also keeps me from betraying her trust and pushing her. I would never. Not with any girl. But especially this one.

"You make me feel safe," she says, sliding her arms around my body and hugging me tightly.

I relax into the seat, maybe a little surprised to hear her say that out loud. It's all I want—her to feel safe. Even before we were a couple, I wanted that for her. I always wanted to protect her. I should have known it meant so much more.

"Okay, well, you know about Tatum. She was my first. And, well, that's because I was an adolescent teenaged boy with hormones busting at the seams and…hell, you know the rest." I stop there, not really wanting to hurt her with the rest. It will hurt her, too. Maybe that's why I did it. I don't deserve her, and the fucked-up way I dealt with my jealousy was just that—fucked up. I glare out the window, feeling the weight of her body against mine and praying this will end here.

"And…numbers two, three, and four?" She asks so quietly, afraid to know. God, Nolan—you don't want to. I know what it's like, though, to need to know. Even when it hurts.

"I said I wasn't proud." I pause with my eyes on her, but I can't tell her this and see how it hits her. I look to the side, to nothing.

"Morgan was my second…you know? The lifeguard that worked with us this summer?"

I can see her throat move as she swallows. I hate this. So much. I glance at her, and her eyes are still on me, waiting for the next two names—girls that deserve more respect than a high-school boy knows how to give them.

Fuck.

I look back down toward the floor of the bus. It's too dark to see my feet, but I mush the toe of my shoe into a small space where the seat in front of us is bolted to the metal.

"Well, Morgan had a friend named Mandy. We were at a party one night and I sort of found myself with her." I scrunch my face because I sound like such a dick. I was a dick.

"That's sort of when Morgan told me to kiss her ass," I admit.

"Good for Morgan," Nolan says quickly. She means it, too. She slaps her hand over her mouth again and flashes her eyes. "Sorry," she squeaks out, smiling bashfully. I squeeze her because she's not the one who should be embarrassed here. What's terrible is I think Morgan and Nolan would have been really good friends. They like a lot of the same things. If I saw them together now, though, I think I'd start to run. There's no way Morgan would be telling Nolan anything nice. I'd deserve it all for cheating on her with her friend, too.

My gaze shifts back to the darkness outside, little glimpses of the mountains and brush lit up by the side lights of the bus. I wish I could lie to this girl. This last name is one I don't ever want her to know, and it's going to break her. I suck in my top lip and try to breathe, even though the air immediately around Nolan and me is suffocating. There's a shortage of it. It's strangling me—my punishment.

"I have to know," she says, her fingers wrapping around my arm. They feel so small and timid. I can feel the vibrations—the worry.

"Calley," I say, ripping the bandage off quickly and instantly wanting to put it back on and hide the truth away forever. Calley is Sarah's sister. A friend. A *close* friend.

Calley was a huge betrayal. It was on both of our parts. It was careless of me—heartless. It was desperate and foolish, and I know if Calley could erase it from history, she would. I'd let her.

I feel her start to tuck into me, hiding, so I flatten my palm against her cheek, my touch gentle. Her head pushes against me and her eyes slant with the pain. Her eyes are starting to water, and goddamn do I hate seeing it. I force myself to look, though. I need to know intimately what hurting her looks like so I can keep myself from doing it again.

She lifts her arm, wiping her eyes along the long sleeve of her sweatshirt, the cuff tucked around her knuckles.

"Sorry, I didn't mean to cry, that one just…surprised me. I just thought Calley knew how I felt about you." Her voice quivers at the end. The knife in my chest grows hot.

She shrugs, trying to pretend that the hurt was temporary—that it isn't real. Before she can look away, though, I lift her chin with my fingers.

"Don't do that. Don't run away from me. And don't blame Calley. She was at the desert party the night you picked me up. She was drunk. I was…drunk."

That's the night I told her I loved her. The words fell out of me in a dream, only I said them out loud. Mostly, I knew she was hearing them. I was a coward, though, and I needed that mask to get through it—to tell her the truth.

"I was running my mouth to her in the back of her car, telling her how you were with this dickhead and I fucked everything up and she was consoling me and then we both did a bunch of shots of what-the-fuck-I-don't-know." I stop suddenly, my mouth watering a little from the wave of nausea. That night was both the worst and the best of my life—the best because she was there. When I needed someone, Nolan was there.

"It sort of happened somewhere after that. And that's when I started texting you because I just wanted to erase it, knew I was fucking everything up…even more than I had already, if that was even possible."

Her eyes sag, maybe with pity for me. She's feeling sorry for me, though she has this all backward.

"Calley started crying, telling me never to tell anyone and to pretend it didn't happen. Noles, she never wanted to hurt you either. You have to know; she was so drunk. She got sick after that, passed out in her backseat and shit."

I stare at her, needing some sort of absolution. *Say it's okay, Nolan. Please…say it's okay.* The quiet drags, and after nearly a minute of staring at her and willing her to forgive me, I realize that she isn't going to. She probably doesn't think she needs to. I'm not really asking for it, but I'm sorry all the same.

She sinks back into me, and my palms tentatively cup her shoulders, then run along her arms.

"I'm never going to be what they were," she says, and my eyes close hearing her hard truth. That's what this is about for her. It's about the experience, and all of that bullshit that we think we need to impress someone. She doesn't need any of it. All she needs to do is be this, to be her.

I lean forward and press my lips to the top of her ear. So small and innocent. So unspoiled and precious.

"Baby, you're so much more." I stop and take a sharp breath, the truth of what I'm saying hitting me hard. "You have no idea. You're so beautiful, and I love you, and if you ever want to be with me, I'll be the luckiest dude on earth…but not unless you want to share that with me."

I kiss her neck and bury my face in it, breathing her scent in until I'll smell it in my dreams. I memorize it. Not that there is any way in hell there is anything about Nolan Lennox that I could ever —*ever*—forget.

Chapter Sixteen

Nolan

THE EMPTY HOUSE IS STRANGE. I guess it isn't completely empty. Buck and Rose are here, and Peyton's locked away in her room swearing off boys forever. I'm okay with that. Maybe she'll be one of those people who swears off intimacy of the romantic kind. It will be so much easier to guide her through that.

It's a pipe dream. I know it is, because my girl is a dreamer. Whether she'll admit it to me now or not, she's just like me. She used to *want* to be just like me. It made her proud. We'd make up fairytales, and while our girls were always strong and independent, they also liked to fall in love. Love was real.

Love *is* real.

It just isn't easy.

I tap on her door on my way back downstairs, one last attempt to bring her out of her misery. The one thing she's missing is a core of friends. I don't know how I would have gotten through half of the shit that comes along with being a teenager without the girls and Sean. The thought brings Sarah racing to the forefront of my mind as Peyton groans on the other side of the doorway. I know I

157

promised not to say anything, but that was just about the ring. I think the rest is fair game. It's not like Peyton didn't see their naked bodies flailing around the hallway either.

"Hey, I have news on Uncle Jason and Sarah."

She perks up.

"Come in!" I smile behind the door and start to giggle.

She loves gossip.

She hasn't gotten out of bed today, and she's wearing the same T-shirt she had on when I said good night yesterday.

I move to sit on the end of her bed, and she pulls her comforter in over her folded up legs and quirks a brow at me.

"Well?" She's hedging a little, expecting this to be a trick to get me in the room so I can talk to her more about Bryce. She's done talking about Bryce though, and I get it. I wouldn't do that to her. I just need to talk to her and feel her out, make sure she's okay. And when I have actual gossip to share, she's going to be glad.

"Six months," I say. Her eyes squint. "That's how long they've been together," I fill in. Her eyes widen.

"Six months?" Her mouth pauses open, and I can see her mentally ticking back through every time we've been with Sarah and when Jason's been here to visit. How did we miss this? I can't stop doing the exact same thing.

"Sarah can keep a secret after all, it seems," I say, pursing my lips.

"I guess so," she says, bunching hers then laughing.

"Uncle Jason told Daddy," I explain. "Apparently, they're *in love.*"

I say it like a joke, but only because it will make Peyton laugh, which it does. Having heard the details from Reed, and judging from the fact that Sarah is still avoiding me, I know better. My best friend is going to be my sister...I think. I'm not sure how that works, when friends marry brothers, but I'm sure, legally, we'll be connected somehow.

"Your dad's game is on soon. Grandma Rose is making snacks. Come on down," I say, tugging at the corner of her blanket. She lets one leg slide out, begrudgingly. I reach for her hand and she gives it to me, letting her body slump backward as if moving out of this bed is impossible. "Come on…you can do it," I tease.

"It's not like Dad's going to play," she says.

I puff out a small laugh, but an itch tickles in the back of my mind because for the first time in weeks, it's possible. It's not likely, but it is…possible.

"You know he likes to give us little signs on camera. Let's see if we can see him holding up fingers and scratching his nose."

My daughter finally gives in and brings both feet to the floor, standing on her own.

"Last time it looked like he was picking his nose. My friends saw that. It was so embarrassing."

I snort laugh, a little proud of my husband for embarrassing our teen. It's a rite of passage, and it's the one benefit from dealing with the drama.

Peyton and I make it downstairs just as Rose is settling Buck into the comfortable chair closest to the TV.

"Dah dah dah dah," he cries out, his pathetic attempt at singing. He's playing the football music with his mouth, and it isn't his stroke that made it sound so awful. His musical skills are genetic, and his son got the same exact ones.

"I made caramel bars," Rose announces, slipping around the counter in the kitchen and pulling a tray from the fridge that I have no idea how I missed. I bet she had those hidden in the garage to keep them away from my friends—from Sarah.

"Where's my girlfriend?" Buck is asking about my friend. He and Sarah are close, and she's usually here for the evening games—especially for Reed's.

"She's tied up. Hopefully, she'll come a little later," I say, glancing at Peyton and widening my eyes in warning. She understands and nods. We won't ruin this for Jason. It's his to tell his dad, and I think Buck is going to be both thrilled and sad that he's losing a pretend girlfriend and gaining a daughter.

Peyton nestles into the corner of the couch closest to Buck, and I watch from the back of the room, near the kitchen, as he struggles to reach for her hand. I can barely hear them, but I get just enough to know he's consoling her. He's always been good at making heartache hurt less.

"You want me to…let one of those…Tucson coaches know his weak side?" Buck jokes, and Peyton smiles.

"Maybe," she says, taking his hand in both of hers. She leans against the sofa's arm and hugs her grandfather's arm completely, leaving her head to rest on his bicep. It's sweet, even if it's to comfort her broken heart.

She thinks Buck's kidding about calling the coaches, but if she asked, I know that he would or he'd have one of us send an email to a friend he has. He has friends everywhere when it comes to high school football in the Southwest. There isn't a team he can't help or hinder. Even now, as a senior citizen. I heard once he found out about a team that was stealing plays from their rival and he got involved by cancelling their uniform order. That team had a hard time finding anyone in Arizona or California willing to print their jerseys.

I got Buck up to speed on Reed, so he isn't surprised to hear his son talking with the sideline reporter for our local broadcast of the game. We get special highlights of Reed, and Buck counts on them, hopping around the channels with deft. He can't drive a car any longer, and walking is hard to manage, but he can run the Sunday ticket with no trouble at all.

"He looks good," Peyton calls over her shoulder after we listen to her dad talk about how much he appreciates the team putting the work in for him and helping him get healthy again.

"He always looks good," I smile.

I stay in the back of the room, wanting to have a little privacy while I stare at my husband through the screen. He gives me a few hints, like the way he brushes the end of his nose with his knuckle and pulls his beanie from his head and scratches at his mussy hair. Those gestures translate to a lot of love for me. They still tickle my heart and make my entire chest warm, even after all these years.

Buck switches over to the game's station when Reed's interview is done, and the first quarter is already in progress. It's only been a minute, but Duke Miller's already thrown one touchdown. I scan the sidelines as the camera rushes to follow him back to the bench as he celebrates, and I sit up higher and smile when I see Reed clasp hands with Duke.

When the camera view cuts Reed's face in half, though, I fall back and grab the underside of my seat. It's such a foreign tightness in my chest. I'm too far to really hear anything clearly, especially with Buck and Peyton talking over the announcer. I know that the announcers are probably talking about Duke, rattling off stats and expectations for today—this season. Suddenly, seeing the frame centered around this young quarterback, working to remove Reed from the view completely...it stings. And it's not my own need to be married to the superstar stud athlete. It's the way Reed is being cut in half, no longer the most important piece of the team—no longer the heart.

I get it. This has to be killing him.

The defense takes over, and the focus is back on the game. I listen close, waiting to hear a mention of Reed's name. Anything. A comparison, or a mention of his mentorship. They probably talked about his leg being better before we switched the channel over, but even if that's the case, it was a small mention. It wasn't what was important. Duke is what's important now.

Reed is what *was* important.

The first quarter passes without a lot of excitement, and by the time halftime rolls around, I realize I've been plastered to this stool with ears intently listening with hope. I just wanted him to be safe. I didn't want him to be forgotten.

I find myself drawn closer to my family, slipping between Rose and Peyton on the couch as I kick my shoes off and curl my legs into my body. Rose is working on her latest knitting project, and my daughter is playing some game on her phone where a little man falls from cliffs over and over again, dying when he lands on cactus. Buck is tuned in, though. We've all given up on really paying attention to every little thing, but not Buck. He knows where his son is at all times. He catches every camera pass, rattles off the stats that the announcers don't know or miss that relate to his son. When Duke Miller is suddenly flattened about fifteen yards behind the line of scrimmage in a way that tells my gut he isn't getting up, Buck…he stands.

My eyes are wide, and things outside of my head begin moving in slow motion. The feeling makes me sick because everything in my head is on overdrive, speeding through thoughts and conclusions, coming up with frightening results.

My father-in-law just lifted himself from his chair onto his own two feet. He's holding fists clenched in front of his body and his lips are parted, waiting to either exhale his nerves or inhale in preparation for what just might come next.

My eyes blink to the screen.

Reed is shedding his jacket.

He's throwing.

The camera leaves my husband and moves back to the field, where Duke is sitting up. I have hope—I have guilt. The cart is coming out, but he's waving it off. He doesn't want it, but it's coming for him anyhow.

"He's okay," I whisper, just loud enough that Peyton hears me.

"That didn't look good," she says, worried for all of the right reasons. She doesn't like that a young athlete in his prime just possibly took a season-ending hit that bent his leg in two different directions.

I'm praying for all of the selfish reasons. If Duke is out, Reed is in. That next hit could happen to him. One more hit…in the wrong place. One break or snap, or one more concussion might change him forever.

Not ever playing this game again, though…he's already changed.

"I'll be right back," I announce, leaping from the sofa and grabbing my keys from the counter, marching through the side door to my Tahoe. I climb in and twist the radio up as loud as it will go after I crank the engine. I whip around in a half circle, heading around the curved driveway forward, leaving a trail of dust in my wake as I fly through the line of trees, branches beginning to bare as golden leaves fall to the ground. I have no direction in mind, so I turn left onto the main highway road and press the pedal to the floor, hitting ninety-five to an old Pat Benatar song.

Brush thrashes as I drive down by the two-lane road. Nobody is on the road with me, so I push the gas to go faster, feeling it rattle the boxiness of my SUV. I travel more than ten miles into the desert, beyond the lines of housing projects graded out in the dirt and sand. I pass only a single car—a minivan that forces me to slow down when the woman driving glares at me as I pass. Maybe she didn't glare. We flew by each other so quickly, it's impossible for me to really have seen her features. What I probably saw was my own warning to myself, the risk and the fear all at once, forcing me to ease back my pressure on the pedal until I'm finally driving at a crawl and pulling off to the side of the road.

My breath is hard, and my knuckles are white from my grip on the steering wheel. The biker bar ahead is filled with football fans. Sundays are the one day you can't get a seat, because every landowner, prison worker, biker, and old-timer in Coolidge has come out to drink away their reality and live vicariously through these boys living the dream on one-hundred yards of turf.

Boys.

Reed isn't a boy anymore. He's a veteran. This game is for rookies and fools, and he's no longer prepared to be on the battlefield.

I drive forward slowly, gently making my way back onto the road for the few yards I need to travel to pull into the last open space in the dirt lot. It's me and a row of Harleys, and I'm sure when I leave the confines of my car and enter the Old Route Draft House, I will be incredibly out of place, yet my legs carry me forward. It's dark inside, and the buzz of mounted televisions and rowdy customers fills my ears like cotton, almost cutting out the stream of my own worries.

Almost.

I feel them too heavily in my chest, like a shiv digging into the soft center between my middle ribs. The feeling cuts my breath, but somehow, I'm able to say "beer" to the bartender as I take the last stool on the very end of an extremely crowded bar. The entire place smells of motor oil and sweat and a faint hint of whiskey. Every television is showing the same thing—the two announcers from the Sunday night game—except for the one in front of me that's showing soccer. It makes me chuckle to myself, because if I could just pay attention to this instead, then I'd be all right.

That's not going to happen though, and I know it. I tried to run and still I found myself in a place where I had to watch. I have to watch because…because it's him. I have to watch because I'm scared, and because I also believe.

I take my beer and point my finger to the TV, knowing I won't have to mention it out loud. The bartender laughs and grabs a remote, bringing this screen in sync with all of the others.

"Some guy sitting here earlier wanted soccer. I wonder why he left," he laughs out, pointing around the room behind me with the remote.

"Yeah, right?" I say, taking my beer with two hands.

"Wanna start a tab?"

I sip the foamy top and consider his offer for a second. A tab…

"Just the one," I answer. He runs off my receipt and folds it in half, sitting it upside down next to my mug.

I'm not the only woman in the joint, but I'm close. I'm the only one not wearing leather or a shirt with fringe. I'm also the only person not smoking.

What I'm *not* is the only person who realizes who that quarterback is—the one running from the sidelines into an offense that isn't the one he molded. This entire room knows what's happening as drunken celebrations turn into rehashed stories about "that one time he threw for four-hundred yards."

Our golden boy is giving it one last shot. The town hero is back, even if it's in someone else's town. He's still ours.

He's still mine.

And there is still nobody better to watch with the ball under the lights.

"Goddamn," I hum, half in awe and half terrified.

I swallow the bitterness of my beer and feel the frost of the glass on my fingertips as number thirteen steps into the huddle and does what he does best.

He claps a few times, his hand grabbing the shoulder of his receiver then his running back. It's all for show—meaningless. It's a stupid trick that works, one he got from his brother of all people. The other team is always watching. They evaluate everything. And if they think you're comfortable with one guy more than the other, then that's where they're going to focus.

Nobody is looking at the tight end. But Reed is.

The first play happens so fast, I nearly miss it by blinking. A ten-yard pass turns into twenty-two thanks to a tight end that Reed has played with before. The same play gets them four more yards, and then Reed scrambles for the first down on the next.

My mouth is sour. I sip at my beer again, sloshing it between my teeth in an attempt to taste anything other than my fear.

My family is watching this without me. Buck is standing—or he was. Peyton is getting to see her father do something he wasn't supposed to be able to do again. And I ran away to watch this with strangers who have no idea what any of this means to me.

My phone buzzes, and I know it's Jason. I wonder how many times he's texted, how many times he tried to call. This is our arrangement, and even getting caught having sex with my best friend wouldn't keep him from following through. I can't look now, though. I can't take my eyes off Reed.

Ten yards after ten yards repeat until he's carried the team to the fifteen-yard line. A lead of fourteen to seven is set to become twenty-one to seven. All he has to do is show them all that he can do it. But Atlanta is ready. They've seen enough to know his weaknesses now, and his first two attempts end up with him running out of bounds for no gain at all. No loss either, and I guess that's something.

The crowd around me has gotten quiet, rooting for Reed even though his success means nothing for our own team. Reed comes first. The man before the business. He's one of them—one of us. The called time-out feels like it stretches on for minutes, and I finally set my beer down, too nervous to drink anymore.

I pull my phone into my palm and see four missed calls and a string of texts from Jason. Peyton is asking where I am. I tell her that I have the game on and I'll be right back. I open Jason's texts, and they're nothing but the same thing over and over again.

Are you all right?

I'll answer him in a few more seconds because by then…I should know. I'm living and dying by every move Reed makes on that field.

They go in without a huddle, wanting to rush the play and get Atlanta off balance. The snap is fast, and Reed takes five or six steps back. I hold my breath and let the smoke burn my eyes rather than blink. His calf is holding steady. His body is shifting just as it's supposed to. He ducks and jerks right, breaking a tackle and running to his strong side with the impossible touchdown in his sights.

The crowd around me has started to give up. They're expecting the fail—a last-minute scramble from a man who doesn't want to get hit.

They don't know where to look.

He'll be there. He'll be there just like Trig would have been there. If he does his job, then Reed will make impossible happen, and everyone in this bar will feel like assholes having doubted him.

I dig my fingers into my thighs, his window closing, the tackle rushing forward. The hit is coming, and I'm glad that the camera moves with the ball rather than forcing me to watch it happen.

His target is a rookie too, just like Duke. His name is Waken, and his number is eighty-one. I know nothing about him, or where he came from—other than those few details I tucked away from earlier and the ones I see on the screen now as his fingers spread wide and bring the ball in. His toes drag across the corner of the turf, leaving no questions for the replay booth.

Touchdown.

The bar has erupted, and the man next to me punches my shoulder and holds a palm open for me to slap. I do it and plaster on a smile that can't possibly look real. It won't be real until they flash back to Reed, until I see him get up.

He's running toward Waken and my heart kicks back to life. My lips puff out. I suck in a hot breath laced with nicotine. Reed's chest collides with Waken's, and he slaps his receiver's helmet as they both run in for what is the beginning of a long relationship. I've seen this before, too. One catch has made him Reed's go-to. If Miller is out for more than today, Waken is going to see a lot of those passes, and he's going to be pushed to his limit. Reed won't expect anything less, because that's what he gives.

That's what he crosses.

His limit.

He doesn't set any.

My phone buzzes and I pick it up on the first ring, pressing it hard to my right ear and shoving my finger in my left.

"I'm okay," I pant out.

Jason shouts on the other line, asking if I saw that pass.

"Of course I did," I shout back. "I gotta go, though. I'm at the biker bar."

Someone shoves into my back, pushing me hard into the bar and spilling a good portion of my beer. The rowdiness of the crowd is growing because this is the kind of place that lives vicariously through the success of one of their own.

"You're in the Draft House. Ha! I'd like to see that." Jason says.

"Maybe we can have your wedding here," I throw back, not thinking hard enough before I speak. "I'm sorry…"

"Nah, it's okay. I'm glad you're all right. And we were going to tell you, it's just…"

"I know," I cut in, not wanting to have this conversation with my brother-in-law while I huddle for protection in the middle of a biker fight.

"You sure you're okay?" he asks again.

I slip out a ten from my purse and leave it for my beer that I abandon to head back out to the mix of coolness and heat in the desert. Everything quiets the moment I push through the doors and head back to my car.

"I got out of there…sorry." I haven't really answered him again. I don't want to, but he asks one more time anyway.

"Nolan...do you need me to stay on the line?"

I breathe out a laugh. This is probably the only time I really do need that. Jason isn't my favorite person to talk to, just because we don't really gel. I do love him, though, and he was there for me when I was scared beyond anything that I would lose Reed.

"I'll be fine. Thanks, Jase." I sink into the seat of my car and turn the engine on, jumping at the blaring stereo I left behind. I push the power button fast, deciding silence for a dozen miles might do me some good.

"Of course. I'll have my phone. I'm in the booth, so call or text. I'll never leave it out of my sight."

I smile at his offer.

"I'll be okay," I say.

"Even still..." he interrupts.

I nod and sit in the silence, hearing the chatter in the background of the phone for a few seconds. In a matter of minutes, that ownership suite went from thinking their season was lost to thinking they won the Cinderella-story lottery.

They did.

Instead of glass slippers, though, their princess wears New Balance with orthopedic inserts for some serious bone spurs.

"It was a really pretty fucking pass," I sigh out.

Jason chuckles quietly, just for me.

"It was," he says. "You drive safe, okay?"

"Mmmm, yeah," I acknowledge, feeling stupid for the way I got here.

I hang up with Jason and toss my phone into the center console, and I start to back out from the parking lot before I stop and stare at my powered-off stereo. Like an addict, I punch the power button again and hit the scan button until I find the sounds of cheering crowds and testosterone-fueled announcers. I find the OKC game on the fourth try, and I stay in that parking lot just like this until Reed throws two more touchdowns and the clock is counting down the final seconds of the fourth quarter.

Chapter Seventeen

Reed

I CAN'T WAIT to get through with the damn media room. I'm amped up with this toxic mix of urgency from just getting off the field and needing to call my family.

Nolan. I'm panicked, because fuck...that was amazing! And she's going to hate how I feel.

My brother's hovering behind me. I'm glad he's serving as a human barrier. The questions are coming in shouts. It's been a while for me to have a circus like this. When someone gets knocked out and rushed to the hospital, they sorta get to do the talking through their publicist. I'm not sure I'm ready for the front line again.

We get to the media room and I file into the long row of chairs behind the table covered in mics. The flashing never stops.

My body hurts.

"All right, we've got a lot to get through here, so let's just settle down and take this a topic at a time. That all right with y'all?"

Our head coach, Lowell Simms, is a lot like me. We were both brought here to send this ship out with some senior leadership behind it. He's committed for three years, but the man is sixty-four and been around the block a few times with two heart surgeries and a hip replacement. Granted, coaching doesn't have the same physical risks as playing, but I can't believe any of this is good on his heart. The man knows how to win, though. And he knows how to work with young quarterbacks. He's here for Duke, just like I'm here for Duke. And now here we both are...without Duke.

The room quiets down, and the training staff steps up behind Coach to help him answer questions.

"Here's what we know. Duke is getting care from a great medical staff at Southern Bell Hospital undergoing evaluation. We can't speculate how bad the injury was and what it means in terms of him being on the field when we play next Sunday in L.A. I can promise you this, though—we aren't going to put him back on that field until we know he's ready and can handle it."

The room lights up with questions. Even though they're all asking the same thing, they talk over each other and make everything sound jumbled as they jockey to be the one to be plucked out of the audience to ask the question on their own.

"Mark, go ahead," Coach says, pointing to the man from ESPN. They always pick ESPN.

"Are you going with Johnson under the presumption that Duke Miller will be out next week?"

Coach levels Mark with a serious gaze and wraps his hands around either side of the podium, shifting his weight and sighing.

"Mark, we go way back. What part of what I just said do you think means I can say anything for certain to that question? Use your damned logic, would you? We have three quarterbacks. Reed's in the two-spot. If Duke's not ready, then yes...you'll see Reed. Do I know if Duke will be ready? No. Can I pull a crystal ball out of my ass and rub it to see the future?"

The crowd chuckles at Mark's expense. Mark grimaces.

It's a formality, and he was the one to have to endure it. I'm taking the field next week. Duke was in excruciating pain. There is no humanly possible way something in his knee didn't tear. I saw it bend the wrong way. Preliminary scans and MRIs are already in.

The conversation happening right now is between Duke's agent, the management and ownership offices, and Jason—who has not taken the phone away from his ear. The rehearsed answer is "We're waiting for them to finish evaluating." The real answer, though, is "Yes, Reed Johnson is now the starting quarterback. We're seeing what all of this shit means for everyone's contract."

"Jim, go ahead." Coach takes a huge chug from the Styrofoam cup next to him that I know is filled with Mountain Dew. It's his vice. Because he can't smoke anymore.

Jim, from *USA Today*, stands next.

"This question is probably more for Reed."

Coach steps to the side and gestures his hand for me. I sigh as I stand, mostly to mask the groan I want to give because my muscles are so goddamn tight I'm not sure I can stand straight.

"Hey, Jim," I say, leaning my weight onto the podium and nodding to my old friend. Jim did a great piece on my rehab and comeback story. I have a feeling he's going to roll that out again with a new ending. I hope it's not a tragedy.

"Hey, Reed. Long time, huh?" He laughs lightly and I smile.

"Two years, I guess, but that's a long time in football."

He nods and holds out his phone to record me.

"Two years is a long time. You didn't look very rusty out there, though. What was it like stepping into an offense for the first time in…"

"Two years," I break in, finishing for him. The room laughs hard this time. I wait for it to settle down.

"I don't know that I really had time to think about it yet, to be honest, Jim. Duke went down, Jenkins smacked the side of my head and shouted to start throwing, and then about a second later I was staring at the Atlanta line."

"It was a little more than a second," Jim corrects.

I shrug.

"Yeah, but damn did it feel like a second, man." I laugh looking back on the last hour. It was a rush—a flash. It was the thrill of my life, and my body has never felt more alive, even if it feels like it's been beaten in a back alley.

"How do you prepare for situations like this?" Jim continues. A few more reporters stand and hold out phones. Here comes the soundbite they'll use for the ten-o'clock.

"I think it's just the job. It's just like everyone in the organization —we all know our jobs. My job is to be ready and to step in when they call on me. It could have been dozens of situations. It just happened to be this one, today. I've worked closely with Duke, and Coach Jenkins makes sure we all know the offense well so we can have seamless transitions. I just wanted to get in there and support the guys and finish the job Duke started."

"And what if the results today come back and Duke's cleared to start Sunday?" I pull my lip in at Jim's last question. We all know that won't happen, but he's pretending because it puts that thought out there. What if it's between me and Duke? Who gets the start now that I've shown what I can still do?

"Well, I guess that's a question for Coach. And I'm pretty sure he was clear about not answering things about the future, so good luck with that conversation, Jim." I wink at my old reporter friend, and he points his phone at me and winks back, turning the recorder off and taking his seat.

He's already got his lead—he probably has his story completely written, minus the few bits I just gave him to fill in for quotes. He cowers back into his seat, balancing his notebooks and stat sheets on his jean-covered knees and begins to feverishly type with his thumbs on his phone. I miss the days of paper.

Coach Simms clears his throat as he takes over the mic again. I breathe easier when my ass hits the chair, glad my time is up. With his bald head reflecting the camera lights, Coach delivers seven or eight more perfect answers that will get sliced up and shown over and over again for the next week. With Duke going down, we became the big story in sports. Even with the blowout of a game over a team we were supposed to beat, we're still newsworthy.

"Thanks, guys."

I jostle from my trance hearing coach virtually end the press conference, and I file out behind him and the training staff. I lift a hand to Jason in the hallway but keep going where I know I'm wanted next. Everyone peels off one by one, but I follow Coach all the way to his back office, shutting the door behind us once we get inside. He goes right to the leather sofa in the middle of the room, kicking his shoes off with his toes on his heels and flopping down and folding his arms over his eyes. His sweatshirt lifts enough to show the white undershirt covering his belly, and he moves one hand to his waist to unbuckle his belt and give himself a little more room to breathe.

"I'm too old for this shit, Reed."

I laugh as I sit back into the chair opposite him, sinking in so deep I might need help up when we're done.

"That's what that guy on *Lethal Weapon* always says."

"Yeah, well he's right. This is a young man's game." He starts to rub his thumbs into his temples, and it moves the loose skin on the side of his head.

I let him rest for a few long seconds, wishing I had the patience to wait longer. I don't, though. I'm teeming with curiosity. I need answers.

"What are we looking at, Coach?" I ask, expecting more of a reaction from him. His breath remains steady though, his eyes closed and his hands still working to rid him of a headache. His mouth twists a little, like he's thinking.

"He's done for the season," he finally says, and my chest lights up with the beats of a thousand butterflies.

I run my palm over my mouth, not sure if I should smile or vomit. Done.

"Tear?" I ask, already knowing.

He tucks in his chin, a crease forming at his neck as he lifts his head enough to meet my gaze.

"Double tear. He's fucked."

The butterflies drop dead; my lungs feel thick all of a sudden. Breathing instantly gets harder.

I've never been one to be affected by other athletes' injuries, but that was all before. Now, it is impossible not to internalize what happened to Duke and imagine how my own legs feel. I can feel the tear, the throbbing, as I imagine that linebacker wrapping me up and driving me into the ground. I can hear the sounds the body makes when it's breaking.

I smell the hospital, taste the meds, feel the heavy drowsiness and despair.

"Fucked, huh?" I respond finally.

"Yup," Coach says, lying back and folding an arm over his eyes again.

I hide in the solace of his office for a few more minutes then finally pull myself from the comfortable hug of the chair and make my way to the door. It's a posh office—everything in here new, like the rest of the building. There isn't anything very personal in here, which makes me think Lowell isn't planning on putting down roots. There is a photo on the wall by the door, though. It's him and Trig, and I stop to honor it for a few seconds before opening the door to leave.

"Get some rest. We've got a lot of work to do," he growls behind me.

"Right," I answer, turning around before closing the door behind me. "See you at the service?"

He lifts his head again and meets my eyes. We linger in our connected gaze for a long breath, and finally he gives me a little nod. I leave him to nap and dream of what to do next. That's about as rattled as that man gets, and I can't help but wonder if Trig would have been all right if he just would have had Lowell around to give him advice when things got really bad. He was always Trig's favorite coach, and they were a team for seven years. Maybe the best team in the sport for the last decade.

Duke Miller's shoes aren't the only ones I'll be filling.

————

I texted Nolan immediately. I finally took a breath when she wrote back a full minute after. I made it through meetings with management, with Jason, with the small team of people that work with him who said I apparently have sponsors interested, and then I agreed to whatever Jason suggested because, ass-hat or not, he always has my best interests at heart. It's freeing to let him make decisions.

I kept checking my phone, comparing the time that passed with Nolan's one-word text: K. I told her I would call soon. That was two and a half hours ago.

OK.

It's such a short response. She's been waiting for a long time. I doubt anything is okay.

I climbed into my Jeep and ducked low in the seat so nobody felt the urge to stop and talk to me on their way out. I finally called as promised. I've been passed around to everyone in the house, shocked they're all still up, given that it's almost midnight for them. I'm staring down one o'clock.

I knew Nolan would be up, though. I've run out of people to congratulate me, and Peyton lost interest several minutes ago. Nolan takes the phone in her hand and tells everyone else goodnight while she climbs the steps with me on the line. She doesn't talk until she's in our room, and I picture her climbing into our bed, a giant sweat-shirt, leggings, and those fuzzy socks she lives in on her feet.

"How are you? Really?" Her breath buzzes against the line as she settles into bed. I sink lower in my Jeep, wishing I was joining her.

"I don't know." There are a lot of answers to that question, but that one seems the most accurate since I don't know which answer is the most right about how I feel right now.

"Leg feel good?" She means neck, and back, and head.

"Yeah, it hasn't hurt in a while. I didn't have to scramble much."

"Liar," she says with a giggle.

"There were a few plays, yeah…" Really, though…today was nothing. She knows it too. It's about next week, and the week after; that's what she's thinking about.

"So, no celebrating with the boys, huh?" Her tone is guarded, like she's forcing herself to be positive.

"They didn't need a chaperone. And I'm fucking beat," I say through a yawn. It sparks one in her, and I wait for that small little humming sound she makes at the end of her yawns. I barely hear it, but it's there, and I smile.

"Duke's done; isn't he?"

She knows. We've been through this enough.

"Yeah," I say.

Silence fills our connection for a long time, long enough that I sit up and glance at my surroundings in the mirror, relieved to see I'm not the only car in the lot still.

"I'm looking at an extra six or seven mill, Jason says." I know she isn't interested in the money. It's never been about that. I'm not sure why I brought it up, other than needing something to say. It's probably only going to piss her off.

"Mmmm," she says.

Yeah, she's pissed.

"Nolan, we knew this was a possibility." I wince at how that came out, and I try to fix it fast. "I mean… I'm sorry. I wish I could have given you warning, but…"

"It's fine, Reed. I'm glad you're feeling okay, and that your leg doesn't hurt."

"Don't do that." I shake my head and draw my lips in tight. She's saying so many things without saying anything. I hate it when she does this.

The line grows silent again. I notice a bright stream of light in my mirror, so I check to see what it is. A few coaches are leaving the offices, and I know that means Jenkins is on his way out soon, too. If he sees me, he'll want to go into strategy right away. I'm too tired to retain any of that, and I don't want to leave Nolan.

I crank the engine and back out, turning the wheel with one hand, then make my way onto the main road through the city, deciding to take my time getting home.

"You were really great." Nolan's compliment startles me. I wasn't expecting her to talk, let alone say something complimentary. It takes me a few seconds to respond.

"I'm rusty." I puff my chest with a laugh replaying mentally how many major fuck-ups I made.

"You're modest," my wife says. She means it. I can tell.

178

"Thanks," I say.

I chew at my lips, wrestling with what I want to ask her, but knowing we have to talk about it. We had plans.

"So, Thursday…" That's when Trig's service is. Originally, we were going to meet there, then drive on to L.A. I'm going to need to be with the team a lot more now, though. That road trip isn't going to be possible. My leash just got a whole lot shorter.

"I guess I'll meet you at the service." She's already assumed so much; she's given up on any time for us to be together. That's not okay. Before she can say she'll fly back home from there, I take advantage of the one thing I have in my back pocket—my brother. At the very least, he owes me for keeping his proposal plans secret. Maybe it's more of a leverage thing than owing thing, now that I think about it.

"Jason is going to take you with him…from Santa Fe. You'll fly with him." I shove my hand in my center console in search of anything paper. I settle on a napkin from God knows where I stopped on the road on my way to Oklahoma. I find a Sharpie next, bite the cap off and write the word JASON really big. I throw the marker and the napkin on my dash so I have to see it; so I remember to call my brother and let him know I just made all sorts of plans for him—plans that require him cashing in some miles and upgrading a few plane tickets.

"Reed, it's okay. We'll be together…"

"When, Noles?" I interrupt her because she's just going to go back to that complacent place, and I need her to fight right now—for us. Hell, be pissed at me even. Let it out!

"You'll have the Arizona game, and maybe I can get up to Oklahoma once or twice." She knows that isn't going to happen, and I don't even have to question it out loud. She exhales, and I imagine her body sinking more into our bed at home, defeated tears stinging her eyes red.

"Jason has it handled. We talked about it." I lie, but this is one of those good lies. I need to sell it like a deal that's done, and a pain in the ass to undo. "The tickets are bought, Nolan. And me and you…we need this. You know we need this."

I hear her breath hitch. I lower my volume and pull off from the main road into the golf club where my condo is. I slow enough I can hear the crickets outside. She's never even seen this place. She'd probably love it here.

"Nolan, I can't do this without knowing we're good…solid." I slide my palm with the phone along my forehead as I slow to a stop just in front of my place. I lean against the steering wheel and close my eyes to prepare to beg.

"Please, Nolan." It comes out a whisper, and I can tell by the faint, but choppy, breaths on the other line that my girl is crying. I hate how hard this is.

"I don't know if I can see it. I don't know if I can handle the game, Reed," she says.

"So, come to L.A. Fuck, just go shopping when you get there. I don't even care if you enter the goddamned stadium. Just…Nolan, just be with me. I'll see you in New Mexico and then a plane ride later. I'll see you before the game, and after the game."

"When you're all bruised and broken," she chokes out.

"Baby…" I murmur.

The silence takes over again. I focus on the crickets and the smell of wet grass, rolling hills that chew up golfers during the day and fuel wild coyotes in the night. Why couldn't I have been good at that damn sport?

"I'll come," she whimpers. Everything about her promise is so unsure.

"Yeah?" My heart beats in my throat. It's hope pumping in my veins. If we can just have time—time alone to be us. I know it will be okay.

"Yeah," she echoes. "I'm not promising anything…about the game."

"That's fine," I answer fast. I need this guarantee she's giving me. I need her.

"Okay. Tell Jason to let me know what to do and where to go. I'll see you Thursday."

"I love you, Noles." I look up at the open sky—black, speckled with stars and a sliver of a moon big in the middle, like a bowl trying to catch diamonds. "I'm nothing without you."

"I love you, too," she says, ending the call so she can hide the sound of her tears in her pillow.

I sit out here and imagine it, probably exactly as it plays out a thousand miles away. I wish I could hold her—rock her and tell her it's all going to be okay. I honestly don't know that it is, though. Today was a fluke. I got lucky and got a defense that wasn't prepared for me. Duke and I run things differently. L.A. is going to know what they're getting, though. They'll be gunning for me. And that means this tired-ass body needs to be ready right back.

And my girl needs to be on my side, even if she doesn't watch a single play.

Chapter Eighteen

Nolan

PEYTON WANTED to come with me. She knew Trig, or at least the version of him he was before he retired from the game. I think if we all lived in the same place for longer, she and Shayla, Trig's oldest daughter, would have been good friends.

Now that I'm here, though—faced with packed rows and somber faces and waving programs staving off this sweltering heat in an auditorium that really should have better air—I'm glad she's missing this. Some things don't need to infect a mind, and seeing the massive hole Trig left behind won't help her. She's better with the glorified memories that will only get better with her imagination.

Reed has been here for a while now. He drove in to spend time with Trig's family before the service. He's wearing a suit. He's both handsome and unnatural-looking. It's not the right time for me to be thinking this, but I mentally go there for just a little bit as he walks up the aisle toward me and Jason. His jacket collar is folded in. It's a common problem for him, because his arms never fit in the sleeves very well. I can't get him to visit a tailor; he always insists on just buying whatever's on a rack. I think one fitted suit would change his world though. Maybe in L.A.

L.A.

I force air into my lungs through my nose. I haven't been able to get a full breath in days. Sarah said I should just start smoking pot. She just wants me to get a medical license so she has one more thing to snake from my drawers and cabinets. She got over being embarrassed or angry or whatever, and I'm glad because I need her now.

Reed stops a few feet short of my reach and lets out a breath of his own. We're so similar, how we carry the weight of our worlds.

"It's so unbelievably good to see you." Those familiar warm eyes are sad, his lids heavy from a lack of sleep and the responsibility he feels for this day.

"It's an amazing turnout," I say, stepping into him and sliding my arms where they go, under his arms and around his body. My head falls into his chest and his chin lands above me. I'm protected everywhere. This is what safe feels like.

"It is. The girls can't quit crying. It's so awful, Noles." He presses his lips to the top of my head and holds them there.

"We should take our seats," Jason whispers close to us, resting his hand on my back.

Soothing music has started from the organist at the front of the church. I let go of my hold on Reed's chest as my hand automatically drifts to his. My fingers weave with his and I hold on tight as he leads me to the front rows of the church pews. He brings our fisted hands to his mouth as we walk and hugs my arm close, kissing my knuckles. I glance at his eyes when he does, but they are focused on our path ahead.

Reed is scared.

We slip into a space that's been saved for us in the second row. I recognize Stacia quickly. She twists in her seat and reaches her hand for me, so I bend down and embrace her. Divorce doesn't make something like this easier. Her girls lost their father. She lost the man she began motherhood with. And as ugly as their relationship had become, there's always love in there somewhere. All those good memories…

"Thank you so much for coming, Nolan." She speaks at my ear, and I can hear the raspiness in her voice. She's been crying. Her girls are all sitting in a row next to her, their knees pulled up to their chins, arms wrapped around their legs, heads buried in their laps and hidden so they can cry without anyone telling them to stop.

They shouldn't have to. Now is the time to cry. I want to fix everything for them. This entire room of people does, I'm sure of it. But there is no fixing this. This will change them.

"I'm so very sorry, Stacia. If there is anything I can do…" That's what people say, I suppose. I don't finish it because I know there isn't. I also know she would never ask. If she did, though—I would come to her side. Anything.

My chest seizes, as it has done periodically ever since we got the news, because I can't help but switch places with this woman and picture my life in the same circumstances. Life without Reed is not life.

"Thank you," Stacia mutters, letting go of her embrace that has fallen to my hand and turning back to the front for the beginning service.

Reed is stoic. I slide into the space between him and Jason and welcome the warmth of them both at my sides, even though it's miserably hot in this room. I can feel them living and breathing next to me.

Family.

I turn enough to face Reed and reach my hand across his chest to fix the collar I saw earlier. He catches my hand before it leaves and holds it tight against his heart, his gaze straight forward but lost. I curl my fingers under his into a fist, scratching at the fabric of his jacket and shirt, as if I want to dig out pieces of him to keep with me and carry around. He lets go of his hold so I turn to face forward and let my palm rest against his leg. He covers it to keep it there.

Trig's father speaks first. His family was very involved in their church, and I guess his parents wanted to make today as personal as they could. He invites others to share stories about Trig, and one by one, people begin to file up to the side of the stage. Reed has so many, but he stays in his seat, next to me. He doesn't want to share them because they're too close—too much of *him and Trig.* I think he should share, but I won't make him. We talked about it on the phone last night, and he said if he got that feeling that he needed to he would. Right now, I doubt he feels a thing.

Stacia stands last, walking up slowly and leaving her girls in the care of their grandmother and grandfather in front of us. I note how her hands tremble with the folded pages she holds as she takes the steps one at a time. She lifts her long black skirt and swallows down the constantly rebuilding wall that's trying to keep her from making it through this. Somehow, by the time she rests the papers on the podium and pulls the mic in close to her lips, she's found strength. Deep-red lips I've always envied pull into a respectful smile, and her eyes find a sparkle as they sweep around the room.

"Ahhhh," she breathes out, letting her long lashes fall closed against her cheeks. She lifts her chin as if there were a sky above to warm her face. Her smile remains and her eyes don't open until she levels her head and looks at us all again.

"Trig is with us today. Oh yes, he is," she says, her words welcomed with a collective exhale. She nods and I gaze around the room to find dozens of people nodding with her. Hands lift in the air and eyes close as people pray, but not in a way that says anything other than respect and joy.

The room swims in this feeling for a heavy moment or two before Stacia begins to share *her* story about Trig Johnson: how they met on campus, how he pursued her relentlessly, how he proposed. She tells the stories of each pregnancy and how neurotic and amazing her husband—*ex-husband*—was for every delivery. She talks about birthdays and anniversaries, and pranks and vacations. She talks about his love for family, and for his girls. And then…she goes somewhere I thought she would have avoided today. She talks about the end—the divorce that killed them both. I grip against Reed's leg nervously, uncomfortable that she's sharing the sad times with this room filled with people there to love this man. Only, Stacia never makes it feel like those times were ugly, even though many of us know they were. She talks about how hard they were—how marriage is hard for anyone, and maybe just a little harder for people who live in this world. She talks about how football and injuries and retirement changed her husband, and how she lost him a little in the mix of it all. But then she mentions the amazing moments, all of the times that he was there—for his girls, for her, for a cancer scare her father went through and one of her own.

"Our bond was one that could never be broken completely. This man and his relentless pursuit," she stops to chuckle. "Oh, he could even flirt with me after a divorce settlement, I swear."

A chuckle rumbles through the room.

"I know you're still there, Babe. I know you hear me now, and that you're seeing all of this. Always had to have the best parties, didn't you? We'll be talking a lot. I'll still turn to you. Always."

My cheeks are wet before I realize that tears have fallen, and Reed leans into me and runs his thumb along my face.

"I love you," he whispers. I don't look, but just from the texture of his voice I can tell—he is crying too.

The procession from the hall takes nearly an hour, and it is an hour after that for us to make it to the cemetery. They lay Trig to rest in a spot next to his cousin and his great grandfather. It feels like he should have more pomp and circumstance, given how loud he lived his life. But his marker is the smallest among those nearby. The words are simple: HUSBAND, FATHER, SON.

Nothing about this day is about the game. It's about the man.

Reed and I hug Stacia one more time and wait for Jason to give her condolences while we wait near the rental car.

"I'm leaving with Coach in an hour." Reed stretches his arm along the side of the car so I can slide into him. I do, and I let my head fall against the side of his chest. "They have a guy who's taking my Jeep back. It's at Trig's parents' house."

"The team leaving today?" I ask.

"They're already there. A few of the guys came with us. I think maybe seven of us will be flying in tonight." Reed seems so heavy and lost in his thoughts; I worry about him carrying it into the game.

"You know Trig is not you, right? Us...we aren't them." His

head turns to face me slowly and our eyes meet. He blinks and lowers his head just a little to acknowledge me. He never says he believes it, though.

Jason walks to us and I hand him the keys, knowing he's probably the most able to focus on driving right now. Reed climbs in the back, insisting I take the front. I unfold my visor after I buckle so I can flip down the mirror and look at him. His gaze drifts right back to the window, to Trig's resting place, and he brings his thumb to his lips and chews at the nail I've noticed he's whittled down to almost nothing.

Jason pulls us through the serene gardens and out onto the main road where we're instantly greeted by honking horns and swerving drivers rushing out for lunch. Everyone is in such a hurry. I suppose I have the effects of recent perspective, though. Mine, too, will fade. I hope I hold onto enough not to rush through life, though.

"How long until we get to the airport?" I ask.

"It's about thirty minutes. I tried to get our flight moved up. We won't be too far behind them, though," Jason says.

I nod, then shift to get my eyes on Reed over my shoulder. His head turns to meet my gaze when I move and he gives me a soft smile, but quickly drifts back to the window. He must be dying in that jacket. He left it on, even for the car ride.

"You wanna take that off?" I say, reaching through the seats and tugging at the end of his sleeve. He stretches his arms out, then bends his elbows as he looks down at the heavy woolen folds.

"I'm okay," he says.

Okay.

Not even close.

The roadway has an even cut of cracks in it. I start to predict the pattern of the *click* of the wheels. It's like a snap every quarter mile, and I find that when I count in fours, I keep up with the signs posted along the roadway for how far is left to go for the airport. I'm drunk in the numbness of the banal noise when Jason stirs me out of the daydream.

"They're donating him for research." Jason says it quietly, but it's still loud enough that his voice can be heard throughout the car.

Reed hasn't reacted physically, but I know he heard. I won't look because I don't want to have this talk right now in front of him.

"Did they say why?" Reed asks, his sound indirect because he's still looking out at the rushing cars going the other way.

I swallow hard and close my eyes.

"That's a hard decision to make," I say, wanting to steer away from this subject.

From science and bodies and studies of the brain.

Trig's brain.

Reed's brain.

"Stacia told me it was her wish, but when she brought it up to Trig's parents, they were all for it. There's a group studying various brain injuries…"

"Jason," I interrupt, glaring at him so hard he must feel the heat of my stare because he turns to match my gaze.

"Sorry," he mouths.

"I've heard of the study," Reed fills in. My stomach rolls with sickness, and I go back to counting the *thumps* on the roadway. I need forty-eight more of them for this car ride to end.

Neither Jason nor I engage Reed's follow-up, and after two miles in silence, I start to feel like we've moved away from the subject. Reed isn't close to done, though.

"Trig was depressed," Reed says, his voice louder than before.

I pull my brow in, but I don't say a word.

"He'd been through a lot," Jason responds, lifting enough in his seat to get his eyes on Reed in the mirror.

"Yeah…I guess…" Reed doesn't sound convinced.

My lips move and push against each other, chewing on the words I won't say—I *can't* say. I don't want to start comparing Reed to Trig, retirement to playing options, married to divorced. Everything about this makes me sad, and it makes me worry more than I already do. I worry in my sleep—worry about Reed's head being changed forever. I worry about him being sad over his friend, for comparing himself to Trig.

I worry that he's going to play longer than he should because he's afraid that quitting will kill him slowly. The depression scares him more than the physical pains. It's been a long time since I've seen him like this—*distant…troubled*. He doesn't make good decisions in this headspace. After our accident in high school, he got like this—irrational and dangerous. It happened again after we lost a pregnancy when Peyton was two. And again, when she was three.

We're saved by the sound of Jason's phone blaring. He pulls it from his pocket, leaning to one side while he drives, then hands it to me and signals for me to press speaker. I don't recognize the number, so I assume it must be one of his assistants or something. When I press to answer, I act as if I'm his secretary.

"Good afternoon. This is Jason Johnson's line. He is currently… indisposed. May I tell him who is calling?" I play up the sexy voice and pucker my lips to hold in my laugh as Jason takes the phone from me and rolls his eyes. He presses speaker and holds the phone to his ear.

"This is Jason. I'm sorry that…"

His head turtles into his shoulders and his throat makes a faint grunting sound.

"That was Nolan, Sarah." He huffs through his nose, and I cup my mouth to hold in laughter.

"Oh, shit!" I mouth toward my brother-in-law as he shakes his head at me in admonishment. I twist to look at Reed, but he's already checked out, staring at his own phone for his flight information. His expression couldn't be less interested in the funny slip I just had.

"Nolan, tell her it's you." Jason holds the phone in front of my face and I move to look at it.

"It was me. Sorry, I was trying to entertain us during our drive."

"Thank you," Jason says to me, returning the phone to his ear. I stare at him for a few more seconds, and the way his face lights up makes me smile. Reed was right—this is real. My brother-in-law is in love with my best friend. I can hear the sounds of her voice slightly through the phone, but I can't make out the words. I just hear the tenor of happiness piping through the line. I hear them both laugh over stupid jokes—shared, *inside* jokes. I see Jason struggle with not wanting to let Sarah go as we pull into the airport.

Their goodbyes drag on, and Reed pulls on the latch in the backseat and steps out of the car, suddenly in a hurry. In a fit of panic, I grab the phone after Jason's last, cutesy goodbye and press END CALL. When his irritated eyes flash to mine, I strangle them with my imploring stare.

"I don't know how you'll do it, but I need you to get him off that plane. I need you to strand us both here. We'll hit the road the minute you leave. I'll drive all night. But you cannot let him leave me right now, not like this. I don't care what lies you have to tell, but I know my husband, Jason, and he's so lost right now. He can't get on that plane and be away from me. He can't get on a field in three days without me talking to him. And it can't be at the hotel. It can't be near the team and near the game. I need him unplugged. Please, Jason. I know it in my heart."

Jason blinks twice, turning to glance out the back window where the trunk is now open and Reed is pulling out a bag. The brothers are wearing the exact same suit, but Jason seems at ease in his. Reed is strangled, and it's more than just his body frame and muscles. It's his spirit. Jason glares at his brother through the small space between the car and the trunk hood.

"Please," I beg. "Given what he's been through...the team will understand. Call it personal time. Whatever you need to do."

My brother-in-law lets out a heavy breath, probably mentally inventorying all of the dominoes he has to line up to get me what I want. What I *need*. It's not going to be easy. And his ass will be the one that gets chewed because right now—Reed is all that team has. He'll be putting his management rep on the line. His future is just starting, and he has plans to grow.

Plans for after...when Reed is done.

"This is the kind of agent and manager you want to be. Beyond this being me asking, more than the fact that it's your brother. You want to be the guy that does what's best. That's what you said when you sold your shares in the dealership, when you put it all on the line —when you talked Reed into coming with you and dropping Dylan."

Jason's eyes come back to mine and he holds them there for

several seconds. I feel my heart kick in my throat, and I can hear his
—I swear it.

"Take the wheel. We can't park here." He unbuckles and I do
the same, stopping with my hands on the door handle.

"What do I tell him?" I wasn't certain I'd be able to talk Jason
into this, so I didn't bother dreaming up fake excuses. I left that all
to him.

His eyes flicker, and his head shakes a few times in thought.

"Uhhhh," he says as his knee starts to bob. The trunk shuts.
"I'm getting out now. I'm going to tell him I fucked the tickets up.
I'm going to tell him I'm going to fix it, that I'll call soon. But you
need to drive around the airport while I go in. That'll give me time.
Ready?"

My mouth curves in an elated smile that betrays the surprised
look I'm supposed to have on my face in about seven seconds.

"Nolan, are you ready?" Jason is a little harsher now.

"Yeah, uhm…sorry. Yes," I say, timing my door opening
with his.

I round the front of the car and get to the front seat just as
Jason's palm flattens on his brother's chest. I only hear bits and
pieces of his lie, focusing on my role—to get in the car, to drive, to
wait.

I glance in the mirror at the officers now pointing at our car
that's been parked here a little too long. I can hear Reed's voice raise
and I make out "Damnit, Jason. You had *one* job!"

I wince with guilt. I'll make this up to Jason. I'll tell Reed eventually, maybe even soon. I'll tell him as soon as I know he's mine for
the road. And one day, he'll know that his brother did have one job
—Reed's best interest—and he did it.

"Fucking idiot," Reed grumbles as he tosses his bag in the backseat and then slams the back door shut. A second later he opens the
passenger door and climbs in, the scowl creasing his skin deeper
than before. "Drive…I guess."

My insides sting from the attitude, but I know he doesn't mean
it. He's frustrated, and he's working so hard to hold up a wall
protecting him from today and all of the questions it put in his head.

"Jason said he'd take care of it. I'll just circle a few times. I'm sure it will be fine." I have to look to my left to avoid any hint of Reed in my periphery because I swear the guilt is stamped across my face.

"I just don't know how you can fuck something as simple as air travel up so badly. Coach is going to be pissed. I don't need that."

I spare a glance as I merge into the flow of traffic. Reed is chewing at his thumbnail again, his elbow resting on the window edge.

"Jason will figure it out," I pile on. I'm going to have to grovel to both of the Johnson boys for the hole I'm digging for them both with this. I know it's the right thing to do, though. And when we're in our place—just Reed and me—he'll know that it was right, too.

I make it a full lap and start the next one when Reed starts hurriedly texting his brother. He calls him when he doesn't get an answer within a minute. Jason doesn't answer, and it's probably because he's on the other line trying to make a miracle happen with the TSA.

"I'm gonna let Coach know," Reed says. I panic, wondering if somehow Coach will know this is all one big sham. Not giving it much thought—*enough thought*—I reach to my right and punch Reed's phone from his hands, sending it flying over his lap and down the side of the seat by the door.

"What the hell, Noles!" His arms fly out and his eyes widen at me. I stare back at them, stupefied. I have no idea what to say.

"I'm sorry...I thought you wanted me to take your phone, and I guess I'm just nervous because your flight is almost up and you're nervous...I just flailed."

That's the most ridiculous thing I've ever made up. I could have said I saw a bee. I wonder if it's too late to take it back? *Bee? I saw a bee?*

I'm saved by Reed's ringing phone, but unfortunately, it's trapped in the guts of the car, and my husband's massive hands are too big to get it out.

"Unbelievable," he huffs when he misses the call the first time. When it starts to ring again he shouts for me to slow down. I pull into the right lane and slow to a crawl, cars nearly rear-ending me and honking as they swerve around. I punch on the hazard lights and pray I don't have a heart attack from the stress I've created.

Reed opens his door carefully, reaching into the small space and grasping his phone before slamming his door closed again. I turn my hazards off and rejoin traffic while he answers. I fill in the blanks —Jason's blanks, based on Reed's half of the conversation.

"How is that even possible? It's L.A.—they don't sell out of flights. When people want to go there, they just make more. There are literally hundreds of flights."

Reed pinches the bridge of his nose, and eventually he starts nodding. It isn't a happy nod, but it's a resolved one.

"Yeah, that's better than nothing. We'd talked about that. I don't think she made any plans, but I might need you to help her out if she did. Or I'll just go on my own…I'll let you know in a minute."

"Yeah…yeah…"

After one final pause, Reed hangs up and blows out heavily, the force flapping his lips and cheeks. It makes me smile. I turn my face away again until I can get it in check.

"Looks like I'm going back with you. Jason's just going to fly back to OKC, and he's taking another flight on game day. It's booked up, and he offered to call Jerry and see if we could get the private jet, but that feels super diva. You can get to Arizona, unless…how do you feel about driving?"

I furrow my brow to mask my excitement, internally amused that I'm now excited about driving through the damn desert in that Jeep. Karma's a funny bitch.

"I mean, I guess I still could. That was our original plan, and I didn't schedule any sessions yet." My pulse speeds up, like a bomb ticking and ready to blow. I'm on the verge of confessing everything.

"Yeah, all right. If you're okay with it. We'll get our trip after all." There's a hint of my Reed in his response, like he's shedding some of the weight of Trig and the day.

"I'd like that," I say, shrugging a shoulder. "I guess I'll drop the car off then and we'll just hit the road in the Jeep? Maybe get dinner?"

Dinner. Like a real date. Granted, at the airport rental car terminal, but still.

"Yeah," Reed says, already dialing Jason back.

I let my grin spread in front of him now, living on the edge knowing that he might see it. I'm hit with that happy-kind-of-cry feeling, and I think it's a window of relief. Reed tells his brother to set it up and have the Jeep brought to the airport, and I pull into the lane marked RENTAL RETURN. He gets off the phone with his brother just as I pull in and hand over the keys to the guy checking for dings on our sedan. Reed grabs his bag, then opens the trunk to pull mine free along with the one Jason, bless his heart, left behind.

"I'll just give it to him when he gets in Sunday," Reed says, and I wonder if that's true or just a lie Jason told him. I have a feeling he's flying straight to L.A., in the seat that Reed was supposed to be in. Maybe he'll make a few clients on the trip.

We sign for the car and take our things to the bridge that spans from the parking garage to the terminal on the other side of the accessway. The divot between Reed's eyes has grown deeper, and I'm afraid that if I don't do something to loosen it now, it won't ever leave him. We make our way to the people-mover, and both stop on the belt, letting it do the work for us while people in a bigger hurry rush by. I stare at Reed's reflection in the glass overlooking the mountains and sprawling desert city stretching out to the west. I think of a dozen different things to say that I keep to myself—until I come up with the one thing that might just lift this blanket that's smothering him.

"Hey, you know what?" I tug at his arm and he relaxes enough to lift his arm and run his palm over my back.

"What?" he asks.

"I'm actually pretty excited about the Jeep," I say, lifting myself up on my toes.

Reed's mouth pulls in on one side with a grin that says he doesn't need my pity.

"You hate the Jeep." His head falls to the side and his eyes study me like a jury assessing my guilt.

"I don't *hate* the Jeep. It's not my favorite smooth ride, but you were looking forward to this. And I kinda think it'll be fun now," I say, remembering the sound of the soft top flapping in the wind. That novelty wears off after about twenty miles.

Reed eyes me a little longer, turning so his chest is facing me. His smirk grows by a hint, and I revel in it, because I feel like it means progress.

"Yeah?" he leans forward, closing the slight gap between us.

I grab hold of the front of his long-sleeved shirt with both hands, tugging on the gray cotton playfully, then stepping in so my chin is resting on his chest and my eyes are peering up at him.

"Yeah," I breathe out.

He swallows and shifts his weight so his hand can press on my back and draw me close enough to kiss. With eyes staring down at me, he gives in to a full-blown smile. His wavy hair flops over his brow and I reach up to move it, cupping his other cheek in my hand as I kiss his lips and leave my mouth on his for the rest of the people-moving ride into the terminal.

Chapter Nineteen

Reed

I'M RUNNING ON ADRENALINE. It's a potion made of urgency to get to L.A. and anticipation for this drive. I was really bummed when I found out I wouldn't be able to drive with Nolan like we'd planned. I guess my brother's screwup has its positives.

She has to be exhausted. She's been driving for nearly nine hours, and we hit the road pretty quick. She got up at five this morning to make her first flight that brought her to Santa Fe. That's a lot of travel in one day, and it's night now.

"I'm really fine to drive, you know," I say one more time. She's brushed off my previous three hints.

"I'm good." She yawns for punctuation. I lean forward and press my palms on the dash and force her to glance at me. We've long left the city and are hitting the stretch of desert that goes on forever, trailing along the Mexico border and over the Colorado River.

"I just wanted you to get to relax for once," she says.

"Bullshit," I tease. She wrinkles her brow. "You wanted to avoid my back-road hopping."

"Maybe that, too," she grimaces, pulling over to the side of the road and putting on the hazards.

I got this cool book called *Blue Highways* once for Christmas. It's all about the things you see off the main drag and into small, little-known places. Peyton was one and we were doing a cross-country road trip and I decided to get creative. I drove us about seventy-six miles before the road we were on just dead-ended in the middle of nowhere, Wyoming. Nolan was hungry and desperate for a bathroom. She's never forgotten.

I keep maps now, though. You can't count on internet access for your map app out in nowhere...or Wyoming. I keep a list of the roads I've been on, too. I've only hit about five percent of them.

"I'll stick to the plan. Besides, you know I love this drive at night," I say.

She smirks and flings her buckle free.

"The ship is yours, Captain."

She kicks open her door and I do the same, meeting her in the light beams by the front bumper. She drags her hand over my chest, but before she can get by me completely, I wrap her up in my arms and swing her around, sitting her on the front of my Jeep just like I did when this thing was new.

"Goddamn, you're pretty out here." I palm her knees, then run my hands down her jeans to the ripped cuffs just above her ankles. I grab the threads and shake her feet a little, then pull them around me as I scoot in as close as I can. She lets her head fall against mine as her arms wrap around my shoulders.

"Just out here, huh? Smooth talker." She giggles.

I roll my head against hers back and forth and squeeze at her sides in her ticklish spot until she lunges into me and pants out for me to stop.

"You're *especially* pretty out here," I clarify.

She leans back, holding onto my arms to brace herself, and looks into my eyes. I love the way her gaze flits from my right eye to my left, a suspicious smile on her lips.

"All right, Johnson. I'll let you off the hook...this time." Her sleepy eyes blink long and slow.

"Phew," I tease.

The desert wind carries a chill and it pulls her hair loose from the band at the base of her neck. I tuck the wild strands behind her ears and pull her rolled-up sweater sleeves down, then rub the top of the knit with my palms to warm her up. She leans forward into me, cuddling and shivering at the same time.

"Your Jeep's heater is shit, ya know," she jokes.

I bust out a heavy laugh and rub her back.

"I'll have the boys take a look."

Never, not once, has she suggested we get rid of it. We could own a garage full of Jeeps at this point, but I don't think I would ever want any other one.

"We should probably hit the road," she says, her tired gaze tilting up to meet mine. My thumbs run along her cheeks and I slide my fingers into her hair and dust her lips with a kiss.

"I'm already late. What's a little later?" I say, going in for a second kiss. We're the only fools out on the road this time of night. I'm taking advantage of having this little slice of moonlight to call our own.

I feel the curl of her top lip lift, the way it swings up in a perfect letter *M*, between both of mine; I grab on with my teeth and hold it hostage for just a beat. Her tongue slips out, urging me to kiss her deeper. I slide my hands around her back and pull her into me completely and take her mouth with mine.

She whimpers when my hands find the bottom of her sweater and feather their way up her ribs to the lacey trim of her bra, and her fingertips loop into the top of my jeans, unbuttoning them just enough so she can reach inside and feel how ready I am for her.

"How much do you hate this Jeep?" I chuckle the words against her lips and she laughs against me in return between heavy breaths.

"I could learn to love it," she says.

I pull her against me tightly, sliding my hands under her ass and lifting her from the Jeep until I've carried her to the passenger door. I glance to the left and the right, not a hint of light glowing in either direction. I bring my hard gaze to her hazy one.

"Get in," I order.

Her breath hitches as I set her in the seat. She lodges her feet just inside the door and scoots back until her spine is resting on the center console; her body is arched and waiting for me to taste it. I pull her sweater up swiftly, and she lifts her arms until I free her of it completely. I rest my knee on the seat between her legs and kiss the pale skin between her breast, my scratchy chin running along the silkiness of her bra as I kiss her hard nipple only half-hidden under thin lace.

"I like this one. It's new," I say, biting her hard peak through the fabric. She pushes up into my mouth and cries out lightly.

"I got it months ago. I've just been saving it," she confesses.

I growl like a caveman because I'm stripped to my most basic needs right now looking at her—feeling her.

With tortuous strokes of my tongue, I work the peak of her breast until I'm sure it's raw. Impatient to do the same to the other one, I run my palms up her stomach to the cups of silk and lace and pull them up over her swollen breasts so I can kiss her other nipple skin to mouth. I suck it hard, until she cries out under my control and raises her hips with need.

I lift my head and pull her bra up until it's free from her body, too, discarded in the driver's seat along with what is now my favorite cream-colored sweater. She pulls the band from her hair, letting her hair spill out over her shoulders and the inside of the car. It's gotten longer since the last time I saw her—maybe I just haven't noticed. I see her now, though. I see us. I've missed this.

I stand as she leans up on her elbows, her lips red and raw from our kissing and the places where her teeth bit down to hold back her cries. Her naked breasts are rising with each breath, a steady pace that's somehow speaking to me, telling me to hurry it the fuck up.

I unbutton her jeans and unzip slowly, letting my hands trail down the front of her panties as I tug her pants down to the curve of her hips, and she lifts enough for me to drag them down her thighs and knees until she can kick them away completely. Her hands reach up, fingers flexing, almost dancing with passion while she squirms in her seat and lies back over the console so far that she's no longer looking at me. It's the hottest goddamned thing I've ever seen.

"You ruin me, woman," I growl, grabbing at her flesh above her knees and sliding my hands up her legs until I find the warm center between them.

I slide my thumbs over the soft strip of cotton as she writhes under my touch and trail my fingers up to the band of silk that cuts just below her bellybutton. Slipping my fingers underneath, I roll the lacy top down until I can almost see the soft pink skin. If I didn't look up, I never would have noticed. The car's lights shine enough, though, that the glow traces my profile.

"We have company," I say, chuckling sinisterly. I feel dizzy, not really in a position to cool down but knowing I'll need to. We've been interrupted…again.

I expect Nolan to sit up and curl into a ball or to drop to the floor of my Jeep, mortified. I prepare myself for it, stepping in closer to give her cover, but soon, I feel her hands cover mine where they rest on her hips. She begins to urge them down, taking her panties off more until she brings her knees up high enough for me to slip them away completely.

This is a colossally dangerous idea. It's also the hottest fucking thing we've ever done. Our first time on a mountain has just been eclipsed. I am never selling this Jeep. If it catches on fire, I will have the scraps welded into a piece of art.

The car heading our direction is maybe a mile out, the lights a dim glow in the distance that flickers with each tiny hill the travelers roll over.

"Are you sure?" I ask, running my finger over her slick pussy just to add to the persuasion. Her breath leaves with a whimper as she lifts her head and bites at her bottom lip.

"God yes, Reed," she begs, her toes curling at the edge of the seat while her knees fall open for me.

I look to my left at the growing headlights as I unzip my jeans to pull out my cock, wrapping my hand around it and stroking twice. I grab Nolan's hips and slide her toward me, hooking one leg with my hand and holding it to my side, my fingers digging into my favorite muscles on her body and moving up to her ass. I grab my cock with my other hand and guide it into her warm center, pushing deep inside as I let out a groan.

"Goddamn," I say, my eyes unable to stay open, drunk on the euphoria of just how amazing it is to be inside of her. I pull out completely and wait while she pants with need until I can't take it anymore, and I fall back inside.

Her body arches more and her hands form fists that pound against the driver's seat and steering wheel just as the car that was in the distance lights us up for anyone to see. It flies by with a roar, the motor rushing to the next mile, the tires eating up pavement. I pull out of Nolan again and push back inside harder. She cries out a "Yes!"

"Come here," I beckon her, scooping her into me, lifting her with my cock pulsing inside until I'm holding her in my arms along the side of the Jeep, hidden from the road. I walk us to the wheel well and brace her body against the cold metal as her hands fall onto the hood to hold herself in place while I slide my cock in and out at a frantic pace. She hums out our sweet rhythm, breathing out a chorus of *pleases* and *yeses* until her head snaps forward and her eyes meet mine.

Her gaze is determined, chasing that ultimate bliss that I get to give to her. I'm the only man who gets to give this to her, and I'd almost forgotten how much pleasure I get from just watching her come undone. My hips rocking in and out, I pull my shirt up and over my body so I can feel her hands on my bare skin. Our breath is turning to fog, and our bodies are damp with a sheen of sex and sweat.

I can feel it coming, but I hold on long enough to push Nolan completely over the edge, falling deep inside her with almost violent thrusts that slide her body back an inch at a time on the metal of my Jeep. When I feel her body start to tighten and pulse around me, I let my weight collapse on top of her, my tongue tasting the salt and sweat forming at the base of her neck as I kiss along her jawline and run my hands over her breasts, up her arms and to her wrists. I pin her arms above her head as I kiss and continue to push until every bit of me loses control. I come in her hard, my warmth making her slick and soft, sending tremors throughout her body again as I finally let my cock slip from her and slide along the swollen folds between her legs.

I'm out of breath, sticky and exhausted, but so damn happy. And deep in love. This woman is my everything, and I think with all of the shit we've been through, and everything we've avoided, I somehow forgot how perfect every piece of her is for me. How undeniable we are together—physically and emotionally.

"I'm pretty sure that was illegal," she finally says, her voice faint and satiated.

I laugh and kiss at her neck.

"I know it was," I say, stepping back enough for her to slide to the ground and stand between me and the Jeep. "Here," I say, handing her my shirt—literally the only piece of clothing in immediate reach.

"That was hot...but I also desperately wish I had a shower," she says, laughing halfway through her words.

"Blue highway?" I raise a brow.

It takes her a few seconds to get my meaning, but when she does she nods excitedly.

"Definitely," she agrees. I think this might be a first. Nolan is willing to let me explore a back road. It's not completely uncharted territory for us. There are a lot of ranches out this way, and some of them are for tourists. There's bound to be a motor lodge nearby.

I help her gather her clothes and redress then I take a sweatshirt out of my bag and climb into the driver's side.

"I'm too sleepy to drive now anyhow," I say.

"I'm fucking exhausted," she yawns.

I laugh quietly because she's been exhausted all night. She's also stunning like this—after that. When she's sleepy. When she's mine.

Blue highways. Is it bad that I'm rooting for another dead end?

Chapter Twenty

Nolan

THE SADDLEBACK INN has the worst mattresses on the planet. There was one room left, with a single full bed, because for whatever reason, people *flocked* to the Saddleback Inn this week. I don't think Reed slept at all, and I maybe slept two hours. My neck feels like it got kicked, so I can't even imagine what his muscles feel like. I keep offering to drive, but he refuses to give up the wheel.

He's going to be tired when he reports. Maybe I should have let him go on his own. This was probably selfish—this time I took from him.

His hand moves across the center console to my knee, and Reed flips his palm over and stretches his fingers, begging for my hand to rest in his. I smile at the age lines in his skin and draw a line along the three wrinkles that are set deep with calluses.

"Did you ever have your fortune told at the Spring Fling?" I think Sarah played the part of the psychic our junior year, which means that any of those fortunes were complete BS.

"Nah, I never believed in that crap. Why?" He squeezes my hand and glances at me, his eyes scrunching in the morning sun. I reach up with my other hand and find his junky old sunglasses clipped to my visor and hand them to him.

"Thanks," he says, sliding them on his face. He's had the same pair for the last decade, and even though they're too big to be in style now, he keeps them because Peyton hates them.

"Sarah had a book about palm reading that she took out from the library. She got it so she could run the booth that one year. And those lines are supposed to be how many children you are destined to have."

He slips his hand from mine and flattens his palm along the steering wheel to examine it. He shrugs and quirks his lip.

"We better get to work then, I guess," he says, winking.

"Uh, no, buddy," I shoot back.

He reaches over to brush his fingertips along my face next.

"My life is perfect," he says, and a warmth fills my chest that I haven't felt in years.

I hesitate to break this moment up with things like the real reason I needed to make this drive with him, but I know if I don't broach the subject, then he's just going to fall right back into that place when I'm no longer here to be a distraction.

A few more miles pass before I find the courage, and I don't bring it up gracefully.

"We should talk about Trig," I say, instantly wanting a do-over.

Reed's staring at the road ahead, and if I weren't so finely tuned to his subtleties, I never would know that his heart and mind just did a shift. His brow dents and his lips pinch tighter in the corners, like he's pretending to think about what I'm asking. It's a mask he wears sometimes when I force him to get raw with his feelings.

"What do you mean?"

I expected that response, so I shift in my seat and bring my leg in, tucking it under the other so I can face him more.

"Trig's death scared you." I know it did. Hell, it scared me, too.

Reed blows out a short laugh and bunches his face.

"I'm sad, sure. I'm really sad. A little angry, too…maybe confused, but scared? Nah," he says. I think he might actually believe that.

"I think, though…" I breathe in long and slow through my nose, ready for a fight. "I think maybe you are."

He shoots me the look I expect, one eye closed more than the other. It's the, "Stop being crazy, Nolan" look. Nine out of ten times, that look means I've touched a nerve. It means I'm right.

"I know you don't want to deal with this now, but if you don't, Reed, I'm afraid it's going to become a thing that eats away at you. And I'm afraid you won't be sharp. I'm afraid you'll get hurt," I admit.

"Ahhhhh," he snickers. "I see what this is about. You're the one that's afraid. I'm not Trig, Babe. I don't get hit the same way, and our offense runs differently. I'm going to be okay."

"Reed, that's not what I'm saying." I twist back in my seat and sigh, sinking in and gripping the strap of my seatbelt across my chest.

"I can't have you not believing in me, Noles. That…*that* is what's going to get me hurt. Not some psychosomatic stuff or memories and regrets…it's me worrying about you that's going to be the thing that gets in my way out there." His tone has gotten a little angry and his volume louder. His nostrils flare as his eyes shift from me to the road and back.

"Reed, I'm pretty sure I'm here with you—*for* you." I'm starting to get mad now.

"Yeah, but you don't want to be. You haven't watched me in years. You know what that feels like?" His words cut to a raw space in my chest. A tornado snakes up my throat and wrecks my heart.

He is my everything, and I always want to be with him. I'm just too terrified to see something awful happen to him. I've admitted that to him! I can say when I'm scared.

"You really think I'm not here for you?" I ask.

He shrugs, a flippant gesture that goads me into pushing us over the edge.

"Why the hell do you think I made Jason fuck up your flight? You think I wanted to ride across the desert in the most uncomfortable car known to man? I left our daughter at home with a broken heart, and I know what those feel like, Reed. I've been there!"

Shit, that was dirty. My breathing has gotten faster, like I've run a sprint. I've landed in the irrational and this is when I get messy and mean.

"You told Jason to cancel my flight?" He zeroes in on that one piece first, his eyebrows high with his question.

"Yeah, but only because…"

"Are you serious?" He shouts his question, interrupting me.

"Reed, listen. I only did it because I saw how you were, and I was…I *am*… worried." I'm stammering.

"Do you have any idea how bad that looks for me? I'm never going to be able to convince people that I have my act together if I can't show up for things when I'm called on to lead. Noles, that was a really fucked-up thing to do, and I can't believe you didn't know better!"

I start to blink tears. He's yelling now, and he's right about a few of the things he's mad about, but also…he's so very wrong!

"Why does it matter? They need you? Reed…if you aren't on your game it won't matter anyway, and this Trig stuff…it's messing with you! I see it!"

"It matters because if I do good here—*now*—maybe I get a contract extension, or better…picked up by Arizona. They love veteran quarterbacks, and I've still got so much to give. I do good here, I get everything I want, Nolan. This is my shot, my last shot, and I can't take things for granted by skipping out on warm-ups and practices and shit."

I'm stunned silent. My tongue feels fat, swollen with the sickness now choking away my air. I blink and the tears that were threatening my eyes slip down my cheeks.

"Extension."

The word falls from my lips so emotionless. No question, just fact, in the way I say it. Reed lets out a heavy breath.

"I don't know. I was just thinking about it, but it doesn't matter now." He's speaking away from me, and the wind attacking the Jeep from the mountain pass has drowned out most of his sounds. I'm glad. These miles will be for reflection. For both of us.

When we clear the Palm Desert, the traffic picks up to that

frenetic L.A. hustle, and Reed's attention turns to the busy lanes. He has a new distraction, and he's playing up how intent he needs to drive, overacting with his expressions and remarks to other drivers. I've quit waiting for our conversation to continue, instead turning my attention to everything I'm missing at home right now.

To Peyton.

I text her a few times, asking if she's all right, and when she doesn't answer after thirty minutes, I refresh our family tracking app to see where she is, relieved when she shows up at the house. She's probably asleep. I wish I was. There's no chance of that happening now, though.

I keep trying to get Reed to connect with my gaze, to notice how much I'm staring at him. I know he feels it, but as much as I'm working to find him, he's running away. He'll look to the right, but only so far. His arms flexed and tense with their grip on the wheel. My master of avoidance.

When his phone rings with Jason's call, I know that I've lost him for the rest of the day, maybe even the weekend. He starts in with questions about his schedule, interviews and meeting times to catch up with the coaching staff. I sit on my hands and wait for him to give up the fact that he knows what I've done and to get angry at Jason for it. He doesn't, though. He doesn't bring it up once, instead pretending he's still in the dark and our little plan is still fully intact.

He's so good at pretending everything's fine.

We exit the freeway after thirty minutes of harsh start-and stop jams, and I'm nauseated and hot when we pull into the hotel valet. I get out and Reed unloads my bag, then steps close to kiss my cheek as if this is just another day of work. I suppose for him it is.

He turns and gets one foot back in his Jeep, and the boiling in my belly reaches my throat.

"That's it? You're just gonna leave? Like that?"

I'm clutching my purse in one hand and my bag handle in the other, a set of doormen holding an overpriced glass doorway open for me on both sides about ten feet behind me. They know who Reed is, and they've figured out that I'm his wife. Of course, now that I've gotten all vocal, I suppose there is a chance that they think

I'm a scorned lover. Maybe the rag magazines are around taking photos. I've always been amused by the made-up headlines.

CINDERELLA QUARTERBACK IN LOVERS' QUARREL WITH MYSTERY WOMAN

Reed steps back out of the Jeep completely, the motor still rumbling feet away from me. His toes match up with mine and his hand brushes the tangled hairs from my face. Our eyes meet a second later, and I catch the flicker in his—he's forcing this.

"We'll have dinner tonight. Somewhere nice," he says, leaning down and kissing me with a little more passion than before. I'm sure to the onlookers everything seems just fine. I feel it, though. Or rather, I *don't* feel it.

My hand grasps the front of his shirt in a bunch and I hold on tightly, urging him to stay. I step up on my toes and tilt my chin to meet his stare.

"Now you're mad, and I guess that's better. We aren't done, though. Not even close," I say.

His mouth twitches, and he turns to the side, his smile rising on the side closest to me but only a little.

"I'll be a few hours," he says. With nothing more to add, he shifts before he buckles up, then drives away.

I turn and greet the doormen with a fake plastered-on smile, and as I walk by them I lean to the side and whisper to one, "Don't tell his wife." I wink and head into the lobby hoping that one of them gives the tabloids a tip and that I show up in a blurry photo online later tonight. It will be amusing, and we'll both laugh about it.

It will be the only thing we'll laugh about.

Chapter Twenty-One

Reed

MY HEAD ISN'T in this.

I was a dick.

Why did she do that?

I should blame Jason. It's easier to blame Jason. Jason would never do this on his own, though. He wouldn't do it unless he was really worried about me.

Nolan wasn't wrong.

Jason's late, and when this happens now, I automatically think he's either planned some secret with Nolan to keep me away from practice or he's off hiding in his hotel room with Sarah. I doubt she flew in for this, though. They don't really have to hide anymore, anyhow, so I guess he's just late.

I should go to the hotel, but I'm not ready yet. I don't want to keep saying stupid things.

Almost everyone else is gone, and the visitor clubhouse at this place is not exactly homey. The brick and concrete are a stark gray with water stains and crumbling bits of sand and cement chips. It's cold, and every sound I make echoes so much I think it must careen into the concourse and circle the concessions.

I could spend an hour running on the treadmill to stress test my leg, but really…that's just going to make me tired. I pull my towel from my neck and toss it in the general direction of my cubby before laying back on the wooden bench.

"I barely fit, but this plank of wood feels better than that mattress did last night," I muse to myself.

"You figure you make up your time sitting in here nursing your sore-ass muscles, then Coach won't notice that you weren't taking snaps today?" I let my arm fall from its rest on my eyes and crack one lid open while smirking at Coach Simms.

"If that's my excuse, what's yours?" I pull myself up to sit and face him and he takes a spot on the bench opposite of me and across the room.

"Lot on my mind, I guess. And I don't sleep on the road games. Never have," he says, clearing his throat through the last few words. I know he used to smoke like a Texas barbecue joint, but from what I gather, he quit six years ago after his first heart surgery.

"That's something like a hundred and seventy nights of insomnia," I say, doing my best to impress him with my estimating skills.

"One sixty-four, actually, but close," he says.

I wince and snap, just missing a perfect guess.

His eyes meet mine and he chuckles once to himself, leaning forward and resting his elbows on his spread-apart knees. His skinny legs are draped in black pants that rise at his ankles, showing off his pink socks. I point to them, and he lifts his pant leg just a little and chuckles more when he sees them.

"Breast cancer socks. My wife beat it, so I wear nothing but pink socks. I wore them all through her treatment, and you know how we get with that superstitious crappola. Whatever, made-up or not, I'm not messing with it. I've got drawers full."

I admire his answer, and I think I'd probably dedicate my life to something like that too if I almost lost Nolan to something like cancer and associated her recovery to something I did. It never would be something I did, though. It'd all be her, because she's the strong one. I just fumble through things.

Coach and I sit in silence for several seconds, both avoiding each other's gaze like Clint Eastwood and Chuck Norris trying to prove who's the bigger man. His head snaps up first, and I'm pretty sure it means he is.

"That was some service." My head tingles with a dose of adrenaline as he pulls me back to Trig and the service. I've never really left I suppose, but I've been doing so well not talking about it.

"It was," I agree. It's the polite thing to do.

We sit in more silence, only Coach leaves his eyes on me while I stare at the lines on the carpet, realizing the subtle pattern of the L.A. skyline woven under my feet. They should go back in and add some smog.

"You're gonna meet with Gary tomorrow. He likes mornings, so get in early." Coach stands and lets his open palms fall against his sides.

My brow pulls in.

"With...Gary..." He means *Chaplain* Gary Cruz.

"What's with people not hearing me lately? Press didn't hear me either the other night...yeah, I said Gary. Be here bright and early. And go home and get some sleep. You look like shit," he says, leaving before I can question him anymore.

I let the melancholy in a little more. It feels like I swallowed a rock and it's stuck just beneath my breastbone. It's sharp and heavy, and I can't get a full breath. The dizzy feeling has gotten worse.

It's seven at night, and Jason, even if he makes it through traffic, isn't going to be here in time to talk to anyone or walk through anything. And it looks like I'm going to be getting in bright and early, so I may as well go back to the hotel—just like I promised.

I flip my phone around in my palm a few times, not surprised that there aren't any texts from Noles. She's likely pissed off. She also knows what Fridays and Saturdays are like before a game. It may have been a while since she's been on the road with me, but the routine is so messed up that she'd never forget how it interferes with regular life.

Hungry?

I set my phone down on the bench while I gather up my things. After a few seconds of trailing dots that tell me she's typing, I get a simple response.

Sure.

Yeah. She's pissed.

Meet me out front in 20.

I grab my bag and toss my phone in the pocket on the side, slinging it over my shoulder as I head into the guts of the stadium toward the garage. I remembered seeing a little shopping center right on the corner by our hotel, and I know I don't have a lot of time, but if I want to ease my way out of the dog house, I should at least try.

I pick up my step and toss my bag in the back of the Jeep, pulling away with a squeal that gets the attention of the security guard who steps out of the small four-foot-by-four-foot box where he keeps an eye on everybody's keys.

I zip through four or five streets before I find the shopping center. I park a little out of the way, trying to avoid two men fresh from the Milk Maiden Café that I see stumble into the parking lot. They're wearing their blue and gold L.A. jerseys; I know they've seen me when, from the corner of my eye, I catch one of them slap his arm against his friend's chest. I almost make it into the mall, but not before one of them turns around, his arm swung around his buddy's neck for balance, and yells "Reed Johnson is a pussy!"

Rather than indulge them in any way, I decide to find the honor in being hated by a rival again. My smug smile feels right, and I start looking people in the eyes when they give me doubletakes in the mall. I let most people wonder, but when a kid who looks like he's about ten or eleven lifts his eyebrows practically to his hairline, I give him a nod. He rolls his shoulders and gives me one back, then walks a little taller into the department store with his parents.

I'm oddly good at picking the perfect thing for Nolan. I kinda suck at shopping otherwise, but something about getting things for her just comes naturally. I see things that feel like magnets to her personality in almost every city I go to. I usually pick something up when I know I'll be seeing her again soon, but I need *this…whatever I find* to be more than a charmingly perfect gift. It has to be an apology, and a story, and maybe another apology.

I pop into the first jewelry store and circle the counter so fast I must look like I'm playing a game of hide-and-go-seek. It's rare that I find something in a place like this that's the right fit for my wife. Department stores are out, and I got her a bunch of new, clever T-shirts a month or two ago. I'm now twelve minutes late from the time I promised her I would be picking her up, so I stop in this weird rock store and pull out my phone to text her.

Got hung up. Almost there.

She answers back quick.

It's fine.

That means it isn't fine at all. Fine is a four-letter word that starts with an *F*. When Nolan says she's fine, what she really means is something quite the opposite.

I glance around, feeling desperate and near giving up, when a small wooden box holding a cluster of crystal rocks on a shelf catches my eye and scratches at something deep in my memory. I don't know how it's the same box, but it is—it just is.

My hand collapses the lid carefully, and I start to shake with a dose of adrenaline when I see the pattern I was expecting come into view. The lid is curved, an intricate carving etched along the grain creating a swirl of flowers and vines. Deep turquoise blues stain the flowers and faint greens wisp for leaves. Before I even held it in my hand, I could have drawn this box from my memory.

I hold it in both hands and gaze around the store, looking for an employee. I finally find a woman with her hair twisted in dreadlocks, woven with pieces of fabric that hang down her back.

"Excuse me, but how much is this box?" She turns to me and pulls her small glasses down her nose, deciphering what I'm talking about.

"Oh, that's just a display," she says, going back to sorting a tangle of leather jewelry that some kids came through and messed up.

I swallow, knowing I have to have this box. I'm not leaving this store without it.

"Can I buy the display?"

She turns to me again, a confused wrinkle zigzagging along the bridge of her nose, and before she can say *no*, I sweeten the pot.

"A hundred bucks. I'll give you a hundred bucks for this box." My words shoot out of my mouth all nervous-like and urgent, and she smirks, letting out a short laugh.

Shrugging, she shakes her head a little.

"Just dump the rocks out and take it. If it's that important, I can't charge you for it." Her natural lips pull into a sweet smile, and I nearly lunge forward and hug her. I think she thinks I'm going to, because she slides her feet around the jewelry display to put a barrier between us.

"That's seriously the most awesome thing ever! Thank you... this...just thank you for this," I ramble, still shaking my head, a little in disbelief.

"Just don't forget the stones. Those are worth a lot," she reminds me.

"Oh...right," I say, tipping the box and palming the stones to hand to her. She cradles them and moves them over to the register area while I walk slowly back through the store, holding the box in my hands in front of my face. My thumb rolls over the aged hinges and I flip the lid open and closed a few times, smelling the sweet scent the store left a trace of on the wood.

I've done it again. This actually might be the very best gift I've ever found for Noles. And when I tell her its history, it's going to make her forget all about the douchebag things I said earlier and remind her that she and I are in fact meant to fucking be...for always.

———

The Hail Mary

Reed, 23 Years Earlier

We've been in the mall longer than two straight dudes should be in a mall. My mom used to drag me around from department store to department store, picking up things she had on hold and changing her mind seeing them again two weeks later. I'd sit on bed displays while she ordered employees around to find her something different. Millie Johnson was the queen of changing her mind, and Christmas time kicked her high-maintenance spirit up a big notch.

I kinda feel like Sean, my best friend, is giving her a run for her money right now though. We've visited the same three stores six times. He's picked up the same chain and locket in two of them, and then there's a sweatshirt that "feels nice and soft, just like Nolan likes them."

She does like soft clothing. She has this collection of T-shirts that are all worn and perfectly broken in. I asked her about them once, and she got embarrassed. I think she thought I was teasing her because, I'm guessing, they were probably from the thrift store. I wasn't though. I actually really dig her style. Everything she wears looks like it belongs to her, says something about her—smart, funny, easy-going, sporty.

"You're gonna kill me, but I think…I think I want to look at the sweatshirt and locket together, at that one store that had them both. That way I can, like…hold them up side by side or whatever."

I just start walking the other direction, to the store my friend is talking about. Sean has been dating Nolan for seven or eight months. They're really good together, and I like that he's good to her, because she's a really cool girl.

"What'd you get Tatum?" Sean asks, quickening his step to catch up to me. I'm walking a little faster than we have all day, because the store he needs is on the other end of the mall, which means one more pass through the food court, and I'm really getting hungry. If I have to smell tater tots one more time—without having time to actually stand in line and buy them—I'm going to throw my friend off the escalator.

"I just got her some earrings. They looked kinda seventies-ish to

221

me, but I knew she wanted them, because she took me to the store to visit them twice."

We both laugh. I've been with Tatum for more than a year now. There isn't much we don't know about each other, but there also doesn't seem to be…well…much to know. The sex is great, and often. But it's not really special anymore. Our first time…*my* first time…I guess that was special. I don't remember much of it, though, other than the end because…I mean, come on.

"I wish Nolan was like that," Sean says, and I perk a brow. "You know, like Tatum? Tell me what to do. I have no idea what she wants."

I fall in behind him as we step onto the escalator and think about what he just said. Nolan loves her family, and she loves simple things. She's willing to try new things, like art or seeing some new band coming to the Valley. She loves to bake. Her mom is an amazing cook, and she's always trying to learn how to make things just like her. She also has to carry her phone and wallet everywhere she goes, and I bet if she had one of those small purse things that she could wear over her body, she'd love it.

I shake from my trance as we step from the escalator, and I follow Sean into the store as I try to dust away the rush of ideas I just had for a girl who is my friend—who *is not* my girlfriend. Who *is* dating my best friend.

Tagging along behind Sean as he circles back to the jewelry counter with the big sweatshirt in his hands, I can't help but notice the dozens of things that leap out at me that would be perfect for her. I hardly hear Sean talking anymore, the noise in my head so loud. I've started to fantasize that I'm the one shopping for Nolan—that I'm buying her a special gift for our first Christmas together, and it has to be perfect. My eyes are staring at the heart-shaped locket and the sweatshirt that Sean has rested side by side on the glass countertop. I'm hit with a sudden realization that neither of these things are good enough for Nolan Lennox. While she'd like them and would be happy, they wouldn't be special.

Nolan deserves something special.

From the corner of my eye, I catch a small wooden box

engraved with swirls and flowers, small cuts stained a turquoise blue, others green or yellow. It's the kind of a place a girl would hide her favorite things. It's something Nolan would love. I don't know how I know it, but I just do.

My lips part and I start to point it out to my friend, but something chokes me, and I don't speak. I wait, and when my friend settles on the locket, I smile and nod, happy that he's done.

She'll like the locket just fine. But she won't love it. She'll show her friends…maybe. Probably wear it for a week or two then keep it on her dresser.

The wooden box, though—that she would keep private.

And that's the difference.

I know Nolan.

And just like that locket, I know that I am not good enough.

———

Nolan, Present Day

My stomach is so loud that I'm fairly certain the couple waiting for their Uber next to me can hear my growls. Add this to the fact that the doormen and their friends—who I am sure they told—all believe I'm a high-dollar hooker or the football-floozie-hookup sleeping with Reed Johnson, and I'm literally a walking sitcom.

I can actually pick the Jeep's motor from of a lineup. I hear it approaching the light out of my sight first. I don't even have to guess which direction it's pulling into the hotel drop-off. My doormen pals watch me step from the curb and reach my hand forward to climb in as Reed slows. I play up my charade a little longer, glance over my shoulder, hiding my face with my palm—as if that's really how I would disguise myself—before getting in, slamming the door and ducking down low in the seat.

"Did you see someone from high school or something? Cuz you only do this stuff when you see someone you didn't like from high school," Reed says.

"I do not," I argue, stopping short and dropping my brow low as

I sit up normal and straighten the seatbelt across my chest. "Actually, yeah…you're right. I guess that *is* what I do. But no…that's not what this is."

I wonder if showing up in tabloid gossip with your wife is bad for a contract extension. I decide not to tell Reed about my little game, but he never asks, so I get away with one more, little hoax. I notice a bag rustling in the back of the Jeep; I reach to grab it, curious. Reed stops my hand short, though.

"That's for later," he says.

I pull my lips in tight, suspicious.

"Okay…" I draw the word out. Reed holds this secret close, though. It's a surprise he's picked up, something to smooth over our rough spots—our most recent rough spot. It's probably really thoughtful, which kinda makes me even more irritated, because it won't be the point. The point is the stuff he said and the mess I made by cancelling his flight.

"You good with steak? I'm starving," Reed says.

"My God, yes," I say, flattening my palms on my stomach.

He glances at me and smiles, pulling us ahead quickly to make the light of an intersection.

I've always been a good eater. Reed has always found it sexy, or at least he *says* he finds it sexy. I don't care if he does or not; when I want meat and potatoes, I'm gonna clean my plate. There is nothing delicate about me taking a fork and knife to a fillet.

We pull into a small parking lot about two blocks away from our hotel and Reed rushes around to get my door before I have a chance to completely get out. He grabs the bag from the back, but winds the bag tight around his thumb and holds it slightly behind his back while we walk toward the restaurant together.

The place is crowded, but Reed manages to finagle us a spot with some privacy, out on the back-patio area, tucked behind a tree wrapped in white lights. Fall in California is so different from the rest of the world. It's chilly in the evening, but a light jacket makes it damn near perfect. We can't have a dinner like this outside in a lot of other places come late September.

Reed waits until we've placed our order and gotten our drinks delivered before he brings the bag up to the table between his palms. Wrapped in some gem store plastic bag, he sets it between his napkin, silverware, and the Jack and Coke he had them bring from the bar.

"Before anything else, let me just say this to you," he begins.

I fold my hands on the table and tuck my feet under my chair, leaning in close.

"I'm sorry," he says, not even blinking as we stare into each other's eyes. He's sincere. I don't have to dig in for more, ask him what he's sorry for. I know…*he* knows. He wouldn't have said it if he didn't think he should.

"Me, too," I add. I wouldn't say it either unless I meant it. I shouldn't have cancelled his flight. I should have found another way.

He takes a deep but quick breath through his nose, his lips forming a tight smile that dents his cheeks. This next part is going to be hard. The truth is that way.

"I don't want this to be it for me, Noles. If I can really do this— play at this level, the level I expect for myself—I don't want to stop." He waits for me to react. I'm not sure what expression to give. I can show him the Nolan who always knew this and understands, or I could give him the crazy woman who is secretly praying none of it works out. I'm praying against his wishes. I'm a horrible, terrible person.

"I just don't understand why." He's heard me say that before, but not directly. We need to be direct about all of this.

"I know," he says.

A waiter swoops in and leaves two salads in front of us, food I suddenly don't want. I pick at a few of the croutons while Reed takes large shovels of greens onto his fork and stuffs his mouth.

"You have so much else in your life. I know you could be happy, that you'd find a purpose and a place. Is this about Trig? About you being afraid? You aren't Trig, Reed. His depression—it could have come from a lot of different places." I can see the flashes of pain reflect in his eyes when I bring up Trig so bluntly. I have to, though. Trig's funeral brought so much of Reed's fears to the surface.

"You're right. I can't help but think about Trig. He was really unhappy after he quit, and he didn't know how to live without the game in his life. I'm just not ready yet, Noles. I feel like there are things I have to do in this sport, goals I have to reach for while I still can." He lowers his fork and runs his napkin along his lips before leaning back in his chair to look at me.

I have so many things to say that they all compete for what comes out, leaving me stymied, I say nothing, and instead simply blink a few times and look down and to the side. Reed shifts and brings the bag he's been hiding from me up on the table. When I glance his direction, he slides it across to me. He nods slightly, urging me to open the bag. My fingers tingle with nerves because I'm still upset, but I know he's just being honest, and he's trying to be kind with this gift.

I take the bag in my hands and hold it open at the end, reaching in and feeling a smooth surface, maybe some sort of wooden carving. I pull out a bohemian-style jewelry box that smells of maple and is adorned with splashes of color, shapes cut like vines and flowers. I smile genuinely. I would have bought this for myself.

"It's beautiful," I say, meeting his waiting eyes. He looks so young and innocent, like he's my high-school Reed holding his breath hoping I like something. It somehow makes this sweeter.

"When we were fifteen...maybe sixteen, I found this box at the mall when I was helping Sean pick out something to get you for Christmas. I knew this box was the perfect gift," he says.

My lip rises on the right and I look down from Reed to the box, lifting the latch on the lid.

"So, you decided not to give Sean a good tip and tell him to buy it for me?" I chuckle at the thought. Years of marriage later and I still get butterflies in my stomach at the thought of Reed Johnson having a crush on me.

"Hell no," he busts out in a laugh. "I kept it to myself, and I think he got you a locket. I wanted to be the one to get this for you. I was just too chicken to do it then. But I found this box tonight. And I knew it was a sign."

He pulls the box into his palms and flips the lid open completely to look inside and twist the box around in a circle to view it from every angle. His lips are parted, waiting for the right words to come.

"I knew I had to be completely honest with you…about what I really want. Why this second shot…hell, third shot…is so important to me."

I swallow so hard that I cough from the dryness. I reach for my water glass and down nearly half of the liquid while he chews at his lip.

"And I know that you are not in favor of this choice I'm making, or rather this goal that I have. But I can't give up because I don't want to hurt you, and I think you know that." His eyes meet mine, and as if I knew we would have to have this silent conversation, I meet his waiting stare and break a little in front of his honest eyes. His head falls to the side a little and he reaches across the table to me, turning his palm over for my hand. I give it to him, shifting my focus to the soft strokes of his thumb along my knuckles.

"I would resent it. You would resent me. You still might because of this…"

"I would never," I break through, a hiccup of a cry.

"Shhhh," he soothes, reaching for my other hand now. I hate how worried I am, and how defeated I feel. I hate how selfish I feel for still not wanting any of this. I love this man so much, but he's being so stupid.

"You're right about everything," he says. I squeeze my eyes shut, feeling a wave of vindication wrap my insides in warmth that chills again quickly because me being right isn't enough. It doesn't matter. "But I have to try, Noles. And I want you to be able to do something when you feel like you can't. I thought maybe you could put your wishes and worries in here. Write down the things you can't say. Hell, tell me I'm an asshole and hide it away in this box if you're not ready to say it to my face. This box is for your feelings, and if there's ever a time when you want me to read them, just hand it to me and I will go through every single note. I won't make my final decision, if I have one to make, until I consider everything you want me to consider. For when we can't talk, or when you aren't ready to speak, let it out here."

He pushes the box forward again, the open side facing me. I run my finger along the inside edge then pinch the clasp and draw the top down slowly, snapping it locked again.

"I always want to hear you. Every single thing you have to say. But I need you to hear me too. I promise to talk if you do."

When I look up, hopeful eyes and sorry lips wait for me to say okay. And so I do. I say okay to venting on paper when I can't vent in person. I say okay to what mentally leaves me kicking and screaming. I say okay to risking my favorite person to a game because if I don't, he won't be the same anyway.

Trig scared him, but he was afraid before that. I saw this same boy look at me with a terrified expression when he broke his arm in a car crash and when he had to watch from the sidelines. I can't be the one who takes this game away from him for good.

But one day, time will. It's inevitable.

I think I might write that down for him to read when he needs to.

Chapter Twenty-Two

Nolan

I STARTED WRITING things on slips of paper when Reed went to practice Saturday morning, and I couldn't stop. I filled that box with my worst thoughts, just to get them out. I ripped through an entire hotel notepad, and I started using receipts from my purse and random scraps from magazines next.

By early afternoon, the crumpled pieces of paper were nearing the top. And I felt terrible. Without adding one more, I poured the papers into the trash, then dumped water on them and topped them with the leftovers from my room-service lunch.

I had to go downstairs to get a new pad of paper, and this time, the writing has not come easy. My phone saves me from drowning mentally. It's Peyton, and I hope she's managed to start acting less like a hermit.

"Hi." I'm smiling just answering her call.

"I need advice."

She doesn't ease me into this, and I swallow hard at her statement. The last time she asked me for advice, it was for what color pony she should pick out with her birthday money. I have a feeling this advice is different.

"Okay," I say, trying to mask my nervous hesitation.

"Bryce came by today…a few times, actually." I recognize the weakening resolve in her voice. I've been there.

"Did you see him?" I need to know how far gone she is. First loves are really more like spells. Hell, if mine wasn't a doozy.

"No. I made Grandma Rose answer the door."

"Good. I mean, if you think that's good," I say.

She doesn't answer right away, and I think that means she isn't sure if it's good. I think it also means she *wants* to see him. That's what it would have meant for me, if I were in her shoes and Reed were in Bryce's. Those shoes feel mighty familiar.

"He brought me a present," she says.

"Is it a pony?" I laugh, but when I realize she isn't, I apologize. "I'm sorry. I'll be serious."

"It was a photocopy of this letter his mom wrote to him—more of a list, really."

I'm intrigued.

"What kind of list?" I ask.

"It was all of these things she hoped for him. Things she wanted him to be. She gave it to him for his twelfth birthday, I guess," Peyton says.

"Wow." My eyes go to my once-again empty box.

"He made notes on the copy he gave me, drawing arrows to all of the places he wrote that he failed. His mom wrote that she wanted him to be a gentleman, and he circled it and wrote that he was so sorry he disrespected me. When she asked him to be strong on the list, he circled that and said he had been weak. Mom, I don't know what to do…"

I can hear the tears she's trying to mask. A pair form in my eyes to match my daughter's.

"What do you *want* to do?" I close my eyes tight and think about this question, how I sound. I'm echoing my own mom and the advice she gave me so many times—she still does.

"I don't know; that's why I called!" Her words are laced with heavy, teenaged sighs.

I laugh silently to myself and shake my head, wiping away the beginning tears. My, how life comes full circle. And it's amazing how much wiser a person really is when they're older.

"You know. You're just afraid you'll get it wrong," I say, shrugging. This conversation is as much for me as it is for Peyton.

"He was an asshole, Mom." I nod as she speaks.

"Yeah. He was." I agree, and that frustrates her even more, her huffing sound buzzing the phone line. I chuckle at it, and that only makes her groan.

"You're not helping!"

I press my palm against my mouth to stifle my laugh. I can't believe I'm here, in this conversation, in so many ways.

"Okay, okay," I start, closing my eyes and calming my urge to smirk. It isn't fair to Peyton. This is serious to her. It's serious to all girls when we're in it. It was serious to me, and look at where I am now…look who I married.

"What I mean is this—I think you want to hear him out. I think you'd like to see if you can talk to him and believe his apology. I think you like him a lot and aren't ready to stop liking him, even though you're mad. And I think you should be mad if that's what you really want to be, for as long as you want. I also think it's fine if you want to kick him to the curb."

"Oh my god, we don't say things like that anymore," she heaves out.

"Like what? Kick to the curb?"

"Ugh," she breathes again.

I chuckle silently and wait for a few seconds for seriousness to reclaim its rightful place for this conversation.

"You're not hearing the right part of what I said…" I wait for her to catch up to me. We sit listening to each other breathe for almost thirty seconds.

"I know what you're saying," she concedes. I don't want her just taking my suggestion though. This still has to be her own conclusion; it has to be hers, not someone else's—mine or some group of girls who think they know what's right for her.

"Maybe I'm full of shit, Peyton. But if that is how you feel, what's stopping you?"

It's silent between us for several more seconds, and eventually Peyton starts to hum in thought, stammering and nervous about what to say.

"It's just me. Remember our rules—you can say *anything* to me," I remind her. So far, that's always been the case, but this is the first time that rule is truly being tested. God, do I hope it holds up.

"Other people saw him…with her. She has a lot of friends, too. And what will people think of me…if I just act like it didn't happen? They'll think I'm weak." Her breath hitches at the admission, but my mouth tightens into a proud grin. What she just said out loud was so hard. She's miles ahead of the woman I was. Hell, she's miles ahead of me now.

"So?"

I look at my reflection in the hotel mirror while I wait for my daughter to respond.

"So…people will think that I'm wrong. That I shouldn't trust him, or whatever…"

"Should you?" I keep asking the obvious—the questions she's asking herself.

"I don't know!" she growls.

"How can you know?" I wait again, knowing this realization will take her a little longer. After a few seconds, she breathes out into the phone.

"By talking to him," she says.

And now, for the big question.

"So, what do *you* want to do? Forget about what other people think you should do. Are you safe with him?"

"Always," she answers quickly.

"Do you think he would hurt you? Physically? Emotionally? On purpose?"

"No!"

Those were always the big things my mom asked when we

talked about Reed in high school. That was always her line in supporting whatever decision I made, and that line holds true for me as well. If she decides to forgive him, I can still make him pay a little with those little digs here and there—and by unleashing Reed on his ass.

"I really liked the letter his mom gave him. I was thinking of maybe making my own list...for him. Is that stupid?" I smirk and think about her idea, how we all could use a list like that.

"I think it's good idea," I say, flipping the lid on my box open and drilling my focus into the woodgrain.

"Thanks, Mom."

Something about her saying that hits the center of my chest. It's not that she hasn't said it before, it's just that, yeah...it's been a while.

"Anytime, Peyt. Always," I say, feeling a little more centered when we hang up.

I twist the pad of paper in my direction and hold the pen an inch above the surface, pausing for a second before writing.

YOU ARE AN AMAZING FATHER.

I put the paper in the box and add to it with a few more.

NOBODY THROWS A HAIL MARY LIKE REED JOHNSON.

YOUR FRIENDSHIP GIVES PEOPLE JOY.

YOU MAKE YOUR DAD SO PROUD, EVERY SINGLE DAY.

And finally...

YOU ARE THE LOVE OF MY LIFE.

There. That's enough for now. Quality over quantity, I think. I close the lid and grab my box. It's no longer filled with venting rants but with things I think Reed needs to know—things I think he sometimes forgets. By the time I'm done with this box, he'll be able to take a handful out and see just how much is still inside. He'll see everything he still is, even if he can't always be it all.

Chapter Twenty-Three

Reed

I'VE CHATTED with Chaplain Cruz a few times, but always in passing—his way in, my way out, or the opposite. He's always here for someone else. He's the guy they send in to deal with the death of a loved one. I was gone so long when my mom passed away, by the time I got back, I didn't really need his services.

I kinda don't think I need them now.

"Hey, Reed. Nice to see you throwing the ball. Looking good, man!" He holds out his hand across a small wooden table covered in health magazines. I take his palm and shake before we both sink in to the deep leather chairs that face one another.

"Thanks. Body hurts a little more than it used to, but somehow the guys are catching my crap," I say with a laugh. He joins me, but shakes his head.

"I'm pretty sure that arm of yours is a long way from crap." His smile settles in as his hands fold over his chest, his belly covered with the OKC sweatshirt that most of the staff wears. He has a championship ring on his hand; I nod to it.

"You must have been the man behind the man for that one,

huh?" I flit my eyes up to his then back down to the ring. He splays his fingers out between us then pulls the heavy metal jewelry from his ring finger and tosses it to me. I catch it like an egg.

"That was with New York. Only one I got, but man did those guys keep me busy. Something about New Yorkers, I guess," he says, chuckling while I spin the ring between my fingers. I've held them before—envied them plenty. I nod and pass it back to him, jealous of one more man now.

"Pretty nice," I say.

"The wife hates it," he spits out, a guttural laugh echoing down the empty hallway of the stadium corridor.

My brow wrinkles. How could anyone hate a championship ring?

"I mean, it's ugly as sin. You have to admit that," he says, dropping it back over his knuckle. "And it's bigger than hers, which let me tell you, she brings up every anniversary, birthday, Christmas, Valentine's Day..."

"Ah, yeah. I get it," I say, smiling and instantly appreciating my wife's preference for T-shirts over jewelry.

It gets quiet when our laughter dies down, and we both take turns sighing, readjusting our crossed legs and positions in the chairs. I'm not sure how this works. I'm not even entirely sure why Coach thought I needed to be here. Eventually, I just bring my gaze up to the Chaplain's waiting eyes and shrug with a tight-lipped smile.

He nods with a smirk.

"Football players aren't so great at talking about feelings," he says.

I nod and roll my eyes in agreement.

"To be honest, I'm not really sure why I'm here. I mean, I'm fine..." I glance to my side, thinking about the progress I made with Nolan, the way we talked and the honesty I shared with her. I'm lightyears ahead of my normal.

"Why don't we just talk about how things are going?" His voice is easy, and I admire his way. I'm also a little suspicious because people don't *just talk* to Chaplain Cruz.

"A'right," I say, tilting my head slightly and eyeing him.

"You have a daughter, yeah? What's her name?"

"Peyton," I answer.

He lifts his chin and smiles.

"That's right. I met her and your wife a couple years ago."

"All-Star Game, and it was four years." Four long years since I was worthy of throwing a ball with the best. That's going to change.

"How are they both?"

His question feels natural, so I relax a little more.

"They're good. I mean, Peyton's a teenager, and she is a lot like I was. She thinks she's good and meanwhile…"

"Your wife's going crazy," he fills in for me with a knowing laugh.

"Something like that, yeah," I say.

"Four daughters. My wife is the only reason they're all good adults today with jobs and lives of their own."

I must show my shock on my face.

"What…chaplains can't procreate?" His lips twist in a challenging expression. I hold up two open palms.

"I stand corrected," I say.

He leans forward enough to take out his wallet, flipping it open and pulling out a stack of five or six faded and bent photographs—the kind people don't keep in their wallets anymore. I take them from him and flip through each one, every girl in the photo about college-aged and near matches to their father. The last two photos are of babies, so I hold them up and quirk a brow.

"Grandkids. Those are Jacqueline's. She's this one," he leans forward and taps his finger on the first photo I saw. "She's our oldest, and she was a handful. Probably a lot like your Peyton is."

I smile and look back at the photos, politely sliding through them again before handing them back.

"That's a pretty family, man," I say, taking my phone out and opening my photo app to show him my favorite photo of Peyton. She's flying through the air doing the splits.

"Well ain't that something. She's good, huh?" He hands my phone back to me.

"She competes at it. I swear cheer is more competitive than football."

"Ain't that the truth. Jacqueline did it all the way through college…" He pauses a little in the middle of our connection, and his eyes dip just a hair before coming up to mine again. His head tilts, and a softness takes over his face.

"You see Trig's girls much?"

And there it is. Why I'm here.

I blink, breathing in through my nose slowly, every relaxed muscle in my body flexing at once.

"Not a lot, no. I mean…at the service, but…" My mouth starts to water, so I look to the side and stretch my jaw.

I rub my palm along my cheek then over my eyes.

"Look, I know that Coach is worried or whatever, but I'm okay. I really am."

"Good," he answers quickly, standing and brushing his hands together. "That was easy then, wasn't it?"

I give him a wry look and drag my feet in, waiting for the trick to be revealed before I stand.

"Yeah," I say slowly, meeting his eyes. He's offering me nothing but a smile, and then he reaches out his hand. I take it tentatively as I rise.

"I'm glad your ladies are doing well. I hear Nolan's in town. If I can, I'll stop by the seats and say hi," he says.

I nod.

"She'd like that."

He reaches forward and pats a heavy hand on my shoulder and looks down to my chest.

"Good," he says, patting one more time and stepping around the small table. He gets to the door before something kicks in my stomach.

"That's it?"

He holds a hand up on the door jam and turns.

"That's it. I'm just here to talk, and if you're done talking, then I'll get on and talk to the next guy. Kinda my job, which is strange… talking for a job?"

I chew at my cheek in thought.

"Yeah...strange."

He seems so satisfied, yet everything inside me is growing tighter, as if a vice is screwing my guts and diaphragm and stomach into a braid.

"I mean..." I catch him before he turns the corner. "I miss him..."

He lifts a brow, so I give into the hook.

"Trig. I miss him," I say, as he takes a few more steps closer to me. I'm not sharing anything I haven't shared with everyone. Hell, I shared this with Coach last night.

"We all do," he says, dumping his hands into his jacket pockets and shifting his feet. I'm glad he isn't settling back in. I don't need to sit. *We* don't need to sit.

"I guess I just wish maybe I could've had one more season with him, ya know? It would have been cool to go out together—I mean, I bet Coach wishes I had his hands to hit in the zone, right?" I laugh, but the chaplain only smiles. It puts me on edge, letting in a strange feeling that sort of bubbles up my chest and suddenly makes it hard to talk.

"I don't know why he quit...he still had it, you know?" My voice grows hoarse, and the sound of myself surprises me. I clear my throat, feeling the strangling sensation of wanting to cry. I tuck my tongue in my far-back molars and bite down, trying to stave off the lip quivering while I shift my feet.

"I just feel like if maybe he was still playing..."

My body jerks with an uncontrollable sob, and I fold my arms around my body. Shit. I don't want to do this, I don't want to do this, I don't want to do this...

"Maybe he would have blown out both knees, and then he never would have walked right again...or been able to travel like he did there at the end, or drive a car." Chaplain fills in the fantasy for me with his own logic, and I shake my head because no—*no*.

"He wasn't ready. This game left him behind, and we all just... we forgot him," I say, giving over as Chaplain Cruz puts his hand on my wrist and swings his other arm over my shoulder. He's my height, but outweighs me by maybe sixty pounds, which makes it easy to fall into his comfort. I tuck my head into his shoulder and shake, feeling vulnerable and embarrassed to cry.

"Fuck, man…I mean…I'm sorry, I shouldn't say that in front of you," I blubber. I laugh nervously, but cry harder.

"I've heard worse, trust me. Just say it—let it out."

Both of his hands squeeze at my shoulders and he stands facing me, trying to force my gaze up, but I can't. I stare at my feet, my shoes tapping forward one foot at a time while I rock.

"This game didn't forget him, Reed. And nobody knows what pushed him so far into sadness, so far into his habits. He had demons, and he made decisions—*his decisions* Reed."

I nod, but my head still screams *no*.

"Just like you and Trig are not the same people. You make different choices, walk on different paths. You get to choose, Reed. Only you…Trig didn't choose for you. He chose for him, and that's it."

I look up at that, our eyes connecting, and mine rejecting him suddenly. I shake my head.

"I know that," I protest, and one of his hands slides from my shoulder, but the other keeps a firm grip.

"You sure?" His eyes probe at me, and my jaw works while I consider it for real. My eyes move from focusing on his left to his right, and several seconds pass while we stay in this standoff.

"I'm sure," I say, finally. We both know I'm lying, but we both also know that for now…that's as good as my answer is going to get.

Chapter Twenty-Four

Reed

NOLAN MADE IT. Honestly, I wasn't sure she would show up. She hasn't watched one of my games in person since...well, just since. Really, it was before that, too. Mostly because she has her own things, and they can't thrive if she's locked into living for only my things. I see so many player wives here on the road, from city to city, living this life just because they're afraid if they don't, their man will step out.

A lot of the guys do. They're douchebags. And those marriages, they aren't going to make it. They probably shouldn't.

But Noles and me...we're climbing back out of this. I can feel it. I feel lighter somehow, after giving her the box and after talking to Chaplain Cruz. He wasn't all wrong. Damn, he wasn't wrong at all. I thought about it that night when I got back to the hotel, and I thought about it all morning today—through the breakfast Noles and I got up at four o'clock in the morning to enjoy because we knew the day would get swallowed up if we didn't force in some time to just be a couple. It was so normal, sitting at a table and eating eggs and reading the news on our phones.

I'm not Trig.

But that doesn't take away this itch. I don't know how to explain it to anyone, really. Football is like this piece of me. Yeah, yeah…I hear people make the identity speech all the time, and sure…it's my identity. But it's also like it's in my bones somehow. Like, if I didn't have it, I wouldn't be able to stand up and breathe.

With the crowd booing and smoke hazing the field from the pregame entertainment, I think about what Chaplain Cruz said—that last thing that really stuck with me.

"You look at the game ahead, and that's as far as you look," he said.

I'm looking at it right now, and it's looking brutal.

I'm heading into major enemy territory, with a coach who left this franchise to come to this new one. We're expected to get killed. Even the Vegas odds aren't very nice, putting them up by three touchdowns.

I better ruin a lot of gamblers' days today.

Helmet poised above my head, I follow the booming echo of the growl as our line leads us out into the stadium, a few cups getting tossed at us on our way out the tunnel. The second I break through, the boos get mixed with the sound of polite reverence. That's what they do for us old guys. We might not play for their teams, but damn is it nice to see other dudes with shot knees and torn-up shoulders still living the dream.

That's what this is, isn't it? The dream.

It's warm out tonight. That's L.A.—a late fall game in the eighties. At least it's a night game. This shit in full sun is brutal. My arm feels good. Shoulder pain is right where it should be, which…at least it's not getting worse, I muse to myself.

I hold out my fist for Waken, and he pounds back.

"Gonna get rough out there today. Be ready to stretch." I shout my words at him because it's nearly impossible to hear. That's the extra weapon in this stadium. It should work both ways, L.A. not being able to hear shit either, but somehow it only screws the away team.

I slip my helmet on, and Waken grabs it with both hands and

nods, revving himself up, bouncing on his legs and firing up his muscles as we stare at one another. He's in for it today. This defense plays dirty. They eat up fines for breakfast, lunch, and dinner. I'm gonna try to keep him out of trouble, but I'm gonna have to use him more than normal. Our rushing game is weak against this defense. Coach thinks Waken can hack it though, so I'm gonna let him do the work.

We lose the coin toss so we receive first, L.A. banking on that number-one defense to shut it down. They do. I don't know what it is out there, but it's like I'm tight and uncertain of everything. The field looks so different, and the rush is getting in my head. Three and out and I'm sitting on the bench listening to Coach Jenkins feed me more routes I'm not going to remember and plays that don't make sense. He's off with this. Something today is off.

I'm off. Fuck, I don't know. But if I don't fix it, my comeback story is going to be majorly short-lived.

"You got it?"

I meet Jenkins's eyes and nod. I have no fucking clue what he said.

"Yeah," I bark. Helmet on, I march to the water and douse my face and gulp some down.

It's too big in here to find her, but I know where she is, generally. I glance up to the booths, to the suite Jason's sitting in, and I just stare at it and breathe.

"Come on, Babe. I am nothing without you. This arm is shit without your faith in it," I mumble to myself.

"Huh?" A guy named Shiff grunts at me as he passes. He's on the line. I should probably know him better, given his job is to keep my head attached to my body.

"Just prayin' is all." I smile. He rolls his eyes.

"You better be. They're coming in hard, man. We got you, though. We got you." We pound forearms as he passes, but I laugh to myself because damn was that a contradiction. I better pray, but he's got me. *WTF?*

I think about what he said though while we let L.A. drive all the way to the twenty and kick a field goal. Three is better than seven.

If they're rushing that hard, they're light on Waken. They have no idea how fast this kid is. He had some great catches last game, but damn can he run. It's time we get him some attention.

When we go out again, I grab his facemask in the huddle and stare at him so he gets me. Coach has a list of plays, but I'm gonna skip ahead this time. Veterans can get away with this shit, right?

They're ready for the short pass. Almost everyone's ready for the short pass. But Waken ghosts our tight end and jets out another fifteen yards. I hit him mid-stride just before I land on my ass and lose my breath for a second.

"Fuck, that kid better have doubled that," I grunt.

A familiar face picks me up off the ground. Lawrence O'McCoy has been knocking me down for a decade. He's done it in six different uniforms. Class fucking asshole, he is.

"A'right, man. That's your one," I say, and he just chuckles and pats me on the back with his big-ass hand.

We move up forty yards. That's more than double. Nice work, kid.

I nod at Waken in the huddle and we break again. We're gonna run this until it doesn't work. It's the rock-paper-scissors theory—if you throw that rock enough, eventually the other guy will switch it up and you'll crush his damn scissors. They're gonna keep throwing rock. I'm gonna keep throwing paper.

I hit Waken again, with almost the exact same play; the L.A. defense starts to scramble a bit. Before they have time to think, we hurry and go no-huddle so I can hit Waken one more time, this time gaining seven.

We make it all the way to the ten before they put on the brakes with a timeout. I prepare myself for an ass-chewing on my way over to the sidelines, but all I get is three pounds before Coach holds an open palm flat out between us.

Paper.

I slap his hand, and he laughs, pounding my helmet.

We work out options on the fly, knowing that they're probably going to guard the pass in the end zone, which makes the run a lot more effective than it was before.

"You go with what you see, though, got that One-Three?"

I smirk when Jenkins calls me that. It's been a while since a coach used my number. Been a while since I was the guy they gave the orders to. It feels nice—damn nice.

"Yeah," I say, guzzling more water and heading back out to the field. I'm going to leave it all out there. One game at a time has just become one play at a time.

We line up and wait while L.A. matches us, their shift just a little different—ready. I call the count, but at the last second, I get a glimpse of something in the backfield. They're going to collapse, and it's going to collapse on our run. Waken might get free in the corner, or he might not. I'm not going to have the time to figure that out; the instant the ball is in my hands, *I run*. This wasn't on the table. Probably for good reason. It's like I'm trying to outrun an explosion in one of those action movies, the collapse coming in slow motion, my legs feeling heavier with every step. The goal line seems to be moving farther and farther away. I spin and manage to break a tackle and get a good block from the next, but there's still an unmovable force between me and the end zone. Without pause, I ready myself to push and climb. I find myself flying with the ball cradled in my suddenly puny-feeling arms. Every sound outside my head is gone, drowned by the warning bells and prayers sounding off inside me. This is stupid.

My shoulder hits the ground first, and my body rolls with it until I'm on my feet, stumbling my steps into the center of the end zone like a drunk frat boy just thrown out of a golf cart by his friends.

"Yeahhhhhhhh!" I scream so loud my voice goes hoarse. I toss the ball to the ref and slam chests with my new friend Shiff, who I'm pretty sure threw me over the rest of that pile.

My body is throbbing with energy, my arms and legs pulsing and wanting to go again. Right now. I feel it boiling in my chest, the faith that I can—*I will*—do this. And I'm not just going to do the job. I'm going to win. Everything.

———

The clock tells us that sixty minutes of football is played. The game takes three hours from first snap to final down. My dad always liked to point out that actual ball in play only happens for a total of eleven minutes, though.

Eleven.

That's a small number to have a huge impact on the outcome of sixty. I've always taken that little fact to heart, and today…*today*, I was wicked for exactly eleven minutes.

I'm sure I'll feel it all later. I know Nolan probably left, or at least retreated and didn't watch every play as it happened. I was careless. Wild abandon, I think is what the ESPN reporter said in the media room. Whatever I was, I know this—I was great.

I felt great. I feel it now.

I'm one of the last to leave the locker room. I've been waiting for Jason to do his work, to field the calls and set up the interviews that he knows I'll do. I finally get a text to meet him outside when I'm done. I pull my bag up on my shoulder and hobble into the hall-way. Nolan's waiting against the far wall, her expression one that I think she's worked on for the last hour to perfect. I see the cracks in the slight smile, the tinge of worry in her eyes. They start to slope.

"Come here," I say, dropping my bag to the ground and step-ping into her. She folds into my chest and I wrap her up in my arms. It breaks me to feel her shiver with tears.

"Shh," I hum as I kiss the top of her head. She grips my jacket and sinks into me with all of her weight. I run my hands down her back and hold her steady.

"Baby, I'm fine. It's okay," I say. She quivers again, but nods.

"I know," she sniffles.

I pull back just enough to cup her face in my hands and rest my forehead on hers. Her eyes are closed so tight. I swallow because I've never really seen how this affects her. I was so out of it in the hospital when she showed up, and through recovery I was so focused on…well…*me*.

"I'm sorry," I whisper, rocking us both side to side, alone in the cold concrete hallway in the underbelly of L.A.'s stadium.

"No…don't do that. You don't have to," she says, grabbing onto both of my wrists. She licks at her lips, eyes still closed but working to open. She blinks a few times with her stare at my chest before her eyes flit up to mine.

"Don't apologize, Reed. You are so gifted. You were amazing out there…like you always are. I just…I'm so sorry, but I can't watch."

It breaks her to say it to me.

"I know," I nod, repeating again and again. "I know, and it's okay."

I hold her, swaying like this, for several minutes until the nervous beating simmers in her chest. She grips my hand, searching for it in a panic when we turn to walk out to the lot where Jason is waiting. Her grip gets tighter with every step we take, and when I have to let go at the car she flexes her stiff fingers as we part.

Jason takes over the conversation for the car ride. He's got me doing two phone-ins, one for the ESPN radio show and another for the NFL channel. I'll pre-tape a pregame for next week's Monday night game, and that should do it. It's part of the contract, being the face of the OKC brand. Truthfully, I don't mind that part all the time. But after my injury, the questions got grating—they got personal. I just didn't like people sizing up what they thought of me and deciding for themselves if I would ever be the same on the field. That shit got in my head. I got rid of it tonight, though.

Jason leaves us at our hotel, and I half wonder if he's speeding off to hop a plane to meet Sarah or if she's here waiting for him. I could have teased him, but I wanted to get upstairs to be with Noles and make everything right for her. I need her to be right, because tonight for me was the most right I've felt in a long time. If I'm capable of more nights like this one, I just have to keep chasing them.

Chapter Twenty-Five

Nolan

REED FELL ASLEEP STROKING my hair. God was it sweet.

I know he wanted to make it through the night, but I also know how tired he was. I've been lying here folded inside his arms while I listen to the steady rhythm of his heart. His beat is so pure and perfect. It's so strong. I let it fool me into believing he really is invincible even though I know—*I've seen*—that he's not. Tonight, he was, and I can't deny that.

When Reed is at the top of his game, it's something special to get to witness. His passes cut through the air like bullets, yet somehow float down like feathers into his receivers' hands.

Trig loved his passes best. And tonight, it felt a lot like that's who Reed was throwing to. I wonder if that's who he was playing for.

His breathing starts to deepen. I roll to my side to check the clock. It's roughly two in the morning, and I know that no matter how exhausted he is now, his body will be ready to go again by six. The game did that to him—put his body on this demanding schedule.

I make my move to slip from his arms, but he starts to stir, his fingers curling around my bicep, the tips tickling against me like a feather.

"Too early," he grumbles, pulling me into him.

His body is so warm. I love the way his chest feels covered in the thin layer of jersey cotton. He smells of my favorite shampoo and expensive hotel linen; rather than leaving his warm embrace to go pace and over-think more, I turn into him and kiss the dead center of his chest.

"Sorry, did I wake you up?" I whisper.

He shifts his hands until they find my lower back. He slides them underneath my sleep shirt all the way up to my shoulder blades. His hands feel so warm and strong.

"Maybe. I was dreaming about you, though, so this is better… the real thing," he says, his gravelly voice vibrating in his chest.

I can feel him hard against my thigh, but I also know he's really only half-awake right now.

"Dreaming about me, huh?" I say, tempted to see if I can wake him completely.

"Mmmm, you were giving me a strip tease," he says, a mischievous tugging at the right side of his cheek.

"Yeah?" I lift a brow, suddenly feeling a different kind of restless.

"Uh huh." Hazed eyes sink down my body while his grin stretches. His hands slide around from my back and run up the front of my cotton shirt, his thumbs rubbing over my breasts and incredibly hard nipples.

"Was I wearing something like this?" I bite at my lip and push myself up on my palms, moving one hand to the other side of Reed's face as he rolls to his back underneath my arms. I have him caged, dragging my left leg over the center of his body so I can straddle him, setting my weight directly on his hard cock.

He nods slowly, but says the opposite.

"No, but I don't care what you wear," he growls, rolling his hips to push up against me. The feel of the pressure sending a wave of pulses up my body and through my legs.

I arch my back and look up to see how much room I have. When I'm satisfied it's enough, I carefully get to my feet while hovering above him. My fingertips can barely touch the ceiling, so I let them when I reach up to steady myself.

Fucking hell is he sexy on the bed. The cover is twisted along the side of his body, and his gray shirt is pulled up enough to show off his impressive set of hard-earned abs. It's always been the way his sweatpants hang low on his hips for me, though. That line that dives down inside his pants, the curvature of his stomach muscles and golden color of his skin.

I sway my hips slowly and drop one hand so I can bite my finger, teasingly showing the tip of my tongue. Reed's hands slide up the bottom of my legs.

"Goddamn, this is a good dream," he jokes.

"Shh, don't wake up then," I say, lifting my foot and pushing lightly into the center of his chest. He lies back, completely flat and I continue to roll my hips while my hands slowly work on lifting my night shirt up and over my body. I don't have much to work with, so within seconds I'm straddling him with nothing more than my favorite pair of lace panties. They're deceptively comfortable, and they get worn on every date we have just in case we find ourselves in a situation like this.

I lean forward and lower myself so my palms reach his chest. He grabs them before I can take them away. I follow his lead and lower myself slowly until I'm sitting on my knees again.

"I hear in the champagne room they let you touch," Reed says, sucking on one of his thumbs then the other.

"I don't know if that's all...allowed," I stutter, instantly arching toward him as his cool, wet thumbs graze the pink tips of my breasts. My thighs squeeze and I sink onto him more, needing to feel him between my legs.

"I'm pretty sure it is," he says, his voice suddenly a lot huskier.

As my skin dries, his thumbs and fingers position perfectly around my cherry red nipples until he starts to apply the sweetest amount of pressure.

"Harder," I beg, really wanting him to bite them, and hard.

He does the next best thing, pinching them tightly between his thumbs and middle fingers, allowing him to flick the tips until my hips can't help but grind down on him.

"Shit, QB one…you know what you're doing," I murmur, loving this side of him—the one that always showed up after a really good win. A dose of confidence in the testosterone cocktail does incredible things.

In a swift movement, Reed shifts himself so he's sitting, and his mouth is pressed firmly against my right breast, his teeth grazing against the hard but sensitive skin and driving my lower body to writhe against him.

"I love you so fucking much, baby," he says against my body, his tongue taking a long, sensual taste of me while his hands travel down my sides to my hips.

His thumbs hook in my panties and drag them down my thighs as I lift myself and work them off one leg at a time. I come back to him instantly, needing to ease my hunger fast. My wet center is drawn to him, and his cock sinks in as I let my weight fall onto him completely. His palms grip at my ass and pull me into him in a swift movement that drives him deep inside, and I can't help but yelp out with the relief.

"Oh God, Reed!"

"Like that, baby?" he growls, pulling me again and again as he buries his mouth into my neck, leaving hungry kisses behind in a trail that sucks every inch of my skin, from the curve of my neck below my ear all the way to the center of my chest.

"Touch me, more…everywhere," I beg, arching so he can taste me while his hands cup my ass.

I help him lift and rock me faster, chasing after that sensation that teases me deep inside at first, then spreads to every inch of my body. I can feel Reed growing more rigid, his cock flexing while it slides in and out of me. I know we're both nearly gone. With my head slung back and my hands holding onto his shoulders, nails digging into his skin, I take him as deep as I can, letting him rock his hips and pull at me violently while my breath nearly disappears.

"Like that…like that…" I become desperate, terrified of missing it—the feeling going away—but then ah…I fall into the temptation completely. My body grinds against him while he pulses inside of me, hot liquid sticky against my thighs.

"Champagne rooms are the best," he says, and I roll my hips one last time in bliss before giving into the laughter he ignites.

"God yes, they are. Where's my tip, buddy?"

Reed lifts his hand from my right ass cheek then brings it back in a heavy-handed slap that I'm sure left a print but that I wouldn't mind wearing for the day. I fall against his chest, lying there with him inside me and my clothes tossed who knows where.

It takes him minutes to fall back into his dream, and I hope it's a lot like the last one, but nowhere near as close to the reality. When I think he's deep enough into slumber, I slide my weight from him and make my way to the bathroom to freshen up. I manage to find my shirt on the floor at the foot of the bed, so I slip it back on and glance around for my panties. I give up after a few minutes, but before I slide back into the warm spot next to his barely bruised body, I pull out my box from my suitcase and sit at the small desk in the corner.

His perfect abs have a deep purple spot that I know he got from getting punched on his way into the end zone, and his throwing arm is bruised as well. Anything that he has that's a weapon is under attack—including his weaknesses. His body feels strong, though, and his head seems right. I hate that I pay attention to those things, that I question it when all I should be doing is making love to the love of my life. But Stacia always said that's when she noticed things on Trig the most, when they were being intimate. Where he was once sweet, he started to show rage. Reed doesn't ever show me anything but love. If that ever went away...

I click the pen and flip the desk lamp so I can see while I write.

YOU GIVE THE BEST HUGS IN THE WORLD. THEY'RE LIKE MEDICINE.

I fold the paper and put it in the box. Then I chew at the end of the pen while I toy with writing the next one. When my smile spreads into my cheeks, I decide that Reed should know this too.

YOU ARE A REALLY GOOD LAY.

Chapter Twenty-Six

Reed

I KNEW brutal hits would start to add up, and they have. Those first few games back felt easy, but that was also the adrenaline and dealing with defenses that didn't quite know how to handle me. I'm different from the guys running the games out there now.

Fuck, I'm old. That's what's different.

I was talking to my dad after last night's game against Dallas, and he said he had to laugh when the local sports guys started going on and on about how patient I was in the pocket.

"Patient, my ass. He's just slow!" my dad said, reenacting the whole thing for me—him pulling off a two-minute comedy set based on talking back to the evening news sports desk and making cracks about how old I am.

I laughed with him because deep down, old or not, I know he believes in me still.

"Older and smarter," I said back to him, stealing the line he always used on me.

I miss him.

I've been looking forward to this week's Arizona game for a lot of reasons, but getting to spend a little time with my dad has shot to the top of the list. I met with the chaplain a few more times, and I've gotten a little more honest about the number Trig's death did on my head. More than my mortality, I think…it got me really thinking about death in general. It got me thinking about loss—*all that I have to lose.*

My dad's survived a massive heart attack, strokes, and a car wreck that he shouldn't have walked away from. And he's stubborn as hell. I know he tries to do more when Nolan and Rose aren't there to assist him. He pushes himself; it's where I get it from. I know he sneaks things he shouldn't eat, too. What I've come to terms with is the fact that he won't be here forever, and that…*that* scares the hell out of me.

We're all so temporary. What's wrong with wanting to live forever?

I flew out early, and Noles is picking me up. No time to drive the Jeep back across the country again. I'm pretty sure I've pushed its limits with the thousands of miles I've racked up over the last month or so. It's due for a really good overhaul over the holidays anyhow… unless of course we make the playoffs.

It's all up in the air. We're five and five. It's better than one and nine, but it's not undefeated like Atlanta or nine and one like New Orleans. It's a long shot, which I used to say was right where I liked to be. Right now, though, sitting comfortably in first would be mighty nice. Sitting in third feels like…well, like sitting in third. Mediocre.

We touch ground in Phoenix just as the sun is setting, and the orange hue makes me feel warmer already. It's deep into November —close to Thanksgiving, which means my brother is running short on time to spill the beans to Dad.

The plane *dings* when we reach the gate and every person on board stands up at the same time. This is the best part about sitting in first class. I don't have to endure the wait that comes along with getting off a damn airplane. I swear, it's just grabbing a bag and walking. Why it takes so long is beyond me.

I'm through the gate first, and my strides get bigger with every step until I clear security and start scanning the seats for my girl. My eyes land on Peyton first, and it surprises me.

"Hey, Daddy!" Fifteen now, she's suddenly looking less like the little girl whose knee I had to bandage after our first outing without training wheels. That girl's still in there, but there's this other creature there, too—one that looks like maybe she doesn't need me so much anymore.

Her arms swing around my neck, and I drop my bag and wrap mine around her to turn her in a circle, planting her by the chairs right where I picked her up.

"Where's Mom?" I glance around.

"She's waiting in the car. She woke up feeling like crap," she says.

Nolan never gets sick, but when she does, it hits her like a sledgehammer. That's rotten timing.

"Well, I guess it's gonna be movie night for us then, huh?" I pick up my bag and open my arm for her to tuck herself at my side. We start walking to the elevators at the end of the concourse, and she grows fidgety and quiet.

"Uh," she starts.

I push the elevator button and look down at her.

"I kinda have a date," she eeks out, the side of her bottom lip lodged tightly between her teeth. She's nervous.

"With Bryce?" I have no idea how I remember that dick hole's name!

"Dad, don't..." she sighs, stepping into the elevator first. I drag my feet in behind her, warring with myself mentally. I'm a little pissed Nolan didn't tell me that there was still a Bryce and Peyton in existence.

"Will he be picking you up at the house?" My chest is thumping with a sense of urgency. I want to greet him, then pound him into the ground. It's not illegal to imagine it. It's a father's right.

"Ha, definitely not." Peyton folds her arms over her chest as the elevator doors close and we begin to move.

"Where are you going then?" I ask.

"I don't know yet. He didn't say?"

I shake my head with wide eyes.

"And you'll be home when?" I follow up my line of questions.

"When...the date is...done?" She glances at me sideways, and her smugness makes me laugh.

"Yeah, this isn't happening," I say, getting out of the elevator first. I find Nolan's Tahoe a few spots away, so I pick up my pace and ignore my daughter's whines behind me.

"But Mom said, but—Dad? You can't do that...and you don't know..."

I toss my bag in the back then slam the hatch closed. Peyton is still pouting at the back-passenger door when I pass her and open mine to lay eyes on Nolan.

"What's this date business?" I wave my hand toward our daughter, but when I get my eyes back on my wife, I realize exactly how out for the count she is.

"It's not a big deal, Reed. She's going to eat dinner at his mom's house...just get in the car..." She's pale, and her eyes are darker than normal.

"Babe, let me drive," I say. She gives in easily, clicking open her door and getting out. I meet her at the front of the car and walk with her back to the passenger side, helping her in and getting her buckled. She's clammy when I put my palm on her head.

"What's wrong?" I lean forward and kiss the top of her head, feeling a little guilty that I'm not kissing her lips but hell, I don't want whatever this mess is.

"I think it was Sarah's food. She made fish, and..." Her throat reacts to the word, her closed mouth puffing with air and a dry heave.

"I get the picture. Just Sarah's cooking is enough. Let's get home and sink into bed, huh?" She's already half asleep, awake barely enough to nod at me.

I point at Peyton to climb in and quit moping, then round the car to drive us home. Nolan is shivering in the seat next to me. I reach over to hold her hand, but just the act of moving seems to make her feel nauseous. My phone buzzes in my pocket, so I work it out of my jeans and hold it in my hand by the wheel to see who it is.

Jason. I let out a short puff of a laugh and answer.

"Your future wife might have killed mine with her cooking. Just thought you should know what you're getting into," I joke. Nolan winces and I mouth to her "Sorry."

"Good thing we both like eating out I guess. Hey, listen…that's why I'm calling actually," he says. "I finally told Dad the news, and needless to say—I'll be proposing this weekend."

"Let me guess—Dad wasn't crazy about you missing Thanksgiving," I say.

"Bing, bing, bing…show the man his prize," my brother says back in a wry tone.

I feel for him. Dad likes family, and he likes to be there for the important things. It makes it hard to deviate from our pop's prearranged plans.

"Maybe you can head out for the beach house after turkey?"

"It's fine. I cancelled. Besides, this ring is burning a hole in my pocket, man! I can't wait to ask her."

I smile at his excitement, because I remember what it was like for me. I was so nervous.

"So, what's the new plan then?" I glance to Nolan when I reach the parking gate.

"Ticket, babe," I whisper. She lets her arm flop toward the middle, pointing to the little cubbyhole under the stereo. I grab the parking pass and hand it to the man at the gate, working my wallet from my pocket next.

"Well, I was thinking tonight, but if Nolan's that sick…maybe tomorrow? Dad wants it to be at the house, for dinner…so he can film it, of course." I laugh at my brother.

"I'll keep you posted, but tomorrow is probably looking better." I chuckle. "And you know it makes his day to watch his son's best moments over and over again on video," I add.

"Yeah, yeah…but it's usually football highlights. I'm nervous enough as it is. Cameras make me act dumb."

"Oh, it's not the cameras, I assure you," I tease.

Jason fires back a quick "Fuck off," then hangs up.

I hand the parking attendant a twenty and wait with my palm

open for my change when I hear Nolan frantically trying to undo her seatbelt and kick open the passenger door. She gets her head out, hung over the roadway, just in time to throw up all over the ground.

"Ewwww!" Peyton screams from the back, folding her arm over her face.

"Don't be a jerk, Peyton. Your mom's sick." I scold her, but hold my own fist up to my nose because sympathy vomiting is a thing, and this entire family is susceptible to it.

"Babe, do you need to lay down in the back?" I press my palm on Nolan's back, ignoring the attendant trying to give me change and hurry me through the gate. I rub in small circles along her spine, and she shivers with my touch.

"I'm fine," Nolan manages to grumble out.

"I'm not sitting back here with her. What if she throws up on me?" Peyton says. I glare at her in the reflection of the mirror.

"Nice. Real nice, Peyt," I say.

She rolls her eyes and flops back into her seat, cupping her nose again even though she no longer has to. Nolan twists back in her seat and manages to refasten her buckle and pull the door closed. She holds the inside of her long sleeve against her bottom lip. I finally turn to grab the change from the parking lady at my window and hurry out of the way of the line of waiting cars.

"Babe, how long have you been sick? Do you think we need to stop at the hospital?" I rub my hand on her thigh gently, happy that she can stand to be touched now.

"I don't know...I woke up like this. I seemed fine yesterday. Sarah cooked, but that was it. I was mostly just tired all day." Nolan mumbles out the words, still not quite over that last stomach attack.

"You better not be pregnant." Peyton's protest cuts through the air inside the car. She's joking and being sharp-tongued, because she's mad at me for not being happy about Bryce and her date. But her idea sticks to Nolan and me; we both drag our gazes, meeting in the center and widening our eyes at the math.

The road trip...four weeks ago. The hotel, days later. This is not possible. We were done. That was all we could have because...

well…I don't know why really. I lift a brow as Nolan's sink to the center, creasing the skin above her nose.

"Fuck," she mouths.

"Oh my god, are you serious?" Peyton chimes from the back.

"Peyton, if you want to go on this *date,* then you'll cool it. Sit back so I can get us home. We'll figure out what's going on with your mom after that."

I'm lecturing my daughter, but it's also a good reminder to myself.

One play at a time. One game at a time.

One major life-altering WTF at a time.

Chapter Twenty-Seven

Reed, Fifteen Years Earlier

"REED JOHNSON, if you don't get your ass to this hospital right now, I swear to god I will gut you."

Sarah has always been good in crisis situations. That's why she was in charge of getting everything Nolan needed to the hospital when her water broke. I should have put her in charge of me. I'm a mess.

"Sar, I'm trying. This San Diego traffic is shit!"

I'm gripping my hair so tightly with a fist that I can feel the strands being yanked out. I glare at my panicked face in my rearview mirror, willing myself to get a handle on things. I can't miss this—I can't miss the birth of my daughter.

"Unfortunately, this is not one of those things that you get to call a time out for, Reed. This ball's in play with or without you."

"Football references are not cute right now, Sar," I shout, looking in both directions and spotting a garage to my right.

"I'm not trying to be cute, Reed. Your wife is losing her shit. I need backup."

"Right. Backup." I look ahead at the traffic I'm facing. I'm at least two miles away, and this road is not going to move anytime soon. I've tried to outsmart this area enough to know that none of these roads are going to help me out either. They're either going to dead-end at an ocean or back up into some crazy one-way drive filled with parallel parkers. My only shot is to run.

I hate running. This is why I throw things, dammit.

"Fuck it. I'm gonna run there." I hang up to the sound of Sarah's laughter and make a hard, fast right toward the parking garage. It's for State's campus, and it's permits only, but I'm desperate. I find an open spot at the end of the first row, and I pull in, grab the plastic bag of things I could be trusted with, and beep the locks.

I use the little bit of downhill slope on my way out to my advantage, and I'm full-on sprinting when I hit the main sidewalk along the road I just abandoned. Now that I'm out of the traffic, I get a clear view of the backup ahead, and I feel good with my decision when I see a pile of flashing lights, and a tow truck trying to work through the bumper-to-bumper line of cars.

The first mile goes down easy, but I hit my wall just after that. My feet feel a lot heavier, like my shoes are somehow suctioning to the pavement with each and every step. I get to the park and file through my mental snapshots of the route I used to take with Nolan on our walks and runs. She hasn't been running much lately, being pregnant and all, and I'm just up for any excuse to put this stuff off. I get enough work in on the field.

I duck through the small patio area where the restaurants cluster, then break it open when my feet hit the grass. The park is empty, minus a few people out walking their dogs, so at least there's nobody to get in my way to slow me down. There also aren't any witnesses to see me stop mid-sprint in the middle of the soccer field to walk a few steps with my hands on my head. I am breathing hard; I really think I might throw up. My pocket vibrates with a new text from Sarah. I kick it back in without even reading.

I can't miss this!

I slide to a stop at the glass doors of the main hospital entrance, and I luck out and find the stairs right by the reception desk. I know where I'm going...*mostly*. Noles and I took our parenting classes here and half of her appointments were here because she was so high risk.

This baby girl we're having is going to be such a miracle. She's going to be a fighter, I can tell. She's already fought through so much. One week early is a lot better than six, like they predicted.

I pop out on the maternity floor and I'm sure I sound like a grizzly bear. My chest is heaving, and I can't work my tongue to form words. I grasp a paper cup from the dispenser mounted on the wall just outside the waiting room and I fill it four times, gulping down water as fast as I can. Eventually, Sarah spots me and waves her arm emphatically.

"She's pushing!" She takes the plastic bag from me and tosses it on the chair for later, and with a quick jerk on my arm she sends me up to Nolan's face—red and sweaty, just like mine.

"Why do you look like you just ran a marathon?" Nolan huffs at me.

I give a pathetic, exhausted laugh that only lifts one side of my mouth.

"Left the Jeep on sixteenth at a garage. Traffic was shit. I wasn't missing this," I say, finding more of my smile.

Nolan's hand grips mine sweetly at first, then starts to squeeze so hard that my fingertips turn purple. She begins to yell like a warrior and sit up.

"That's it. One more like that, Nolan. You're doing great," our doctor says somewhere below Nolan's knees.

My wife collapses back on the hospital bed and pants. I find myself starting to breathe with her, and it's making my head light.

"How'd it go?" I have no idea how she's having a normal conversation right now, so I quirk a brow. "You signed. Yeah?"

I shake my head quickly.

"Oh…yeah. We can talk about that later, Noles. You're kinda busy…" I stop when her hand starts to tighten again, and I rub her back as she sits forward. Her back has been killing her, so it's the one thing I know might be helpful. She screams out and grunts for a full fifteen seconds, then sucks in a long breath as she falls back into the pillow.

I'm feeling nauseous. If I throw up, she and Sarah will never let me live it down. I reach for the cup of ice on the table and pour a few pieces into my mouth. Sarah jerks the cup away from me and glares into my eyes.

"That's her ice, you ass," she says.

I lift a shoulder.

"Sorry," I mumble.

Nolan jerks on my hand to get my attention.

"How did it go?" She's right back into our previous conversation. It's weird. Her focus is crazy.

"Oh, uh…fine. We got exactly what we wanted. Three years, forty-two." I feel weird talking about this in a room full of other people, but nobody else seems to care.

"Three years. Here, in the same place," Nolan says, her hand softening for just a moment. A smile starts to dust her lips. More than anything, Nolan wanted us to find a steady place to start our family.

I smile back and lean forward to kiss her head.

"Three years, same place," I say, readying myself for the next push I know is coming.

"Come on, girly. This is the one. I know it," Sarah coaches from the other side. Nolan's mom wanted to be here for this, but Peyton is showing up ten days early, three days before they booked their flights. I got Jason to get their flights changed the second Nolan called me and said it was time. They should be here tonight.

Nolan growls on this push, and her entire face, neck, and chest go beet red. I step closer to the doctor on a hunch, and I look just in time to see our baby girl's head, then shoulders and body slip out for the world to welcome.

"Oh God, thank you God," Nolan pants. I start to laugh, a little hysterically, and tears pool in my eyes at a rapid pace, sliding down my cheeks as my laughter picks up even more.

"You did great, babe. She's amazing. So great," I say just before kissing Nolan's head. I brush her hair back from her face while the doctor works to clean up our baby and make sure everything is as it should be. A sharp cry pierces the air, and Nolan's breath hitches.

"That's her?" She looks at me and grabs my arm.

I nod.

"That's her," I smile.

"Mom? Someone wants to meet you," the doctor says, bringing a perfect tiny human that is somehow ours to Nolan's chest. We're both a mess of tears, and someone hands me a pair of odd scissors and holds my hand through cutting the cord. I don't know how clearly I'll remember everything that happened in the last two minutes, but I'll remember this right here.

Two loves of my life, breathing, cooing, looking around wildly and not sure how they got here. I'm not sure how I got to be theirs, how I got so lucky.

"Peyton, meet your daddy," Nolan says through half laughter and half tears.

"Hey, baby girl. You ready to run my world?" I whisper, kissing her damp but perfect head. I kiss Nolan's next and slide into the small space on the bed to be with them.

That's all I need in this world. To be with them.

Chapter Twenty-Eight

Nolan

I ALWAYS HATED those rides at the fair that spun me around and made my world crooked. I've somehow found myself on one now, though. Not a *real* one, but also not one I can get off. My world is tilted.

"Congratulations. You're pregnant."

Reed and I sat, dumbfounded, in the doctor's office for what felt like an hour. It must have been less, but I swear time has slowed down completely.

Pregnant. I'm coming up on forty. My daughter is fifteen. I wasn't supposed to be able to do this.

Reed drove us home, and we've been sitting in the driveway filled with cars. We dropped Peyton off and got in at our doctor right away, mostly because Reed can call in favors. While we were here, everyone else was arriving at our house for dinner—for the big engagement surprise. I was so excited for this about three hours ago. Now, I have no idea what anything is or feels like or means.

"It was probably that night in the Jeep," Reed says, and I

swallow and let my eyes flit closed. Thank God I'm done throwing up.

"What are we going to do?" I ask the question we've both been thinking.

We both just breathe. The longer the silence goes, the more scared I become. There was a time when I would have cried with glee at this news. It's happy news. It should be, at least. No…no, it is. It's just…*unexpected*. It's scary. It's…

"When Peyton's a sophomore in college, this baby will be starting kindergarten." Reed rattles that off like a simple fact, emotionless. We both think about it for a few seconds and simultaneously burst into laughter.

"That's ridiculous," I say, tears of madness filling my eyes. I'm hysterical. I wipe them away but keep laughing, unable to stop. Reed joins me for the first minute, but while I continue to titter and feel sick, his face grows serious. His smile settles into a barely there kind and his eyes study me without blinking.

He shifts his weight and leans over the center console, moving his left hand to the side of my face, sweeping it into my hair as he moves in to brush his lips on mine.

"It's going to be okay," he says against me. I quiver with hope and hopelessness, then let out another small laugh.

"You can't say that," I say, pulling back but holding onto his wrist. His eyes dip as he shifts his palm to my chin, forcing our gazes to connect.

"I can, because it will, Noles."

I stare at him long and hard, waiting to see the crack in his resolve. It isn't there, but it's because he's not thinking about this through my eyes. It's not his fault. I don't let him see things that way sometimes. But this…it's too big. I'm carrying so much.

"You'll be starting camp for…who knows where…about the time this baby is born. You'll be deep into a season when we're working on crawling here.

"So, I'll come home more." He wavers a little, starting to understand. "Or maybe I'll land Arizona…or we can split our time."

"And let Jason and Sarah move in here to take care of your dad?

And I'll just cancel my clients for four months out of the year. And we'll hire more people to tend to the horses. And Peyton…she'll figure out how to manage herself when we're gone so she doesn't have to change schools or take high school online. She won't miss cheer…"

"Okay, okay. I get it. But we always figure it out, Noles. You're just looking at the bad…"

"I figure it out," I interrupt. It stuns him and there's a flash of defensiveness in his eyes, but then it fades with understanding. He sinks back into his seat, still facing me, while I stare through the window behind him.

"I'm not looking at the bad, Reed. I'm just looking at the parts of life. I'm looking at reality. This is going to be hard—*on me*. And I've got to come to terms with that in my head, because I want this baby, Reed. I've wanted this baby for a long time, and you know that."

I move my eyes to his in time to see them become glossy. He flits his gaze to me but looks back out the front window with a hard breath. I've started to cry, and I'm so mad that our house is full of people right now. I—*we*—can't leave this damn car until we get our shit together. This kind of news needs to be shared just right. The questions all need answers. And then there's the certain bit about certainty—me and pregnancy has always been so uncertain.

"I'll retire," Reed says, his voice soft.

"Don't make that choice right now," I answer before he can say more.

"Noles, you can't do this alone…" he says, finally turning to me and reaching for my hand. I give my palm to him and watch the way our fingers blend together perfectly and move, caressing—loving. I love this man with every bit of my soul.

"I *can* do it alone, Reed. You forget that I have," I say, feeling his muscles flex as he winces. "I didn't mean it like that. I'm sorry."

"No, I know what you meant." He twists again, this time pulling my hand into both of his, bringing it to his mouth and pressing a soft kiss against my knuckles.

I feel him swallow.

"You're an amazing woman, Noles. An amazing mother... wife..." His eyes close and he brings our tethered hands up to the bridge of his nose, resting his head against them and closing his eyes.

"You cannot make a decision about football because of this baby," I say. I feel him nod slightly against our hands.

"I know," he says, his voice hoarse.

"It's not fair to him or her. This baby cannot be the reason that you stepped away, because there will always be the ghost of resentment. You won't want to, but it will linger there. You know it...I know it..."

"You're right," he says.

He breathes in deeply and kisses my hand again, turning my wrist to his mouth and holding his lips there long enough to feel my pulse.

I reach up with my other hand and thread my fingers into his hair, bringing his head to my lips to kiss.

"You're an amazing man...an amazing father, and son, and husband," I say. I mean every word. I also mean this.

"And you're a great quarterback, Reed. Maybe one of the best. I love you, and whatever decision you come to...none of any of this —of *us*—will change." I make a promise that will feel impossible in nine months. I make a promise that we've already broken, two years of a strained marriage have been so hard. We've changed from that alone. But I know that through it all, we won't quit on each other. We can't. I won't let us.

———

After another twenty minutes in the car and two texts from Jason asking when the hell we're coming inside, we finally look normal enough to walk in and make jokes with our family as if earth-shattering news isn't breaking in my womb.

I'm glad I know what's about to happen, because it makes watching Jason nervously twitch around the kitchen so much fun to watch. He's sweating, and I feel so bad for him that I have to tell him that his shirt is starting to get damp. He's still wearing his dress clothes, and I'm sure it's because he wants to look his nicest for the proposal, but another minute in that button-down and tie, and he's going to look like he's been on a safari.

I step up to Buck, knowing he's the reason we're doing this here and not on Thanksgiving on the beach.

"Your son is not gonna make this. I think you need to intervene," I say against his ear.

He chuckles and turns to me, giving me a wink. I should have known, he was going to run this show his way all along.

A few seconds pass and Rose starts to clank a spoon against her wine glass. I look to Reed to do the same, panicking because no more wine for me—*bloody hell!* He takes a quick spoon to his beer bottle, which only makes it foam. The sight of him licking up the side and trying to contain the overflow amuses me and settles the massive, mega butterflies trying to break free in my chest. I breathe, and just as quickly, they're back.

"You all know...how I like to talk...some say a lot," Buck begins. It's the usual crowd gathered—Jason and Sarah, Reed and I, Peyton and a few of her friends—who I am sure she told. No Bryce, though; Bryce will have to wait.

What Sarah doesn't know, though, is that Reed's aunt and uncle are here along with Sarah's parents and her sister, in the garage. They've been stashed in there for probably an hour. We saw their cars parked a property over, behind the construction trailers that have taken up the edge of our residence.

"I'm not going to talk..." Buck pauses because he has to, but the timing makes us all giggle. "Much...ah you thought...you were off the hook!"

"Not a chance," Rose says, taking an early sip from her glass and rolling her eyes to exaggerate.

"Wow, tough...room," Buck says, good at taking her teasing. She squeezes at his shoulder with adoration in her eyes. This will be Reed and me one day. I hope.

"I just want to say...how proud I am of my...boys. Reed... Jason...I love you. You are my life's...best achievement. I had very…little to do…with how great you turned out…too…ha!" His belly laugh is still the same, a punch at the end of a very sweet joke. He had more to do with the men those boys became than he knows. Hell, he's had a hand on the person most of us became.

"Reed…what you've done…in life…and on that field. It gives me such joy, son. Watching you play…live your dream. It's…it's everything," Buck says, a little choked up by the end.

This night isn't about Reed. It's about Jason. But Buck always talks about them both when they're together. And he probably doesn't want to tip Sarah off to what's coming. But he has no idea how deep he's dug with those words just now. I see it in the tight smile Reed offers with the slight lift of his hand. He's showing modesty on the outside, but inside he's living tug-of-war. Buck just voiced one more thing that makes it hard for Reed to walk away.

The more time that passes with our new reality settling into my chest, my heart and mind, the more I think there's no easy way through the near future. It's going to hurt, and it's going to test us —*test me.*

I wish I could have a glass of wine right about now.

Buck's been talking up Jason for the last few minutes. I've been zoned out, noticing the details in every flick of Reed's eyes, every bend of his lips and twitch in his cheeks. He's not taking any of this night in like a brother. He's in his own head, thinking about us. I step closer to him when Jason begins speaking, and without looking my fingers brush his until his hand grabs a hold of mine tight.

"Sarah Perez, as my father and brother would say, you've knocked me on my ass…" Jason pauses just long enough for Sarah to understand what's happening. My friend covers her mouth and looks around the room, crying hard when she sees her sister Calley and her parents now standing in the corner behind her. Her wide eyes swing to mine next, and I smile as she shakes her head in disbelief.

Jason pulls the ring from his back pocket and gets down on one knee, which only makes my best friend shake more.

I can't believe I was ever against this happening. Seeing it here now, how he's asking, the words he's saying about her, and more than anything, how happy my friend is—this was meant to be. I'm sad it took so long.

"I love you so much that I'm willing to be whatever man it takes to be worthy of being yours. I'm done hiding how I feel—how I know we both feel. I want the world to see me kiss you and take your breath away. I want to know my home will be wherever you are. I want to have kids, and build a family, and learn how to make that amazing soup you make, and to worship you and brag about you to every single person I meet. Sarah Perez, I want you to be a Johnson. I want you to take me as your husband because breathing without you is hard...and it's quickly becoming impossible."

My eyes are tearing as I watch this guy—who I have seen fail and make an ass out of himself so often—bare himself raw for a woman I know is the best one there is left on the planet.

Jason's hand trembles as he holds the ring forward and leans his face toward his bicep, running his sleeve along his damp eyes.

"Will you marry me?"

She answers in an instant, her voice gone and unable to make a sound but her emphatic head nod leaving nothing to question. In a blink, she's being swung in Jason's arms, clawing her legs around his waist while he kisses her like the princess she is. He slides the ring on her finger while their lips dust one another's with words and kisses.

That's love, the realest kind.

I squeeze my hand to feel Reed, to know he's there. We have that. I know we do. I trust it more than I trust anything, and when the night is done, I'll put that in the box about him, too.

Chapter Twenty-Nine

Reed

SIX WEEKS.

That's what we said was the magic number.

I marked it off on the calendar a week ago, and I know Nolan's keeping better track than I am. That six-week date came and went, and for whatever reason, I'm too chicken to ask her if she's ready to tell everyone. Maybe I'm not ready to tell everyone.

I don't know what I am.

"You ready?" Jason asks. I hold up two fingers while I walk back into my bedroom to find my phone. I left it charging because I'm obsessed with hearing from Nolan lately. I need to know she's okay. I worry about her and the baby constantly. It's literally wrapped up every synapse in my brain.

It's the last game of the year. It's Baltimore, and they're vicious. Neither of us has anything to play for or anything to lose. Our playoff hopes are gone, but barely. We were in it until the very end. Well, almost the very end. Last week the wrong teams won, making our six-game streak meaningless for the team. It means a lot for me, though.

The interviews have all been the same.

"Where are you finding this renewed energy?"

"How do you think you've been able to step into a role you've been away from for two years?"

"Why do you think the players respond to you?"

My answers are so memorized, I'm not sure they're real anymore.

"I've always had the energy, but just not the opportunity. It's what I've worked hard my whole life to be able to do—to lead a team. I'm honored to lead this one."

And… "I just love the game. I think I've been lucky enough to find other players who love the game, too. We've been able to bond quickly here in OKC. There's a real passion for what we do out on that field, and I think it's less about me leading and more about what we do together as a unit, you know?"

I guess that last part is true. I've grown close to Waken. He's going to be a Hall of Famer one day. He's the Jerry Rice of now. I can see it in how fast he grows, how quickly he learns. He's a different player by the end of every game. It's a beautiful thing for a quarterback to find hands like his. He's football purity—through and through.

I flop on my bed and reach over to the night table, my room still sparse of anything but the basics. I flip over my phone and wish for there to be a message from her. When there isn't one, I send her a quick note.

Feeling ok?

She hates the doting. I don't just sense it; she told me last night that she hates the doting. It makes her think about how she should be nervous, which only makes her nervous. But if I don't ask, it builds up in my head to the very worst.

When she doesn't write back right away, I shout out to Jason.

"Got it, be right there," I say, pausing for a few more seconds, considering calling her.

I give up after a few more seconds and follow my brother out the door.

"Chicago wants to talk," he says.

I bite my lip, mentally adding that to the sick game of Jenga indecision happening in my gut.

"That's good, right?" Jason leans into me a little at the elevator bay.

"Oh, yeah…no…it is. I was just thinking about all of it. Hey… you hear from Noles today?" I'm not even hiding my preoccupation.

Jason rubs his palm over his face and sighs.

"I'll ask Sar. I'm sure she's fine. Dude, you need to tell me what you wanna do. How do you want to handle this? Because I've got interest, Reed. I've got a lot of interest. It won't be here, unfortunately. And Arizona's tied up. But you've got a two, maybe a three-year deal in the blueprint if you want it. A good deal, too. Like…*ca-ching*!"

Jason rubs his thumb to his fingers and I smirk.

"What if I'm a fluke?" I shift my eyes over to him in the elevator.

"Fuck that. You're a Johnson." He lets out a laugh and goes back to looking at something on his phone. He's not just filling my head; that's what Jason truly believes. I think half of me believes that, too. The other half is thinking about having another baby, and missing more of the other half of my life.

Jason's smiling with tight lips, so I lean to my side to get a glimpse of his phone. I see Sarah's name, but that's all I get before he jerks his phone away and tells me to get the fuck out of his business. I hold up my palms and laugh. He's smitten, and it's so cool to see it from this perspective.

I was smitten once too. Now I'm just terrified.

What if I'm messing all of this up?

I flip my phone in my palm all the way to the stadium. Jason set up a service to clear out my condo for me after the game, and I'm showering and heading right to the airport to go home—my real home. The home I'm dying to hear from.

Jason drops me at the back entrance for the players and drives on to the executive lot. He said he has to take a few calls but I think maybe he's just taking one—and I think it will probably be a Face-Time with Sarah.

The underbelly of the stadium is cold and empty. Almost everyone's already arrived and either getting work or being taped together so they can get in one last game, a final performance for the next year's paycheck. This part of the season is always hard. You're always playing for something. And if you're not playing for a title or a spot, then you're playing for yourself. Team goes to shit on nights like this, and this is when that leadership job becomes real damn essential. I better get my head in the right place.

I notice Coach Simms sitting in the boardroom on my way to the locker room, so I pause. He's in the dark, only lit by the fluorescents of the hallway.

"This a new interrogation tactic you're testing out? I gotta tell you, I think the dark is just gonna put them to sleep," I say, taking a chair next to him and rolling it out so I can extend my legs. I'm due for the trainer soon, my turn to get taped back together.

"Ha, you're funny, Johnson," he says, tilting his head back with a hard laugh and turning his chair a little to face me more. He leaves his gaze up at the ceiling and stretches his hands behind his head, interlocking them.

"I was just thinking about how it's been a good run."

I let his words sit with me for a few beats. I know the deal he was given. They want him back here in OKC, and it's a pretty penny— two years, twelve mil. That's almost New England money.

"Good run, huh?" I bait him.

He swivels a little in the chair, then levels me with his eyes.

"Yep, I'm done. Money's nice and all, and the job is the best there is, but I'm tired Reed. I've got things to do, other things to get to, ya know?"

I smirk and nod slowly.

"I know a thing or two about that," I say.

Our eyes rest on each other for a long pause, and eventually his hands let go of their grip on one another and he leans forward to rest an elbow on the shiny, glass table. My contract was signed in this room. I remember how uneasy I felt in my own skin. I feel at home right now, and I wonder if that's because there's nothing at risk. There's nothing to lose here now.

"I hear Chicago's interested. Baylor's a good coach. You'd work well together," he says, clearing his voice with a hard cough.

I nod.

"That's what my agent says."

He chuckles.

"Ain't that your brother?"

I laugh a little in response.

"Yeah, it is." Coach's laugh breaks for just a breath then starts in again, and I join him.

"He's actually good at the job" I sigh, the itch of laughter leaving my chest. Silence settles into the room, and I get the sense that Coach Simms is content just letting it be there. He's at peace with it all, even the outcome of today.

"You wanna win?" I ask, lifting a brow.

He mimics me.

"Reed, son. I always wanna win. Even when I don't really give two shits."

I lift my chin and smile to the ceiling.

"Ahh, yeah. I think maybe I like how you roll," I respond.

"It's gotten me through a lot of tough decisions," he says.

"What has?" I ask.

"My gut. Gut instincts, really. My gut's just fat as hell, ha!" I glance at the bulging belly for a second and smile.

"Your gut, huh?"

"Yep." His answer is concise.

I flit my eyes up to his, and he leans back, this time folding his hands together on his belly before crossing one leg over his knee.

"When you need to make the choice, Reed. You'll know. It will hit you like a fucking Mack truck. I promise." He holds my gaze at that, and I take it all in. He must sense my struggle. I must be wearing it more than I thought I was.

I reach to the center of the table and snag a piece of chocolate from the bowl that's always full. They're probably old as shit, but I want one. I stand and hold it up to him between my finger and thumb.

"Gut says I want this," I say.

He lifts one side of his mouth.

"Well then, best give it what it wants."

He winks at me and leans back a little more, diving back into his blissful bubble.

I knock on the door as I leave and walk slowly down the hall, picking at the tinfoil wrap around the chocolate. I pop it in my mouth and am instantly disappointed. So much for my goddamned gut. I spit it out in the trash by the locker-room door.

My phone doesn't leave my palm the entire time I'm with the trainer, propped on my thigh while they work my shoulder with deep massage, and then right back in my hand when my ankles get taped. I'm sure everything's fine, but I just wish she would tell me something.

Eventually, I have to give in and put my phone away to head out to the field. The unsettled feeling grows with the clock's countdown. By the time I'm lined up for the anthem, my feet can't stay still. I'm like a kid who has to pee at a wedding. I'm on edge.

The feeling sticks with me out on the field, and I start with a dismal three and out. Six wins in a row will buy me a little forgiveness, but this crowd will start to boo if I go out there and do that shit again. I wish there was some way I could just know. I need to know she's okay, that my family is okay. I start to pace the sidelines, stopping when others start to notice, but starting again the second they look away.

I bet the color commentary guys are loving this. Shit…I bet Dad's seeing this. I take a seat and stuff my hands into the pockets of my jacket. I've never felt the cold before, but for some reason, tonight it freezes me to the bone.

"Come on, Reed. Out of your head." Jenkins slaps the top of my helmet as he walks by, my cue to follow him. I try to shake off the strange sensation eating at me and join him to watch tape of my pathetic first set of downs.

"You're sinking into the pocket. Look…there." He pauses the video on the iPad and zooms in, pointing out shit I already know.

"Yeah, yeah," I say, which irritates him and he steps more directly in front of me, between my body and the field.

"Yeah," he says again, firmer this time.

My eyes lift enough to see how serious his are and I crack my neck to one side and blink as I lower my gaze.

"Sorry, I've got some personal things. You're right. Off the field. I'm focused." I almost believe my promise to him.

"Good, now the pocket…you have too much faith in our offensive line. I don't want to get you killed. So how about we start pivoting out, moving those legs a little," he says, face tilted and brow raised.

"Got it. Lemme watch again."

I didn't really watch the first time. This round, I focus, and I see just how slow I am. It's like I'm carrying elephants around the field, and I hold onto them all the way to my knees until I'm under the two-hundred-forty pounds of flesh that wrapped me up twice in a row last time out.

Our defense recovers a fumble and I get my redemption, this time heading out with nothing but my dad in my thoughts. He never misses a game. He's watching, and if this is it—if this is the last time I decide to take the field—then it's going to be damn near perfect from here out.

My time in the pocket only gets shorter. Jenkins was right. After a thrown-away pass for the first down, I roll out for the second and spot Waken about twenty yards out, a foot away from his defender. My window is shrinking; number sixty-six is coming at me with wide-open, angry arms. The next half-second feels like it takes thirty. My eyes look for any other option but going down. All I need is to buy Waken a few…more…steps…

My body going down, he turns just enough that I get a view, and I throw the ball like a third baseman from my knees, whipping it with my elbow as hard as I can and somehow cutting through two defenders reaching in to intercept it. I don't know if it got caught at all. I know my arm hurts like hell, and I know that sixty-six is heavy as fuck. He pushes my shoulder into the turf hard as he stands, offering his palm to help me up as if that makes it okay. I take it, because I need it; I jump to my feet just in time to see Waken breaking the last ten yards free and into the End Zone.

My body feels an instant injection of victory, however brief, and nothing hurts anymore. Nothing feels impossible, and my problems stay over there, to the side, for the next forty minutes.

There's no reason for my eyes to focus on the man in the suit. Well-dressed business types float around the space behind the side-lines all the time. The list of VIPs who bought the right to walk almost wherever the hell they want is long. But this guy—he looks different. He's here for a reason. He's looking for someone.

I start to stand before I see the Chaplain walk toward the man. My chest empties, and my heart stops. My stomach drops to my feet, and I'm frozen where I stand, somewhere between ready to go in, and ready to collapse.

Coach Jenkins gets waved over; my feet start to dig more into the ground. Suddenly staying right here, in ignorance, feels like the best option. It's not a practical one, though, and their faces all turn to me in slow motion.

It feels like I've been shot—the pinpoint sharpness hitting my chest, knocking the wind from me again. My knees buckle and I lose my balance for a moment, catching myself with a flat palm on the metal bench.

They're eyes are full of warning and all of that junk that comes along with not wanting to give someone bad news. Jenkins starts to jog toward me. I shake my head in response, as if I can somehow request that we just don't do this.

"Just tell me." I must look rabid, because my quarterback coach has gone ghost white; he's looking over his shoulder for backup.

"You need to talk with Greg real quick…" He's bad at this. He doesn't even know how to deliver bad news on his own.

"Jenk, just tell me. Is Nolan all right?"

"What? Nolan? No…oh, no Reed. She's fine, she's totally fine. I mean, as far as I know. This is about Jason—" He shakes his head, wanting to take it back the instant my brother's name falls from his lips.

My head turns a thousand directions. There are seconds left in the half…there's a whole other half. I can't though; I can't. Why would they talk to me now if it weren't terrible? They always wait for the end of the game for news like this. The team always wants their commodity sharp—why would they make me dull?

"Reed, let's head in…let me get you inside…" Jenkins urges me to follow along behind him, and my head plays the running commentary.

Johnson's leaving the field. I wonder if time's finally catching up to him. That arm only has so many throws left in it. And some of those hits he's taken today—a man who's been through what he's been through can only be sacked so many times before he breaks. I wonder if that's what we're seeing here?

I guess we'll know if we see him at the second half or if they go with third-stringer Jackson Barrett. Good enough time as any to break in the youth.

I make it three steps into the locker room before I insist I get all of the details.

"What the hell's going on? Does Coach know you pulled me?"

Jenkins's hands are on my biceps, almost like he's holding me back from a fight. His eyes are searching mine, trying to lock on.

"Gary's telling him now. Reed, listen. I need you to listen."

I can hear my own breath flaring my nostrils, coming out in angry, panicked streams. My cheeks puff out a few times and I feel dizzy. I turn to the bench near us and move to sit, holding my knees with a tight grip and staring at the giant *O* pattern on the carpet.

"Reed, Jason suffered a major heart attack. Someone found him beside his car in the parking lot…" More words leave his mouth. I don't hear them. I'm instantly sixteen, waking up in the back of Nolan's car with my world rocked.

———

Reed, seventeen years old

My head is pounding. My mouth is dry. I think maybe at some point I threw up, though I don't remember doing that. I remember Nolan.

Shit. Nolan!

I crack a lid and slide my hand along the velvety cushion that feels only faintly familiar. There's a beam of sun filtering in through something in front of me. I let my hand explore while I try to force my left eye to open completely. Shapes start to make sense, a car seat head rest—the sunlight glinting off the chrome in-between. Damn, that's bright!

"Ugh," I growl into what I have figured out to be a backseat. I pull both of my arms into my body, pressing my palms flat under my face and pushing up until I can sit. That small movement feels like death.

I drank last night. I drank a lot. And Nolan…shit…this is her car.

She came.

Did I call her? I think I called her.

I was so jealous last night…*angry*. I still am. That's the only feeling I'm sure of right now. I hate the thought of Nolan being into anyone else. I hate this Tyler guy she's dating. He's not right for her, which…gah! Like I am. Look at me. I woke up in the back of her car, and I'm hungover.

Why would she deal with me like this? I must have said something awful to get her to come to the party. I bet I was an ass.

I push my fists into my temples and smack my lips, both wanting and never wanting water. I raise myself enough to catch my wild hair in the reflection of the rearview mirror. My eyes refocus on the hospital outside the window. I blink a few times, willing my memory to replay anything that might give me a clue.

EMERGENCY ROOM

I swallow, splices flashing in my mind. I remember the stairs. I remember Nolan being there. I…I told her I loved her. And then my dad.

"Dad!" I feel a jolt to my heart, my limbs suddenly getting enough life to pull myself from the car—Nolan's car. I find a sweatshirt on the floor before I shut the door, so I slip it over my head and attempt to hide the wrinkled clothes underneath while I untangle my hair with my fingers.

Nolan drove me here. She took care of my dad. I'm at the hospital…where he is.

I shuffle my feet forward and through the sliding doors at the front entrance and look for my next clue—something familiar. Her brown eyes are all I need, and they're waiting for me.

She's sitting next to her parents. I tilt my head trying to piece together how they're all here and I'm not. She untangles her legs and jogs over to me, reaching for my hands. The way they look together is so familiar and right, and it's so scary. She's holding my hands with love and sympathy. I feel her nerves in her touch.

I can't quit staring at them, but my confusion craves more—I need to know. My mouth open, a question hanging on my lips without the right words to frame it, I look up and meet her waiting eyes.

"Reed, listen to me. Your dad had a heart attack last night. They are performing surgery, but we should hear something very soon."

She stops there, waiting for me to digest and not knowing that my insides are literally tumbling in on themselves. My dad is everything!

My eyes start to sting and that brief feeling hits my chest, telling me I should push back, keep myself from crumbling, but her hands are on mine, and she's here—and she took care of my dad. She's taking care of me. She brought me here. My world is in that room —under a knife.

I step into her, and she knows I need her. Her arms wrap me up and her hands hold my head tightly against her shoulder. I hide myself under the shadow of her long hair and I cry so hard I think I may frighten people coming in. I can't stop, though. I have never hurt like this. I feel like a failure. I wasn't there. I was fucking drunk.

She took care of me. Of him.

I love her...so, so much.

Her hand moves along my back and I try to right my breathing with her touch, but I keep slipping back into a wrecked version of myself.

"He's going to be okay, Reed. I called nine-one-one. They came in time. He's going to be okay," she says.

"Reed, son. Come sit with us. We should hear something soon." I recognize her dad's voice, but I'm too ashamed to look at him.

Her hand finds mine as she slips from my arms, and her fingers wrap mine up as she leads me to the chairs where her parents are. She moves a few seats down to a couch that looks cold and lonely, almost a hard-plastic material that's a blue from the seventies. This is the kind of place where people get horrible news. It's all I can think until she pulls my body toward hers and gathers me up in her arms. I fall into her lap and let her soothe me. I need it, and she knows I do. She knows me—all of me. She knows my worst, and she's seeing my worst fear.

My dad might die. He's all I have.

Him, and this girl who I don't deserve.

This girl who is taking care of me.

———

Present Day

"Heart problems run in the family," I say, slipping back into the conversation. I must have missed a question or not have said the right thing because Jenkins is looking at me oddly. Chaplain Cruz is here now, and I realize he was speaking and I interrupted him.

"I'm sorry. That thought just flew into my head. I…I'm sorry. I don't know what to do," I ramble.

"It's okay, Reed. Who can I call for you? Brad from the front office has a car ready. He'll take you to Samaritan, where Jason is. It's important that you take this one step at a time…"

One play at a time.

I close my eyes as those two thoughts intertwine. Funny how that rule runs my life.

"Right, well…he has a fiancé. I should call her, though. My dad will want to know. And Nolan. I just…I don't know what to do."

"Call your wife," Chaplain Cruz interrupts. My eyes flash to his, and his are so certain that I finally get a full breath.

"Call your wife, Reed. Always call your wife," he smiles.

I pull my lips in tight and take my bag of things that Jenkins has pulled together for me. I fish inside for my phone, my fingers fumbling it before I can get a look at my screen where I see three missed messages from Nolan.

She wrote me back. She's okay.

A tear starts to slide down my cheek, and another one follows so fast I can't stop them. I lean forward and cover my face, feeling the force of my emotions in one heavy rush.

"I'm sorry. I need a minute," I say, shuddering with sobs and an overwhelmed feeling that has me grounded and unable to move. "I'm so sorry."

"It's all right, Reed," Chaplain Cruz says, sitting next to me and putting his arm around my body, holding me close to keep me present. I want to drift away, but I can't. I have to call my wife. I have to call Jason's fiancé. I have to find my brother. I have to pray.

I let it all out hard for about five minutes, and like a performer, I suck it in and run my arm over my eyes a few times trying to erase the evidence that I felt something so awful. I can't completely, and when guys start to come in and get immediately directed away from me, I feel the weight of it all starting to crush me again.

My thumb dials feverishly as the chaplain escorts me to Coach's office, and he closes the door as soon as we get inside. I pace, ignoring his request for me to sit. I walk from one corner to the other, counting the rings until Nolan picks up, her voice confused because I'm sure the game is on there. This is going to freak her out, and I can't have that.

"Reed?"

"I'm fine. It's okay, Noles. I'm fine." I hammer her with those thoughts, but I'm so manic that the effect is the opposite.

"What's wrong?" There are hints of hysteria in her tone.

"Noles, it's Jason. He...he had a massive heart attack. I'm going there now. It's fine...he'll be fine. I have to tell Dad. And I need to tell Sarah, but it's fine. He'll be fine..."

I'm not making sense, but Nolan gets the message, and then she takes over the ship.

"Reed, Reed...listen to me..."

I breathe out hard and lean into the wall, resting my forehead on the cool plaster while I look down at my feet. I want to kick a hole through this wall.

"Yeah…" I exhale.

"I'll tell everyone. It's going to be fine. Call me when you get there, and I'll keep everyone here informed. Sarah's here, Reed. I'll take care of it all. Just…is someone with you?"

I shudder with a cry again, but my eyes are just raw and dry.

"Yeah, Jenk is here. And the chaplain. A guy from the front office is driving me. I'm good, I'm good."

I'm nowhere near good. She knows. As if she's trying to force me to follow her, she takes in a long deep breath. I can't help but do the same, and my dizziness lifts just enough to turn to look at the coaches all now standing in my office with sympathy and genuine worry etched into their frowns and sagging eyes.

"Okay, you need to call me when you get there. Every time you find out more. Every time you just need to call me. I'm plugged in, and I'm not leaving this phone. I got you, baby. I got you…"

My eyes flutter closed and I pinch at the bridge of my nose.

"Right. Okay. I'm going."

"I love you, Reed."

I vibrate at her words, a deep tickle at my chest.

"God, I love you, baby."

I end the call after a few seconds because if I don't we'll just stand here listening to our quiet lines. She would never hang up first —not now.

"I'm ready," I lie, meeting Coach Timms's eyes. He nods once, and the sourness only gets deeper as I get closer. His hand grabs mine before I can get through the door. I pause my steps just long enough to squeeze him back so hard that my knuckles turn red.

One play at a time.

Chapter Thirty

Nolan

I'M NOT SHOWING YET. My jeans will barely zip, but that's what hair ties are for, right? I need bigger hair ties because I'm gonna need to stretch this button a lot more pretty soon.

The trip here was brutal. Everyone had to come. Buck was coming no matter what, which I expected, and Sarah had to be here. I guess I could have stayed home, but I wanted to be here for Reed. And Peyton and Rose didn't want to be left behind, plus I really needed Rose's help with Buck. Why is it that a family emergency turns into a vacation?

I'm not sure this is what Reed expected, but it's what Buck insisted on—a family invasion.

It's just after midnight, and my feet are killing me. I drove the rental van all the way to the hospital, and there were times I only could keep one eye open. It's a miracle I didn't turn all of us into emergency-room patients by driving off the road.

Reed's waiting for us at the entrance as I pull up. He comes to my door, opening it and burying his head in my lap. He's so lost and frightened. I can tell he never showered from the game, and he's wearing borrowed clothes from the hospital. The media is camped out just a few car-lengths away, and photographers are catching all of this—seeing him hurt. I hate that. I'm just grateful that the hospital won't let them get closer. And at least it's just photos. Nobody's shouting questions. It would be just like them to ask him how he's coping, then start drilling him about his contract.

"Reed, is he out yet?" Sarah's body is hanging over mine from the seat behind me. I lift Reed's head and our tired eyes meet.

Jason went into emergency surgery almost instantly for a massive blockage in his heart. He's fitter than most, but a genetic predisposition to blockage really ramps up the effects of steak dinners and beer, I guess. That's how the doctor explained it. He was still in when our flight took off.

"The doctor said it went well. We can see him in a few hours. Maybe you should rest, Sar…"

"I'm not leaving." My friend's insistence is met with under-standing eyes. Reed nods.

"I know," he says, his eyes somehow sagging even more.

He's worried. I can tell there are things he isn't saying because of Sarah, but I don't want him carrying it all on his own.

"Let me drive. I'll park and meet you inside," Reed says, taking my hand and helping me from the driver's seat.

"I'm not letting you walk back up here alone," I say.

He gives me a small nod.

"They found a private waiting room for us on Jason's floor. The nurse at the desk knows who you all are, so just tell her," he says to Sarah as she slips out first. She's shivering with fear, and without pause Reed takes her into his arms and holds her tight. He doesn't say anything or make any promises. He just knows she needs it right now. He needs it too.

I help Rose and Peyton with Buck's chair and Reed helps his father get out of the van, stopping before he jogs back to the driver's side to hug his daughter. He kisses her head as if she's been missing and was just found.

I climb in to the passenger seat and we circle around to the garage and begin weaving for open spots.

"Hospital feels busy for such an odd hour," I say through a yawn.

"You should get to the rental, get some sleep. Babe, this isn't good for you," he says, glancing my way and grabbing my hand. He doesn't let go, and I don't let him. It feels desperate, this meeting.

Reed finds a spot on the third floor, and before I'm even able to open my door, he's rushed around to the passenger side to open it for me.

"I just need to hold you for a little while more," he says, pulling me to him. My feet slide to the ground and I fall into his arms just like I did when we were kids. When we went through this with his dad.

"He's gonna be okay." I know he is. Jason's too young—too stubborn.

"Your dad is insisting Jason sees one of the U of A doctors down in Tucson when he gets home," I chuckle, feeling Reed shake with a laugh against me. Buck is of the opinion that any doctor that didn't graduate from U of A is simply pretending.

"Jason's gonna be out of commission for a while." Reed pulls away but keeps my hand. We shut the passenger door and lock the van to begin the long trek inside.

"How's Sarah?" he asks.

I shake my head. Sarah's never really faced something like this. She's been through it with me, but that's about it. Her family is small and tight, and healthy.

"I think she's better now that she's here. She felt helpless," I say, feeling the sting of that word. That's how I feel sometimes with Reed, when he's hurt, or when my imagination just thinks he will be.

"Mmm," Reed hums with a nod. He feels the sting, too.

We've both felt helpless at times.

Our brief alone time ends the moment we step back inside. Reed shifts into caregiver mode for everyone. I've never seen him like this, almost manic about making sure everyone's all right—including his brother. It's like he's trying to hold the entire world together all by himself. Whenever I try to help, he just starts focusing on me, and our baby—something we haven't told anyone else in this room about yet, and that's on me. I've been too nervous. I don't want all of the questions that come with it.

"Do they know if you're high risk?"

"Aren't you a little old?"

"What does this mean for Reed's career?"

Reed's career. Not mine.

I breathe in and hold it in my chest, exhaling all of the thoughts as I sink into the stiff waiting-room chair and lean my head in a miserable crick to get a few minutes of sleep.

———

I feel his breath first, against my cheek and neck. It's warm, and it smells like cinnamon. Reed has probably chewed through an entire pack tonight.

"Mmm, I just dozed off." I blink my eyes open wide and shift in the chair to focus my vision on him. Sun is spilling through the blinds to my left and there's a buzz of people out in the hallway. Reed and I are all alone. He's smiling.

"You were so tired. You slept for four hours," he says with a breathy laugh.

I stretch out my arms and notice that somewhere along the way I unbuttoned my jeans from the makeshift hair-tie device. My mouth is dry, and I know any minute I'm going to be sick. Happens like clockwork every morning right about…now…

I push past Reed and rush to the bathroom, flinging open a stall door only to throw up what little I ate the night before. Reed's hand is on my back a second later, his other hand gathering my hair away from my face.

"You probably shouldn't be in the ladies' room," I say, shaking a little from sudden weakness. Reed helps me up from my knees and leads me to the sink.

"I'm pretty sure they get a lot of pregnant ladies in this place, and I think they'd understand," he says, wetting a paper towel and running it along my lips. His touch is so gentle and sweet. For the first time this morning, I realize he's happy. The worry isn't there.

"Jason's okay," I say through a stretched smile.

Reed nods.

"He'd love to see you," he says, his head falling to the side.

My body tingles with happiness—for Reed, for Sarah…for all of us.

"Yes! Where? Do I look okay? Do I smell?" I tuck my nose to my shoulder and sniff. Reed lifts my chin with a laugh.

"Not that anyone will care, babe, but you look great. You smell fine," he says through a chuckle. "Now, come on."

"Okay," I say, wide-eyed and sure he's lying about all of that no-smelling business. I'm in forty-eight-hour-old clothes, and I slept on orange vinyl.

I follow Reed through a pair of doors when a nurse buzzes us through. We get to a round bank of rooms around an incredibly busy nurse's station. It's the CCU, for cardiac care. It doesn't look much different from the rooms I've been in with Buck.

"Is everyone in there?" I scan the area trying to pick out Jason's room.

"No, Rose drove Buck and Peyton to the rental to get some rest. It's just Sarah, and she's not leaving," he says, holding open the last door we get to on our right.

My best friend looks up at me, lifting her head from Jason's chest where he rests on a bed, a million machines beeping, dripping and pumping at his bedside.

"Hey," my friend says, standing and hugging me harder than she has in our lives. Her voice is so raspy. She's been crying all night. "Did you hear? He came through like a champ. Doc said he was lucky, and that with a little diet change, he should be okay."

"They said no beer," Jason says with a gravelly voice behind her. I move closer to the bed and reach for his hand.

"I think you Johnson boys could all use drinking a little less beer. It just gets you in trouble," I say, lowering my eyes at him. Reed rubs his belly at my other side and lifts his shirt.

"Are you saying I have a beer belly?" he jokes.

I pat it with a cupped hand, making a smacking sound.

"Not at all," I deadpan. It makes Jason laugh but then wince.

"Sorry, I'll try to be less funny," I say. I move up to his head and hug him, kissing his cheek.

"Hey, did you hear the news?" I step back and pull my brow in, my own belly quivering with nerves all of a sudden. Did Reed tell them?

I glance to my husband, and his expression is tight, his shoulders hunched. I'm about to slap his arm for breaking the news without me when Jason shifts everything.

"Dallas wants him. Three years. I couldn't take the call, obviously, but my assistant did. It's on the table—the dream gig."

My breath stops along with my heart. I can feel the rush of blood leaving my face and chest and dropping down my legs. I steady myself on the edge of Jason's bed and beg myself not to say the words streaming through my head.

"Oh," I blink rapidly and shake my head.

Smile, Nolan. Make your lips curve up.

"That's…" I look to Reed, his eyes squinting more with the lift of his cheeks, his own brand of pretend smile covering his teeth. This isn't how he wanted me to find out about this.

I swallow rocks. With another shake of my head, I will away the sting of tears, and without even thinking, my hand moves to my stomach. Reed's eyes catch the motion and his fake smile breaks just a little.

"That's…amazing. Just…wow," I say. I know Sarah can hear the difference in my tone. She won't question it now, not with Jason where he is and with all of us in the room together. She knows how I feel, how I've been hoping. She just doesn't know about the pregnancy, and now I really don't want to tell anyone.

I let Jason share a little more. I stare at things in his room until my vision starts to blur and I have to move my focus on to something else. I nod and smile, and I grab Reed's fingers loosely, then let my hand fall. It happens a few times, like the will to hold on just isn't there. When a nurse comes in and sends Reed and me away to give

Jason rest, I'm grateful for the break from faking it. But I also don't know what to say to my husband. I don't know anything.

He waits until we get to the elevator. Once we step inside, behind closed doors, his breath shakes and his body turns to me.

"It's just an offer. I didn't want to get into details with him... now, ya know? I haven't decided anything..."

"Sure...yeah," I say, my brow bent and my heart burning.

"Noles, I didn't know this was coming. He was just excited and I think he's scared after everything that happened."

"No, yeah...I get it," I say, flitting my eyes up to him and reaching for his hand. I squeeze it hard this time, but I still let go.

"I think I'm just...I'm exhausted. That's all. My neck hurts and I'm really hungry, so...yeah. We can figure it out later, or after..."

I swallow and Reed does the same when our eyes meet.

"After," he nods.

My lips pull into a tight smile, more pretend, and I say that meaningless word again.

"After."

Chapter Thirty-One

Reed

MY DAD and Rose went back home with Peyton a few days after the surgery. Nolan's been gone for a week. I'm flying home with Sarah and Jason. He just got cleared after four weeks. To think he's the same man who was pale and weak in that hospital bed blows my mind—he looks so different now.

Maybe it was the fright. I remember how our dad changed after his heart attack. Jason's seen the long-term effects with me, too, as our dad slowly slipped back into old habits and then suffered debilitating strokes. Four weeks and he's become a health nut.

Jason and Sarah are waiting downstairs in the car. I've scoured the rental several times already to make sure nothing's been missed, but I want to give it one more pass. I found one of Nolan's bags the last time, a few sweaters and the box I gave her tucked inside. I've been so tempted to look inside, but those thoughts are personal. I'm sure she added more worries after Jason gave away the news about Dallas, too.

I haven't signed anything. They've been understanding because of my brother's situation, but tomorrow—at home—a decision needs to be made. I want Nolan to make it. I know it isn't fair, but I just can't.

Satisfied that I've snagged everything left behind, including one of my charging cords, I shut the door, lock it, and drop the key into the small metal box for the Airbnb owner. This house served us well for the last month.

I slide into the front seat with our driver and leave Sarah and Jason to the back.

"What asshole thought it was a good idea to book a flight this early?" Sarah gripes from the backseat. The frightened woman from a month ago is long gone. The sass is back, along with her mouth.

"Hey, it was this or six layovers and four times the price," I say from the front seat.

I feel the driver's eyes shift to me. I lift my hand and smile with a nod.

"Hi, how ya doin'?" I say. He recognizes me, and he probably thinks I'm being cheap and should just have a jet at my disposal. He's fucking clueless about the jet, but yeah…I'm cheap.

"There are not six layovers for any flight anywhere, cheap-ass," Sarah groans. Our driver laughs and turns his face from me to hide it.

"You're lucky I didn't book us on a prop plane," I say, turning to glance at my future sister-in-law over my shoulder.

"Reed, we're lucky you didn't hire a crop duster," she says, this time Jason laughing hard.

"Shut up." I roll my eyes, but I laugh silently. She's right. I would have considered it.

We get to the airport in minutes, and after clearing security, we make it to the gate just as people are starting to board. Seats were limited, so I got Jason and Sarah together near the front. I got the last spot, in the middle in the back, by the bathroom. She won't notice, and I'm tempted to snap a photo to show her what a good guy I am, but I decide Sarah's been through enough. I let her be grumpy about this trip home.

I'm between two women, both of them dressed in business suits with laptops waiting to be fired up once the pilot gives the all clear.

They don't seem to care who I am, just that I take up a little too much room on the armrests. I tuck my elbows in as much as I can and thank God it's a two-and-a-half-hour flight.

I kick Nolan's bag deeper under the seat, and my toe rests on the hard surface of the box. I close my eyes through takeoff and try to think about anything but Dallas and the wooden container next to my foot. I pull the magazine from the seat pocket when I can't seem to keep my eyes closed, and the cover story about things to do in Dallas makes me laugh.

"Of course," I breathe out, dropping the magazine back into the sleeve and catching odd glances from my seat mates on either side.

I try to stare straight ahead for a while, not wanting to look over the woman to my left so I can watch clouds out the window and not wanting to appear nosey to the woman on my right, her laptop turned slightly away from me as if she's hiding some erotic novel she's writing.

My eyes keep going to my feet, to the box I know is buried in that duffel bag, to the words written on papers inside. I finally give in and pull the bag between my feet, unzip it and bring the box to my lap. I run my thumbs over the wood a few times, flirting with the latch until I finally open it and push the lid back.

The box isn't overflowing, which gives me a twisted sense of relief. I convince myself that she must not hate the idea of me playing *that* much…she would have filled this box to the top if she did. Guilt seeps into my chest next, so I slap it closed again, but not before one torn paper flutters out from the top. I catch it as it slides down my leg, static clinging it to my jeans at my knee.

I cup it in my hand, feeling where it's folded. It's like I'm holding a fortune from a stale cookie—one I'm not so sure I really want to read. The box in my lap, I run my other palm over my mouth as I stare at the curled paper that looks to have been torn from a magazine. I can see the page number and the word HEALTH printed along the edge.

She probably ripped this one off at the hospital.

My stomach tightens. My thumb runs along the edge of the box, my nail feeling the seam where the lid meets the rest of the wood. This box was my dumb idea. Serves me right.

I scrunch my eyes tight and hunt for inner willpower to act either way—to just make a damn decision. The irony is that decisions are the very center of my problem and my fear of this box.

My gaze fades into the seat back in front of me while my fingers work together to flatten out the paper. When I feel it open, my pulse ratchets up hitting a deafening thump within my chest when I dip my chin and look down at the words written in black pen in Nolan's handwriting.

I WISH YOU KNEW HOW PROUD I WAS OF YOU.

I stare at it for several minutes, trying to connect it to something—an argument we had, something I did. It's just a bunch of words that I can't fathom she means, but also know she does. Why would she write this?

We never fought about the Dallas topic while she was here. We barely brought it up other than her telling me to think it through and do what I thought was best and what made me happy. I quit broaching the topic, because I knew her answer would always be the same. I figured we wouldn't talk about it again until I made a choice, and then we'd probably talk about it a lot.

She wrote this when we were visiting Jason at the hospital, on some random morning or afternoon. I didn't see when, but she was so compelled to put this thought down that it's more meaningful than most.

Guilt crawls into my veins and my heart rate fires up again. I instantly feel like the women next to me must know the horrible trust I broke. I look to my periphery, my flannel shirt suddenly way too warm. Neither of them is looking at me, busy in their own words, so I crack the box open enough to slide the note in, then shut it, clutching it in my palms with every intention of putting it back in Nolan's bag and forgetting I ever saw anything.

Only I did. And I can't stop now.

In a breath, I'm in the box again, first pulling out a small stack of folded papers to read one at a time.

YOU HAVE A HUGE HEART.

YOU'RE FUNNIER THAN MOST MEN.

YOU THINK IT WAS YOUR LEGS AND ARMS, BUT IT WAS YOUR EYES I SAW FIRST.

I BRAGGED TO GIRLS IN GRAD SCHOOL ABOUT YOU.

YOU'RE MY QB1.

I WAS SO AFRAID TO KISS YOU, BUT YOU MADE IT OKAY…THAT FIRST TIME…IN THE POOL.

SOMETIMES I JUST OPEN UP PICTURES OF US ON MY PHONE TO FEEL HAPPY.

The next time I open the box, I leave the lid open and just start sifting. I'm like an addict in a poppy field.

YOU ARE A REALLY GOOD LAY.

I laugh at that one, knowing exactly when she wrote it.

I DON'T REALLY HATE YOUR JEEP.

OKAY, I LOVE THE STUPID JEEP.

I pull out at least five or six I LOVE YOUs and some oddly flattering ones like YOU HAVE THE BEST HAIR and I'M GLAD PEYTON LOOKS LIKE YOU.

There are at least twenty left when I read it.

One small square of paper, a folded Post-it with a little sticky left on its edge, holds the truth I needed to hear. I don't know when she wrote it, and really, it doesn't matter because I know just seeing it that it's the one thing she would have written no matter what the date, what the time, and wherever we were in our lives. Amid all of these sweet nothings, she's hidden a confession. She's somehow reached into my chest and pulled one from me as well. She's made everything abundantly clear.

I REALLY WANT ANOTHER BABY, AND I THINK YOU DO TOO.

I set that paper, unfolded but creased, on top of the pile I've stirred in the box. The words begin to grow bold and everything behind them fades. My head gets dizzy with memories of the times we tried and failed, of the time Nolan lost our first without me there to stand by her, of the times we were afraid we weren't ready, the sleepless nights with Peyton, the high fives when she walked and said a word—*touchdown!*

The setbacks.

The milestones.

The ride.

The motherfucking ride.

This life, it's hard on a marriage. It's hard on the mind and the soul. You have to be something rare just to survive it and I did.

We did.

I shut the box and hold it in my hands, never wanting to let it go. I can't sit still. I drive the women next to me nuts with my nervous legs, my bobbing knee that I stop and restart every time I glance at it. I'm sweating; I'm nervous.

I'm happy. I've never been happier in my entire life other than the two times my girls changed everything. The day Nolan said "I do" and the day Peyton cried to welcome the world.

After another torturous hour and a half on the airplane, stuffed in the very back, and third from the last to get off the plane, I catch up to my brother and Sarah. They can barely keep up with my enormous strides. They make jokes about how manic I've suddenly become. I want to shout everything that's suddenly filled my heart to them—break the news. But I can't. Nolan deserves to be there for it. She deserves to be the one I talk to first.

Our bags are the last to drop onto the return, and it's pouring rain when we get out of the terminal and wait for the car I arranged to find us. The windows are almost impossible to see out of, gale-force winds pushing the rain sideways. The freeway is at a standstill for most of the ride, and by the time we break into the desert, the sky is a perfect swirl of cream and deep gray. It's that kind of winter storm that brings hale to the sand hills and soaks the ground back home. I roll down my window and ignore Sarah's protest as I breathe it in, pulling myself up enough in my seat to put my head outside and feel it pelt me with icy cold shots. It's just like they say in that Eagles song, the smell of the desert's earth mixed with the crisp dry air.

This is home. Where have I been? This is it. I'm here.

Home is here.

With her.

"We're having a baby," I say, suddenly overcome with the need to share this joy bursting out of my chest. I fall back into my seat and smile to nobody at all, experiencing the stunned silence in the backseat.

"Did you say…"

I turn to face them both.

"We're having a baby." My smile starts to hurt my cheeks. "You can't say anything. And…shit…you're gonna have to pretend you don't know because Nolan is going to be hella pissed I told you without her, but I just can't not."

"Dude!" Sarah's eyes light up and she looks to Jason then back to me.

My brother reaches a hand forward and I turn enough to grasp his hand in mine and hold on.

"Congratulations, man. That's…"

"I'm done," I say before Jason can get any deeper in the conversation.

His eyes still on mine, studying me to see just how absolutely serious I am. He chews at his cheek for a moment, working his jaw as his left eye closes just a hint.

"All right," he says, lips tight as he nods.

He turns to Sarah and threads his hand with hers. Didn't take him a note in a box to figure his shit out.

I can't handle the speed the driver is moving along our driveway, the line of trees dead from winter, clawing up the sides like fingers trying to keep me from getting there—to her. I'm out of the car before it fully stops, leaving the door wide open and the bags in the back. My clothes are drenched by the time I get to the door, and I realize it's locked and I don't have a key. I ring the bell and start to pound like a maniac. When Nolan opens it, I rush at her, my hands on her cheeks, my lips on hers, moving her all the way back to the wall that backs the stairs.

"Miss someone?" My dad jokes from the living room, but I don't stop kissing her. My lips caress against hers, feeling her gasp for air because I surprised her. Nolan's hands give in quickly and hold on to my sides first before sliding up my damp T-shirt that clings to my chest to the water droplets on my jaw then into my soaking hair.

Hair she loves. Because she said so. She wrote it down.

When my breath runs out, I hold my head against hers and open my eyes just enough to see her suck in her bottom lip and let go. That sexy little pout drives me to kiss her again, to suck that lip in-between mine until I think I might just suck it raw. I hear Jason and Sarah step in behind me and pull back to let her breathe. Instead of letting go, I lift her up slowly, her long ribbons of hair spilling down to hide her face, covering us both in a private moment where she smiles down at me and I circle her around like the queen she is.

Hopeful eyes meet mine as I lower her back to her feet, nervous lips twitch, afraid to hear the answer, but anxious all the same. I start to nod, and she starts to cry.

"This is enough for me. You...Peyton..."

"We're having a baby!" Nolan shouts before I can finish.

Laughter brews in my chest and spills out loudly, a duet with my wife's gleeful laugh that comes out in hiccups in-between happy cries.

"I'm done, baby. I'm home, and I want you and this perfect little family. I want another baby so much," I say, letting the flood of tears blur everything now.

"Oh my, a baby!" Rose cries out, stepping into us both with wide, open arms. We hug her together, then separately. When I turn to face my dad and see him standing, his hand over his heart and tears in his eyes, a smile broad from cheek to cheek, I begin to cry more.

"I'm gonna be a dad again, Pops," I say, leaping over an ottoman to get to him faster. I grab his hand but he quickly pulls me in for a hug in celebration. He's weathered so much but somehow still stands tall over me—he stands, when he shouldn't. On his own.

Sarah holds a phone in the air as she whistles, and it draws everyone's attention.

"Sean, Reed has something he would like to tell you," she

shouts, passing the phone to me with my friend's face lit up on the screen. He looks confused as hell.

"How do you feel about Arizona in say…" I glance to Nolan, not really sure of my math.

"July. The fourth, actually," she says through the most perfect smile. I haven't seen her face shine like this in months.

"What she said," I say, leaving my eyes on her while my friend continues to shout confused questions from his phone. I look back down to my palm, Becky now standing behind him.

"We're having a baby!"

"Oh my God!" They both scream, and Sarah takes the phone away from me to join them.

My brother steps up behind me and pulls me into a bear hug that I cut short and yell at him for, reminding him of the surgery he just had.

"I guess we're gonna have to get busy to catch up to you!" He pulls at my shoulders and our heads press together while we hold each other's biceps and laugh like loons. It's such a show of masculinity, proving that we can make life. Hell, Nolan really does all the work.

"Babe, we have to call Micah and Sienna," I shout, letting go of Jason's arms but leaving my arm around him.

"Already on it!" Sarah says, passing the phone with Sean and Beck to Nolan while she takes over Jason's phone to call the rest of our friends.

We spend the rest of the night looping everyone in, and making plans for Nolan's parents to visit along with her brother and his wife and their kids. Our house will be full. Her mom promises help, but I don't want to miss any of it this time. I want every awful job, every late-hour cry. I want to kick myself for wanting it, then thank myself when I'm refreshed after a nap. I want to live every moment, the ones I missed with Peyton and the one's that we'll all make together.

I want to be the man my daughter tells her secrets to, the one who threatens the boys who will never be good enough, then gives in to the one she begs me to accept. I want to watch her be the best at what she does, to be the reason I show up to a football field and stand under the Friday lights.

I want this town. This small town that I've promised to give back to in the name of one of the best men I ever knew. I want to live in Trig's honor and do all of the things that he never got to because this game, and his mind—it stole it away.

More than anything, I want to live.

This life, with this girl—it's my passion.

I'm nothing without her, and everything when I'm wherever she is.

All the games couldn't compare.

She's my hail Mary.

Epilogue

Nolan

"YOUR MAMA LIVED IN THIS TRAILER."

I bounce Ellie in my arms, her sleepy eyes barely holding on. She doesn't understand anything I say yet. She's only two months old.

They're tearing down the manufactured homes on my old street, making way for a business park and some condos. It's strange to see, and it makes me a little sad, honestly. I want progress, but I also want my town to stay small. I guess it doesn't work that way.

Change.

We've been part of that. The school fields are transforming on a pretty tight schedule, with the promise of being ready by game day in September. The view from our property is already obscured by steel frames that will soon become an advanced medical complex and homes.

Until my old street is gone, though, I've decided to make it a part of my daily morning walk. We'll stop and say goodbye when the bulldozers come, but after that, I just don't think I'll be able to see it disappear. I'd rather just wake up and see something new, like a dream.

"You ready to go see Daddy?" I bounce Ellie at my hip and she coos. I put her back in the jogger and strap her in, giving her the small teddy bear she got from Peyton as a present. If I make it to the high school before she throws it on the ground, I'll be amazed.

I started running again. I haven't really run since, well...high school. It was always good for my head then, though. More than the mental benefits, I think what Jason went through really scared us all. Reed hasn't stopped training like he's about to start for an NFL team. But instead of pro-players, he throws the ball to teenagers now.

He's not officially on the coaching staff, but he just shows up every day. They let him because hell, his presence is pretty freaking good for fundraising. He's actually really good with the offense. I think Coach Baker just likes having him around to talk to. I've asked him if he thinks he'll take the head job when Baker steps down next year, but he insists he won't.

"I'm retired," he always says.

World's busiest volunteer, more like it.

I make the final curve around the back of the school with the jogging stroller and slow to a walk, weaving through the portable buildings that are being used while the main gym and health classes get a new home. Reed won't be happy until this entire campus is new and better than any other campus in the state.

Always the competitor.

Reed is leaning against the wall in his usual spot, right by Baker's office. I stroll up quietly and whisper, "Boo!"

"Hey," he says, an instant smile on his face. It's not there for me. It's there for Ellie. Okay, well maybe it's partly there for me, but I know what really makes his heart melt.

"You waitin' on Baker or something?" I ask while he takes his daughter from me and holds her up high above his head until a string of drool drops to the front of his chest. He brings her in to cuddle at his side and chuckles at me while he smears the damp spot.

"I deserved that," he says.

I nod with tight lips because I know better.

"Oh hey, step in to the wall. You're going to blow my cover," he whispers quickly. He grabs the sleeve of my T-shirt and pulls me close, which irritates me at first until I follow his gaze to the main courtyard filled with grass and picnic tables

"You think he's asking her?" I whisper.

"I don't know. I'm not sure I want him to," Reed whispers.

Bryce spent the summer at a football camp—one Reed recommended him for. I was never quite sure if he really believed in the kid or just wanted him away from his daughter. But Bryce's first letter showed up about a week after he left, and he sent one religiously every few days. Every single letter was about something that Peyton put on her list for him. The very first item—sometimes a girl just wants a letter. Not everything was a simple task. She asked him to really think about why he messed around with another girl but still wanted her. She also asked him to do something for the community. When he was at camp in San Diego, he volunteered at the Boys and Girls club and coached a youth football team. He sent her a picture from their last game.

He hand-delivered his last letter a few days ago. He gave it to Reed and asked him to read it then and there, and somehow my husband didn't crumple it up and throw it back at him. I think because deep down he sees himself in the kid. Heck, *I* see Reed in Bryce. The letter was for us, and he asked us if it would be all right if he asked Peyton to homecoming.

Reed's immediate response was "That's in like six weeks, man." After I elbowed him, though, and he cleared his throat of all the damn masculine hostility, he shrugged and said "We'll see."

I guess we're seeing right now.

"She's a lot like you, you know," he says, and I loop my arm through his and squeeze, kissing his bicep. She's not. She's like him. She's so much more secure and confident than I was. I'm glad she is.

"I think he's asking now," I say, suddenly nervous for her —for him!

Our daughter takes a deep breath and folds her arms over her chest. I start to feel bad and a little guilty for spying. She lets her arms fall to her side, though, and steps toward him with a hug.

"Damn," Reed says, and I jerk his arm because he forgets that Ellie's here sometimes. Not that she can talk yet, but I swear her first word is going to be a doozy.

I watch a little longer, and I see the little things I can't verbalize to him, but they're special things that let me know Peyton…she's gonna be okay. Bryce's eyes close as they hug, and his face dips into her hair. That smile is the kind I always wanted Reed to have for me when I was our daughter's age. The way his hands flex then fist at her back says this is important to him. It also says he's scared and probably full of adrenaline.

"Well," Reed says, turning into me and grimacing.

"Oh, come on. Don't be such a skeptic," I say, tilting my head.

"I'm not. I'm a romantic," he says with a wink and a laugh. I join him as I take our daughter back and put her in the stroller again. He was making a joke, but he really is the romantic one. He always has been.

I turn the big wheel around and push back the way I came, this time with Reed at my side. I think about how hard I thought this all was going to be. Funny how easy this life is, though.

"You know, I haven't had a dream since you've been home. Not one that I can remember," he says. I smile to myself because while he's just musing about things, like he always does, he has no idea how deeply those words resonate.

I look up into his perfect green eyes while we walk, and he takes over pushing duties so I can link my arm with his.

"Probably because you don't have to," I say.

His crooked smile comes fast.

"I like that," he says, looking ahead.

"Me too," I say.

Me, too.

THE END

Acknowledgments

And now for the most difficult part to write...

Sigh.

There is so much to say about this book—this family and series. I don't want to double the size of this sucker, even though I could. I've shared my writing journey and the roots of Waiting on the Sidelines often, so I won't go deep into it here, but for those who may not know, Book 1 - Waiting on the Sidelines - was my first published novel. I carried it around for more than a decade half finished. I was terrified to share it, afraid of rejection and being judged, I suppose.

It came out on Tax Day 2013. Good news on a shitty day haha. Turns out, that little book of my heart was the best news ever for me. It opened up the possibility of my dream. I'm living it. And those of you who took a chance on that book, back in the day; those of you who I have grown epically close to and call friends—you are my fairy godmothers. For real.

This gets said a lot in acknowledgements and it's said because it's true. You—the reader—are everything. That's it. Not one single title fits what you are to those of us who toil away with carpal tunnel and insomnia, hovering over our keyboards, manic on Diet Coke and Teddy Grahams while we talk to ourselves to make sure the dialogue sounds just...right... You are everything. We do this because you let us. I do this because you made it possible. I can't thank you enough. All I can do is promise to keep creating, always with you in mind. I do, and I will.

I have so many people to thank. This first one might seem strange, but I'd like to thank Kurt Warner. You see, Reed was number 13 for a reason. Kurt is the kinda guy who breaks the mold. In the world of football, he was not just exceptional—he was an exception. Driven, yes, but grounded above all else. I admire him, and as much as I wish we had gotten one more year of him on the field…I'm glad he knew when to quit. His story inspired this one in many ways.

I'd also like to thank my family—my parents for giving me such an amazing life, my brother for molding me into the Tomboy I am, my husband for loving me and believing in me fiercely, and my son for being my very best friend. My family also includes my home. This series is very much about Arizona. I know Coolidge, Phoenix, Tucson, the desert—every dusty nook and cranny that somehow produces the most spectacular earth and sunsets. This place is the heartbeat that's steady under my prose.

To my betas—Bianca, Shelley, Jen (I'll get back to more on you, missy) and to TeriLyn. You put up with me doling out words to you bits at a time. You help me make sure they're just right. Endless thanks! And please don't ever close your email inboxes lol!

Now Jen, I call you out because in 2012, you were my very first beta. My bestie. We were working in a place that felt like it was on fire, and I had this dream and you needed an escape. In pure Jen fashion, you not only took my manuscript in to read as a favor, you made it your goddamned mission. You made *me* your goddamned mission. I can never thank you enough for believing in me, for pushing me, and for tirelessly telling people I'm your favorite author, even though you're biased as hell haha. I love you, my friend. For your encouragement, and just for who you are.

This bookish world was forever changed by those of you who give your time and effort through blogging. I was forever changed by your work. There are so many of you who have lifted me up, and I want you to know that your work is so vital to this community. You, more than any of us, changed this romance business landscape. You knocked down doors and reshaped the rulebook. All because you wanted to find ALL OF THE BOOKS. And you wanted to share them…with the world! Thank you for sharing mine. Thank you for every single small and large thing you do. You work harder than me. And thank God! I will forever be your fan.

To my editors: BilliJoy Carson of Editing Addict and Tina Scott. You're my bullet-proof vest. To use a Waiting Series-themed analogy: You are my offensive line. You march me down the field with the confidence that I can score. Thank you!

Now, Autumn… You, my dear, are my Tony Dungy. I'm pretty sure I was a fan of you first. Your belief in me is one thing, but the fact that you also know when I need to just stop and breathe is beyond. You roll up your sleeves for me and have not just allowed me to stand a little straighter…taller…but you've made me start to believe that maybe I'm a'right at this book stuff after all. That right there, overcoming that doubt, has been the mountain in the way of everything for me. You came in with dynamite and blew it to shit. Thank you, my friend. You are so special.

Like I said, I have a ton of people to thank. I could go on and on. My husband really deserves his own chapter of thanks, but since he's right here, I can just tell him. I'm gonna wrap this up, as hard as it is because in doing so…I'm also closing the final chapter on characters who have become family.

I hope you enjoyed this coming-of-age ride. I hope I served Nolan and Reed well with this final book. I've never felt so satisfied in telling a tale. Honestly. Something about these two and where they are now feels just right. It's like ahhh. They literally fade into our epic Arizona sunset. And kinda like them, I don't really have to dream anymore. I've already gotten there.

XO

Til next time.

Ginger

About the Author

Ginger Scott is a *USA Today*, *Wall Street Journal* and Amazon-bestselling author from Peoria, Arizona. She has also been nominated for the Goodreads Choice and RWA Rita Awards. She is the author of several young and new adult romances, including bestsellers Cry Baby, The Hard Count, A Boy Like You, This Is Falling and Wild Reckless.

A sucker for a good romance, Ginger's other passion is sports, and she often blends the two in her stories. When she's not writing, the odds are high that she's somewhere near a baseball diamond, either watching her son swing for the fences or cheering on her favorite baseball team, the Arizona Diamondbacks. Ginger lives in Arizona and is married to her college sweetheart whom she met at ASU (fork 'em, Devils).

FIND GINGER ONLINE: www.littlemisswrite.com

facebook.com/GingerScottAuthor

twitter.com/TheGingerScott

instagram.com/authorgingerscott

Also By Ginger Scott

Newest

Southpaw: An enemies-to-lovers sports romance

The Boys of Welles

Loner

Rebel

Habit

The Fuel Series

Shift

Wreck

Burn

The Varsity Series

Varsity Heartbreaker

Varsity Tiebreaker

Varsity Rule breaker

Varsity Captain

The Waiting Series

Waiting on the Sidelines

Going Long

The Hail Mary

Like Us Duet

A Boy Like You

A Girl Like Me

The Falling Series

This Is Falling

You And Everything After

The Girl I Was Before

In Your Dreams

The Harper Boys

Wild Reckless

Wicked Restless

Standalone Reads

Candy Colored Sky

Cowboy Villain Damsel Duel

Drummer Girl

BRED

Cry Baby

The Hard Count

Memphis

Hold My Breath

Blindness

How We Deal With Gravity

Made in the USA
Middletown, DE
14 October 2023

40564592R00186